CODE OF
MISCONDUCT
Conduct Unbecoming

A Novel

by

C.A. Griffith

Doris,
My very to
best
you always!

Published by
Brighton Publishing LLC
501 W. Ray Road
Suite 4
Chandler, AZ 85225

CODE OF MISCONDUCT
Conduct Unbecoming

A Novel

by

C.A. Griffith

Published by
Brighton Publishing LLC
501 W. Ray Road
Suite 4
Chandler, AZ 85225

ISBN 13: 978-1-621830-15-3
ISBN 10: 1-621-83015-2

First Edition

Printed in the United States of America

Cover Design By: Tom Rodriguez

Reader Reviews

THIS BOOK HAS IT ALL!

I couldn't put it down! Code of Misconduct has it all...you will remain on the edge of your seat from beginning to end. The characters are complex and human. The writer has all the skills of a seasoned author, with exciting plot twists that remain realistic and true to life. I can't wait for the next novel!

— Amazon.com

GREAT BOOK!

Chris really uses his law enforcement experience to write a great book with really good characters. His knowledge of all parts of law enforcement shows through in the main character. I am looking forward to the next book.

— Amazon.com

GREAT READ!

Could not put it down! I loved it! I love the storyline, and kept thinking that it would make a great movie as well. I loved the main character, Grey Colson. I can't wait for the next one to come out. Great work from a new writer. I highly recommend this book.

— Amazon.com

LOVED IT!

Code of Misconduct was a great read! I had a hard time putting it down! I can't wait for the next book to come out! I really appreciate the attention to detail, which you only get from someone who has actually been in law enforcement. I highly recommend it!

— Amazon.com

YOU WON'T PUT IT DOWN!

Chris has a great skill in keeping the storyline going. You won't put the book down once you start reading it because from chapter to chapter you can't wait to find out what's going to happen next. Get this book! You will love it! I am excited to see what Chris writes next!

— Amazon.com

A MUST READ....MYSTERY, SUSPENSE, AND MORE!

This author has a natural way of writing. Slick and fast-paced, with in your face characters that jump off the page. As a writer, I really appreciate how he made the characters come alive.

— Amazon.com

THE REAL DEAL!!

A must read for those who love a fast-paced crime thriller. The characters come to life within a storyline that will make you peek around every corner to see what is coming next. Having recently retired from a law enforcement career myself, it is evident Chris has drawn upon his professional and personal experiences to make the main character, Grey Colson the "Real Deal." Can't wait for another Grey Colson novel.

— Amazon.com

⇛ Introduction ⇚

For centuries, the Office of Sheriff has worked to maintain safe communities. The men and women deputized to serve are critical to the positive quality of life experienced by our citizens. Major Griffith has worked in all areas of the Cobb County Sheriff's Office, including Detention Facilities, Field Services, Investigations, undercover narcotics and Internal Affairs. He has performed his duties as a Deputy Sheriff with honesty, integrity, and commitment to objectively enforce the law. These experiences have given him an exceptional insight and knowledge of the responsibilities and duties of the Sheriff's Office, as well as the consequences that occur when some people make the wrong choices in life. In this profession it is important for those that serve to have compassion, understanding and a clear dedication to their oath of office. Major Chris Griffith is one of those unique individuals who has unselfishly served the people and accepted the sacrifices associated with putting one's life on the line for others.

Sheriff Neil Warren

Cobb County, Georgia

❯❯ Foreword ❮❮

by

LOU REITER

DEPUTY CHIEF LOS ANGELES POLICE DEPARTMENT (RETIRED)

Why do some cops turn bad? Men and women become cops for various reasons. Many are simply looking for a job that's somewhat steady, pays well, sounds exciting, and is a change from the cubicle. Others are driven by a sense of calling; to be a protector and serve their community. But then there are the few who look at the role of a cop to get laid, steal what they can, and use the badge to reinforce their personal prejudices.

Most people in police work say you weed the bad ones out at the front end, during the hiring process. Their background and job experiences will predict those who will most likely become bad cops. The psychological screening will find the deviants. Many times this is true. In law enforcement each time we lower our entrance requirements we know that three-to-five years down the road we'll face the residue and cancers from that knee-jerk reaction to get more warm bodies into the police cars.

Yet, many of the really bad, nasty cops are successful candidates at the front end. They have stellar backgrounds. They are often church-going family men and women. But the nature of the job changes them. The hard drinking. The access to easy or vulnerable women. The cutting of corners and trashing the Constitution because of their belief that the "Noble Cause" serves the community and only scum, dirtbags, and criminals are affected. The access that the badge suddenly gives them entrée to money, sex and power.

Police misconduct and bad cops aren't found only in the big, urban cities. It permeates even the smallest agencies. It can be found in farm country, idyllic communities, and those that few outsiders ever get to. Most police or sheriff agencies never make the local newspaper's front page with a scandal. Others seem to fight each other to get a more atrocious scandal. So what seems to determine why some are successful and others are not.

The departments that rarely face scandals are well-run. The Chief or Sheriff sets the tone. The Chief or Sheriff knows what's happening in the field when his cops are out there alone, often without any supervision. The Chief of Sheriff continuously talks with their officers; asks about their personal life; knows the good deeds each one has accomplished in the past week. This kind of Chief or Sheriff puts on the same uniform the field guys wear and not just for a press conference. The Chief will be with the street cop on routine calls, not just the hot calls. This Chief or Sheriff demands the same from every other supervisor and manager in the department. They all care about their people and their community.

And what about the departments that seem to continuously have scandals and breed bad cops? The Chief or Sheriff in these departments may have an open door policy, but is never in. He's constantly out politicking, worrying about his job, wondering whether he has a majority at the next Commission meeting. This Chief or Sheriff hogs the limelight and news media events at the expense of the cops actually doing the job. This Chief or Sheriff only comments on things that went wrong and never seems to even know the good things the field cops are doing. This Chief or Sheriff wouldn't even know how to audit the work of his cops or special units, either—because he never did the job or has forgotten.

And then there's the Internal Affairs Unit who's supposed to police the police. In the well-run police department this unit knows that complaints, even from the dirtbags and criminals, are valuable information. Bad cops usually abuse those who are have little or no credibility and are on the marginal side of the community—not the bankers or PTA presidents. The well-run IA Unit sees their job as being impartial fact finders. They work as hard to protect the name of good cops as they do to uncover misconduct or mistakes. They treat complainants and cops equally and professionally. They are the guards who protect the reputation of the Chief, Sheriff, and agency. The Chief or Sheriff in the well-run agency knows that IA protects his back and aren't just yes men who pat their backs.

In the malignant police agencies the Internal Affairs Unit is either nonexistent, works only to clear officers, or is known to be simply "badge/tin collectors" or "headhunters," getting a thrill when they uncover a cop who makes a mistake or is caught engaging in wrongdoing. IA in these agencies abuse citizen complainants. These agencies create hurdles for anyone who might be interested in filing a complaint.

In every police or sheriff department, other cops know the bad cops. They know the skirt chasers, the heavy-handed brutal cops, those who make "hummer" or bad arrests, those who are on the take, the cops who sleep through the shift, and the ones who are racists, homophobic, or sexist. All anyone has to do is mingle with the cops and keep your ears and eyes open. The bad cops often believe no one is looking and no one cares. When no one looks or cares, the bad cops now control the agency.

❧ Foreword ❧

by

BOB BARR

FORMER CONGRESSMAN AND UNITED STATES ATTORNEY FOR THE NORTHERN DISTRICT OF GEORGIA

Chris Griffith has written a suspenseful and action-packed novel; but the real value of Code of Misconduct is that it reminds all citizens—law enforcement and civilian alike—that it is neither equipment nor manpower that forms the foundation for good law enforcement; it is integrity.

From 1986 to 1990, I was honored to have served as the United States Attorney for the Northern District of Georgia under two presidents—Ronald Reagan and George H.W. Bush. As the chief federal prosecutor for north Georgia, I realized early on that ultimate success rested not on the number of defendants prosecuted or on the value of assets seized; but on the integrity with which those resources were marshaled and directed. Both Attorneys General under whom I served— Edwin Meese and Richard Thornburgh—regularly reminded me and my colleagues from across the country, that any prosecution, no matter how large, must be constructed of trustworthy evidence, developed in a fair and objective manner, and presented with no motive other than seeking justice and protecting the lives, values, and property of the people of the United States.

As an earlier Attorney General, Robert Jackson noted to United States Attorneys assembled in the Department of Justice on April 1, 1940: The prosecutor has more control over life, liberty, and reputation than any other person in America. His discretion is tremendous...While the prosecutor at his best is one of the most beneficent forces in our society, when he acts from malice or other base motives, he is one of the worst.

The qualities of a good prosecutor are as elusive and as impossible to define as those which mark a gentleman. And those who need to be told would not understand it anyway. A sensitiveness to fair play and sportsmanship is perhaps the best protection against the abuse of power, and the citizen's safety lies in the prosecutor who tempers zeal with human kindness, who seeks truth and not victims, who serves the law and not factional purposes, and who approaches his task with humility.

It is axiomatic that for a prosecutor to bear true faith and allegiance to this eloquent charge from former Attorney General Jackson, those who work with him and at his direction—the law enforcement officers on the street and in their offices—also must base their actions on integrity and respect for the law. Like the prosecutor who takes the investigations they develop, and then presents the cases to judges and juries for resolution, the law enforcement officer cannot be blinded by statistics or the lure of dirty money or other false rewards. It is of these ingredients—integrity and respect for the law—that public support for laws and law enforcement is born. Without them, the confidence in our justice system that is essential for a fair and free society vanishes.

This process has nothing to do with political party or politics generally. As Attorney General Janet Reno said in a 2001 memo: "Policing...when done well, brings a community together to solve problems, reduce crime, and inspire us all." When done poorly or dishonestly, it eats away at the very fabric of our society as rust might quietly but destructively weaken the infrastructure of the tallest skyscraper.

These fundamental principles are reminded to us through these words from real-life Attorneys General; but they also are illustrated for us through the pages of Chris Griffith's Code of Misconduct. Griffith's lead character, retired Georgia Sheriff Grey Colson, finds himself drawn back into the intrigue of police undercover work through a sense of civic duty and law enforcement instinct. Ultimately, he prevails over corruption and scandal in much the same way that in my experiences and—even more so—Chris Griffith's, led us through the labyrinth of real-life corruption investigations and prosecutions.

It is a fascinating read that Griffith has laid out for us, and the many twists and turns in the plot will hold the reader's attention from the first page to the last. But do not let the exciting plot and well-constructed prose blind you to the very real and vitally important message in Code of Misconduct: corruption in public office—whether large or small—is inherently and inevitably destructive of liberty, and rooting it out in all its manifestations is a job as vital to our nation as is maintaining a strong and effective military.

Neither Chris Griffith nor Grey Colson apologize for their staunch support of this principle. As former President Theodore Roosevelt said in 1903 in his Message to the Congress, "No man is above the law and no man is below it; nor do we ask any man's permission when we require him to obey it." Teddy Roosevelt, too, would have enjoyed Code of Misconduct.

≫ Acknowledgements ≪

I have always heard that no man is an island unto himself and I have come to understand the meaning of those words. The people who make up your family, friends, and co-workers have a direct effect on either your happiness and success or your distress and failure. In my case, I have been blessed beyond measure and thank God for all those people in my life and for giving me the very breath to pursue my interests.

To my beautiful wife, Beverly, who has suppressed the urge to roll her eyes at the mention of all my eccentric projects and has stood by me each step of the way. You are the love of my life. To my lovely daughter, Brittany, whose encouraging words and smile make me believe I can do anything. And to my dear mother, Eileen, who encouraged me as a young man to pursue my dreams. I love each of you more than you will ever know.

Thanks to my agent, Anita Melograna, for her encouragement, guidance, and faith in me.

And thank you to three honorable gentlemen who graciously gave of their time to contribute to this work: Cobb County Sheriff, Neil Warren; former Congressman and United States Attorney, Bob Barr; and former LAPD Deputy Chief, Lou Reiter. You are each true examples of men who have dedicated themselves to justice, integrity, and public service.

The words of honorable men are more valuable than gold.

⇒ Chapter One ⇐

It was stark, light coral in color, but functional. The small bath in the enormous beach house was the best Jay Taylor ever had. The room and bath were rent-free. He stood in his boxers, motionless in front of the large mirror spanning the width of the wall above the double sinks. He lifted his left palm and covered his left eye. The same view as before. He lowered his arm, took a deep breath, and slowly raised his right hand to his face, covering his right eye. Nothing. No matter how much he willed himself to see the image from moments ago, there was still nothing. Only the slight-pink glow of light that seeped through the imperfect seal his hand made over his good eye.

The ophthalmologist blamed it on a fungus. A damned thing called fungal keratitis. All from a single, stray fingernail scratch to his cornea. Grappling maneuvers were at least half of the mixed martial arts game and the open-fingered gloves were necessary for fighters to grab and throw opponents. The punch thrown by Antwon Silva didn't faze Taylor at the time. Larger men had hit him harder. He didn't even blame Silva for the inadvertent pinky to the eye as the punch glanced off Taylor's nose. He had made the same accidental contact countless times. As always, he shook it off, touched gloves, and resumed the fight.

No, not Silva's fault, but the young optometrist was a different story. For days following the fight, Taylor's eye was swollen and slammed shut, so the optometrist prescribed antibiotics and told him not to worry. Looking back, Taylor realized the young optometrist was examining his assistant's legs more than his swollen eye. Things were looking up, so to speak, during the following week, but the blurred vision worsened so he returned for a follow up examination. "Nothing to worry about" said the playboy optometrist as he scribbled a prescription for alternative antibiotics.

Another month passed. More pills and a patch over his eye. Taylor continued to work out and grapple with his trainers. He gave his eye the recommended period of rest; but on the fourth of July, exactly one month before he was scheduled to compete for a shot at fighting in the main octagon and winning a six-figure salary, he woke up with the eye completely and totally blind.

The specialist didn't offer much hope of recovery. He was a steady man in his sixties. A confident and mature professional who wasn't distracted by female office assistants. The subconjunctival injections and topical fortified antifungal drops he prescribed were a day late and a dollar short. Taylor continued to hope—and even pray, but his depth perception was gone and so was his chance for a heavyweight title. Instead of psyching himself up for a fight on August first, Taylor was in Wal-Mart buying a new pair of dark sunglasses. He walked out of the store and threw his eye patch in a garbage bin as the old door greeter bid him a nice day. He didn't respond. Rage built in Taylor as he power-walked to his car. He had previously exploded on opponents who threatened his chance at victory, but this was different. This was flagrant incompetence that ruined his future. Taylor slammed the car door with a jerk as he dropped in the driver's seat and drove straight to the young optometrist's office.

Taylor didn't recall the drive. His trainers called the adrenalin rush "tunnel vision." They were right. He swung his car nose first into a handicap space at the front entrance, next to a black, sporty, Mercedes coupe bearing a personalized Florida tag that read SEE ME. The building contained four business offices that appeared to have been converted from another grocery store gone belly-up. They appeared identical in size from the outside, but he was only interested in the one located on the far right.

He shoved open the driver's door and heard a dull thud as he threw the gear into park. The door had rebounded from its impact with the Mercedes door and almost closed on his left ankle when he began to step out. He quickly caught the door with the toe of his shoe, and then shoved and held it firm against the sporty black car. He stepped out and caught a glimpse of the damage as he slammed the door. A three-inch vertical crease from the violent sheet metal contact, highlighted by the blue metallic paint transfer from his door. He hoped it was the right one.

He pushed through the glass office door to the familiar waiting room. He made a quick survey of the room, but didn't remove his new glasses. An older man seated next to an elderly woman peered at him through thick soda-bottle glasses. The couple was seated across from a young woman reading a Hollywood-type magazine. All three patiently waiting for their appointment with the young doctor. The waiting room setting was typical, but low rent. Nine uncomfortable chairs with worn, wooden armrests lined three walls. Two cheap end tables were set in the

2

far corners. A similarly cheap, wooden coffee table was situated in the middle of the room with three-year-old magazines strewn on top.

He stepped to the translucent sliding window at the counter. No bell to ring and he couldn't see the form of a human being through the frosted glass. To the right of the window was a solid door from which the young assistant would summon weary patients. Taylor recalled waiting no less than thirty minutes past each appointment time before being called, but he had no intention of waiting today. He rapped his knuckles loudly on the counter and waited. No response. He popped the frosted glass five times with the knuckle of his index finger, clapping the sliding panes against each other in protest.

A figure moved on the opposite side of the glass and a delicate hand slid it open. The scowl on the young assistant's face disappeared when she recognized the large man. She forced a smile.

"Mr. Taylor?" The girl said, pulling her long hair back with both hands and tying it with practiced ease. Taylor breathed hard through his nose and glared at the young assistant.

"Where's Cooper?"

"Doctor Cooper," she corrected, and looked at a day planner. "Do you have an appointment?"

Taylor continued to glare and said nothing. The assistant stared back for a moment, then cut her eyes away.

"Just sign in and he'll be with you."

"Let me back there," Taylor insisted and nodded at the inner door.

The girl straightened and froze. Her smile vanished. "I'll tell him you're here," she quipped, and then slid the glass closed.

Taylor spun and froze. His eyes landed on the older man and woman seated along the left wall. The old man peered at Taylor through his thick lenses until their eyes met, and then his gaze shifted quickly to the floor. The old man rested his hand on the woman's hand who sat seemingly unaware of the tension filled room. Taylor realized the old man was being intimidated.

"Don't worry, old man," he said, and turned back to the window. From the interior office he heard muffled laughter. He leaned closer to the glass and recognized the voice of Cooper and the young assistant.

Taylor concentrated. He heard only three words. "What...Cyclops ...Want..." Then faint chuckling. He slipped into tunnel vision again. He had never considered suing Cooper for his lazy incompetence and now he fully understood why. He wasn't someone who did his best, but fell short or made an honest mistake. Cooper was a condescending, money-hungry fool who didn't take his patient's needs seriously. No, this man had to be dealt with outside of a courtroom.

Taylor slid the glass open and stuck his head through, toward the sound of the voices. Cooper stood in front of a photocopier at the end of the hall, one hand around the young assistant's waist and the other cupping her ear as he moved close to no doubt offer another insult about Taylor. The assistant leaned back and covered her mouth with both hands, suppressing a laugh. Taylor left the window open and charged the interior door. He turned the knob and pushed, but realized it opened outward and pulled hard. The cheap, hollow-core door opened with a whoosh of air. The knob struck the opposite wall, making a clean hole in the sheetrock and lodging in place. Taylor was greeted with the shocked faces of Cooper and his assistant as he stormed through the opening and down the hallway.

The young assistant frowned and marched toward Taylor. "Mr. Taylor, you can't just..." was all she could get out before Taylor gave her an easy shove with his left hand, propelling her small frame back against the wall and down to her knees. Taylor didn't break stride or take his eye off of Cooper, who stood motionless against the copier.

Cooper raised his hands in a gesture of surrender as Taylor approached. "Look, Taylor. I don't know what your problem is."

"Shut up!" Taylor shouted, stopping toe-to-toe with Cooper. He breathed hard for a moment, staring down at Cooper, who was a head shorter and easily eighty pounds lighter. Taylor reached for the copier lid and flipped it open, and then reached around Cooper with his right hand and pushed the one and the zero for ten copies. Cooper looked from one side to the other, confused.

"What the hell are you doing?" he demanded.

Taylor stared down at Cooper and pressed START. "You'll want to give these to the district attorney."

A green glow of light began its methodical sweep across the copier glass as the counter on the screen began a backwards count,

10...09...08... Sheets of black-tinted paper began slipping from the copier into a side holding tray.

"What the hell...?" Cooper demanded again. Taylor grabbed Cooper's throat in his left hand, causing him to expel a loud gasp. Cooper's eyes shot open wide as he struggled to grasp Taylor's wrist. Cooper felt he was being lifted to his toes and couldn't concentrate on defense. He felt a hand on the back of his head. Taylor planted his large right hand around the base of Cooper's skull, turned his head a few degrees to the left, and then slammed Cooper's right temple on the copier glass. A spider web crack instantly appeared in the glass as small jets of blood shot from the point of impact.

Cooper's body wobbled and then went limp as he blacked out. Taylor leaned against Cooper's legs to keep him upright and moved his left hand to hold his head firmly on its side. He knew from years of fighting how much trauma a head could take and he didn't intend on killing the young optometrist, but he would teach him a lesson that he would never forget. Taylor struck Cooper's left orbital bone repeatedly until he felt it collapse into fragments rupturing the eyeball.

Taylor ceased his flurry and stood motionless for a moment. The green glow from the copier had run its course. Blood covered the glass and was dripping onto the floor and into the paper tray. He stepped back and watched Cooper crumple to the floor, resting in a gurgling heap. Breathing heavily, he turned to an empty hallway and walked to the waiting room. The assistant was nowhere in sight and the room was vacant. Taylor paused to wipe blood from his hands on a cheap curtain by the door and stepped out into the sunlit parking lot. He saw the assistant standing in front of the adjacent office door, desperately talking on her cell phone. She pointed at Taylor as if the person she was speaking with could see him, and then she ran inside the building. He knew he had a few minutes, but that's all he would need.

Taylor walked to the black Mercedes and admired the dent he had left in the door. It seemed like an hour ago. He noted the sleek side mirror on the driver's side. In a fluid move, Taylor raised his right leg in a side stance and kicked the side mirror with his heel, leaving it swinging like a pendulum against the door. Cooper wouldn't be using it, anyway.

Taylor's breathing had almost returned to normal when he pulled into the parking lot of Cash's Liquors. He found the fifth of vodka he was looking for on the back isle, carried it to the counter, set it down with a thud, and dropped a twenty dollar bill next to it. A greasy-haired young man in his twenties walked from a back room and used a wireless device to scan the barcode on the bottle, swiped up the twenty, and then stuck it in the register drawer. Taylor watched with mild curiosity as the young man appeared to be calculating the change in his head instead of entering the twenty dollars and allowing the machine to do it for him. Without looking up, the young man pulled bills and coin from the drawer and handed them to Taylor.

"I'd like a receipt," Taylor said evenly. The young man left the cash drawer open and looked at Taylor.

"Why?" he asked. "You paid cash."

Taylor took a deep breath through his nose and gritted his teeth. "You heard me you little, greasy bastard."

"What's the problem?" another voice said. The second man, this one in his thirties walked to the counter. He looked at Taylor and back at the young man. Without a word, the young man closed the drawer, pulled a receipt from the register, and handed it to Taylor.

"I don't have a problem," the young cashier said, rolling his eyes and walking away. "I was gonna give the guy a receipt."

Taylor blew air from his mouth and looked down at the counter. His adrenalin rush subsided and sweat ran into his eyes. He pulled off his new sunglasses and wiped his brow with his sleeve. The thirty-something man watched him closely from behind the counter for a moment, and then a grin crept across his face.

"Jay Taylor?" the man said with enthusiasm. "Jay 'The Terrible' Taylor."

Taylor slipped his glasses back on, lifted the vodka bottle, and turned. Before he could escape the conversation the man said, "Hey man, no disrespect or anything. I saw what happened to you with Silva and I hate it, I mean really hate it. I was pulling for you."

Taylor faced the counter. "Fine. Thanks," he muttered, and then moved toward the exit.

But the man wouldn't shut up. "What are you doing now? I mean, if you don't mind me asking."

Taylor stopped and turned. "I'm trying to get home and drink this bottle," he said.

6

"I was just going to say that my boss has been looking to hire someone like you. We, I mean he…needs someone with your expertise."

"For what?"

The man brightened. "Different things. He could use a bodyguard. He's got money and enemies."

Taylor chuckled. "Like your greasy headed cashier?" he said sarcastically.

The man looked toward the back room where the boy had disappeared, and then back to Taylor. "Worse than that. That is, in case you were looking for work."

"I have a feeling I'm going to be tied up for a while"

The man nodded and extended his hand. "Whenever you're available. Randy Fuller."

Taylor hesitated and the, stepped to the counter. What could he lose? Maybe he'd have the opportunity to pound another optometrist. He shook Fuller's hand. "I may stop back," he said. Taylor drove back to his apartment, his right hand now throbbing. He walked through the cool living room and into the kitchen where he plucked a shot glass from the counter and two aspirins from a bottle by the sink. Taylor plopped down on the recliner, switched on the television, poured a shot, and waited for the police to arrive. It took them twenty-five minutes.

Taylor hated criminals but believed in street justice. He had worked hard his entire adult life and had exacted payment for what had been stolen from him. He wouldn't deny it. In fact he was proud to take full responsibility for his actions. His public defender told him he was an idiot for wanting to plead guilty at his first appearance, but Taylor insisted. The stunned judge was obviously unprepared for the swift guilty plea and set a sentencing date two weeks later. Taylor was convicted of aggravated battery and received a ten-year sentence with two years in confinement and the remaining eight on probation. The judge made it clear the prison sentence would have been a minimum of five years if Taylor had a previous record. With good behavior, Taylor was out in thirteen months and five days. His Florida criminal history would forever reflect a conviction for aggravated battery. Taylor called it an eye for an eye.

✥ Chapter Two ✥

The highway known as A1A or Atlantic 1 Alternate is one of the most famous stretches of road on the eastern coast of the United States. The northern end of the five-hundred-plus mile route begins in Fernandina Beach, Nassau County, Florida and ends at its southern point on Bertha Street in Key West. Two miles of A1A will live in race enthusiasts' memories as being part of the Daytona Beach Road Course. It saw its end in 1959 with the construction of the Daytona International Speedway and the first Daytona 500.

The Volusia County sheriff's motor unit cruised in the left lane of A1A just a few miles north of the famed road course, and swung left on International Speedway Boulevard, traveling over the Broadway inner coastal waterway bridge on its three mile trip to Cash's liquor store on Nova Road. The Harley Davidson rolled into the parking lot and came to a stop next to a dark gray sedan. At nine a.m. there would be no customers. The deputy swung his leg over the seat and stretched. He glanced at his short sleeves and smiled. The temperature in Daytona Beach should reach the low nineties today. Had he still been living in Michigan, he would be thawing from a seemingly never-ending winter. The deputy could see his reflection in the twelve-foot high tinted windows of the store. His vanity slowed his pace so he could check out his reflection. To stop and stare would be too obvious. He reached the entrance, rapped the glass door with his knuckle, and then waited.

Randy Fuller slid a cash tray into the register and pushed it closed. He muttered a sharp, "Damn" at the tapping. The store hours were clearly displayed at eye level on the door.

OPEN MON - SAT
10 AM to 11 PM
CLOSED SUNDAY

But the person at the door continued as if they were blind, illiterate, or just plain stupid. Fuller decided to ignore it and walked toward the rear office. He saw the uniform in his peripheral vision and stopped dead in his tracks. Fuller walked to the door, spun the deadbolt counter-clockwise, and pushed it open.

"What's going on, Pickett?"

The deputy shouldered his way past him. "The checks were not in my box this morning."

"That's because your boy didn't show up last night to pick them up," Fuller snarled.

"Damn it"! Pickett said sharply. "I'm going to fire that idiot before he pisses Cash off and we lose this security job."

Fuller was back behind the counter before Pickett finished his tirade. He lifted a green bank bag from under the counter, pulled out a handful of envelopes, and waved them in the air. "Don't lose your mind, man. They're right here."

Pickett walked to the counter and took the stack of envelopes. "There's just no excuse. These guys come begging for part-time work, so I hook them up. Then when I give them the hours, they take a dump on me."

"I wouldn't worry about it," Fuller said dismissively as he pulled a manila envelope from the counter drawer. "As long as you take care of these, Mr. Cash will overlook a guard not showing up now and then."

Pickett's eyes narrowed. "We're not guards. We're state mandated deputy sheriffs. You want guards, call rent-a-cop. They're not going to save your ass when some gangbanger walks in here with a shotgun and turns you into a twenty-four hour ghost."

Fuller dropped the envelope on the counter and rolled his eyes. "Come on, man. Don't blow a gasket. You know what I mean."

"Fine," Pickett replied. "What's this?" he said, eyeing the envelope.

Fuller exhaled. "You know what it is. Cash wants you to run another one." Fuller handed Pickett the envelope. Pickett pulled the contents out and glanced at the face of the document. He shoved it back in the envelope and shook his head.

"Tell me something, Randy," Pickett said. "With all the money Cash has, you'd think he would just send one of you guys down to records and pay the measly twenty bucks for the NCIC check. Your employees handle money, so it's perfectly legal to check their criminal backgrounds."

Fuller shrugged. "I have no idea. I just do what I'm told and don't complain. You shouldn't either, considering the bonus you get for each one."

Pickett slapped the envelope against his free hand and stared at Fuller. He held the envelope up and pointed at it. "This is the third check I've run in…what? Two months? The first two girls had felonies on their record and one was wanted. That put me in the trick bag when I had to respond to the wanted hit. What kind of applicants are you getting here"?

"Look, you gonna run the criminal history or not?" Fuller held out his hand. "If not, I'll let Cash know."

"I've got it," Pickett snapped. "But something is starting to smell about this, Randy. You better not be jerking me around."

Pickett folded the large envelope around the stack of small ones and walked to the door. He turned back to Fuller as he pushed it open. "Tell the night guys a different deputy will be here next Friday. The no-show is fired. I've got ten others wanting his night." Pickett stepped out into the glaring sun and mounted his bike.

Fuller waited until the door closed with a click. "Like I give a shit," he mumbled to himself.

Fuller watched Pickett climb on the bike and kick-start it. It came to life with a plap-plap-plap. He slipped on his helmet and opened a side compartment where he dropped the envelopes and slapped the lid shut. He walked the bike backwards, turned the wheel, and cranked the accelerator repeatedly, waiting for an opening in traffic. Pickett enjoyed watching the widening eyes of motorists when they recognized him as a motor cop. One who is to be feared and respected. As usual, a driver would slow and motion him out. He nodded a short thank you, released the clutch, and shot into traffic as if being propelled by a catapult.

⇒ Chapter Three ⇐

Which part of large coffee, cream only, remotely sounds like large coffee, cream, and a pound of sugar?

Colson almost made a U-turn on International Speedway Blvd. Twice in as many weeks he had been to the Speedway Cafe drive-through for a morning cup of his favorite mild brew and twice they jacked up his order. "Just let it go," Colson said to himself, and maintained his direction of travel. The little girl at the window couldn't have been more than sixteen years old and it wasn't in Colson's nature to stir up a stink with her boss over a jacked up cup of coffee. A young person not taking their job seriously was one of his pet peeves. Didn't they realize their generation would be running the country one day? It was obvious what happened after all the hippies became of-age and acquired power. God help us all when the Goths and pants-on-the-ground generation take over.

Every time Colson saw a school-age girl, Nichole immediately materialized in his mind. His now twenty-two-year-old, newlywed daughter. But she was over three-hundred miles away, back in Georgia, and he was just the retired old man in Daytona Beach.

"Why don't they listen," Colson said aloud. Partly referring to the coffee girl and partly referring to Nichole. He admittedly talked to himself on occasion, especially in the car. At times he chastised fellow drivers for their inconsiderate driving as if they could hear him and benefit from the advice. But at present there was no one else to talk to and he wanted to stay in practice. He was satisfied that he was the most interesting person he knew, frequently sarcastic, and often amusing.

Although Nicole was the most wonderful daughter a father could ask for, there was always that piece of advice here or a strong suggestion there that was summarily ignored. Such as his latest suggestion that she and her husband move into his home. The home she grew up in. The home where he taught her how to ride a bike, where they threw the softball in the back yard, where he built her club house, where she primped and prepared for senior prom, and where she was presented with her engagement ring. "It's just the memories of Mom," she told him. "Maybe in a few years." Colson couldn't bear selling the house to a stranger. He and Ann had spent nearly twenty wonderful years sitting on the screened porch, talking about new home projects, their daughter, watching the dog's antics, and listening to '80s music on the radio. He found it difficult to stay there, and really didn't blame Nichole for being uncomfortable with the idea—but she was finally convinced that moving into her childhood home was the best decision.

His mind was still on Nichole as he cruised through the yellow light at Ridgewood Avenue. The morning temperature was hovering at seventy-five degrees according to the screen on his vehicle information center, and the sun reflected off the inner coastal waves like daytime fireworks as he topped the causeway. A marvelous June morning, with the exception of the blue and red LED lights in his rearview mirror from the motor unit that was closing in fast on his tail.

A gotcha grin formed on the lips of the Volusia County motor unit deputy on his fast approach to the green Corvette.

"1701 to radio. I'll be Code 18 on Florida plate Charlie-Alfa-Golf-Two-Three-Three on Speedway at North Palmetto Avenue. Will advise final stop location," said the deputy into his helmet microphone.

"10-4", responded the female voice in his headset. To those who don't routinely listen to police radio traffic, the reply would have sounded like: "Chaw."

Colson glanced at his speedometer. Fifty-two miles per hour. Short of ten over the limit, but he was used to the hassle. He had been guilty of instigating the same type of hassle years ago. Many years ago, and only when he was bored or the offense was blatant and dangerous. He lifted his foot from the accelerator but didn't brake just yet. Braking immediately projects the message: "Yes officer, I'm the idiot who knows he's been caught speeding," even if it is just seven over the posted limit. Colson steered right into the Subway parking lot, providing plenty of safe space for the deputy to swing in behind and park his bike.

Colson was a uniform critic of sorts, but admired a well-pressed and smartly decorated uniform. Not overly burdened with shiny metallic attachments, but short of the commando uniforms reserved for tactical units such as SWAT. The uniform of a peace officer should command authority, but reflect a professional image instead of a military presence. The badge denotes the agency represented, the nameplate provides the officer's name, and the pen is a necessity to record information. Last name preferably on the plate, because it's not a good practice to develop a first name relationship with people you encounter in the course of the job. Offering your first name to relatives during a death notification, a lost child, or an elderly person broken down on the road was perfectly acceptable. Under some circumstances you'd give them a business card and tell them to call you directly if they need anything. Additional metal attached to the uniform is totally unnecessary and can only pose a safety hazard when attempting to apprehend or fight a suspect. Mirrored sunglasses were a no-no. Southern sheriffs have spent years trying to shed the Hollywood stereotype with mirrored glasses, southern drawls, and exaggerated racist attitudes. As Florida is not technically a southern state, given the massive migration of snow birds to retirement golf communities, one would certainly expect an officer to be far removed from the likes of Buford T. Justice.

The deputy spoke into his helmet. "1701 to radio. Final stop is the Subway, one hundred block of International Speedway. Cross street is Beach."

The eight-hundred-megahertz helmet radio came to life. "10-4. Twenty-eights return on a 1994 Corvette to a Grey Colson, 1303 South Atlantic Avenue, number five-ten, Daytona. No wants."

"Received," was the deputy's one word reply.

This deputy failed the first part of the Colson test the moment he glanced at his driver's side mirror and watched the deputy lower the kick stand. He permitted the bike to lean a few degrees until it came to a rest and dismounted. Colson took silent inventory of the deputy's uniform which immediately reminded him of a walking Christmas tree, complete with whistle, star on the helmet, star on the chest, star tie pin, and every conceivable association and commemorative pin an officer could either be awarded, pilfer, or purchase on eBay. He cringed at the sight of the deputy's green uniform shirt. Only park rangers and forest rangers were supposed to wear green. The deputy approaching his driver's side window could have posed for the squirrel patrol recruitment poster.

The deputy made the standard cautious approach from the rear of the vehicle. Body bladed with his weapon side slightly angled to the rear. His hand hovered near what appeared to be a Glock 17 nine millimeter semi-automatic. He slowed his pace somewhat as he pressed down on the rear glass hatch, assuring himself a mythical midget with a machine gun wouldn't pop out at the last moment and cut him down. Colson could not prevent his eyes from rolling but closed them briefly to allow himself the satisfaction as Mister Green Jeans arrived at his window.

Colson respected law enforcement officers to a fault because he had spent his entire adult life as one. However, his twenty-eight year adventure had taught him how to identify the good ones from bad ones and the dedicated ones from the worthless ones. He knew from working Internal Affairs there are three basic groups of people who enter the law enforcement profession.

The first is the worst. Group number one is those who are hungry for the power of the badge and gun, thinking those items alone demand respect from the public and the admiration of friends. Group one officers have five-inch-thick file jackets in Internal Affairs filled with reprimand, suspension, and demotion letters. When progressive discipline failed, a termination letter would complete their file for storage, awaiting the lawsuits that would probably follow.

Group number two consists of those who simply have no idea of what they are getting themselves into. Maybe they watched too many episodes of *Cops* on TV, or were laid off from more lucrative employment and needed a paycheck. The disciplinary and termination letters for those in group number two were not as numerous because they would resign the moment another job opportunity became available, leaving little or no work history.

The third group consists of those who enjoy the command structure and job security that exists in the law enforcement community. They have a desire to do the right thing and it's not about the paycheck or perceived power associated with the position. Colson didn't buy into the "Save the World and Serve Society" crap he heard from most job applicants during employment interviews. He knew they were only saying what they thought he wanted to hear. "To Protect and Serve" is the ultimate goal of all law enforcement agencies, but if you sat across the table from him during an employment interview and expected him to believe that line of bull as being the driving force behind wanting the job, you would eventually receive a "Thanks, but no thanks" letter in the mail. Colson knew he was from the third group. Not because he lived and breathed the job as some pretend. There was nothing supernatural or superhuman about police work. It was simply a reputable job and didn't require a master's degree.

Within the fifteen or so seconds he had been observing Mister Green Jeans, Colson had him identified with the category one crowd and immediately didn't like him. The deputy took the correct position slightly behind the driver's side window. He didn't bother to remove his helmet or glasses, which were thankfully not mirrored.

"License and insurance," said the deputy in an even tone.

Colson couldn't place his accent but with only three words spoken, knew the guy wasn't a southern native. He had already removed both requested items and handed them to Deputy Pickett. That was on his nameplate, surrounded by a "Serving since 2006" rider. *Wow*, thought Colson sarcastically, *a whole four years of service.* Colson also glanced at his seven-point sheriff's badge, identifying him as a reserve deputy sheriff. Just a small indicator probably missed by a majority of citizens, yet a very important indicator that separates full-time cops from the wannabes. Two bright gold sergeant chevrons were affixed to each collar, separated only by Pickett's skinny neck. *Wow*, thought Colson a second time. *I may be experiencing the pleasure of speaking with the King Wannabe Reserve Deputy.*

"Do you know why I stopped you?" asked Pickett.

"Because I'm driving a Vette?" Colson replied. To admit he was seven over the posted limit would make Pickett's job too easy. He still didn't like Pickett and sarcasm wasn't a crime—yet.

"You were driving fifty-five in a forty-five," Pickett replied, seeming to ignore Colson's preemptive poke.

"Interesting," Colson said. "Okay."

Pickett glanced at Colson's insurance card and gave his Georgia driver's license a long look. Colson would never defame his precious ride with stickers of any sort. No political endorsements, funny quotes, or catchy phrases, and especially no law enforcement identifiers such as "Blue Line" or "Fraternal Order of Police" stickers. Not because he was ashamed of his job, but because it was nothing more than an open invitation for human debris or cop haters to vandalize the car or break in, hoping to find a firearm concealed in the glove box or under the seat.

"You a cop?" asked Pickett.

"I was," Colson replied.

Pickett had taken note of Colson's uniform in the license photo. He had been on duty the day he renewed his license several years ago. The State of Georgia had been permitting renewal of licenses by mail and his was on its third reissue, making it thirteen years old. His hair was partially brown at the time. Now, it was mostly gray.

"Until when?" asked Pickett.

"January, this year."

"Retired?"

"That's what they told me at the party."

"Why the Florida plates and Georgia license?"

"I moved in two weeks ago. Got the plate Monday and am planning on camping out in the license line tomorrow. Rumor is I've got thirty days by Florida law and I didn't feel like investing an entire day to get both."

"Did they give you any retirement I.D. when you left? You know the crap people pull to get out of a ticket."

Colson removed his retirement credentials from the center console and handed them to Pickett.

He casually flipped it open and read aloud, "Deputy Sheriff Major, Clay County, Georgia, Retired. What was your assignment, retired Major Colson?"

"Well, Reserve Sergeant Pickett, all assignments at some point or another, but finished the last five as Commander of Internal Affairs."

Pickett didn't miss the "reserve" comment. His eyes darted momentarily at his reserve badge, and then back to Colson. "I don't know about Georgia, retired Major Colson, but reserve officers in Florida are certified peace officers through Florida Peace Officer Standards and Training, just like the full-timers."

"I never doubted it," said Colson.

"Okay, Colson," Pickett said, "I can appreciate your service. I'll do you a professional courtesy and only give you a warning if you'll do me a favor and drive your little sports car within the posted limits."

Colson formed a small grin. "Sounds fair to me, but could you do me another favor?"

"What's that?" Pickett's reply hinted annoyance. Colson couldn't see his face from behind the sunglasses and the shroud of his helmet. His tone was enough.

"You think you could hook me up with one of those sweet beach patrol jobs? I could outfit this baby with blue lights, remove the targa top, cruise chicks, and work on my tan at the same time."

"Enjoy your retirement, Colson," Pickett said with no hint of amusement and handed back the license and insurance card. He casually returned to his bike, mounted it, and then eased back into traffic. Colson watched him disappear into traffic and then turned his attention to the young lady unlocking the Subway entrance and pulling the chain to illuminate the OPEN sign. *Already ten-thirty,* Colson thought. He decided to grab a foot long, loaded with extra onions. He got out of the car, discreetly poured his coffee with extra sugar on a nearby shrub, and then went inside.

◆◆

The office was only two years old, but it felt older to Sheriff Stuart Langston. He sat behind his flat screen computer monitor with his second cup of coffee, looking between two names in a list of five. It dawned on him that almost everything came in pairs. His second cup of coffee, his second marriage in the last two decades, his second divorce looming, and running for a second term in office as sheriff of Volusia County. Now he had to decide between two fine-looking deputies to promote to Lieutenant. *Decisions, decisions,* he thought with a chuckle. He pressed the button next to his secretary's name displayed on the IP smart phone.

"Good morning, Sheriff," Hannah Sparks said in her bubbly voice.

"Hannah, I need the file jackets for the five employees I sent the email about yesterday," he said to the speakerphone.

"They're in your in box, Sheriff."

Langston glanced to the corner of his desk. "Okay, I see them, thanks."

"No problem, Sheriff," she said, and the line went blank.

Langston lifted the five brown file jackets and sifted quickly through the stack. He laid the two files of interest in front of him and tossed the remaining three in his out box. There was no need to review the other three; they were all men. Promotional testing in Volusia County was similar to promotional testing for police agencies across the county.

17

A written test was administered that varied from year-to-year, but the subject matter remained constant. Multiple-choice questions regarding agency policy and procedure. Series of questions regarding civil liability, use of force scenarios, and amended state and federal law updates. If the candidate successfully passed the written test with a score of eighty percent or better, they moved on to the second phase of the promotional process. It also varied from year to year. One year the candidate may be required to deliver an oral presentation, a written project, or an oral examination in front of an assessment panel of seasoned officers from various jurisdictions. Most candidates dreaded the idea of the oral exam. There was nothing more stressful than to be given a one-minute time limit to answer an incredibly complicated scenario and deliver it with confidence. The assessment panel scores were averaged for the second score of the process. The third portion was a review of the employee's past evaluations. Only those with acceptable evaluations for the past two years were eligible for promotion. A recent unacceptable evaluation or formal disciplinary action was an automatic disqualifier.

Eight sergeants had participated in the assessment process and five had made the cut. Those names were placed on an eligibility list for the sheriff's consideration. The two files in front of Langston at the moment were the only ones he was interested in. He could make his selection from the files in front of him or make no selection at all. There was only one vacancy for lieutenant due to the resignation of Lieutenant Phillips three months ago. He had accepted a position with Orlando P.D. for the extra money and better benefits. "Good riddance," Langston said to his Chief Deputy at the time. Phillips was a slug inherited from the previous administration and hated Langston. The feeling was mutual.

Langston leafed through each file, skimming over the performance evaluations, attendance reports, commendations, reprimands and miscellaneous personal information without interest. He passed the employee's photograph and had to flip back two pages. Langston read the name under the photo: Kimberly Sue Reese. He had known her for three years, but only as Kim. Langston knew she had attended the University of Florida, Jacksonville and had been a lifeguard at Ormond Beach for a year prior to the sheriff's office. He didn't have a photo of Reese in her lifeguard uniform, but could formulate one in his mind. At five feet, she was petite and had a figure that would make a man beg to be arrested. Her dark shoulder-length hair and tan looked of middle-eastern decent. "Finer than frog hair," is what Langston's father would have said. He dropped the image of her from his imagination and glanced at the file photo. The uniform and tied-back hair didn't do her justice, but she looked good, the uniform notwithstanding. If she was given the promotion, she would work in plain clothes every day and her office would be a five minute drive away. She would look good on television, but the opening was in Investigations, not Public Relations. One of the best features about Kim is that she was single. No murderous husband to worry about.

Langston laid the Kim Reese file on his desk pad and flipped open Heather McFadden's file jacket. Equally attractive, but scored less than Kim by one point. That, being she was married and had a young kid. She married a paramedic just a little over a year ago and couldn't shut up about their honeymoon in Mexico, a year and a kid later. Langston dropped the file with the other three in the rejected pile and flipped open Kim's file again. *That settles it,* Langston thought to himself, and pressed the button on his phone for Hannah. She answered in the middle of the first ring.

"Yes, Sheriff."

"Hannah, call dispatch and tell them to have Sergeant Reese work a thirty-five to my office," Langston ordered politely.

"I'm sorry, Sheriff," she hesitated a beat, "work a thirty-five?"

"Just tell radio to have her report to the executive office," Langston replied, and then thought better of it. "Disregard, Hannah. Just pull her cell number off the employee rolodex and tell her to report to my office at fifteen hundred...ah...three o'clock."

"Right away, Sheriff," she said with a tone of relief, thankful Langston hadn't bitten her head off for not memorizing all those ridiculous cop codes and signals.

He depressed the button to the right of the LED display next to Hannah's name. The line went blank and her name disappeared simultaneously. Nice phone system when it worked. He glanced at the plaques Hannah had situated on his office wall. The FBI National Academy was elevated above his Peace Officers Standards and Training certificate and class photograph. The frames to the left formed a second triangle. His certificate of graduation from the DEA's basic agent's course, 2001 Chamber of Commerce Officer of the Year Award, and a Bachelor of Arts in Political Science degree from the University of Florida at Jacksonville. There were many other training certificates, three or four more plaques for various recognitions received over the years, and more photos than Langston had time to count, but he didn't bother to shuffle through them or hang them on the wall. Not enough space. He could have chosen the large inner conference room for his office, but he preferred windows, sunshine, and a view of the tall palms between the street and the parking lot.

Langston was silently celebrating twenty-five years in law enforcement. The first five years were with Daytona Beach PD, but a better opportunity for advancement came available with the larger and better-funded sheriff's office. It wasn't an easy adjustment for a much younger Stuart Langston. The deputies spent their first couple of years working the jail before moving on to serve warrants and ride patrol. He had already been riding patrol with DBPD. Babysitting inmates felt like a step down. He was handing out dinner, or "slinging trays" as the other deputies put it, to the same slugs he had been arresting five years prior. The inmates wouldn't let him forget it either, calling him their "bitch" or "boy" every day. He recognized they were trying to push his buttons to make him go off and do something stupid, but he kept his cool.

Eventually his tour in the jail ended and he was back on patrol. Two years later he made detective and in eighteen months he was assigned to represent the agency with a small group of other local officers in the Group 3 DEA Task Force in Orlando. Langston enjoyed the five years working undercover, but was more than ready to move on with his promotion to sergeant in the uniform division. The next ten years saw Langston promoted to Lieutenant in the uniform division. As Watch Commander, the troops admired and respected Langston.

Like any Watch Commander, he had stacks of administrative paperwork to approve at the beginning of each shift. Vacation requests, attendance reports, scheduling, overtime reports, citizen complaints, worker's compensation forms, statistical reporting for the feds, and arrest reports. No one ever saw an officer or detective write a report in a movie. They participate in a torrential gun battle for fifteen minutes and go to lunch. The only time Langston ever saw a cop take notes on TV was in an episode of Dragnet. What his deputies admired was not his administrative abilities, but that he finished by six p.m. and hit the road with them until midnight or whenever the job was done.

Lieutenant Langston became Captain Langston in 2001 and was assigned to the Administration Division as Public Information Officer. His weaknesses were the top two items his first supervisor warned him about years earlier. Liquor and women. Not that he was told never to have a relationship with a woman, but to avoid dipping his pen in company ink.

"It causes nothing but trouble," old Sergeant Bacon had told him in his rough smoker's voice.

"It will draw negative attention to you, son, and your career will go down the toilet." Sergeant Bacon told him liquor in moderation was no problem, but he'd better not be acting the fool in public and get caught.

He thought back to one of his first days as a recruit in the jail, looking into the booking desk cabinet for property forms, only to discover partial bottles of liquor scattered in the back. "What are these for?" he asked Sergeant Bacon.

"Oh, there's no nurse on night shift, so we just keep those around to give to the drunks when they're in detox," was his stuttered reply. Langston was naïve and actually bought the explanation. He still believed it to an extent; however, Bacon's rosy cheeks confessed liquor had more important uses on night shift than keeping the drunks from having seizures. Langston stayed careful over the years, played the game, and locked up the bad guys. Now he was in charge and if he wanted to dip his pen in a little company ink, he had earned the privilege.

❖ Chapter Four ❖

G rey Colson's condo was nothing spectacular, but it was on the beach and that's all he wanted. He and Ann didn't take extravagant vacations, nor could they afford them on a deputy and payroll manager's salary. They spent their annual one-week vacation at the beach for twenty-five years and those were some of their best memories. This would have been the first year Nichole wouldn't be with them. This would also be the first year without Ann since cancer took her life and changed his forever.

Colson intended on staying on with the sheriff's office for a full thirty years. That was a good round number and the thirty-year mark would max out his retirement pay and medical benefits for both he and Ann. When Ann passed, he still planned on staying thirty years, but it only took a few months alone in the house to change his mind. Their Jack Russell terrier, Marty, and miniature pincher, Bella, did everything in their power to entertain and keep him company, but they couldn't fill the vacuum created by Ann's absence. The condominium association had strict rules against animals on the property, so Marty and Bella moved in with Nichole and her husband without objection. They actually appeared to be as happy as clams about the arrangement. No one could blame them. Colson hadn't been very good company for several months.

Colson made his decision one Friday evening while watching some worthless and unbelievable action movie. He would use the bulk of the life insurance to pay off the mortgage. Nichole and her husband could move in and pay him a very affordable rent. He would use most of the remaining funds for the condo down payment, and help Nichole through college. The retirement checks would sustain him. Property values had dropped across the nation and Daytona was no exception. He preferred to remember Ann in the sun, not in a dark bedroom with the dread of death hanging in the air. He wouldn't sit idle. He had to stay busy, so he'd find employment somewhere, even if he had to pick up cans on the beach to recycle. *Earth tones,* Colson thought. *I'll paint the entire condo in earth tones. That's just what Ann would have done.*

He tossed one half of the sandwich on a paper plate, slid the other half back into the plastic bag, and laid it in the refrigerator for later. He grabbed a glass, poured it full of two percent milk and stepped out to the balcony. It was simple, but perfect by Colson's standards. Five feet deep and twelve feet wide. A white aluminum railing prevented the constant Atlantic breeze from sweeping the four plastic chairs and two end tables onto the sunbathers five floors below. A metal plate covered a void where a wall light used to be, thanks to the animal rights activists who were convinced that exterior lighting at night would drive sea turtles out of existence. Colson was shocked there were any lights on the property that could be seen from the shore. Florida property owners adapted by installing shrouded covers so any light cast would be directed inland. *Maybe that would drive rats and cockroaches inland toward Orlando,* he thought, but then the activists would have two more critters to protect. Who were these silly taxpayers who preferred security lighting over getting raped, mugged, or murdered?

Colson turned the radio on and finished his sandwich. He found it difficult to believe that late '70s and '80s hits were considered oldies, but he overlooked the announcer's comment and enjoyed the music. A car insurance commercial interrupted his listening pleasure, then one promoting a male enhancement drug. There were at least three other commercials Colson ignored while taking in the ocean view and the vehicles driving slowly up and down the beach. The last commercial briefly caught his attention because he had just experienced a close encounter with Reserve Sergeant Pickett. He didn't begin paying attention until the commercial was about over. He picked up the female voice saying: "Sheriff Stuart Langston. Consistent, fair, professional, and ready to continue his service on behalf of the citizens of Volusia County. Vote this November." The disclaimer followed with a speedy male voice. "Paid for by the Committee to Re-Elect Sheriff Stuart Langston." Colson admired the man's strong name. "Good name for a sheriff," he murmured, "but your judgment was lacking the day you gave Pickett a badge and gun." He raised his binoculars to check out the rectangular shape on the horizon. He guessed it was a tanker ship.

He lowered his binoculars after being satisfied he was wrong about the huge barge being a tanker. His attention was drawn by the boy standing and flailing his arms, shouting at the young girl seated on a towel next to him. He lifted the binoculars and adjusted the focus to bring them in close. Colson estimated the boy was twenty years old. Skinny, but toned. Black shoulder length hair, a three day growth emphasized by a little goatee-looking beard and black stud ear rings. The boy sported black swim trunks being worn too low and hanging below his knees. The girl's back was to Colson, but it didn't appear she was troubled by the fire and brimstone lecture being delivered by skinny boy. He watched the girl stand, turn, and start to walk away. Skinny boy was pretty quick. He grabbed the girl's right wrist with his left hand and spun her around to face him. The girl was a head shorter than skinny boy and had short, straight brown hair. She wore a yellow bikini and looked to be around eighteen.

Colson counted one or two additional words from skinny boy an instant before he slapped the girl across the face. He instinctively lowered the binoculars as if looking over them made the scene real. He didn't need the binoculars to see the young girl struggling to escape the boy's grasp. The couple was only a hundred feet away, but five stories down. Colson dropped the binoculars on his chair and sprinted through the condo and out the door. Condo 510 was conveniently an end unit directly across from the stairwell door. He took the stairs two at a time until he reached the bottom. He crossed the rear parking area to the beachfront gate, punching in the code, 2-3-2-4-#, on the keypad. He ran down the concrete steps to the sand and covered the remaining dozen feet to the couple. Had his old physical training instructor been timing him, he would have been impressed. Twenty-eight seconds flat. Little else appeared to have transpired in that time. The girl continued to struggle and skinny boy was still shouting. He raised his hand to launch slap number two, or three, depending on what Colson missed on his way down the stairs. Skinny boy didn't notice Colson running full speed in his peripheral vision. His anger kept him focused on the girl. The boy's next sensation was hot sand on his stomach and in his mouth. Colson body blocked him from his left, breaking his grasp of the girl's arm and hurtling him to the sand face first. The girl raised her hands to her mouth and stepped back in momentary shock.

"What the hell do you think you're doing?" skinny boy screamed, and jumped to his feet.

He spit out grains of sand that had lodged inside his bottom lip. The boy appraised his sudden opponent. The man was probably older than his own father, gray hair, five-ten or eleven, but not out of shape like his old man. He had broad shoulders and was thick in the chest. For whatever reason, this guy seemed controlled, not a hot head like his dad. If his dad had been pissed enough to knock him on his ass, or in this case on your face, his next move would have been an immediate fist fest to the head and ribs. He knew from personal experience. Not this guy, he just stood there with his right hand raised as if he were taking an oath in court.

"This is not your business, old man," skinny boy said through gritted teeth.

He assumed the best fighting stance he could, considering his slight stature. Both fists clenched, but held low to his side as if fighting an urge to raise them. Colson noticed the boy's swim trunks had slipped a few inches lower from his slide in the sand.

"You should think seriously about pulling those britches up, son, before you end up in jail for indecent exposure as well as battery," Colson said without intended sarcasm.

"I'm not your son and you're not my old man, old man. My old man will bury you," skinny boy retorted.

"I consider myself fortunate that I'm not your father and you should consider yourself fortunate that I'm not HER father," Colson said, and turned to the girl. "You know this punk's name, honey?"

The girl lowered her hands and nodded.

Thinking back, Colson had just reacted. No gun, no handcuffs, no flex cuffs, no radio, no cell phone. He supposed he could take his shirt off, use it to tie the punk's hands together, and march him barefoot to the nearest precinct. Where was Reserve Sergeant Pickett when there was a real crime taking place? Imagine all the authority Pickett could abuse right here, right now. And what about the other two or three hundred people scattered along this quarter-mile of beach? There must have been a dozen who heard the boy shouting and saw the girl struggling. And of course, witnessed the slap. He already knew the answer. People talk a big game, especially men. They brag about critical incidents *after the fact* and make statements such as, "By God, this is what I would have done if I saw him slap that little girl." In reality, most people are professional bystanders and won't do squat on their own. They wait until the police are on scene and all the bad guys are in cuffs before they sneak out from behind wherever they were hiding and begin speculating about the exciting details, boldly proclaiming what they would have done had the police not arrived. It was a fact that a majority of the population are busybodies.

If the girl knew the punk's name and where he lived, making the police report would be easy enough, especially after Colson provided a detailed witness statement. If the case went to trial, he would happily testify. He figured the punk would run down the beach any second, but he just stood defiant with his bare feet in the sand.

Skinny boy took three fast strides at Colson with both arms extended to return the shove. Colson took a quick step backward and grasped the boy's left wrist in his right hand. As the boy's momentum carried him, Colson rotated the back of the boy's hand clockwise, placing him in a reverse wristlock. The movement spun the boy face down on the sand again. Colson continued to torque his wrist, straightening his arm, and locking him flat on his stomach. The boy released an exasperated, "Ahhhh," followed by a muffled expletive.

"You just don't know when to quit, do you boy?" Colson said, keeping pressure on the boy's wrist. "Your experience must be limited to slapping young ladies around." The boy responded with a groan and sporadic leg jerks.

∽

The Daytona Beach Police Patrol unit turned onto the packed sand for a routine five-mile-per-hour tour down the length of the beach roadway. Officer Matt Sanders started his shift at three-fifteen p.m., and it was just about lunchtime. His plan was to drive one last run down the beach road, turn south on A1A and stop at Buddies Burgers for a half-price meal. But unfortunately, the man controlling a struggling kid in the sand could ruin his dinner. *Could be horseplay,* he thought. Father and son roughhousing, but he had to check anyway. Sanders used to believe he had seen it all over his dozen years, but every situation differed to some extent. Just as sure as he ignored it and chalked it up to an innocent wrestling match, he would either be disciplined for dereliction of duty or sued by grieving parents. Why can't people just behave and enjoy the beach? He switched on the blue lights and stopped.

"504 to radio. I'll be out on a possible affray, behind the Sundowner complex, north of life guard station five," Officer Sanders said in an exasperated tone, reflecting his need for dinner. "White male, mid-forties, wearing a white t-shirt. Second subject is a white male in his twenties; no shirt, dark shorts." The female voice in radio simply replied, "10-4," or "Chaw."

The beach police truck was a gleaming white, multipurpose Ford F-150 with standard six-inch dark green lettering. Being cross-trained as a paramedic and police officer, his truck was equipped with a surfboard, first aid kit, an automated external defibrillator, and rescue tubes.

Colson relaxed his grip on skinny boy's hand and pulled him to his feet when the officer walked toward them. Skinny boy decided to offer his own unsolicited version of events.

"This moron came from out of nowhere and tried to kill me," he shouted. Sanders stared at the boy, momentarily distracted by the dime size holes in both ears. The holes were formed by black rings resembling the washers he'd recently replaced in the kitchen faucet. Colson caught the officer's glance and looked for himself. He was wrong about the earrings from a distance and in all the excitement he hadn't noticed. They were not earrings, but ear holes. Colson silently offered a little prayer of thanks that Nichole had not selected her husband from the beach.

"You just sit your butt down in the sand and exercise your right to remain silent," Sanders commanded. "I'll talk to you in a minute. Sit on your hands." He turned his gaze back to Colson. "You have I.D.?" Colson handed his license over. Sanders examined the license, not missing the photo of Colson in uniform. He said nothing about the photo, only a glance back at Colson to satisfy himself that he was looking at the same man in the photo, several years older. Colson provide a brief, concise report of the incident, just as if he was Sander's partner. No emotion, no conjecture, nothing but facts as if he were writing a police report.

Sanders turned to the girl. "Is that accurate, Miss?" Sanders took note of the palm-sized red mark on her right cheek as she nodded. "You need medical attention, Miss?" he asked. The girl shook her head in silence. "Stay right here," Sanders told the girl. "I'll need your information."

"That's bullshit," skinny boy shouted and shot to his feet. "She won't sign a complaint against me."

"I didn't tell you to stand up. Sit your ass back down, straighten your legs, and bend forward," Sanders said sharply.

He was already stepping toward the boy with handcuffs removed from his belt. He was cuffed before he could protest further, and on his feet with one fluid jerk of Sanders' arm.

"She ain't gonna sign no complaint," the boy repeated. Sanders marched him to the truck, stuffed him in the passenger side, and buckled him in.

"No, she's not going to sign. I am," Sanders explained and slammed the door.

Colson liked Sanders' efficiency and simple manner. He simply gathered the facts and made a decision. He hadn't tried to play counselor, teacher, or preacher. He had just done his job. The counseling, teaching, and preaching were better left to professionals in those fields, not the beat officer. The judging was to be handed down by the judge, not the dirt road deputy, or in this case, the sand dune cop. Colson placed him in group three. A far cry and a darn sight better than Pickett.

Sanders flipped open his field pad and jotted down the basic information. Colson didn't see what he wrote, but knew it by heart. The location, date, time, Colson's and the girls' name, dates of birth, address, and contact numbers. He received a case number from dispatch and flipped the pad closed. He handed both Colson and the girl a business card with the case number scribbled on back, saying they would be contacted at a later date by the district attorney's office, and if they had any questions they could contact him through headquarters. He told the girl the boy would be prohibited from making contact with her as a condition of bond, but it would be wise to obtain a protective order. All the steps followed without fail. The officer knew his job and did it well.

Sanders handed Colson's license back and said, "Where you from in Georgia?"

"Clay County," Colson replied.

"On vacation? Retired?"

Colson grinned. "Do I really look that old?"

"Just curious," Sanders said.

"Retired since January."

"You didn't get enough of this?"

"I have a daughter," Colson said without the grin.

Sanders returned the serious look with a nod of understanding. "Yeah, me too. Take care," Sanders said, and walked to the truck.

"Do you know Reserve Sergeant Pickett with the sheriff's office?" Colson asked.

Sanders paused and glanced over his shoulder. "Sure. Why?"

"Just curious."

"We all have a sergeant Pickett," Sanders replied. "If you know what I mean."

"He's the reason we all have an Internal Affairs Unit," Colson agreed. "Have a good shift."

"I probably don't have to tell you," Sanders said as though it was an afterthought. "You'll get a subpoena. Your statement will probably be sufficient, but you know these assistant D.A.s. They occasionally have to do something to justify their existence," Sanders said with a smirk.

Colson nodded. "No problem—and I understand. My daughter just married one."

"Sorry," Sanders lifted his left hand in a lazy wave and climbed into the truck. He lifted the microphone to inform dispatch he was on his way to the county jail with one in custody.

∽↝

Colson slid Sanders' card in his pocket and turned to walk back to the condo. The girl had already made it to her car, which was a black Acura NSX parked twenty-five feet away. No tears, no thank you, no nothing. That's the gratitude you get from spoiled, young people. Colson hoped she realized her poor judgment in the boyfriend selection department, but doubted it. She backed the car and drove toward the beach exit.

Mrs. Charles Alexander Cox, known by most residents as Faye, watched the excitement from her ground floor condo, number 105. She didn't like heights and preferred easy beach access. With all the resident beach goers, the elevators stank of sweat and suntan lotion most of the time, anyway. Mr. Cox died at age sixty-five, leaving the leathery, tanned, fifty-eight year old Faye with a home in Circleville, Ohio and condo 105 on Daytona Beach. She hated the frigid Ohio weather from October to May and decided to sell their home of thirty years and take permanent residence in Daytona.

"You're that policeman," Faye said from her deck chair as Colson walked past the ground level balcony. Her low conversational tone didn't catch his attention at first. She could have been speaking to a friend inside through the partially open screen door. Colson caught himself and turned. She stood and dumped her partially smoked cigarette in a wine glass sitting on a side table and walked to the edge of the curb.

She wore a white bathrobe, no shoes. Colson estimated she was sixty years old, but the leathery tan and cigarettes may have added a few years.

"They told me a cop moved in upstairs," she said.

"I'm retired," Colson said, matter-of-factly.

"You couldn't tell, the way you handled that man on the beach," she said with an admiring smile.

Colson returned her compliment with a small grin. "He was just a boy. He's got a long way to go to become a man, if ever."

"Either way, very impressive and no one else was going to do anything about it."

"Well, thank you for the kind words, ma'am," Colson replied, and then turned and took another step.

"You ever been down to the Space Coast, you know, the beach down from Kennedy Space Center?" she asked.

Colson stopped again. He would try not being rude to his neighbor during his first month in residence. He stepped back to the curb. She may be on the homeowner's association board and he may want to break out his gas grill on the balcony. Clearly against the rules, but the two poolside grills were usually occupied by timeshare residents and their hoard of screaming rug rats. He decided to be polite, but was tired from having to talk nice to every nutcase, hoodlum, and busybody for three decades. For the purpose of self-preservation, he decided not to crap in his own back yard and put on a friendly face.

"I watched a shuttle launch from the balcony a few years ago," he finally replied.

Faye moved a little closer to Colson, cutting her eyes briefly from side to side as if checking for eavesdroppers. *Was she going to impart some state secret? Maybe information about a neighbor who she saw smoking weed?* Colson thought. All information Colson was no longer interested in.

"No, silly. Not the shuttle," Faye said in a whisper. "It's the beach that's on federal property. You know, no state laws. It's the only nude beach in Florida. There's no federal law against nudity, but you probably knew that."

Colson was not familiar with federal law regarding nudity. For some reason, there never was an issue he could remember requiring such research in middle Georgia.

Colson played the whisper game, just for fun. "I didn't know about that, sorry."

"Well, I go down there about once a month. It's exhilarating," she said with a wink.

Colson said with feigned surprise, "Is that a fact? Well, your secret is safe with me." He returned the wink and spun to walk away.

"It's Faye Cox," she half-shouted as he stepped around the corner.

"Nice to meet you," he replied, not offering his name in return. His beautiful Ann was always the recipient of come-ons from men when he wasn't around. That's why he always wanted to be with her in public. To shield her from the flirting that certainly occurred on a daily basis. He never thought of himself as the one who needed shielding. He wished she were with him today. Especially if she was wearing her slinky two-piece bikini. Other women would have been too busy hating her guts to give him a second look. He was a big boy and could take care of himself, but there's nothing like a good-looking spouse to stifle the aggravation of such conversation. He and Ann were never social animals and didn't particularly enjoy the company of other people, including family. He made a mental note never to venture onto federal beach territory.

∾

Colson heard the sound of Steely Dan's *Hey Nineteen* as he reached the door to his condo. It had been his ringtone for three years. Time to change it, he supposed. It was well into the second verse when he pressed the touch screen to answer.

"Cole Slaw," the male voice said in a chipper tone. Only two people on the planet referred to Colson as Cole Slaw; one was his first patrol partner—he'd lost track of him years ago. The other was former Lieutenant Mike Beavers of the Bibb County Sheriff's Office in Macon, Georgia. They first met ten years ago while attending Internal Affairs training at the University of North Florida's Institute of Police Technology and Management in Jacksonville. He liked the guy, but he was a little too goofy. Colson thought "shifty" was a more accurate description.

31

Beavers was a little hard to figure out. Colson couldn't put his finger on what exactly bothered him about the man. He just knew he wouldn't hire him to feed the tracking dogs at the prison. Just a gut feeling. As misfortune would have it, Beavers retired two years ago and settled in the Daytona area. Ormond Beach, Colson remembered, just north of Daytona.

He saw Beavers at a sheriff's fundraiser six months ago, quite by accident. He made the mistake of telling Beavers he intended to move to Florida, not knowing he already lived there.

"What are you doing back up here?" Colson had asked him.

"Just staying in touch with my buds. Networking you might say. You know how cops are. Always fooling around and getting divorced," Beavers explained as he pulled a business card from his pocket and handed it to Colson.

Colson glanced at the card and read over it twice. *Fonda Beavers Investigations, LLC,* with an address of Ormnod Beach, Florida.

"Who's Fonda?" Colson asked.

Beavers produced a belly laugh. "Fonda's my wife." Beavers finally caught his breath. "The name is quite fitting, don't you think? I mean, especially since most of our business is from scorned women whose husbands are getting a little on the side. Women trust other women investigators a lot more than male investigators. She doesn't do the legwork, just the books, but it's a good business move and the name is priceless." Beavers started laughing again. Through his choking he said, "Fonda Beavers? I sure am!"

Colson recalled chuckling about it later that evening. What a goofball. Colson paused a beat as he held the phone, wishing he had let the call go to voice mail.

"You get settled in yet?" Beavers asked.

"For the most part," Colson replied

"What have you been up to?"

"Beach Patrol."

"You're kidding? Don't tell me you hooked a job with DBPD," Beavers said in disbelief. "You haven't been retired a full six months."

Colson chuckled. "Not really. Just people watching."

"Good, cause I've got something for you. You have a digital camera? If not, don't worry, I've got three."

"What are we talking about, Mike?" Colson asked.

"Did you apply for your P.I. license yet?"

Colson sighed. "No, I've decided I'm not…"

Beavers cut him short. "Forget it, you can work under my license."

"Look, Mike," Colson said firmly, "I've had enough of investigating, snooping, and digging up other people's dirt. It's depressing."

"C'mon, Colson. Listen, if you don't do a little part time, you'll sit around and rot. The wife and I are going on a cruise and I need this one favor. Just a small job. Take a few notes, a few photos, and it'll make you five hundred in mad money."

His pleading sounded pitiful. "You'll make an employer happy and maybe land a thief in jail without laying a hand on him."

Colson remained silent for a long moment. "When?"

Beavers' voice turned peppy again. "Great! How 'bout we have lunch day after tomorrow at Inlet Harbor and I'll give you the particulars. Eleven-thirty good? Any later and the stupid tourists will make it a forty minute wait."

"I was one of those stupid tourists just six months ago, Mike."

"You know what I mean. See you then."

"Sure, later." Colson pressed "end" on his phone.

❧ Chapter Five ❧

T he six-thousand-square-foot beachfront house belonged to Martin Cash. So did two restaurants, a popular beachside bar, and five liquor stores in Volusia County, coincidentally named "Cash's." He sat in a large rectangular hot tub perched on the flat roof, providing him a fabulous view of the Atlantic Ocean. Thick glass panels around the entire perimeter functioned as a windbreak, but didn't obstruct the view for those enjoying activities on the five-story roof. Those who Cash entertained enjoyed high definition movies projected on a theater-size screen, steaks grilled to order from the outdoor kitchen, and dancing on the ornately designed party area adjacent to a fully stocked bar under a stylish pergola.

The girl with straight brown hair sat in her yellow bikini on a beach chair five feet from the edge of the hot tub. Her slightly puffy red eyes were an obvious clue she had been crying. Her hair was longer in her driver's license photo and her eyes weren't red and puffy, but shining with the excitement of being a newly licensed driver. The excitement had long gone since her second underage drunk driving conviction and license revocation. In some file within control of the Alabama Department of Drivers Services, the license revealed her name as Tina Crowder, but all her friends called her T.C.

Cash placed his Long Island iced tea in one of the ten smartly arranged drink holders built into the spa and cut his eyes toward Tina. "So the police just happened by? You expect me to believe that?"

Tina crossed her arms as if chilled. "No, not at first. This other guy ran up and knocked Jason down and held him until the police got there."

"What other guy?" Cash insisted.

"I don't know. I've never seen him, I swear, but…"

Cash cut her short. "But what?"

"I don't know for sure," she said with hopes the information would be appreciated. "The guy may have been a cop. The beach cop and him either knew each other or something because what little I heard sounded like cop-to-cop talk."

Cash spread his arms, palms up, as if confused. "You didn't tell them anything? You didn't press charges? You didn't give a statement?"

"The cop said I didn't have to. The other guy told him what happened and gave a statement," she explained, trying to avoid the rage she saw building is Cash's eyes.

He stood in the tub and pointed in her face. "Then you should have said the guy saw wrong and you two were just horse playing, you stupid little bimbo. Get the hell down stairs and don't go outside this house, you understand?"

Tina rolled her eyes, spun on her heels, and jogged to the roof elevator. Cash watched her disappear behind the elevator door and sat back down in the spa, cursing under his breath. He glanced out over the ocean and considered his next move. He dried his hands on a beach towel, grabbed his cell phone, and touched the speed dial for the manager of his largest liquor store. The cheerful answer came before the second ring.

"Cash's on Nova Road, this is Randy."

"The security guy, get in touch with him," Cash said without a greeting.

"Oh, Mr. Cash," Fuller said respectfully. "You mean the off-duty sheriff's guy that's here tonight? You wanna talk to him?"

Cash gritted his teeth and took a deep breath. He hated it when stupid people assumed one thing when he obviously meant another. "That's not what I asked you, is it? Call the guy you hired to run the backgrounds and have him come to the house."

"You want to deal with him direct this time? I didn't think you wanted to be direct…"

"Just do it," Cash snapped, cutting Fuller off mid-word. "What's his name?"

"It's Pickett."

⁓

Tina rode the elevator to the second story of the house. The door opened to a twenty-five by thirty-foot media room. She stepped out onto the rich, tan terracotta tile. The view through the floor-to-ceiling glass paneled walls was almost identical to that from the roof, but at a slightly lower angle. It was a strikingly beautiful view of the Atlantic over the balcony railing, depending on your perspective. Beautiful and totally relaxing to a tourist sipping a margarita by the pool, but the sun beating down on the sand and through the glass was nothing more than a glaring reminder of the six months she had been Martin Cash's captive.

She recalled what an unusually cold January it had been, hitching rides from Montgomery to Orlando. All she wanted was a warmer climate, better friends, and a new life. The judge at the initial hearing didn't buy her defense attorney's argument that the meth wasn't hers, but it was true. It had been the week between Christmas and New Year's over two years ago when her former best friend and two of her guy friends picked her up for a night at the twenty-four hour bowling alley. At eighteen she could not legally drink, but that didn't prevent the older guys from slipping a few ounces in her soft drink cup on occasion. No one ever gave them a problem, if they even noticed.

The cop who stopped them on the way home that night was a smartass. He wanted to know where they had been, where they were going, and why they were out so late. The guy driving didn't help matters by giving the cop a false name and insisting his driver's license had been stolen. She thought it odd at the time, because they had been doing more karaoke than drinking and he obviously wasn't slobbering drunk. Surely he could pass a breathalyzer. The second cop car was driven by a female. She saw the second set of blue strobes pull in behind the first cop car. The first cop didn't ask about searching the car until the female cop was standing just to the rear of her side window.

The driver, Kyle, was an idiot. He kept repeating "why" each time the officer asked to search his car. Kyle and his friend were searched and put in the back of the first cop car, and then she and Kellie were put through the same routine by the female cop and stuck in the back of her car. It seemed like an hour before the police dog arrived and sniffed through the car. She couldn't see what the dog was doing, but remembered the cop saying the dog "alerted" during the preliminary hearing. She also remembered the short little celebration and high fives the cops gave each other over that little bag of powder she had never seen before. She would be home in Montgomery right now if Kellie's boyfriends had grown a couple of balls and claimed ownership of the meth. But they didn't, and she certainly was not going to admit to something she wasn't guilty of, so everyone went to jail.

Her court-appointed attorney couldn't convince the district attorney to drop or lower the charges. They said something about the meth being "within the span of control by everyone in the car." She didn't have the money for a good attorney, so she had to settle with what the county gave her. The case took over eight months to be indicted and it took another month to set the trial. She couldn't stand the thought of being convicted of felony drug possession and made her decision to run a week before trial. She hated cops, she hated attorneys, and she hated her former friends. So maybe this dude on the beach was some kind of off-duty cop, supposedly coming to her rescue. "Well, thanks a lot," she mumbled sarcastically, a lot of good that did her. It just created more trouble than it prevented.

The last hitch of her journey was with the Nelson family, who picked her up while driving down Interstate 75 to Universal Studios with their sixteen-year-old daughter and her girlfriend. They left from a restaurant in Valdosta, Georgia after she spent her last ten dollars on breakfast. Mr. and Mrs. Nelson seemed quite concerned about her situation during the brief drive. Tina contrived a story that her widowed mother had recently died from heart problems and she was trying to locate her cousin who lived in the Florida Keys. The part about the cousin and her dead mother was a lie, but the part about going to the Keys was true. Mr. Nelson apologized that they couldn't take her any further than Orlando as they exited onto the Ronald Reagan Turnpike.

"The kids want to go to Universal," he said, rolling his eyes.

"That's fine," Tina assured him and thanked them repeatedly for the ride.

Mrs. Nelson scolded her husband when he handed Tina a twenty-dollar bill, insisting he should give her at least fifty. "Twenty's more than plenty," Tina told them.

Mr. Nelson wrote his cell number on a Universal Studios brochure and handed it to her. "If you need us, we'll be down here for the week." He looked genuinely concerned. She gave them both a hug and waved to the girls before she walked away from the minivan.

Tina walked down the ramp from the Universal Studios parking deck on South Kirkman Road, toward the Interstate. She intended to start hitching south once again when a black Acura NSX pulled up next to her and slowed. At first she wouldn't make eye contact with the driver or turn her head in his direction. She was tired of the whistles, predatory glares, and sexual comments from truckers and weirdoes. She suspected the driver was another dirty old man, but as the car moved past her and came to a stop on the shoulder, a younger guy was waving at her in the side mirror. Tina wasn't interested in sports cars, but knew this one was very expensive. She wondered how he could afford it. Tina walked to the driver's window as it slid down.

"What's up?" the guy said with a smile. "Need a ride?"

Tina didn't answer, just looked up and down the length of the freeway below her. She guessed the temperature was around 90 degrees, but the humidity made it feel like 110. The tight little cockpit of the Acura would be cool, but awfully close quarters for a ride with a stranger.

The young guy broke the silence. "I'm headed back to my old man's place in Daytona. You wanna ride, 'cause I need to get back?"

Tina finally looked at him and paused for another moment. She gave a brief nod and walked around the front of the car to the passenger side. To Tina it felt more like she was putting on the car instead of getting into it.

"Thanks," she said, closing the door and dropping her bag between her feet.

$$\sim\!\sim$$

The trip from Orlando to Daytona on Interstate 4 took a little less than an hour. They sat in silence for the first five minutes.

Tina broke the silence this time. "So, what do you do?"

"I work for my old man. Pretty much run one of his restaurants, but he has a bar and some liquor stores in Daytona that I'll be running in a few years," he bragged. "By the way, my name's Jason Cash."

Tina looked straight ahead, even though Jason turned to check her reaction. When he saw none, he turned his attention back to the interstate.

He said, "So, what are doing hitching rides?"

Tina gave him the same story she shared with the Nelson family. The death of her widowed mother and her plans to hook up with her cousin in the Keys to find a job.

"No jobs in the Keys unless you want to dig swimming pools or sell ashtrays to tourists."

"I'll figure it out," she said. "I always get by."

"We always need good part time help at the liquor stores. I have to stop on the way in and you could fill out an application if you want," he said enthusiastically. "You could build up a little traveling money in a few months during tourist season and set yourself up in the Keys next winter."

"Maybe," Tina said. "I'll think about it."

"Probably should think quick. We'll be there in fifteen minutes, unless you want off on 95 to catch a ride south."

Tina exhaled and thought for a long second. "That's fine. I need someplace to use the bathroom anyway."

"Cool," Jason exclaimed and turned up the radio, blasting a type of grunge music Tina didn't recognize. She guessed it must have been some local knock-off band, because it almost made her ears bleed. The sports car lurched forward as Jason shifted into third gear and sped around the International Speedway exit loop and onto the four-lane surface road. The sudden acceleration snatched Tina back in her seat. She thought for a second they had been struck from behind, but realized he was just trying to show off. She had to brace her right hand on the dash to fight the centrifugal force.

"If you want me to wait until we get there to use the bathroom, you'll stop trying to kill me," she said with mild frustration in her voice.

Jason chuckled while moving the shifter into forth, accelerating to seventy-five miles per hour. The NSX jerked into the left lane and emerged from under the I-95 overpass. A few seconds later he gestured to his right.

"The Daytona Speedway," he said as if he were a tour guide. Tina couldn't make herself look. The fear of imminent death locked her eyes forward.

"Will you keep your eyes on the road?" she snapped. "You're going to kill us both."

Jason laughed and pressed the accelerator to the floor.

"You'll get stopped," Tina shouted as the NSX exceeded ninety, darting into the right lane to avoid a motorcycle and just as quickly back to the left lane.

"Who cares?" Jason said nonchalantly. "My old man owns the cops here." The car mercifully slowed to fifty, swung right onto Nova Road, and then jerked left into the parking lot of Cash's Liquors. Tina wished a thousand times she hadn't let Jason talk her into filling out that employment application.

✺

Sheriff Langston watched Sergeant Kim Reese walk out of his office. A better description would have been skipped out the door. Reese had given Langston a huge smile and handshake when told she was being promoted to Lieutenant. Of course she promised him one hundred and ten percent of her effort and loyalty. Langston was counting on the loyalty part. He could care less how much actual police work she would do. Reese was a smart girl and good cop, but those traits didn't top Langston's "highly promotable" list at this point. He smiled to himself, remembering how her face lit up when he assigned her as a supervisor with the organized crime task force.

Reese would have been happy with the reassignment alone, but the promotion was icing on the cake. Langston warned her about the long, late hours. She responded with one of those smart, professional, serious looks he expected. "I understand sir. That's to be expected and I am eager for the challenge." Langston remembered making almost identical statements when accepting his numerous promotions and reassignments, as every other cop in every other agency had for a hundred years.

"We have initiated a high profile case in OCU, so I'll need and expect your full commitment to the agency. I'll get you started. Maybe ride with you a couple of shifts," Langston explained to Reese with a smile.

Her smile widened. "I look forward to it, Sheriff."

"This is serious business," Langston said. "You're familiar with Martin Cash, correct?"

Reese matched Langston's serious demeanor. "Yes, sir. Hard not to know about him around here."

Langston pursed his lips. "He's dirty and we're going to put him away. Drugs, possibly meth and God knows what else. So we're going to be working this from both the narcotics and organized crime angle."

Reese nodded. "We'll make it happen, Sheriff."

Langston replayed the memory of Kim's grateful smile and snapped back to the present as he remembered to call the property room deputy. He pressed another speed dial button.

"Deputy Duncan. Lieutenant Reese is on her way right now. She'll need new credentials, photos, and uniforms, so get on it," he ordered.

Langston pressed a new line and waited two rings. A familiar male voice answered.

"Organized Crime Unit, Sergeant Cantrell."

"It's Langston, Cantrell. What's the status of the Cash case?"

Cantrell cleared his throat. "Yes, Sheriff. Ah, we've kicked it off and run histories on all his people. Not many red flags. Most have misdemeanors convictions, but one is on probation for carrying a concealed weapon out of Alabama and has a conviction for a rolling meth lab down in Hollywood. There's a second guy who has an aggravated battery conviction. One of the agents said he was a promising contender as a UFC fighter a few years ago."

"What's the meth lab guy's name?" Langston asked. He could hear Cantrell rustling paperwork.

"Meth lab guy's name is Randal James Fuller. The second guy, the fighter, is Jay Taylor, aka Jay "The Terrible" Taylor in fighting circles."

"I remember him," Langston said. "Almost killed some doctor. I was there when he was arrested. He didn't run, fight, or resist; but who would with six SWAT guys standing around you with AR 15s pointed at you?"

"This Randy Fuller guy," Cantrell continued, "he was just down at the jail posting bail for Cash's kid, Jason. Some domestic spat."

Langston sat up straight and barked into the phone, "So just when did you plan on telling me his kid was in jail? When I retire?"

Cantrell hesitated. "I'm sorry, Sheriff. I didn't, I mean I didn't know that you didn't know. I didn't think you'd want me to do anything with him. You know, I thought it would burn the investigation."

"Think Cantrell. Use that investigative head of yours. You take advantage of all available opportunities and resources. All the jail lines are recorded. It's possible that idiot kid could have said something useful on the phone. We could have delayed the bonding process and put him in population, at least for a few hours."

"I'm sorry, Sheriff," Cantrell apologized. "It was my screw up. Won't happen again."

Langston's voice resumed a normal tone, but still carried the heavy weight of an elected official who was very comfortable with authority. "You put surveillance on those two convicts Cash hired and report back to me. If Cash is dirty…" Langston corrected himself mid-sentence. "Not if, I know he's dirty—and I want to know what he's got these guys up to. He'll be using them. The meth guy is our best bet. He's either using Taylor as a heavy or bodyguard."

"Understood," Cantrell said. "I'll get two agents on them."

"Damn it," Langston snapped again. "Do you need to be re-trained, Cantrell? You can't conduct an effective surveillance with two agents. You'll get burnt. You put at least three on him. I've got to be out over the weekend. I'm gonna raise you on the radio and you better be out there when I call for a report."

"Yes, sir," Cantrell said and braced for the next barrage of insults, but the line went dead.

⁓

The newly promoted Lieutenant Reese could not suppress her beaming smile as she collected her new badge from Deputy Duncan. She had her sergeant's badge already in hand to relinquish even before Duncan removed the new one from the large jeweler's zip lock bag. The not-quite-as-excited Deputy Duncan maneuvered the desk-mounted camera to project a red laser dot in the middle of Lieutenant Reese's forehead and asked her to smile for the camera. He wanted to tell her to drop the smile, but decided against it because she outranked him and he was just a road deputy, pulling property room duty because of two at-fault traffic accidents on duty last year.

Duncan clipped Reese's photo to size, carefully placed it on the top, right corner of her new credentials, and fed it into a small laminating device on the counter. The small machine hummed, pulling the card through one end and spitting out the other. Duncan handed the warm, new identification to Reese without a word. She examined the I.D. for a several seconds, focusing on her new title, Deputy Sheriff Lieutenant.

Reese pushed her I.D. behind the clear plastic window in her wallet, opposite the polished gold badge. "Anything else?" she asked, still smiling at the property officer.

He forced a smile his eyes contradicted, and with every ounce of his being attempted to contain his sarcasm. "Not until they make you a Captain."

She recognized the jab, but was in too good of a mood to berate the officer. She knew not every officer could rise through the ranks. She had earned it, and she knew this guy wasn't pulling property room duty because he had arrested one of America's ten most wanted.

She forgot about the property guy by the time she stepped into the blistering June sun and crossed the parking lot to her Jeep. She pulled her cell from her purse and pressed the number two speed dial. She turned the air conditioner to high while waiting for an answer.

"Hey, babe," the male voice said in greeting.

"I got it," Reese said with enthusiasm.

"I knew you would."

"And how would you know that for sure?" she said suspiciously. "There were at least five or six sergeants going for promotion and he gave me the supervisors spot in O.C.U. What, you think I wasn't qualified?"

"I didn't say that."

"Langston said he'd be willing to ride a couple of shifts with me himself to bring me up to speed."

"I bet," the man mumbled.

"What?"

"You know he's going to try to get in your pants. I'm happy for you, but—"

"Stop worrying about it," she interrupted. "He has too much personal baggage."

"Is that the only reason?"

"Of course not. Besides, I'm already dating the next sheriff."

"I'm going to win the election."

"You mean *we* are going to win the election. If Langston finds out I'm helping you oppose him, I'll be writing parking tickets at the pier."

"You'll do great, don't worry. I'm anxious to hear about your cases."

"Langston ordered an investigation on Martin Cash. It'll be my first case." There were several seconds of silence. "You there?" she asked.

"Yeah," the man replied. "I was just thinking a second. Good for you."

"You want to celebrate...have dinner?" she said excitedly.

"Yeah," the man said again.

"Okay, you can come by at six. Bye," she said, and closed her phone.

On the opposite end of the line, Pickett pressed "end" on his phone. He rubbed his chin with the palm of his hand and narrowed his eyes. His phone rang again an instant later. All he did was move his finger a fraction to the left and press the little green icon to answer.

"You change your mind?" he said.

After a long pause: "Is that you, Pickett?" a confused male voice asked.

"What? Yeah, who's this?" Pickett demanded, embarrassed.

"Randy Fuller, from Cash's."

"Oh, what do you need, Fuller? Is there a problem with the security? Don't tell me one of those slug deputies didn't show again. I'll fire his—"

"No," Fuller interrupted. "Martin, ah, Mr. Cash wants you to come out to the house."

"What does he want now?"

"I don't know, Pickett. If you want to keep the security job, you won't keep him waiting."

"I'm on my way."

"I'll let him know," Randy said and disconnected. Pickett waited for oncoming traffic to pass, made a U-turn, and then crossed back over the Port Orange Bridge. *What the hell*, was all he could think.

⟫ Chapter Six ⟪

The Savannah College of Art and Design, known more prominently as SCAD to its students and alumni, is a type of urban college with its campus spread across various locations in Atlanta. The main campus is located in Savannah, but metro Atlanta was just too lucrative an area not to host a satellite school. At an average of thirty thousand dollars tuition per year, most middle-class students would have to be recipients of very generous scholarships or have parents who were willing to sacrifice their lives working extra jobs. The multiple areas of study prepared graduates for professional life in the fine arts, media design, and marketing.

Twenty-two-year-old Nichole Colson Walker had dreamed of attending SCAD since she first heard about it from her high school art teacher. Money had been an issue then and she couldn't attend straight out of high school, even with a superior transcript. She grew to understand that being the daughter of a deputy sheriff and a payroll manager wasn't conducive to the price of such an expensive education. But she determined to make the best of it and had proven herself in high school, graduating with honors and being awarded a partial state-funded scholarship. Nichole attended Kennesaw State University and maintained a 4.0 average in hopes of attending SCAD as a graduate. However, no matter how much she aspired to attain a degree from SCAD, she would gladly give up it all up if she could have Mom back at home, alive and well.

When her mother was dying, SCAD was the last thing on Nichole's mind. In addition to her grieving, she witnessed her father's near breakdown and his broken heart. She had never known such anguish, and hoped to never experience it again. Even as a newlywed, Nichole could not imagine the pain of losing a spouse. Her father was strong, but Ann's passing brought him closer to breaking than Nichole ever expected. Even when death is imminent, a person is never really prepared when it comes. Never.

When her father informed her of his decision to move to Florida, she felt like she was becoming an orphan. She loved her husband deeply, but it was her first year of marriage and she hadn't completely broken the bond of living at home for the first twenty-one years of her life. Through private tears she supported her father and knew it was best for him to get away. What she didn't expect was for him to offer her and Bobby the home she grew up in, or the college fund he set up to cover her first two years at SCAD.

Nichole accepted the offer to take care of the house because she couldn't bear the thought of him selling it, but she expressly declined the tuition gift. "That's yours and Mom's insurance money," she insisted. "She wanted you to be taken care of. I'm married now, and you'll need it."

"Look, Nichole," Grey countered, "nothing would have made your Mother happier than for you to attend SCAD. The reason she became so frustrated when you talked about it was only because we couldn't afford it then," he explained. "It would make her happy."

It was bittersweet when Nichole and Bobby moved in, but they didn't miss the apartment for an instant. She had no difficulty being accepted to SCAD. Her portfolio was exceptional and her transcript from Kennesaw State was outstanding.

They were standing in the driveway on the day Grey left for Florida. Holding back tears again, she managed a smile. "I'll take care of the house, Dad. And I'll be responsible with the tuition."

He smiled and gave her a hug. "I know you will, Babe."

Nichole gave him a smile. "I'm glad you trust me."

Grey glanced up to the second story of the house as if examining a loose shingle on the roof. He chuckled.

"What?" Nicole said.

"When your mother was pregnant everyone wanted to know if she was having a boy or girl, but she wanted to be surprised."

Nichole grinned. "I remember her saying that, but what's funny?"

"When people at work would ask if Ann was having a boy or girl, I didn't know."

"What did you tell them?"

"I told them of course I knew. I said we were having a republican." Grey's chuckle turned into a burst of laughter. Nichole laughed and they hugged again. Grey slipped into the car and Nichole bent over to kiss him on the cheek before he backed out of the driveway.

"You be safe and call when you get there."

Grey waved and shifted into reverse. "I'll do it, Babe. You call me every weekend."

"I will, Dad. Love you," she said.

"Love you more."

Colson let the Corvette roll back into the cul-de-sac, and then drove away.

Nichole chuckled again at the memory of the day her Dad left for the beach as she opened the door of her VW Beetle for the hour drive back to Clay County. She picked up her phone and pressed the contact listed as "Dad."

∽

The whistles were blowing in stereo to Colson's left and right, up and down the beach. The one he heard most clearly came from the direction of the lifeguard stand five stories down and thirty yards directly in front of him in the sand. The dark storm head had been creeping from south to north on the horizon for the last hour. In the last fifteen minutes the dark mass took a sharp western turn and was gaining on the shore like a locomotive. Colson lifted his cocktail from the side table and took a sip while gazing at the approaching storm. Ann would have scolded him for having a drink before noon.

He didn't mind the storms. In most cases they swept in from the Atlantic, dumped thirty minutes of cooling rain on the beach, and ran inland to Orlando. The sun would be back in all its glory within the hour and he could admire the deserted beach, its then gray sand punctured by a million raindrops. Rainwater would rush down the length of the building in the gutter attached to the stucco finish of the condo wall just inches from the balcony railing and slow to a lonely trickle.

Colson relaxed in his chair and admired the storm hovering miles offshore. He could only see as far as the first row of pines in the woods behind his house in Georgia. Here, he could see the curve of the earth. Silent lightning bolts traveled at the speed of light to the ocean below; the resulting thunder absorbed by hundreds of cubic miles of dead air and dying before reaching the shore. A thin veil of rain—like a sheer curtain—slowing became visible. It appeared as if it were being towed across the water by the towering storm. A staggered line of large gray seagulls glided above him with the tips of their wings almost touching the roof as they rode the updraft deflected skyward by the five-story structure.

The lifeguard now stood in his perch, waving a red flag in sharp motions from left to right, and blowing his whistle with new urgency. Reluctant swimmers, inner tube riders and hip waders made their way to the shore and began gathering towels, beach chairs, Frisbees, and drink coolers. With armloads of equipment, parents motioned for children to follow them—some to vehicles whose interiors had reached a hundred-and-twenty degrees in the relentless Daytona sun. Others climbed concrete steps to condominium gates, stopping briefly at knee-high shower faucets to spray sand off their legs and feet. Colson still lounged on the beach occasionally, but only when he felt like erecting his ten-foot square canopy and dragging a cooler and beach chair down the elevator and across the scorching parking lot. It required two trips and Ann had always helped him erect the canopy and carry the equipment. Most days Colson conducted his people watching from the fifth floor balcony. If it meant he had grown lazy in his early retirement, then so be it.

He knew retired cops who did nothing but sit around, collecting their pensions, and piddling around the house. Within five years they became fat and miserable individuals whose marriage had developed into a cold war and their children long since gone. Colson knew he had to stay active, but had always promised himself he would no longer do police work. Problem was, he didn't know anything else. Colson wished he hadn't agreed to meet Mike Beavers. The man would pester him until he took the job. Beavers' earlier persistence guaranteed it.

The storm moved in fast, but the thunder and lightning didn't perform as advertised from several miles off shore. Large, heavy drops pelted the sand as several drivers moved their vehicles slowly toward the access road. Others remained parked in hopes the rain would move on and allow them to capitalize on another couple hours of sun. And move on it did. He checked his watch. Eleven-twenty. He would never make the meeting by eleven-thirty. Beavers would wait, or he wouldn't. Colson sighed and set his glass down. "One job, Beavers," he said. "I don't like it already."

He rode the elevator to the underground garage and walked to space number sixteen. He slipped into his car and drove to the roll-up steel gate. It began its slow ascent when the tires reached a spot on the concrete above the pressure plate. The sun was high and hot again as he ascended the driveway to the street. Colson turned south on A1A and gunned the car into the left lane. The traffic was nothing compared to metro Atlanta gridlock. That alone was reason enough to move here. Just past the Port Orange Bridge, A1A narrows to two lanes, with private residences lining both sides of the road. Some large, some small, some modest, and some extravagant. No matter their condition, the location eliminated the possibility of Colson owning one. Location, location, location is what he'd always heard, and the realtors were correct, even in this recession. He was searching for the pre-set '80's radio station when his cell rang.

"Hey, Daddy," Nichole said in a cheery tone.

Colson grinned. "Hey, babe. It's so good to hear your voice."

"I miss you, Dad."

"I miss you more than you know, honey. When are you coming to see me? The weather's great. You can bring what's his name...ah, Robert."

"Oh, Dad," she said sarcastically, "don't act like you forgot his name. Bobby just started his new job, but I'm going to try and make it down in a few weeks."

"You better," his voice taking a fatherly tone. "You know how old I'm getting."

Nichole chuckled. "Right, Dad. Darn near ancient at fifty. I'm surprised they still let you drive."

Colson laughed. "Yeah, don't forget to bring my bedpan. You know my favorite one with that picture of the president in the bottom."

She laughed with him for a moment, and then a serious tone returned to her voice. "I love you, Dad. I want you to take care of yourself."

"I will, honey. You come see me when you can."

"I will, Dad. I'm about home, so I'll let you go. Love you."

"Love you back."

‿◠◡

Colson turned right into the Quik Mart convenience store. He thought it truly amazing how many convenience stores didn't upgrade their gas pumps to accept credit and debit cards. He walked up to the straggly teenage attendant to prepay, and pulled his debit card from his wallet. His retirement star was hidden behind a leather flap and he tried to keep it that way. But as luck would have it, the boy must have caught a glimpse of his ID on the opposite side as he pulled the card from behind it.

"Cop, huh?" the boy said with an obvious sneer. Colson tilted his head with slight disgust as he handed over the card. The young attendant wore a tan shirt with a Quik Mart logo on the left breast and a plastic nameplate over the right. He looked slightly of middle-eastern descent, but his accent suggested he had lived here all his life. His black hair was just long enough to cover his ears. He read the boy's nametag and tried to sound it out silently in his head. *Raja.*

"Just put thirty on the card for gas," Colson said flatly.

"Which pump?" the boy answered.

"How 'bout the only one with a car sitting next to it."

The boy glanced out the front window, slid Colson's card across the counter, and then punched in numbers on the point of sale device.

"What would you do if I got robbed right now?" Raja asked.

"I'm retired."

The boy looked at Colson and cocked his head with his own look of disgust. This young man's encounters with law enforcement must not have been very pleasant. Colson was perfectly content to let it go. He had seen the attitude so frequently over the years he'd almost be shocked and disappointed if it was different here. But Raja wouldn't to let it go.

"I thought you guys were like on duty all the time. You still got ID, so like don't you like have to do something? So what would you do?"

Colson took his receipt, sighed and glanced at the boy. "Well, Roger. Like, I'd make an excellent witness."

The boy spoke up as Colson walked to the door.

"It's Rah-Jah."

Colson waved back dismissively. "Whatever."

As he turned south on A1A, he made a mental note to pull all the cards out of his ID and put them in the three-dollar Velcro wallet he bought his first week in town. It wasn't worth the trouble.

One of the more extravagant homes on the beach side of A1A was located two miles north of Inlet Harbor and approximately three miles south of the Quik Mart where Colson met his new best buddy, Raja. It was equally impressive from the street as it was from the beach. Ten-foot-high stucco walls stretched the length of the property as a backdrop to thirty tall palm trees. A passing driver could view the top two stories of the massive residence over the front walls. Most men would testify the structure was a hideous pink color and wouldn't be caught dead living in it. On the other hand, most women would argue the color was an appropriate Florida mauve and would live there in a second.

Martin Cash sat in an oversized, distressed, dark chocolate leather recliner. The floor-to-ceiling tinted windows on the opposite side of the large living area provided a full view of the private beach beyond, but Cash was concentrating on his laptop instead of admiring the view. The email currently open had Cash's undivided attention and was the highest bid of the day. Fifty-five thousand upon delivery was being offered by "Darkhorse121." Reasonable, but the bidding would continue until midnight and Cash was patient when money was involved. He minimized the email and selected a photo file. A grin formed as he admired the girl in the photo, allowing his eyes to trace her figure up and down. The bidding will be strong tonight. The beach photo of Kara in her bikini accentuated every curve of her young form, framed perfectly by her long dark hair. She had been living at the beach house for three days at the time and could still produce a convincing smile, especially after being told the photos would be used for liquor store advertisements in the Daytona Beach News Journal.

A SecureTech alert window popped up in the middle of the screen. He touched the window and a moment later the girl's photo was replaced by a full screen view of a motorcycle rider at the front gate. He touched the speaker icon.

"Yes."

He watched the rider's head turn toward the external intercom mounted within a stucco pillar adjacent to the driveway.

"Sergeant Pickett here to see Mr. Cash. He's expecting me."

"Pull up to the right side entrance and park. Someone will show you in," Cash instructed.

The black iron gates swung inward. Pickett hit the clutch and drove through the gates toward the front of the residence. The driveway looped around a water fountain to his left. He veered right on a secondary drive and parked under a portico covering the side entrance as instructed. A wiry young man stepped out the door and stood with his arms crossed.

"You Pickett?" Jason asked.

Pickett nodded. Jason motioned to the interior of the house, and then turned and walked inside with Pickett in tow. They passed through a kitchen that would be the envy of any chef. Stainless steel commercial appliances gleamed among cream colored, distressed French country-style cabinetry, accented by black granite countertops. A large man devouring a sub sandwich glanced at the pair walking by from his perch on a high seat at the large kitchen island. Picket returned his glance. He appeared to be over six feet, but it was difficult to estimate accurately since he was seated. His broad shoulders and thick chest were typical of a career body builder or a prizefighter. His cauliflower ears and bent nose answered Pickett's question. He turned his attention back to the sandwich as Jason led Pickett into the adjacent great room.

Martin Cash hadn't moved from his recliner and his focus remained on the computer screen. Pickett was briefly captivated by the ocean view through the two-story floor-to-ceiling windows. It would forever ruin the puny view of thick grass and shrub through his inland bedroom window. He was determined to own a house such as Cash's, but the prospects didn't look good considering his suffering insurance business. It wasn't showing improvement in spite of the "Hope and Change" economy. Maybe he shouldn't be wasting his time playing police and spend more time busting his hump selling whole life policies.

"How do you know Randy?" Cash asked.

"I'm sorry," Pickett said, turning his attention to Cash and away from the view.

"From my main store," Cash said with mild irritation. "Where we pay you for security."

Pickett's face registered recognition. "Oh, Randy. I sold him insurance a couple of years ago."

Cash squinted. "Insurance?"

"It's what I do for a living. That's my main source of income. Reserve deputies donate their time. Well, except for the part-time security I arrange for you and a few other businesses."

"You work free for Langston, but you don't seem to have a problem charging me thirty dollars an hour for security."

Pickett shrugged and took a breath. Cash waved his hand. "It doesn't matter. That's not why I called you out here. I need you to check into someone for me."

Pickett clasped his hands in front of him and rocked back on his heels. "Mr. Cash, I spoke to Randy about this. Running criminal backgrounds on your employees is understandable and I've been glad to help, but it's kind of a gray area—legally, that is."

Cash stood to his feet, glared, and pointed his finger in Pickett's face. "Gray area, hell," he shouted. "You didn't score well at the academy, I suspect. You know as well as I do it's straight up illegal, and one word from me could land you in your own jail. Who will they come looking for, me? Even if you say I asked or even paid you to get the information, it won't matter. You are the person with the access and you are the one who is breaking the law."

Pickett's eyes widened just enough to alert Cash he hit the nail on the head. He couldn't immediately form a response.

"And help me out," Cash mocked sarcastically. "You've been paid five hundred apiece for those records, and then you come in here talking to me like I'm an idiot and don't know the law."

Pickett stepped back. "No, I didn't say anything like that." The big man moved into the room, apparently drawn by Cash's raised tone. He took a position at the door, blocking the entire frame with his shoulders. Pickett took a second step backwards, not noticing the leather chair behind him, and collapsed into its soft cushions. Cash lowered his arm and settled back in his chair. He glared at Pickett for several moments, sighed, and slapped both armrests.

"That's not what this is about, Pickett, but now that we know our positions on the food chain, I'm assigning you a project."

Pickett raised his eyes to Cash, wondering what was next. Another girl's history to check or license to run? It had confused him as to why Cash even bothered since all the histories he provided so far revealed some type of past criminal activity involving drug use or theft. He always assumed it was for employment purposes since he was given copies of employment applications to draw their personal information from, but what were the odds his business would attract that many with such histories? A couple were wanted out of state, but all were at least on probation or first offender status. The wanted ones were tricky since they weren't in custody. By NCIC rules a response had to be sent within minutes of receiving the wanted hit. Pickett always had the technician respond that the person was not in custody and the query was run for information purposes only. One anonymous word from Cash and his certification would be pulled, at best; and if Langston was pissed off, he would see him prosecuted. It would probably be jail since Sheriff Langston hated him. He needed time to think, but it wasn't now. Pickett was looking at Cash, but not focusing on him. His mind was a swirl of activity. All he heard was "beach bum."

Pickett refocused his eyes. "What about a beach bum?"

"Get the shit out of your ears," Cash snapped. "There's a beach bum out near the Sundowner condos who thinks he's a hot shot. Probably some type of rent-a-cop. Snatched Jason around and got him arrested. I want to know who and what he is."

Pickett sat up straight and spread his arms slightly, turning his palms upward. "When was this?"

Jason walked to the back of Cash's chair and rested his hands on the headrest. "Today around eleven. Bastard nearly broke my arm. The beach cop didn't even let me tell my side, just took this guy's word for everything."

"So what were you doing?" Pickett said.

"Nothing. We were just having an argument."

"That's all, just arguing?"

"It doesn't matter, Pickett," Cash commanded. "No one jerks my son around and gets him arrested without answering to me."

Pickett shook his head. "Influencing a witness is a felony, and if you—" Cash cut him short.

"Do we have to go through this again, Pickett? You just find him, I'll deal with him."

Pickett looked at Jason. "I can get a copy of the report from the PD, but did you hear him give his name to the beach cop?"

Jason looked at the ceiling for a moment, then back at Pickett. "Something Colson. I can't remember the first name, it was weird."

Pickett squinted in vague recognition, trying to remember where he had heard the name. "What did he look like?"

"Gray, short hair. Forty something. Kinda thick."

"His hair was thick?"

"No, thick in the chest."

Pickett strained to remember, and then his eyes widened.

"What?" Cash demanded. "You know him?"

Pickett looked back to Cash. "Maybe. I mean, I don't know him, but I think I know who he is. I can't remember his first name either. I stopped him the other day for speeding."

"Well, who the hell is he?" said Cash.

Pickett's gaze steadied on Cash "A retired sheriff's major from Georgia."

⟫ Chapter Seven ⟪

The Volusia County Organized Crime Task Force office is located in a storefront in a strip shopping center at an undisclosed location. It consists of a dozen officers assigned from various agencies in the county. A sheriff's office lieutenant commands two sergeants, one on day watch, and the other on night watch. Four of the agents are employees of the sheriff's office. Two are assigned from Daytona Beach Police, two from De Land Police and a single agent from Ormond Beach Police. The police officers assigned from their respective agencies carried sheriff's office identification. During their assignment to the Organized Crime Unit, they're sworn by Sheriff Langston as deputies with statewide jurisdiction in the event their cases extended beyond the boundaries of the county. The task force was about to be blessed with its new Commander, Lieutenant Kimberly Reese.

Sergeant Cantrell sat at his desk with his head resting in the palm of his left hand and a pen in his right. No matter how long he stared at the roster, no new names appeared. He crossed off the names of two agents who were on leave and another who was on light duty with a broken ankle after a foot chase with a suspect, ending with both jumping off a ten-foot wall. Bad guy gone; agent on light duty. Cantrell shook his head. Langston expected day and night surveillance on Cash's goons. No one even knew what they were up to, if anything. The financial records hadn't turned up any red flags other than Cash was losing his ass like everyone else in the recession. There was no confidential informant giving up information and no probable cause to go up on a wiretap. That added up to zero. A wiretap wasn't even in the cards and a judge wouldn't even consider it unless they had exhausted all other reasonable investigative means to begin with. They weren't even sure what Cash was up to, but Langston had a bug up his butt about him.

Langston had been right about surveillance. Two car leapfrog surveillance might work on the naïve, low-level, first-time criminal, but most others were paranoid and suspected a tail. With a minimum of three vehicles, the possibility of being burnt was reduced. If one car was behind the target with another running parallel, and the target quickly jumped into the left turn lane, the tail could drive on past and alert the other two to pick him up down the road. Each undercover vehicle had a toggle switch under the driver's side dash to extinguish one headlight and one tail light. At night, three cars magically became a six-car surveillance if conducted properly. That still didn't solve the manpower issue. Maybe this new Lieutenant Reese could crap out a couple of extra agents. Cantrell thought maybe when she finished arranging the photos of her two dogs on her desk she may offer some words of wisdom from her vast experience. He had hoped so, because his six years supervising these agents was getting him nowhere.

Reese saw Cantrell glaring at her. She stopped arranging the photos and walked to his desk. Cantrell turned his attention back to his paperwork.

"What are you working on, Sarge?" she asked.

"The surveillance schedule we've been ordered to start tonight," Cantrell said flatly.

"Is there a problem?"

"Not if these guys don't mind giving up all their personal life working twelve hour shifts."

"This case is priority, Sergeant. Every officer who accepts this position understands that coming in."

Cantrell looked up from his roster and eyed Reese. "I do understand that… ma'am. We're just shorthanded, that's all."

"Let me see."

She leaned over and examined the roster. Cantrell had made hand written notations next to the agent's names, indicating the hours they would be assigned. She tapped the schedule with her right index finger and looked at Cantrell.

"How long have you been assigned to OCU, sergeant?"

"Six years, why?"

"When did you stop being an agent?"

"Excuse me?"

"I don't see an assignment written next to your name on the roster."

Cantrell glanced back to the schedule, and then back to Reese.

She let out a sigh. "You write the day shift sergeant in. He can give some of the administrative duties to the agent on light duty until this is over. You write yourself in three nights this week and four the next. I'll be out there five nights a week at minimum, so we'll have it covered in case one falls out on sick leave. Three extra bodies, just like that."

Cantrell examined the schedule and nodded. "That should work. I didn't think to include supervisors."

"I'm here to help, Sarge," she said with a smile. "We're a team, right?"

"Sure," Cantrell replied, "a team. Do we kick this off tonight?"

"In the morning at five. Put one car at the residence, one at the liquor store, and the other can rove until someone moves."

"Can I ask something, Lieutenant?"

"Sure."

"What are we looking for?"

Reese looked at the floor, and then back to Cantrell. "Hell if I know."

❧

Tina entered the bedroom off the common area. The oversized bedroom was at least thirty by sixty with a fireplace on the north side, flanked by slender, floor-to-ceiling tinted windows. She was warned any attempt to open them would result in an alarm and immediate discipline. Instead of a king-size bed and lavish sitting area normally expected in such a room, four twin beds were situated against the perimeter walls. One was hers, one was empty, and the remaining two were occupied.

Kara was coiled in a sheet from head to toe and Lacy was sleeping soundly on her back. It was four o'clock in the afternoon and the two didn't look like they had changed positions since before she was ordered to go with Jason this morning at ten o'clock. Both girls were nineteen. Kara was a heroin addict when Jason found her on the run from a possession with intent to distribute charge out of Texas. Tina didn't know Lacy's story. She would hardly speak, but something held her here, just like her and Kara. Cash had something on her and made it clear to all of them they would live here and cooperate or be turned over to the cops. But cooperate with what? They were not being sexually abused. Cash wouldn't let anyone touch them. A constant supply of heroin was made available to both Lacy and Kara. Tina couldn't stand it and did everything she could to avoid it. Cash didn't seem to have a problem with it, but promised if she attempted to escape, she wouldn't run beyond his reach. He said jail would be paradise next to what he would do to her. He didn't have to explain. She didn't doubt him.

She sat on a wooden chair next to the fireplace, shoved aside the heavy curtain, and looked out over the ocean. Such a beautiful day, but there was no room in her mind to admire the day when she was filled with despair. Taylor was standing at the rail of the upper deck. The curtain movement must have caught his attention because he snapped a glaring look in her direction. She quickly dropped the curtain closed, crossed her arms and rocked back and forth in short, quick motions—and cried.

✄∾

Pickett's breathing went from relaxed just a few minutes earlier to short and rapid gasps. His hands trembled at the prospect of losing his badge, his business, and going to jail. Thoughts raced through his head. He had been coordinating on-site security for this man. Nothing wrong with that. In return he ran a few criminal histories. So what? Cash could have legitimately run the histories due to nature of his business, so why did he need him to do it? He had done nothing Cash couldn't have done, so no problem, right? Wrong. He was being set up, entrapped, and he should have recognized it from the beginning. They warned of such things in the academy. Taking gratuities was taboo. Taking just one seemingly insignificant gift or bribe could enslave you from that point forward. But this wasn't about a convenience store clerk giving you a free cup of coffee for stopping by at midnight. Providing sensitive criminal histories for illegitimate purposes was the mother of all screw-ups.

The National Criminal Information Center became fed up with cops running pickup truck tags they saw in their driveways, convinced their wives or girlfriends were getting some on the side. Then there were cops who stopped good-looking women and ran their tags for information so they could contact them later for a date. The list of violations went on and on until laws were enacted to prosecute those who used NCIC for anything other than official business. *No*, Pickett thought, *there was no way out.* Even though his name wasn't in the NCIC

60

logbook, the technician would give him up in a heartbeat to keep her job. There should be no problem unless someone had a reason to look for it. As long as he was valuable to Cash. But if they did, it wouldn't take Sherlock Holmes to figure it out. There was nothing more exhilarating to an Internal Affairs Investigator than to bust a dirty cop. No, he was either all in or he might as well write out a confession and be done with it.

"What the hell's wrong with you, Pickett?" Cash demanded.

Pickett attempted to compose himself. "There's something else that will concern you."

"What are you talking about?"

"Just before you, I mean, Randy, called…"

"Well, what the hell is it, Pickett? I don't have all day."

"Organized Crime is looking at you."

"What do you mean, looking at me and how would a motor cop know about that?"

"I know the new lieutenant over the unit and we were talking about it."

Cash walked to the wall of windows and stared at nothing. "Damn Langston," he said just loud enough to be heard, and then turned back to Pickett.

"It looks like you're going to be a busy man," Cash said.

"What do you mean?"

Cash's tone turned nonchalant. "You're going to get rid of him for me."

Pickett stood and raised both hands as if to push himself away from the situation. "I know you got me on the histories, but I'm not hurting anyone."

"Did I say that?" Cash quipped back. "If that was my intent, I'd send Taylor after him, not your puny ass."

"What do you expect me to do?"

"You figure it out, but make it happen. And get me an address on Colson. I'll handle him."

Pickett dropped back in the chair and put his head in his hands.

"Well," Cash said. "What are you waiting for?"

൜

Inlet Harbor Restaurant was located on the inland waterway near the southern tip of Ponce Inlet. It was a fairly large restaurant specializing in fresh seafood, and an equally large outdoor Tiki bar overhanging the inland waterway. Bright tropical-colored umbrellas shaded outdoor patrons from the intense Florida sunshine, and live entertainment was provided from the covered stage most evenings until midnight. Charters were available for rent most months of the year for avid and novice fishermen and women anxious for a day of sea and sun.

Colson went through the intersection of South Peninsula Drive on Inlet Harbor Road at twelve fifteen according to the digital clock on his dash; the sun beat down through the tinted-glass panel above his head. The isolated storm had passed to the north, depriving Ponce Inlet the benefit of a brief cooling off period. He couldn't remember ever being late for an appointment, but he didn't care this time. If Beavers had given up and gone home, or if his obvious nonchalant attitude about the meeting ticked him off, so be it. Being on a strict schedule was a habit Colson had intended to break and today was as good as any day to start.

He grimaced as he turned into the large gravel parking lot. Dozens of cars were parked nose-in against old railroad ties, suggesting where one space began and another ended. The gravel popped and cracked under the weight of the wide Corvette tires. He coasted in slowly, unable to prevent the gray gravel dust and swirling airborne particles from settling on the polo green paint like a fine dusting of snow. He made a mental note to stop at the car wash on his way back.

His cell started playing Steely Dan as he backed into what appeared to be a space at the furthest point of the parking lot. He dared not pull the delicate fiberglass nose anywhere near the railroad ties. He set the parking brake and unclipped the phone from his belt.

"Coleslaw," Beavers said.

Colson squinted with disappointment. "I'm in the parking lot."

"Sorry I'm running late," Beavers said. "I've had someone in my office, but I'll be there in fifteen minutes."

"Listen," Colson said, giving Beavers an excuse to cancel, "we could meet another time when you're not tied up."

"We're good. I really need to get with you on this. You shouldn't have waited in the car. It has to be a hundred degrees. Go in and have a drink. I'll catch up when I get there."

"Fine," Colson said, and then disconnected the call.

∽

Mike Beavers' office was nothing more than a spare bedroom in his small, two-bedroom house on Oriole Avenue, one street west of South Atlantic Avenue in Daytona Beach Shores. The pale blue ranch would have sold for over a half-million dollars in 2006 during the expansion of the housing bubble. Beavers' timing was more luck than planning. He and his wife had purchased the house for a fraction of its 2006 value in late 2009 during the economic collapse, using his retirement savings and her 401K as a large down payment. Pickett followed Beavers out of his office, through a modest kitchen, and out a side exit to the carport.

Beavers stopped in the middle of the carport with his back to Pickett. "This is a little last minute, Pickett. I'm busy on another case." He turned, looking at his watch. "And I'm late for an appointment right now, as a matter of fact."

Pickett crossed his arms. "I understand, but you're the only one I can trust for this job."

Beavers shook his head. "This seems a little, I dunno, it just doesn't seem right." He looked directly at Pickett. "It's a fellow cop. Why would you agree to it?"

Pickett smiled. "I'm not doing it. You are."

"You know what I mean. Same thing."

"Look," Pickett turned serious. "His wife's been a good friend. She just needs to know for sure, that's all there is to it."

"If she's been such a good friend, why take her money?" Beavers asked.

"I wouldn't accept her money, but I wouldn't do the job either. She wants it done by an outsider and she knows it will cost. So I came to another friend who's an outsider, but if you don't want the two grand I'll go elsewhere. Someone's going to accept it."

"I didn't say no. We can take care of it, but following him around for nights on end will run up to more than two grand in less than a week. You did happen to notice the current price of gas around here..."

Pickett raised his hand to stop Beavers diatribe. "No, no, no, Mike. We're talking about just being on standby. I'll let you know when and where. One night's work."

"How the hell will you know? Don't tell me he coordinates his affairs with you."

"Can you even imagine how pissed off the investigators are, Mike? It's so blatantly obvious the girl was promoted so he could get in her pants. Believe me; they're watching him like a hawk. They're investigators, not morons. When and where it happens will not be that difficult to figure out."

Pickett reached into his saddlebag and pulled out a legal size envelope and handed it to Beavers. "Here's his photo. He'll be on duty, so he should be driving a black Tahoe. It's a UC vehicle. No visible LED lights or anything."

Beavers rolled his eyes. "I think I already know undercover units don't typically sport visible LEDs or strobes. I did do the job for a minute or two in case you forgot."

"Right, sorry," Pickett said and handed Beavers a white letter envelope. "There's one thousand. The rest when you have the photos ready."

Beavers glanced at his watch. "I have to get to my next meeting. Try to give me more than an hour's notice."

"That'll work." Pickett shook Beavers hand, straddled the Harley, and then cranked it.

"Nice bike. How many Harleys does the agency have?"

"It's mine. Old Sheriff Graham let me trick it out with the equipment for donating the time. He was a good man, not a whoremonger like Langston." Pickett kicked and the bike came to life.

"A little loud for my taste," Beavers said.

"Drivers," explained Pickett. "They don't pay attention to motorcycles. The sound lets them know I'm coming."

"I call BS on that one, Pickett."

"What do you mean?"

"If that were the case, the pipes would be facing forward."

"Screw you, Beavers," Pickett said, walking the Harley back into the street.

Beavers just smiled and gave Pickett the finger.

Pickett swung the Harley left onto South Atlantic Avenue and headed north toward the Port Orange Bridge. His head was swimming and he was becoming nauseated. The day began with his normal routine of making sales calls, replying to customer emails, and landing a modest number of insurance policies, but it turned to crap faster than butter through a bulldog. It was 1:45 p.m. and he should be planning the celebration night out with Kim. He loved Kim. At least he loved the thought of her being with him. What he loved the most was playing police on his Harley among the scantily clad female population of Daytona Beach. What would happen to his fun in the sun now that he was sucked into Cash's world of scandal and blackmail? Too late to worry about that now. He pressed the button on the chin bar of his Bluetooth equip helmet and said, "Cash" to the automated dialer.

Fuller answered. "Cash's, this is Randy."

"Fuller, it's Pickett."

"What's the good word?"

"There's nothing good about it, but tell Cash it's in the works."

Fuller chuckled. "Ah, lighten up, Pickett. Another day, another dollar. We all work for Cash around here, get it?"

"Real funny, Fuller. Now let me go before I puke in my damn helmet."

Pickett disconnected and swung left onto the Port Orange Bridge. The traffic was heavy with summer vacation traffic and there wasn't a convertible without the top down. The SUVs were everywhere. He was tailing one with an Ohio tag. Through the medium-tinted rear window he saw two kids bouncing in their seats and pointing at sailboats floating in the inner coastal waterway on either side of the bridge. Another family on vacation. He dropped the Harley down a gear and shot around the SUV. He reached seventy at the crest of the bridge, weaving between the slowpokes and the really slowpokes. Screw the speed limit.

He activated the Bluetooth, said "Kim" and waited for her to pick up.

"Lieutenant Reese," she said, exaggerating her new title.

"Listen," Pickett said, "I've been thinking about the case you're working on and I've come up with an idea that can help both of us out."

"Really? How?"

"I know a confidential informant who feeds me a little information on small time street dealers. I have no doubt he just does it to cut out his competition, but he is in with one of Cash's employees. I can probably get him to meet with you, but he'll probably insist Langston be there. Knowing how he is, he won't do anything that big without something big in return from the sheriff himself."

⇻ Chapter Eight ⇺

Colson walked to the front entrance of the Inlet Harbor. He hadn't visited the restaurant since their last trip two years earlier. Last year Ann was too weak to travel. The vacation week last year went by without notice. Colson was consumed with Ann's care and comfort during those final days. Memories made Colson stand still for several seconds, taking in the scene. Palm trees were scattered throughout the parking area and twin palms framed the front door. Older couples walked lazily into the restaurant ahead of him. Various sections of the restaurant were painted a variety of tropical blues, greens, and orange. Unpainted boards appeared to have been removed from old sailing ships and fashioned into doors, railings, and steps.

He walked away from the entrance to a railing and took in a view of the marina. He stopped counting at seventy-five wet slips where boats of all sizes were docked. He didn't bother to count the stacked dry slips. They were too numerous. The sea air worked miracles on his lifelong allergy to oak trees, grass, and dust. The salty, sea breeze was just the medicine he needed.

He looked at his watch. Beavers said he'd be here in fifteen minutes. That was thirty minutes ago. He sighed, walked back to the entrance, and decided to kill one beer; then he'd leave. He had people-watching to do from his balcony, and Beavers was making him burn daylight. He saw people seated at outside tables under the colorful umbrellas on the large deck. There was no access to the deck area from the parking lot, so he walked through the front door.

A four-foot tall pirate greeted Colson just inside the door. The wooden figure was painted red and black with a hook for a hand, extended in some sort of macabre welcome. He grinned, remembering how Ann chuckled when he told her some kid would lose an eye if he walked into that hideous midget's hook. He made his way through the interior of the main restaurant and around to the waterfront dining and bar area. The bar was at least thirty feet long and most of the fifteen stools were occupied. Waitresses were scurrying from tables to the bar, dropping off used glasses and reloading their trays with full ones. There was no live entertainment at this hour, but Caribbean music played loudly, occasionally interrupted by a popular selection from the '70s or

'80s. Two bartenders alternated pouring draft, shaking mixed drinks, and swiping debit cards. One finally noticed Colson.

"What can I get for you, sir?"

"Anything on draft is fine."

The bartender pointed at bright-colored, translucent glasses on a shelf behind him.

"Would you like that in one of our souvenir glasses, just three dollars more?" the young man said with an unconvincing grin.

"No thanks," Colson said. "I've got the entire collection."

He actually did. Colson would buy one each year and line them up on top of the refrigerator in his garage. In the middle of winter he would glance at them as he left for the night shift and think about the warm, June climate of Florida. Once he had five different colors, there was no need to buy another one. He tried to remember if he had the clear one the bartender had pointed out. But there was no garage refrigerator anymore. He wondered if he still looked like a tourist. He was wearing tan Dockers and a solid white polo shirt, untucked. He surveyed the small crowd around him. They wore t-shirts with advertisements for Disney World, NASCAR, and various beers. A few women wore t-shirts pulled over bikini tops. They had probably been sunbathing on a boat earlier. Maybe he was successful in shedding the tourist look, after all. The bartender returned, placing a square napkin in front of him and a plastic cup of beer on top of it.

"Would you like to start a tab?" the young man asked.

"Don't think I'll need to, thanks."

The bartender turned, worked the register for a moment and laid a little black receipt holder next to the cup. Colson flipped it open and laid his card inside. He raised the cup for a sip and was simultaneously slapped on the back, causing him to slosh several drops onto the bar.

"How you doing, young man?" Beavers said with glee. "Sorry again about being late. Business is booming."

"No problem. I was just trying to figure out if I had a full collection."

"Collection of what?"

"Never mind."

He signed his receipt and followed Beavers to a tall round table at the far end of the deck, next to the railing and away from the outdoor speakers. Beavers laid the folder on the table, slid it to his right, and set his beer in front of him.

Beavers smiled. "I bet you're bored. Ready to get back to work?"

"Not necessarily. I figure after nearly thirty years I could use some time off."

"Sure, sure, you deserve it; that's what makes these little jobs perfect. You work off and on, here and there. It makes the time off even better."

Colson didn't want to make conversation. He just wanted to get it over with. Beavers was beginning to sound like a car salesman. "Tell me what you have, Mike."

Beavers opened the envelope, drew out a photo, flipped it over, and laid it in front of Colson. Half of a five-by-seven photo, showing a man in a black golf shirt. The man had close-cut, dark hair, a trimmed moustache, and was standing against a white background. He looked to be in his late forties.

"This guy," Beavers tapped the photo with his finger, "is a real jerk. In a few days he's supposed to take his mistress to a local hotel for a little rendezvous. His wife needs photos of them going in a room, that's it."

"So she already knows in advance when they'll meet?" Colson said. "Why not confront him there, like on that TV show?"

"I guess she's afraid she'll lose it. You know, kids are involved. She could end up in jail for assault."

Colson looked down at the photo, and then back to Beavers. "Who's in the other half of the picture?"

"I'm thinking it's his wife."

Colson nodded. "So what's his name? What does he do?"

Beavers sucked his teeth. "That's the thing. The wife wants to keep their names out of it as much as possible. He holds a pretty high position in their church or something."

"You're not being much help, Mike."

"Look, it's just a couple of photos. Two or three hours for five hundred."

"When?"

"She's going to call me, and then I'll call you."

Colson sat back in his chair and released a loud exhale. He looked back at the picture and shook his head. "Why don't you just do it, Mike? Anyway, you said on the phone this was about taking photos of a suspected thief."

Beavers cut his eyes to the left and then back to Colson. "Yeah, well that problem was resolved. Besides, this one pays better and I've got other things going that I can't drop at a moment's notice."

Colson rubbed his eyes and sat for a moment. "Fine," he finally said. "I'm not giving you the idea that I'm going to be doing this again. I appreciate the call, but I'm enjoying retirement and have no desire to do things related to my old job. I'd rather cut keys at the hardware store."

Beavers held up his hands in surrender and shook his head. "I fully understand. If you don't want to take any more jobs I won't bug you. So we're good?"

"Just call me," Colson responded, and then drank the rest of his beer in one gulp and stood. "Nice seeing you again, Mike."

Beavers offered his hand and Colson shook it. He slid the photo back in the envelope and handed it to Colson. He turned and walked out the way he came in. Beavers was left sipping his beer and rolling his fingers on the table. Dirty deed done. It was a gamble that Colson wouldn't recognize the man in the photo, but he counted on the fact Colson hadn't lived in the county very long. If Colson was that hesitant to work on a run-of-the-mill infidelity case, he would never have talked him into potentially having to testify in a divorce hearing against the sheriff of the county. Not that Colson would approve of the man's infidelity, just his personal involvement in dragging another cop through the mud. Colson would tell him the same thing he told Pickett. Let the wife do it herself. Beavers felt a headache coming on and rubbed his temple. If Colson sees Langston on TV before he takes the photos, the job will go down the toilet.

The city of New Smyrna Beach is located due south of Ponce Inlet. The dark gray sedan turned right off of North Causeway, onto South Peninsula Drive, and then right onto Oakwood Avenue. The vehicle slowed at the end of Oakwood and made a soft left on South Indian River Road. It rolled to a quiet stop at exactly one-thirty a.m. on the left shoulder, directly across from a covered, one-slip pier.

Fuller watched the sedan park right where they had planned, leaving him an unobstructed view of the pier from the front window of the small, abandoned rental house. He was sitting in a metal folding chair behind an old wooden kitchen table left by the previous tenants. They had been evicted three months earlier, so to speak, when Cash sent Taylor to collect two months back rent. After twenty minutes of intense coaxing by Jay "The Terrible" Taylor, the couple gave him every dime they had on hand and departed the next morning in a pickup full of furniture and personal items, leaving several large pieces behind.

Fuller rested his rifle on a bipod and placed his right eye near the night vision scope mounted on top. He pointed it at the sedan, but couldn't see anyone through the dark windows. He knew Taylor was driving and Jason would be sitting with Kara in back. He swung the rifle to the right. The causeway streetlights glared in the night vision scope. The wide leaves of the huge magnolia tree at the corner of the road restricted his view of any vehicle traffic on the causeway bridge or vessels approaching from the northern waterway. He shook his head. Cash will lose his mind if these guys are a no show.

Taylor killed the headlights and turned off the engine. Jason sat silently in back, keeping a close watch on Kara. She was enjoying a heroin-induced nap, but a gag and handcuffs were in the glove box just in case. Jason checked his watch and looked at the back of Taylor's head.

"One-forty a.m. You see anything?"

"Can't see shit out here. Be patient," Taylor replied and adjusted the Smith & Wesson nine-millimeter pistol in the paddle holster on his belt. Kara moaned softly and rolled her head from right to left, allowing hair to fall in her face.

∽

The Peligrosas Marinero was a sleek, thirty-seven foot, 370 Sundancer cabin cruiser. The pilot reduced speed to just above idle as it approached the causeway bridge. He gave his GPS a quick look to satisfy himself that he hadn't overshot the rendezvous location. The two idling 330 horsepower diesel engines could be heard on shore through the still night air. Their low rumbling echoed down from the concrete causeway bridge above. The pilot placed the palms of his hands against the rich, high-gloss maple dash. He leaned forward and peered through the darkness for a signal to guide him in. And there it was: two short flashes of light.

Taylor lowered the flashlight and set it on the dock. Fuller was alerted when Taylor stepped out of the sedan and walked to the dock, but he still had not seen movement in the water. He placed his eye against the scope and scanned the water. "There," he mumbled. Fuller could just make out a slender white object on the water. Not being able to see the dark blue hull beneath made the object appear to be more of a ridiculous surfboard than a boat. He tracked the boat as it turned to port and eased toward the dock.

Taylor reached behind his suit jacket to satisfy himself the Smith and Wesson was still where it was five minutes ago. He tossed a handful of rope to a man standing on the port side as the boat bobbed, bumped, and settled against the dock. The man stepped down, tied the boat off, and then silently motioned for Taylor to follow him. The man led Taylor across the bridge and down into the main cabin.

Dim light barely illuminated the cabin as Taylor descended, but he recognized the lavishness of the cabin's appointments nonetheless. High gloss maple wood floors, cabinets, and trim surrounded by cream Naugahyde cushions. A squatty figure appeared from behind a set of twin bi-fold doors, revealing a king size bed illuminated by small, inset spotlights in the low ceiling of the cabin.

"Jay the Terrible," the man said in a thick Latino accent as he stepped up and extended his hand. Taylor permitted two short shakes.

"You know me?" Taylor asked.

The man smiled. "Oh, yes. I've watched you fight many times. You almost made it to the heavyweight championship."

Taylor gave him a quick nod.

The man rubbed his chin. "My apologies. I know about the accident. I say it was a shameful waste. You could have beaten Clay Madman Haggert."

Taylor had no desire to talk about what could have been and changed the subject.

"And you are Darkhorse121?"

"He is my employer. You may call me Miguel," the man replied. "You have the order?"

"In the car."

"Very well," the man said, and pulled a black satchel from an overhead compartment. Taylor flipped the top flap and fumbled through the bundles of hundreds. Satisfied with the quick count, he replaced the lid and nodded. The man motioned for Taylor to follow him onto the deck. Taylor lifted the satchel under his arm and followed.

From across the street, Fuller adjusted his scope to include all three men. Man number one on the deck, Taylor, and the new man from below. He saw Taylor give a thumbs-up. Fuller glanced over the scope and watched Jason exit the car and open the rear passenger door. He bent over briefly and rose with an unsteady Kara. Jason assisted Kara down to the boat as if he had met her in a bar and was escorting her to his motel room for a date rape session. The new guy motioned Jason to escort Kara below as Taylor stood on deck with man number one. Fuller placed the rifle's cross hairs steady on the deck hand's head.

Jason stood below deck with one arm around Kara's unsteady waist. Miguel turned and eyed Kara. Her straight, dark hair hung below her breasts and swung slightly as her chin rocked back and forth against her chest.

"What is this?" quizzed Miguel, lifting Kara's chin to examine her face. He lowered her chin and turned his gaze to Jason. "My employer did not bargain for an addict."

"What's the problem?" Taylor asked from the deck.

"The product is damaged. She's nothing more than a dead fish."

Taylor moved to the top of the stairway "You tell your employer this was the only way to deliver her without drawing attention. You'd rather have her bound with duct tape, kicking and screaming?"

Miguel stared at Taylor, and back to Jason as he lowered Kara to the portside couch.

Taylor said, "She's fine. She had to be sedated."

"And if she dies on the return trip?"

Taylor grinned. "Then send her head back for a full refund."

Miguel frowned. "I don't appreciate your attitude, Taylor."

"Well Miguel, I'm not here for your appreciation. Let's go."

Jason stepped past Miguel and climbed the stairs.

Fuller watched their moves from behind the old kitchen table. Taylor and Jason stepped from the boat and walked casually back to the sedan. The slow rumble of the boat's twin engines could be heard through the breezy night air as Fuller watched the cabin cruiser back slowly from the dock and turn in the direction it came. He lifted the rifle, collapsed the bipod, and placed both in a long, nylon gun bag. He zipped the gun bag and walked out to the small front porch, pulling the door closed, and checking the lock. He walked to the sedan as Jason popped the trunk. Fuller tossed the gun bag in with one hand and pulled the lid down with the other. It made a soft click when it latched. Fuller climbed into the back seat as the sedan's engine came to life.

✺

"They're moving," Cantrell said into his radio as Taylor eased the sedan onto the gravel and moved in the direction of the surveillance van. "They'll be moving south, past my position." He lowered his night vision binoculars and eased down behind the empty driver's seat.

"Did anyone get any identifiers off the boat?"

An agent replied from the second surveillance car, "I got the name, but couldn't get a serial number. Nothing at all on the second one."

Cantrell thought he misunderstood. "What second one?"

"There was another cabin cruiser five hundred or so yards north of your position. I saw it from the causeway bridge."

"Why do you think it had anything to do with the meeting? What's the connection?"

"They were running dark and made a hundred and eighty degree turn when your target left the dock?"

"Anything else?"

"Yeah, someone on deck was watching what we were watching with night vision goggles."

➤ Chapter Nine ❦

"What's the case status?" Langston asked from behind his desk. Reese and Cantrell sat in two slightly angled high-back chairs across from him. Cantrell lifted the thick, expandable file from his lap as if to impress Langston with its bulk, and parted his lips to speak. Reese beat him to it.

"Sheriff, we've been out on these guys for the past week," she held her hand out to Cantrell for the case file. She opened the cover to review the status sheet.

"Nothing the first two days—just to the liquor store and back to their residences. Day three, Fuller met with a known small-time heroin dealer, but we didn't see dope or money changing hands."

"Heroin," Langston shrugged. "I thought Fuller was a meth cooker."

Cantrell spoke up, "It's his history. I don't see him as a heroin addict. Him or Taylor either one. And if Cash wanted heroin, he could do a damn sight better than having Fuller buy it from a street slug."

Langston turned his attention to Cantrell. "What's his financials look like?"

"His deposits aren't bad, but not what they were last year. The economy trashed tourism the past two seasons and his liquor business took a hit. Bike Week wasn't near average, so he's barely breaking even."

Reese pulled a grainy photo from the file and handed it to Langston. He laid it on his desk and slipped on a pair of reading glasses. A greenish-tinted night vision photograph of five figures on the deck of a medium-size cabin cruiser. One appeared to be standing partially below deck as the photo only revealed him from the waist up.

"When was this?"

"Last night." Reese stood and moved in behind Langston to point at the photo.

"Taylor on the right, Jason Cash walking with the unidentified female, and these are two unidentified males from the boat."

"There's something to this, Sheriff." Cantrell was tired of being left out of the briefing. "They meet this boat at two a.m., escort this young female below deck and leave without her, but with a satchel they didn't come with."

"Jesus," Langston muttered.

"Here's the next one." Reese pulled out a second photo and laid it on top of the first.

"Boat leaves, Cash and Taylor return to the car, and that's Fuller." Reese touched the figure of Fuller with her index finger.

"Where the hell did he come from?"

"From the small rental house across the street. A Martin Cash rental," Cantrell said while crossing his legs.

Langston looked up from the photo to Cantrell. "I don't suspect he has a beach umbrella in that long gun case he's carrying."

"I suspect you're correct, sir," Cantrell replied. "He was covering them from the house. We went back after we put them to bed. There's an old table pushed up against the front window with a metal folding chair right behind it."

Langston stood and walked to the picture window behind his desk. He admired the half-dozen freshly washed sheriff's vehicles in the lot, baking in the sun. He briefly mused about his days on patrol when he would run his unit through the car wash just to cool it down for the muggy night shift ahead. Simpler days.

"What do we have on the two unknown subjects?" Langston said, still gazing out the window.

"Latino, both early thirties," Reese said, and returned to her seat.

"Anything on the boat? SSR number, name?"

Reese checked her notes. "Not close enough to get the number. The name is the Peligrosas Marinero."

Langston chuckled. "Peligrosas Marinero. Arrogant bastards."

Reese raised her eyebrows. "You know what it means? I hadn't checked yet."

Langston glanced over his shoulder. "Dangerous Sailor."

"There was another boat in the area, no markings at all," Cantrell said. "It was running without lights and there was an observer on deck with night vision."

Langston turned from the window. "Were they Latino?"

"The agent couldn't tell from behind the goggles."

"So you think this was a kidnap-ransom deal?" Reese asked.

Langston sat back at his desk and looked at the photos for a long moment. Cantrell sat silent, shaking his head in slow, short motions. Langston answered with short, affirmative nods. Reese looked back and forth between them.

"What?" she demanded, as if being an outside party to an inside joke.

"Possible human trafficking," Langston said as he met her eyes.

"I don't think big time," Cantrell added. "Amateur operation."

Reese sat back in her chair and exhaled. "My God."

Cantrell moved forward and sat on the edge of his chair. "I think we should get a search warrant for the beach house. Dump his computer and find out what's on it. I can get our computer crimes guy to dissect it on site if we need to. The man is going bankrupt. We could get an IRS investigator to crawl up his ass with a microscope."

Langston raised his hand to stop Cantrell. "Hold on, Sergeant. You're getting ahead of yourself. What probable cause are you going to use for a search warrant on the residence? What do you tell the judge; you observed a late meeting at a dock?"

"We saw an exchange. The girl for a package."

"Was she struggling, screaming, and waving her arms? Have you seen other females being drug into the beach house? Do you have any credible inside information? You can't tell the judge you think Cash is into human trafficking or anything else at this point, even if we both have the same gut feeling. Search warrants are not based on gut feelings, but probable cause."

Cantrell looked at the floor without a word. Reese sat silent with the closed file in her lap.

"Anything else? Is that all you've come up with?" Langston said and waited for a response. He looked from Reese to Cantrell, but neither made eye contact.

Langston fumed, "Am I going to have to conduct this investigation myself? If that's the case, what the hell do I need you two for?"

"I've developed a confidential informant," Reese said with a smile. "Says he can get in with one of Cash's employees."

"What's the C.I.'s name?"

"Marcus Wituka."

"Ah, hell, Reese. You ever dealt with him in the jail?"

"No, sir. I'm sure you have. I was told he wouldn't meet with me unless you were willing to be there. Kind of an introduction, I guess."

Langston shook his head. "Look Reese, I know you don't find informants at the foot of the cross, but this idiot is nuttier than squirrel turds."

"Agreed," Cantrell added.

"I'm not talking to you, sergeant," Reese snapped, keeping her eyes on Langston. "Sheriff, we need to know if Cash has more girls. If he can get Wituka to convince Fuller to get him in there, we could wire him and catch some conversation since the photos aren't enough evidence."

"It's not that the photos aren't useful," Langston said. "Evidence is not links in a chain you put together for a good case. Evidence is a long fiber that can be easily broken. But when you gather enough fibers and tie them together, it makes a rope that is almost impossible to break. You simply have to gather enough of it."

Reese and Cantrell nodded understanding. Langston rubbed his temples and sighed. "Fine. Try to set it up for tomorrow night, but don't get your hopes up. You'll find out he's full of crap, except when he's rolling it into little balls to throw at the jail deputies."

Reese appeared confused. "What are you talking about?"

"You obviously didn't spend enough time in the Detention Division."

Cantrell leaned forward and set his elbows on his knees. "Excuse me, lieutenant. How did you come across Marcus Wituka?"

She looked at Cantrell. "Sergeant Pickett arrested him twice. He said Wituka has given him good information on street dealers."

Langston froze, his face flushed with anger. He fixed his glare on Reese and addressed Cantrell, "Sergeant Cantrell, would you excuse the lieutenant and me for a minute?"

Cantrell looked at Langston, and then at a bewildered Reese. "Of course, sir," he said. Cantrell walked out with a grin and shut the door. He suspected what was coming and wished he could stay to witness it. Langston continued to glare at Reese until the door clicked and allowed a few more seconds to assure himself Cantrell was out of earshot. Reese set the case file on the side table and sat straight in her chair.

"I apologize, Sheriff. Did I say something wrong?"

Langston did not alter his glare. "Reese, what the hell are you doing talking to a reserve deputy about an OCU case?"

"I'm sorry, Sheriff. I didn't realize—"

"You better start to realize," Langston interrupted. "The only reason I've tolerated that bunch of wannabe reservists is because I inherited them from the previous administration. When their operating funds are depleted, they're history. I'm tired of a bunch of insurance and car salesmen running around playing police under my authority. They cause more problems than they're worth, and the very last thing I'll allow is for them to be sticking their nose into an organized crime investigation and bragging to all their wannabe buddies."

Reese looked down at the clutched hands in her lap. "Bad judgment on my part, Sheriff. It won't happen again."

"We'll meet your CI, but Pickett's ass is out of it. You either tell him," Langston reached for the phone, "or I will."

"I'll tell him, sir."

Langston held the phone and pressed a button. "Send Cantrell back in here," he said, and replaced the receiver. Cantrell entered the office, shut the door, and then returned to his seat.

"You know reserve Sergeant Pickett," Langston asked Cantrell.

Cantrell raised an eyebrow. "Somewhat. Actually, he runs the part-time security at Cash's liquors."

Langston snapped his head to look at Reese. "You're shitting me."

⌇⌇

Martin Cash could see the terracotta tile on the floor through his glass-top office desk. He minimized the chat-room screen on his laptop when he heard the door open. His cyber conversation with Avid Collector had ended and a price had yet to be agreed on. The bids for Tina were disappointing, to say the least. They would need to upload better pictures. Sexier pictures. His current negotiation with Avid Collector had not improved his mood. Taylor laid the black satchel on the desk and stepped back.

"Where's Jason and Fuller?" Cash said, opening the satchel.

"Still asleep."

"There's a shock," Cash muttered sarcastically as he pulled the bundles of bills from inside and staked them on the table.

"Since you made it back in one piece, I suspect you didn't have a problem?"

"No problem."

Cash fanned through each of the twelve bundles of bills and shook his head. "We've got to do better than this. You have any more prospects?"

"Fuller said another transient girl put in an application yesterday, but I couldn't get ahold of Pickett to run the information."

Cash looked over his shoulder at Taylor. "I think we scared the piss out of him. You'll have to pressure him to run the histories from now on. No charge."

"Why not just take her anyway?" Taylor asked.

"Don't you understand, Taylor? If we don't have anything to hold over their heads, like turning their sorry asses in for probation violation or a warrant, we'll play hell keeping them here. If the bids don't improve, I'll have to resort to turning them over to their bail bondsmen for reward."

Taylor shook his head. "I understand. I'll find Pickett today."

"You do that," Cash said and turned back to the stacks of hundreds. Taylor turned and walked to the door.

"Hold up, Taylor," Taylor spun on his heels. "Get a few hours' sleep. We have a visit to make." Cash swiveled his seat to face him. "When you find Pickett this morning, get Colson's address."

Taylor nodded and walked out.

∽∾

Tina turned on the small bedside lamp and shook Lacy's shoulder. "Wake up Lacy," she said in a forceful whisper. It was 7:30 p.m., but the room was totally dark. Lacy groaned and instead of opening her eyes, squeezed them tightly closed.

Lacy finally whispered her reply. "What is it?"

"Kara," Tina said with concern in her voice. "They had her out all night and she hasn't come back."

"So?" Lacy jerked from Tina's grip and rolled her face back into the pillow.

"So...everyone else is back and she's not. You have to get a grip, Lacy. You need to talk to me."

Lacy groaned in frustration and rolled onto her back. She opened her eyes into small slits and immediately covered them with her hand. "Turn that light off!"

"No, I won't be able to see you with these stupid blackout curtains on the windows. Taylor threatened to tie me to the bed if he caught me opening them again."

Lacy sat up awkwardly on the side of her bed and rested her head in her hands. Her long, black hair fell forward. "What do you want, Tina?"

Tina squatted on the floor in front of her and held both of Lacy's forearms in her hands. "They've done something with Kara. You and I both know they didn't drop her off at the nearest bus station. Something bad has happened and we need to get out of here."

Lacy shook her head in her hands. "I can't."

"You have to stop doing the drugs, Lacy. We can't stay here."

"You go."

"I can't leave you here. Something bad will happen, especially if I get away. They'll have to do something with you if they think there's a chance I'd tell the cops what's going on."

Tina heard footsteps on the tile floor outside the room and a key sliding into the lock. She ran and sat on the edge of her bed before Jason opened the door. The funnel of sunlight from the adjacent room silhouetted Jason as he stepped in.

"What are you two up to?" he asked suspiciously.

Tina looked at Jason and rolled her eyes. "What could we be up to? Where's Kara?"

"Busy. Get some rest. We have a photo shoot on the beach in the morning."

Tina slapped her hands on the bed. "Are you serious?" She couldn't see the expression on Jason's backlit face. "What do you want with us?" she demanded. "This is insane. A photo shoot? I want to know what you did with Kara."

"Look," Jason held his hands out, palms up. "Nothing happened to anybody. It's just some pictures. Pick out a nice bikini. Use one of Kara's if you need to. She'll be back in a week and won't care. Be ready at nine." He stepped back and pulled the door closed. Tina heard him slide the key in and turn the deadbolt.

She crossed the room to Lacy, who had returned to her face-down position on the bed. Tina shook her again. "Lacy," Tina's rough whisper was more exaggerated than before, "we have to get out of here."

Lacy lazily swatted back at Tina. "No," she replied sharply.

Tina stood straight, defeated, and returned to bed. "Why won't you go with me, Lacy? Why won't you tell me?"

Lacy rolled slightly and lifted her head a fraction of an inch off the pillow. "My boyfriend."

"You think your boyfriend will find you. That can't be any worse than—"

"No," she interrupted.

"Then what is it?"

Lacy paused a beat. "I killed him."

∽

The steakhouse on South Ridgewood Avenue was a popular tourist stop, but small crowds of hungry patrons holding vibrating coasters were the exception rather than the rule these days. The rustic restaurant had been suffering as most local businesses had over the past two years. The black and white nostalgic photos of stock cars racing up and down Daytona Beach, autographed pictures of smiling drivers sporting dark sunglasses, and NASCAR memorabilia hung proudly on the rough, paneled walls, but few admirers enjoyed them these days. Local residents and the dwindling number tourists had found cheaper dining solutions in the slumping economy, such as making sandwiches in hotel rooms and grilling hamburgers poolside.

"Langston is pissed," Reese said to Pickett in a hushed voice. He sat across from her in the booth.

Pickett raised an eyebrow. "What about?"

"He's being an ass, don't worry about it."

"Did he agree to meet Wituka?"

"Yeah, but you shouldn't be there, just set it up."

Pickett placed his hand around his beer. "What's going on, Kim?"

"Langston's got a real problem with people outside of the unit knowing about the cases."

"I see," Pickett said, looking down at his glass. "You sure that's all?"

"That's all I got from him." Kim reached across the table and put her hand on Pickett's wrist. "Like I said, he's just being an ass."

Pickett took his hands off the glass and sat back in the booth. "Not that. Is something going on between you and Langston?"

"You serious?" Reese's mouth dropped. "Of course not. He's married."

"I heard he's getting a divorce."

"It's not like that," she said defensively.

"Fine," he said.

"Fine," Reese mocked.

Pickett held up one hand. "Let's forget it. I'll arrange for Wituka to be at the Rayford Inn tomorrow night at eight o'clock. Did Langston agree to go with you?"

"Yes."

"Go to the hotel office. I'll make sure they give you his room number and a key in case he's late."

"Langston told me about Wituka."

Pickett took a sip of beer and set the bottle down. "What about him?"

"Langston says he's crazy and throws shit balls at the jail deputies when he's in lockup."

"He won't do that to you or I'll beat his ass."

"That's not what bothers me," Reese said. "If he's a psycho and this meeting turns to shit, no pun intended, I'll look like an idiot to Langston. Are you sure you know what you're doing?"

Pickett smiled. "I'm working on something I'll tell you about soon, but I can't right now. Not until I know it's going to work. But if it does, you may be Chief Deputy instead of a lieutenant."

Reese smiled and stood. "I should get back to the office." She stepped from around the table and gave Pickett a peck on the cheek. "Maybe we'll have time for a real dinner next week."

"Promise?"

"I never promise."

She grabbed her purse and headed for the door. Pickett watched her walk out to the lot and climb into her Jeep. He rubbed his eyes and pinched the bridge of his nose. He jerked his hand away and muttered, "Shit," as he pulled out his cell.

"Beavers," he said into the phone. "It'll happen tomorrow night at eight, the Rayford Inn on A1A. I told you you'd get the rest of the money after the meet. All you have to do is be there and take the photos." Pickett paused and closed his eyes while listening, slapped his free hand on the table, and sharpened his tone. "I'll tell you which room after I rent it, you idiot."

Pickett pressed the "end" button and punched a second speed-dial. "It's Pickett. Tell Cash it's set for tomorrow night." He pressed the "end" button again. The waitress appeared by his side.

"You need another beer?" she said with a pleasant smile.

Pickett downed the last swallow and handed her the empty bottle. "Bring a pitcher and a large glass."

➤ Chapter Ten ❦

Colson awoke to the sound of ice cubes dropping in the kitchen freezer tray. The vertical blinds hanging inside the bedroom sliding door blocked a majority of the hot, morning sun—but not completely. He glanced at the clock on the nightstand. 8:20 was ridiculous. He missed watching the ocean sunrise again. There was not a morning when he didn't wake without thinking of Ann in this very bed. It was Colson's pleasant chore to brew coffee while Ann arranged the pillows for them to sit up and watch the daily weather forecast. When you only had a week to spend at the beach, every day was a precious gift away from the routine of work and being separated from each other most of the time. He and Ann would pray that the day would be without rain and clouds. Their second cup of coffee would be enjoyed on the balcony, provided they woke early enough to avoid the June morning's sun turning the concrete floor and white stucco exterior into a blast furnace.

Colson's favorite chore following morning coffee was being Mrs. Colson's cabana boy. She would summon Colson to apply tanning lotion to her back prior to changing into her bikini. She would smile, kiss him, and begin packing her bag with all the necessary supplies for a day at the beach. God, how he loved her and their time together. He would carry on as long as God gave him breath, but there would never be another Ann. She had his love with her and always would. Colson prayed she was with him and loved him as much as he still loved her.

He swung his legs over the bed and grabbed the television remote. The weather woman predicted a slight chance of a cooling afternoon shower as usual, but most of the day would be cloudless with a high of ninety-four degrees. He didn't dare open the vertical blinds for fear of losing his sight for a good five minutes. The light spilling in from the edge was proof enough of the weather lady's prediction.

Colson moved into the kitchen and poured a cup of coffee; cream, and no sugar. He had lost faith in the Speedway Café. His eyes adjusted enough to push the kitchen door blinds aside. He slid the door open and stepped onto the balcony. The morning breeze was light and the sun had starting doing its job on the concrete and stucco. Colson walked to the railing and glanced down to the pool area. The timeshare families wasted no time. Now it was their one and only week at the beach and it wasn't being squandered on sleep. He counted six couples already jockeying for position at poolside lounge chairs, laying their beach towels across them to claim ownership and dropping their beach bags on nearby umbrella-shaded tables. He and Ann had given up on the poolside rush years ago. The beach afforded more room to spread out, and setting up camp under the canopy was much more intimate and relaxing.

He turned his attention to the beach, where morning runners were the first to appear. The high tide had receded, leaving a smooth, glassy surface for the runners to leave their trail. The only vehicles moving on the sand this early were a couple of open trailers full of rental four-wheelers being pulled by heavy-duty pickup trucks. One pickup towed a golf cart on a trailer with a load of green beach umbrellas and low folding chairs. Colson watched the man's daily routine of setting the fifteen umbrellas and chairs out in a row down a small stretch of the beach, approximately fifty feet apart. He had done the calculations several times. The man rented the umbrella and two chairs for thirty dollars per day and at least ten were occupied on any given day, at any given time. The guy made $300 to $450 a day, riding up and down the beach on his golf cart and collecting rental fees from tourists too lazy to bring their own. "Hmm." Colson considered starting such an enterprise, but blew it off in the same instant. Too much initial outlay for the truck, trailer, golf cart, umbrellas and chairs. Forget it.

He took another sip of coffee and sat in the heavy plastic chair. He thought about calling Nichole, but she was probably in class and he didn't want to bug her again. She's new to married life and the last thing she needed was a worrisome daddy calling her every day. He glanced over his shoulder and checked the calendar hanging on the refrigerator door. Thursday is a good day to set up on the beach. Friday through Sunday was out. Too many tourists. He chuckled to himself and smiled. It was nice being a resident.

He closed the sliding door as he stepped back in the kitchen, walked to the storage closet, and pulled out the four-foot-high bag containing the canopy. The cooler in the closet stayed prepared with his preferred beach paraphernalia, just as his go-bag had stayed prepared with the necessary police equipment in the event of an emergency call-out. But instead of a Glock, ASP, pens, blank witness interview forms, handcuffs, and a flashlight, the items consisted of a towel, portable radio, extra batteries, large water bottle, and whatever novel he was reading at the time.

He changed into his trunks and hefted the cooler to the kitchen, where he dropped in two frozen blocks from the freezer and filled the water bottle with ice. He pulled a small folding chair from behind the door, shoved it under one arm, and swung the canopy strap across his back. He lifted the cooler and walked out the door and down the open hallway toward the familiar aroma of tanning lotion and sweat emitting from the elevators. Colson didn't feel the need to apply lotion before he left; there was enough in the humidity of the elevator to cover him head to toe like a spray-on application. Most of the women here wore enough lotion to leave a puddle if they stood still for ten seconds. Colson pushed the button marked "1" and rode to ground level. He walked through the breezeway and emerged in the visitors parking area.

The woman's voice came from the ground-level patio. "You've got a load there, Mr. Colson."

Colson didn't stop this time, suspecting the source of the comment. "It's manageable."

"You need a hand?"

She wasn't going to let it go. *Be nice,* Colson thought. He stopped and turned.

"Ah, Mrs...."

She smiled. "Cox."

The canopy bag strap was beginning to cut into his shoulder.

"Yes, Ma'am, how are you?"

She frowned. "Please don't call me Ma'am. People will think I'm your mother."

Colson smiled. In fact she was almost old enough, but Mom wouldn't have been caught dead outside in her bathrobe. "Sorry. Force of habit."

Mrs. Cox found her smile again. "Well, can you use some help?"

He thought for a moment. *Pulling the canopy apart was really a job for two people, but could be accomplished by one person if patient and not easily frustrated. Colson could use five minutes of assistance, but not from the village nudist and apparent nymphomaniac.*

"I'm good, but thanks," Colson turned and continued his walk toward the beach gate.

"You have a nice one," Mrs. Cox said, as Colson moved past the first row of parked cars. He didn't look back again, but smiled to himself and mumbled.

"That's what I've been told, but you'll never know."

⁓

Tina hadn't slept all night. She positioned her chair to prop open the heavy curtain and stared at the beach. Lacy had barely moved in her bed across the room. The brilliant moonlight made a wavy streak across the ocean and gave the sand the illusion of snow. She watched the tide recede slowly as morning approached. A white police truck moved up and down the beach in predictable twenty-minute cycles. She had no idea if it was the same truck, or if there were two or three in rotation. She counted five times during the night when the trucks would turn at a slight angle, stop, and direct their spotlight at different points on the sea wall. She wished they were looking for her. She thought if she could only get out of the room and out to the beach undetected, she could run out into the truck's path and flag one of the officers down. They would surely find out she was wanted, put her in jail, and send her back to Alabama, but she didn't care anymore. She couldn't run anymore. She couldn't even cry.

At three a.m. another light appeared, moving left and right on the sand directly under the window. It was Taylor making his evening security round, checking windows and doors. Tina slid her chair back and let the curtain fall against the window. She wouldn't risk another scolding and more threats from Taylor the Ogre. She didn't care why Taylor acted pissed all the time; she just didn't want to be his target. She eased the curtain back and watched the flashlight beam dance on the sand for ten minutes before it vanished and she heard him climbing the steps to the lower deck. She pulled the chair forward, propped the curtain and continued her survey of the beach—and her life.

She lay on her bed to think, but drifted off to sleep. The next thing she heard was movement in the common room and men talking. She strained to hear their words, but couldn't understand. What did they want? She needed to talk to Kara, but what had they done with her? There was no use in trying to reason with Lacy. She would have to stay until her family could be contacted—but what could they do? Lacy is an adult and can stay anywhere she wants. Tina shook her head. Helping Lacy would have to wait. She could only help herself now.

She heard a key being inserted in the lock and two loud knocks. There was no mistaking Jason's juvenile voice. "You dressed?" he said, and opened the door a crack.

"No, close the door," Tina said sharply. The door was pulled closed. "Hurry up," Jason said.

Tina moved from the window and picked through Kara's bag lying at the head of her unmade bed. If Kara was going away for a week, why not let her take her only possessions? She found two bikinis; one yellow, and the other blue. She pulled the blue one out and went into the bathroom to change. Jason stood up from the couch holding a digital camera when Tina entered the media room.

Jason said, "Let's go."

Tina reluctantly followed. They were silent until they reached the door leading to the deck.

"What are we doing?" Tina asked.

Jason lifted the camera as if Tina hadn't noticed him carrying it. "I told you, taking pictures."

"I know what you said, but why?"

"I just do what I'm told, and so do you."

Tina followed Jason around a cocktail table surrounded by luxurious wrought iron chairs with bright red cushions. In the middle of the table was a long, black flashlight, standing where Taylor must have left it after his security rounds. They walked down the steps and onto the thick sand. Jason walked to the water's edge, looked up and down the beach, and squinted at the morning sun hanging above the gently curving horizon of the Atlantic. He turned and motioned for Tina to walk closer. She cocked her head in disgust and met Jason at the water's edge.

"So now what, mister photographer?" she said. "Even I know you should do this in the afternoon or evening. It's too bright to take pictures in the direction of the water."

Jason's face turned sour. "Just shut up."

"You gonna slap me again?"

"Maybe. Just stand over there and shut up."

Tina rolled her eyes and turned away, facing the sunrise. Jason fumbled with the small digital camera and held it up to view the rear screen. He lowered the camera and gave Tina a disgusted look.

"Face me and try to smile, will you?" he barked. "The quicker we get this done, the quicker you can go back inside."

Tina forced a smile. "Oh, like I can't wait to get back to prison."

"What?" Jason shouted.

"Nothing. Just take your damned pictures."

Tina turned side-to-side in various poses and made her best effort to smile and act like a happy beach babe. The beachfront was deserted, but she could see the movement of small figures to the north, along the solid wall of condominiums up the coastline. Some thirteen stories and others three-to-five stories high. They appeared a short walking distance from where she stood, but she knew distance was deceiving on the long stretch of the beach. While visiting Daytona as a thirteen-year-old with her parents, she decided to walk to the boardwalk with her girlfriend. From their condo it seemed so close, but thirty minutes into their journey the boardwalk appeared to be running away from them down the beach. She felt no closer than when they began. For a moment she forgot she was being held captive by a deranged liquor store owner. She faced the rising sun again, took a deep breath of fresh sea air, and even forgot about Jason for a second, until—

"Hey." Jason had apparently finished his photo shoot and was standing directly behind her. Tina spun around, startled.

Jason backed up a step. "What's wrong with you?"

"What's wrong with me?" she said sarcastically. "You have me locked in a room and threaten me with jail if I try to leave or even look out the window. You won't tell me where Kara is and then you drag me out here to take pictures." She lowered her head and hoped to appeal to Jason's soft side if it existed. She softened her voice, gave Jason a pitiful glance and pouted her lips. "I'm scared. Just tell me what you're doing so I can feel better. I won't tell anyone."

Jason looked at her for a long moment, as if giving serious consideration to her request, and then laughed. "You're something else. I know you better than that. You're one tough bitch, Tina." Jason turned away and motioned for her to follow, still chuckling as he walked into the thick sand near the deck stairs. "Let's go."

"Hey."

Jason stopped and turned. "What now?"

"Where's your dad and Taylor?"

He cocked his head. "None of your business."

"I really don't care what they're doing. All I wanted to do is watch TV for a while and not be locked down by Taylor the goon. What's his problem, anyway?"

"Fine," Jason relented. "Just until I hear them come in, then it's back to your room."

Tina shrugged. "That's all I asked."

Jason turned again and started up the stairs. Tina moved in behind him. Jason topped the last stair and walked past the first table. Tina quickened her pace up the stairs and over to the table where the flashlight stood. She gripped the metal mag-light at the base of bulb housing and hefted it. It was heavier than she expected with its four D-cell batteries. She paused as Jason reached for the French door handle. "You're waiting too long," she mouthed and screamed in her head. "DO IT"! He was halfway through the door. Tina made herself move quickly. She swung the flashlight hard from right to left, striking Jason's right temple.

Tina felt the flashlight make contact with skin and bone. The metal made a dull sounding thump against Jason's skull. He staggered two steps and fell to the floor of the media room.

✑

Taylor turned the sedan right into the front parking lot of the condominium and pulled into a shaded space against the building. The temperature gauge already read eighty-seven degrees at 11:15 a.m. The Sundowner Condos had received a full-body lift three years ago after tropical storm Fay meandered over the area in 2008, hurtling sixty-mile-per-hour wind and rain against the beachfront condos. There was minimal structural damage, but mold began to thrive in the twenty-year-old walls and had to be eradicated or the Sundowner would be condemned.

Resident owners were informed by county health officials that everything had to be torn out and rebuilt or they would face eviction and condemnation. An additional five grand from each owner would be required for the necessary construction. A quarter of the residents surrendered their deeds in protest. The Sundowner was rebuilt, but the two-year delay resulted in another five residents giving up their deeds. Two vacant lots flanked the Sundowner where older condominiums had stood. There were not enough owners interested in saving them. The vacancies at the facility afforded the opportunity for a new generation of beach lovers to buy units at a reduced price. Grey Colson was one of them. In the end, the Sundowner maintained its late 1980s bones, resurrected with bright new paint, and tiled interior and new furnishings.

Taylor killed the engine and craned his head to see the top level of the building. Cash stepped out, looked at the building, and scoffed.

"This is the best a retired Major can afford?"

"I guess it's the best a public servant can do," Taylor said, climbing out and slamming the door.

"Public servant my ass."

"You want to go through the office?"

"Why?" Cash said. "Condo 510. I counted the floors."

Taylor nodded as they walked toward an exposed hallway marked by blue sign on the wall with "ELEVATORS" written in white letters. They walked single file down the narrow hall. A door swung open in their path, making Taylor stop abruptly. A heavy woman in a one-piece red bathing suit backed out of the door carrying a laundry basket heaping with towels and chlorine-faded vacation clothing. A waft of humid air hit Taylor in the face as the woman squeezed between them and moved down the hall.

"Well, excuse the hell out of me," Taylor snorted, but the woman marched on, oblivious. Taylor found the elevator and caught the door as it began to close. Two soaking wet and barefoot nine- or ten-year-old girls moved to one side of the elevator as the two menacing figures crowded in next to them. Taylor pressed the button labeled 5. Both girls huddled in beach towels and shivered during the cool elevator ride.

"Why are you wearing a suit?" one of the girls asked Cash. "It's hot out."

Cash glanced at the girl but said nothing. The girl cut her eyes to Taylor who looked straight ahead through his sunglasses as if nothing had been said. The girls scurried out on the third floor. When the elevator door closed behind them, a duet of giggles could be heard, but quickly faded as the elevator ascended.

∽

Colson stepped into the thick sand at the bottom of the stairs. He decided not to wear the flip-flops. Just something else to keep up with. The sand was already hot and his heels sank and shifted with every step. He plodded through slowly until he reached the driving lane, where the sand was packed solid by a steady stream of vehicles. He judged his distance from the water and the growing knots of people, and set the canopy bag on its end. He knew approximately how far the water would make its way inland as high tide approached, and he wanted to avoid moving the canopy and his belongings like a naïve tourist. Which he no longer was.

The spot Colson chose was just even with Mr. and Mrs. Hammond. He and Ann had spoken to the couple almost every year. Short, polite, how-do-you-do conversations. Mr. Hammond was a retired engineer from Kentucky. He never elaborated what type. Hammond was older than Colson by at least ten years. He was squat, with a round belly that glowed pink from hours at the beach. He and Mrs. Hammond had a standing date with the little guy in the umbrella cart. The umbrella man would drive by like clockwork to collect the thirty-dollar fee for the use of two chairs and a round beach umbrella that barely shaded the couple. Mr. Hammond would settle in, lay his head back, and rarely move the entire day, while Mrs. Hammond slowly leafed through a novel. The first time Mr. Hammond would move was when Grey and Ann would arrive and set up camp. He would tilt his head to the left and raise a hand of greeting, and then return to the coma position. The second time Hammond moved was to eat the sandwich his wife would bring around three p.m. Other than those two occasions, nothing. If Colson hadn't walked by at least once during the week and spoke to the couple, he wouldn't know his name to this day.

Today was unprecedented. Mr. Hammond immediately stood at the sight of Colson and walked over. He removed his sunglasses, shook his head, and extended his hand. Colson couldn't believe his eyes.

"I'm so very sorry to hear about your wife," Hammond said.

Colson shook his hand. "Thank you, Mr. Hammond."

He half smiled. "Please, call me Roger."

"I do appreciate it, Roger. Ann loved it here, and seeing you two was an expected tradition."

Hammond turned to the ocean and put his hands on his hips. "We were used to seeing both of you, too. Julie and I said a prayer for you last night when we heard."

Colson grinned. "Let me guess. Faye Cox?"

Hammond chuckled. "Yep, the complex busybody. Hey, let me help you with the tent."

"Sure, thanks." Colson zipped open the bag. "Mrs. Cox offered to help, but…"

Hammond's chuckle grew into a laugh. "I'm sure she did."

They both continued to laugh as Mrs. Hammond lowered her book and gazed in their direction. They took sides opposite of each other, held two legs apiece, and stepped backwards. The frame extended into a ten-by-ten square, three feet in height. Colson pulled the black covering from the side pouch of the bag and gave Hammond one end. They lifted the covering over the frame and Colson stooped underneath with the middle extension pole. After the pole was inserted and the sides secured, Colson raised each leg to the highest notch and locked it in place. A couple of adjustments to settle the canopy square and they were done.

"This is a job for two people." Hammond hesitated as if he had said the wrong thing. "Sorry."

Colson smiled. "Couldn't have done it without you, thanks."

"Anytime."

Hammond stepped back to examine the canopy. "Nice. I should get one of these things."

"You'd put the umbrella man out of business."

Hammond shook Colson's hand again. "I'm too lazy to fool with it. You need anything, we're here."

"Same here. Please tell Mrs. Hammond hello."

"I will."

Hammond walked back to his chair. Mrs. Hammond waved to Colson as Mr. Hammond replaced his sunglasses and assumed the position.

Colson placed his chair and cooler in the middle of the shade and set the radio on top. The sun was brilliant and the sea wind blew steady and strong. Sandpipers with unbelievably fragile legs ran across the sand, competing for tiny treats washed in by the waves. Colson loved this beach and couldn't imagine being anywhere else. He turned on the radio, adjusted the antenna for best reception, and then settled into his chair.

∽∾

Taylor followed Cash down the exterior walkway past a support pillar wrapped with thick rope in a spiral pattern from top to bottom, and then another. Taylor watched Cash give the pillar a quick examination and brief head shake in disgust. Taylor found nothing tacky or disgusting about the designer's attempt to give the complex a marine décor. The place wasn't a five-star resort, but it was clean, well-maintained, and surprisingly new looking from what Taylor had seen so far. He hated people who felt they were superior to others because of where they lived, what they did for a living, or how much money they made.

Taylor knew Cash was a little prick like the young optometrist, but he paid well and treated him with pseudo-respect. The only thing he couldn't stand about his job was the dress code. Cash was obsessed with appearances, and was the vainest person he ever met. He had never owned a suit, dress shoes, or a tie until Cash insisted on it. He felt only a few degrees from boiling in the ridiculous jacket and tie. He'd often thought if he ever had to react quickly in this insane outfit, they'd both be dead before he could throw a strike or pull his gun. At least they would already be dressed for the funeral.

They were going in the right direction. Taylor glanced at the brass numbers tacked to the inset doors. The first read "507" and the next was "508." Cash and Taylor arrived at "510" at the end of the hallway. Taylor paused and looked at Cash.

"Just knock," Cash said. "Right now we're just here to talk."

Taylor nodded. "Maybe he don't want to talk."

"Then he can listen," Cash replied, and motioned to the door with his index finger.

Taylor knocked, waited, and then knocked again. He cupped the peephole with his left hand, but didn't see any change in light from the other side. Taylor knocked harder the third time. No sound from the inside. No movement from behind the peephole. He turned to Cash.

"Maybe he's at work."

"He's retired. Anyway, these local government scum didn't actually work when they were employed."

"You want to ask them at the office?"

"So someone can testify we were here to influence a witness? You're not that stupid, are you?"

Cash turned back down the hallway. Taylor followed without a word. They rode the same humid elevator to the ground floor and stepped off. Cash stepped into the hallway and glanced left and right. He retraced their steps with Taylor in tow and stopped at the breezeway leading to the rear parking area. A heavy blast of sea wind struck them as they stepped into the opening. Twenty-mile-per-hour winds striking the seaside of the building were being funneled through the opening, accelerating them to fifty miles per hour. Their suit jackets blew open and their neckties wrapped around their necks.

"Back here." Cash motioned with his finger again. "He could be at the pool."

"We don't know what he looks like," Taylor said.

Cash didn't turn as he walked through the two-lane opening. "So we'll ask around."

✺

Faye Cox finished her third margarita and set the glass on the side table. A roundish, balding man opened the beach gate and stopped to spray sand from his feet at a low-mounted showerhead next to the gate. He reminded her of her late husband, Reverend Cox. A good man who had given up a six-figure career with the airlines to go into the ministry. Faye supported her husband through seminary and the list of churches he ministered in over the years. Congregations loved, but eventually hated him, for his firm, biblical stance. After losing a pastor over a heartbreaking church scandal, a firm hand was what the congregation wanted. But when Reverend Cox refused to bow to the two or three families who actually ran things, he would be run out of town on a rail.

She could see it coming when Reverend Cox felt it necessary to preach his famous attendance sermon. She knew it almost word-for-word when attendance began to decline in the summer months.

"Members who attend on Sunday morning love the church. Those who attend on Sunday nights love the preacher. But those who care enough to come to prayer meeting on Wednesday night love the Lord."

When Reverend Cox passed away, no doubt years early from the stress of battling and worrying over church cliques, she'd had enough. Of course if he hadn't passed when he did, the mere thought of her possessing the ingredients for margaritas in the fridge would have been enough to kill him instantly. With that thought, Faye reached for the pitcher and poured another drink. She noticed the two men in dark suits appear from the breezeway opening and scan the parking area as she set the pitcher back on the table.

She restrained a burp. "You gentlemen lose your car?"

Cash and Taylor turned and walked to the edge of Faye's small patio. "We're trying to locate Mr. Grey Colson," he said in a neighborly tone.

She suppressed another burp and slurred, "You must be some of his police friends."

Cash grinned. "Sort of, but not exactly. It's a family matter."

"You just missed him," she said, and pointed to the gate. "He went out to the beach."

Cash followed the lazy motion of Faye's arm and thought for a moment. "Ah, he was recommended. I haven't met him before."

"You can't miss him," Faye chuckled. "He's the only one on the beach with a big, black Corvette tent."

"Thank you."

Cash turned and walked across the parking lot. Taylor moved behind as if he was on a leash.

She called out to them, "You should take your shoes off. They'll be full of sand if you don't. And you don't know the gate code!"

Taylor dismissed her with a backhand wave.

❧ Chapter Eleven ❦

Tina dropped the flashlight, grabbed a beach towel, and took the deck stairs down two at a time. She saw Jason fall, but was he unconscious? She pushed herself to run hard. The thick sand made it almost impossible. She drove her heels into the mounds of sand until she reached the sandy grass mixture at the side of the beach house. Hugging the exterior wall, she ran the length of the house and stopped to catch her breath at the front corner. No yelling from Jason yet. A sudden thought made her go pale and weak-kneed. *Had she killed him?* The thought terrified her. She grasped the corner of the house to steady herself. The front gate was closed. The ten-foot stone wall prevented her from seeing the road. Cars periodically appeared for an instant on A1A as they passed in front of the wrought iron gates. She looked down the wall to her left. Its sides extended only fifteen or twenty feet from the ends, giving drivers the illusion of a property completely surrounded by a massive wall of stone.

She ran to her left and spanned the half-acre front yard, stopping again to lean against the short outside wall. Now hidden from view of the beach house, she glanced back. Still no shouting and no Jason. Now what? A1A was nothing but two lanes here. She would be easily exposed to traffic going in either direction. Cash would spot her in a second, or worse, Taylor would.

She turned and ran straight toward the shore, and then cut left across the rear of the house. People were beginning to migrate to the beach. She felt confident she would blend in the farther from the house she went. She checked over her shoulder once more, and left the house behind. Her legs began to burn and breathing became painful. Sitting around doing nothing for months was taking its toll. The tourists paid no attention to a beach runner. There were dozens of them this morning, but Tina outpaced them all. She stopped a quarter-mile up the beach and sat in the sand. Cash's house was now a faint outline on the coast. It was difficult to distinguish from other houses and condos she had passed. She held her hand against her forehead to shield the sun and squinted, looking north.

A small, long, gray object appeared to sit on the water in the distance. It was the main pier. Jason made her go there with him the first week. That was when he was being nice to her that first day. When she had been fooled into believing Cash was being kind by giving her a place to stay until she could get on her feet and rent an apartment. They promised her a job and helped her with the application. But when she moved into the beach house, her world changed. The pier was too far. It had to be five—maybe even ten—miles away. She had no money, no friends and nothing on but a bikini. She dropped her head into her hands, thinking she should have planned better.

∽

Five-and-a-half miles north from where Tina sat on the shore, Colson tuned his radio to his favorite station and leaned his head back. The sandpipers landed randomly at the water's edge, plucking at their sandy treats. He wished he had brought a few slices of bread to squeeze into marble-size lumps to throw at them. They would be frightened at first, but once they realized it was food, dozens would swoop in to compete for them.

Normal depends on where you are, what time of day it is, and the activities occurring at any given location. A preacher stepping to the podium to offer a Sunday morning sermon wearing boxers and a wife-beater shirt would be unusual. A preppy, white male driving a BMW slowly through a known crack slum at one o'clock in the morning would be suspect. A haggard, long-haired forty-year-old man sitting for hours in a beat-up Dodge watching adolescent girls playing soccer would send up an immediate red flag. And so did the two black-suited men in their dress shoes walking in his direction from behind Mr. and Mrs. Hammond.

Colson hadn't looked their way, but he didn't have to. Their non-appropriate beach garb caught his peripheral vision ten seconds ago. Colson kept his eyes on the birds, but his focus on the two strangers. Maybe they liked his canopy and wanted to ask where he bought it. Then again, probably not.

He crossed his arms as a pair of now sand-covered dress shoes stopped to his right. The second man had moved out of his peripheral vision. He would be behind him now. At least they knew not to step under the canopy uninvited and Colson had no intention of offering an invitation. No one wears their Sunday best to the beach for a friendly visit, and local police detectives in this county aren't paid enough to wear five-hundred-dollar suits, nor would they in this weather.

Detectives are not that stupid. He was out of clues with these two. Maybe they were salesmen. He stared straight at the birds.

"I'm not interested in a timeshare," Colson said.

"What?" the man wearing the dress shoes asked.

"A timeshare. I don't need one. I'm a resident."

"You're Grey Colson," Cash said, half-asking and half-telling.

Colson looked up at Cash from his chair. "So you already know I'm a resident. I still don't want what you're selling."

"I'm Martin Cash," he said, ignoring Colson's dismissal. "You involved yourself in an incident with my son, if you recall."

Colson adjusted his chair to put both men in his view. He studied Taylor for a moment and grinned. "Well, he's really grown. You must be feeding him well."

"They were right; you must be the retired cop."

"Who are 'they'?"

"That's not relevant."

Colson stood and glared at Cash through his sunglasses. "It's relevant to me."

Taylor took a step and stopped.

Cash gave him a grin. "Colson, I understand, I really do. I know it's in your nature to interfere in people's lives. That's what cops do. But as you can see…" Cash motioned toward the ocean, "you're not in Georgia anymore."

"And I suppose it's in your son's nature to slap teenage girls around."

Cash dropped his grin. "We were both teenage boys, Colson. You remember how it was. Young and dumb."

"Oh, I remember being a teenager, and assaulting women wasn't part of it. Let's be clear, Cash, are you attempting to influence a witness here?"

Cash held his palms face up. "Of course not, Colson. I'm just asking that you consider his age and that he's going through the normal changes a boy goes through."

Colson mockingly agreed. "There's no doubt he could use a change, but it's impossible to change fathers or the way you were brought up. The criminal justice system can't change him either, but it can keep him away from young women for a while."

Cash lowered his hands and stuck them in his pockets. "Fine, Colson. I was asking...now I'm telling you to stay out of it. I'm sure you had enough jollies in your career arresting real criminals."

"And as they told you, I'm retired. That means I no longer take orders from anyone."

Cash sighed. "I don't believe I introduced my employee, Mr. Taylor." Colson looked to Taylor and then back to Cash. "You may recognize him. Jay 'The Terrible' Taylor?"

"The Terrible Taylor? No," Colson replied with a grin, "but I could tell that much by looking at your suit."

"There's that smartass cop humor again. And you people wonder why the public can't stand you. You know, I won't be able—or even willing—to get between you and Taylor if it comes to that."

Colson turned to Taylor. "Get between us? There's nothing between us right now but air and the fear in his heart."

Taylor ducked his head and stepped under the tent. Colson took note of a vein bulging in Taylor's fat neck. Cash put his hand on Taylor's chest.

"No," Taylor shot back, keeping his eyes on Colson. "That's what you'd like, isn't it Colson? Right out here where your beach buddies can help you."

"It's time for you to go, Cash, and take him with you. There are signs all over the beach prohibiting pets."

Colson reached down and cranked up the radio volume. K.C. and the Sunshine Band blared, "I'm your boogie man." Taylor looked at Cash who shook his head and walked away from the canopy. Taylor fell in behind. Colson watched the pair walk easily across the packed sand of the beach roadway, then slow their pace through the thick sand leading to the concrete stairway at the sea wall.

Roger Hammond was halfway to the canopy when Colson eased back in his lounge chair. Colson motioned for him to step into the shade.

"Not trying to be nosey," Hammond began, "but is everything okay?"

Colson grinned. "They were timeshare salesmen."

Hammond tilted his head like a dog reacting to a high-pitched whistle.

"Right. High-pressure sales, I suppose. You must have turned them down and that's why the one with the thick neck wanted to deck you."

"Sometimes I can be a little sarcastic. It's a gift, you know."

"As long as you're okay. Mrs. Hammond was worried."

"Thanks, Roger, and tell her I appreciate it."

Hammond chuckled. "Oh, and will you please turn that damned boogie music down? People are trying to sleep around here."

The ice cream truck rolling up and down the beach road made Colson hungry. He didn't bring a watch, but knew he'd been out for three hours, making it around three o'clock. Mrs. Hammond was leafing through her book, but Mr. Hammond hadn't moved an inch in the past two hours. He stood, stretched, and took a deep breath of sea air. He reminded himself to bring a piece of bread back for the sandpipers. Mrs. Hammond looked over and waved. He made an eating motion with his hand and pointed down to his belongings in the sand. Mrs. Hammond returned a nod and smiled. He knew she wouldn't drift off to sleep and let a bunch of beach trolls steal his stuff. He crossed the beach road and waded into the thick sand to the stairs.

He stepped into the cool air conditioning of the condo and headed to the refrigerator. His cell phone made a faint chirp on the kitchen counter. He picked it up and saw the missed call. He rolled his eyes when he saw it was Beavers. He dialed his voice mail, thankful he didn't have to have a conversation.

"Hey, buddy. Your detail is set for tomorrow night at the Rayford Inn on A1A at eight o'clock. You can set up in the parking lot across the street and get a perfect view of the rooms. The target will be driving a late-model, black Tahoe with blacked out windows. Piece of cake. Oh, I almost forgot. Remember to rent a car. Yours will stand out like a turd in a punch bowl. Bring the receipt and I'll reimburse you. Call me when you get the message."

Colson deleted the message and set the phone on the counter. "Of course I'm renting a car, you moron," he said in a disgusted growl. He opened the cabinet and pulled out a vodka bottle instead of sandwich bread.

～～

Pickett opened his appointment book and placed it next to him on the edge of the bed. Two names, telephone numbers, and locations were listed. One lunch meeting at noon on Monday and another on Wednesday. He rubbed his forehead and let himself drop back on the bed. The ceiling was a cheap, popcorn finish. He noticed it had developed a yellowish haze over the past five years, but adding a fresh coat of paint was not on his list of priorities. Insurance sales had declined just as most other business in the area. If things worked as planned, he wouldn't need to sell insurance and could move out of this dump of a house.

He turned to look at the two frames on the dresser across the room. The woman in the photo to the left had long, dark hair and a radiant smile. She waved at him from the two dimensional photo as if she were literally in the room. Brittany was twenty-five years old in the picture and gorgeous, especially wearing those white shorts and the University of Michigan t-shirt. He smiled at the memory of the early September afternoon before they left for the stadium. He didn't remember the game, only her and the look of envy in the eyes of other men who watched her hang on his arm.

The photo to the right roused very different memories. His father. The six foot, three inch, Michigan State Police Captain in full dress uniform, holding his retirement plaque. His short, but slim, mother with her arm wrapped around his waist and a smile of pride on her lips. Pickett stared back at the popcorn ceiling and closed his eyes.

The years of study and the prospect of becoming the cop his father had been were a waste. He had wanted to do better than his old man. Pickett had promised himself he would make it all the way to the Director of State Police. He had the education his father lacked. Who would have thought one single department psychologist could take that away from him? It had been over five years, but he could recall every word of the conversation.

～～

The psychologist uncrossed his legs and removed his reading glasses. "No one is suggesting you're crazy. If you'll read the summary, it merely states your personality is not conducive to a career in law enforcement."

"But that doesn't make sense," Pickett replied, his breaths becoming deeper and more frequent with the realization of what the summary meant. It didn't matter that he scored highest in the written test and his feverish cardio workouts awarded him with the best time on the physical agility course. His background was unblemished and he was the son of a retired captain in good standing. No, none of that would matter. This one report from this one psychologist could slam the door to his career. He fought to keep his composure. Anything short of that would validate the psychologist's concerns.

"So, do you recommend me waiting what, six months or a year, and take the test again?" Pickett asked.

The psychologist replaced his glasses and crossed his legs. He looked at Pickett for a long moment and steepled his hands.

"If you were twenty-one years old, maybe. Mr. Pickett, you're thirty years old. Your psychological profile is set, for the most part, and is highly unlikely to change."

Pickett slowly shook his head. "You have to help me out here. You just don't understand."

The psychologist closed the file and stood, straightening his tie.

"There's nothing more I can do for you, Mr. Pickett. My diagnosis and professional opinion will stand."

Pickett jerked to his feet and held up his hands. His breathing became heavier and sporadic. "Just hang on. You can't stop my career before it even gets started because of those stupid-ass tests and your supposedly professional opinion."

"We're finished Mr. Pickett," he replied, and took a step toward the door.

The psychologist had heard all the arguments before, the pleadings to retest and the challenges to his expertise. He'd had the same discussion hundreds of times with hundreds of desperate cop wannabes and knew when the argument was exhausted. And this discussion was going nowhere, but neither was he. Pickett grabbed him by both shoulders. He felt himself spin violently, and he stumbled as Pickett marched him backwards to the wall, the contents of the folder spilling onto the floor. The psychologist flailed his arms in an attempt to maintain balance and felt his back slam into the wood-paneled wall.

Pickett's eyes burned into his with rage. No longer attempting to control his breathing, his breaths came loud and heavy, as if he had just completed a half-mile sprint. The psychologist relaxed his arms and let them drop to his side. Pickett's breathing calmed, as they stood motionless and speechless for what seemed to be several minutes. The psychologist spoke first.

"You see now, Mr. Pickett? I would just be setting you up for failure. A favor from me today would be a curse for you tomorrow, or the next day. What I did today was not to deprive you of a long career with the State Police, but to deprive you of many years in federal prison for civil rights violations."

Pickett dropped his hands and stepped back. His head was spinning with fading rage. The palms of his hands were wet with greasy sweat. He wiped them on his pant legs, turned, and then walked out of the office without a word.

The following six months of depression resulted in his driving Brittany further and further away from him. The supportive words of Pickett's retired father felt like the hollow words of a parent comforting a Down syndrome child after losing a Special Olympics race. Even Brittany encouraged him. She first said she would stand by him, no matter what career he chose, but he knew better. A month later she broke the news about a job opportunity in Jacksonville. It was just too good to turn down. Six months and ten days after his shoving match with the psychologist, she was gone.

One year and six weeks later, he found her in Jacksonville, working at the Mayo Clinic Hospital. She was married and pregnant. He hugged her, wished her well, and mounted his Harley. The weather was warm and the road was smooth. Pickett swung out on Butler Boulevard and gunned the bike. He eased into the right lane to exit north on the I-295 bypass and slowed. The warm air had a faint sea aroma he had never experienced. He took a deep breath and downshifted, driving past the exit north, and rode south toward Daytona. He always wanted to see the famous speedway, and this was as good an opportunity as any.

It was the first week of March and eighty-two degrees. Pickett was enjoying the ride immensely and had no desire to fracture the speed limit, knowing that would only shorten the experience. Other riders met him going north and lowered their hands in the universal "bike wave." He returned their greetings in kind and noticed them riding without helmets. It looked odd, but it was legal in Florida. Feeling a sudden rush of freedom, he pulled to the emergency lane, removed his confining helmet, and pulled back onto the highway. He couldn't believe the exhilaration. He felt like a rebellious child, but he liked it. It took sixty minutes before he began riding past signs for the various beach exits and another twenty minutes to the International Speedway Boulevard exit. He was in heaven. It was Daytona Bike Week and they were everywhere, but so was Volusia County's finest. He thought about the nightmare it must be for those officers. He was certain it was no holiday for them. No off days and no annual leave would be granted under any circumstance during bike week. It gave him a revelation.

Pickett made his way over the inner coastal waterway and north on A1A to the Rayford Inn. He pulled his laptop from the saddlebag and paid a week in advance for an ocean-side room. After settling in and running through a drive-thru for a burger, he sat in front of his laptop and began researching the Volusia County Sheriff's Office and the Florida Peace Officers Standards and Training site. He read through the divisions of the sheriff's office and smiled. "They have a reserve unit," he said aloud at the computer screen. He punched in the administrative office number on his cell and requested an appointment with Sheriff Graham. He had an opening on Tuesday morning.

"I have a meeting at nine," Sheriff Graham said. "How can I help you Mister…"

"Pickett."

"Mister Pickett."

"I've moved to Daytona and am going to sponsor myself through the academy."

Graham's response sounded as though he had heard the sales pitch a thousand times. "Well, good luck, but we don't have any openings at this time. You may want to try—"

Pickett interrupted. "Oh, I wasn't interested in a salaried position. I work full time in insurance. An Internet business."

Graham sounded confused. "I don't follow you, Mister Pickett."

"I'm interested in the reserve unit. My father is a retired captain with the Michigan State Police and I've always wanted to serve. I would be a valuable asset to the agency and I already have a bike to volunteer for duty."

"Why not the state police in Michigan?" Graham said.

"I have always dreamed of working in an area like Volusia County. Michigan is frozen eight months out of the year."

Graham chuckled. "The last thing we need around here is another biker. The biker mentality causes nothing but trouble."

"I'm not a biker in that sense, Sheriff," Pickett pleaded. "I've grown up a law enforcement brat and respect my father and all he stood for."

Graham sighed. "I can't guarantee anything. You understand you have to pay for your own certification, pass a background check, everything a full-time deputy goes through."

"Yes, sir. No problem."

"And that doesn't mean I have to offer you a position and allow you to wear our badge. It will depend on how well you perform in the academy and where you finish in the class."

Pickett beamed. "Understood, Sheriff."

Pickett spent the next three weeks making application, establishing state citizenship, and waiting for the next academy class to begin. Another twelve weeks at the Daytona State College School of Emergency Services and ten thousand dollars lighter, Pickett held the required certification and had arrest powers. With Graham's final blessing, Pickett continued through the physical agility course and psychological examination. He was wringing his hands after four hours of testing, but forced himself to stop when he heard the waiting room door begin to swoosh against the carpet. The female psychologist sat in the chair across from him, just as the Michigan psychologist had done. This one rested her elbows on her knees instead of crossing her legs.

"So?" Pickett began.

"We're done. You can go grab something to eat," she said.

"But how did I do?"

"Oh, we don't give you our determination now. I have to examine the test results and how they relate to each other. It will take a few days, but your agency will get back with you."

Pickett tilted his head back and closed his eyes. "Okay, I just thought I'd know today. This is the last step."

She smiled and nodded. "I understand how important this job is to you, but I'm not trying to make the waiting any worse. I really do have to give serious consideration to your test results."

Pickett nodded and offered his hand. "Thanks."

She took Pickett's hand and smiled. "But from what I can tell at this point, you have nothing to worry about."

Pickett returned a larger smile and exhaled. "Thanks for that much, ma'am. I appreciate it."

He mounted his bike outside the office and laughed. "These stupid psychologists are crazier than they say I am."

Sheriff Graham was a firm—but fair—man. A little sloppy looking in uniform and a little overweight, but he was a jolly soul when he got to know you. A career law enforcement man, Graham had over thirty years of service. He was bald, wore thick prescription glasses, and was never seen without his cigar. Old school law enforcement like Pickett's old man. And just like his old man, came up through the job during the years when you didn't have to write a report every time you laid hands on a suspect or pointed your gun at them. You weren't required to check little boxes on reports, giving the federal government running statistics about how many Blacks, Hispanics, Asians, and Anglos you came in contact with to ensure you weren't picking on one certain group. The old guys were taught that a criminal is a criminal, their color notwithstanding.

Pickett was loving life just three short years ago. His Internet sales sustained him, and his dream of being a motor cop had finally come true. Then Graham announced his retirement at the end of his term. He was relieved to hear Stuart Langston was running for the job. He had met him once or twice and heard he would continue the reserve unit. But over the past two years something had changed. Langston became real comfortable as sheriff and started to feel the power of being the chief law enforcement officer of the county. Everyone said his attitude had changed. Langston had become a real hothead. Pickett's plan was to lay low, fly under the radar, and not draw negative attention to himself. But lately Langston was using his name in vain and he didn't understand why. There was one thing Pickett understood very clearly. Things would change when he would be running the department.

❧ Chapter Twelve ❧

Jason squinted and rolled to his side. He raised his head from the floor and saw the French door standing open. A steady ocean breeze blew in his face across the hard tile, and the faint laughing of children could be heard at the beach. He started to push himself up, but a shooting pain above his right ear caused him to slam his eyes shut and drop back to the floor. He pressed his hand against the pain, making it subside for a moment. What had happened? He shoved the long hair from his eyes, pressed his palm against his temple, and rubbed the new knot he just discovered. He jerked his hand away to examine it. No blood.

He pushed himself up again and sat staring at the open door, then quickly looked around the media room. "Hey!" No one answered. A faint "hey" seeped through the adjacent bedroom door. He rolled to his knees, stood, and walked to the bedroom. He jerked the door open. Lacy lay in bed on her side. The sudden wash of daylight made her squint.

"What," she said. He reached for the switch and flipped it. Lacy covered her eyes and buried her head in the pillow. "Hey!" she belted in disgust.

"Where's Tina?" Jason demanded.

"How should I know? Turn off the light." Her voice was muffled by the pillow.

Jason ran out of the bedroom, through the French door, and out to the deck rail. He ran back inside, grabbed his old man's binoculars off the bar counter, and ran back outside. The beach was littered with tourists north and south. He focused the field glasses and moved them slowly in both directions. He thought he found her twice, but closer examination proved him wrong. The sun was high and it began burning his shoulders. He suddenly wondered how long he had been out and stepped back inside to check the bar clock. "Damn, it's been...two hours!"

He heard the side door chime, followed by heavy steps in the kitchen. Cash and Taylor stepped into the media room and saw Jason holding the binoculars. Taylor sat on couch and pulled off his tie. Cash dropped into his recliner and looked at Jason.

"I don't have time to keep trying to fix your screw-ups, boy," he began. "I have a business to run. Several businesses to run and I'm tired of wasting my time cleaning up after you. When is your court date?"

Jason set the binoculars on the bar and stood silent.

"Are you listening to me? When is your court date?"

Jason looked at the floor. "It was six weeks from…well, five weeks from now."

Cash looked at Taylor. "We give him two weeks, and then we visit him again. Or should I say you visit him again. Actually…" Cash looked at the ceiling and thought for a moment. "You and Fuller go next time."

Taylor nodded. "I'll arrange it so he can't identify us."

"He better not be able to identify anyone. Hell, he better not even be able to speak."

Cash looked back to Jason, who stood with a look of bewilderment. "And what's wrong with you?"

"Tina."

"What about her?"

"She's gone."

∽

Tina welcomed the warm, night air. It had been twelve hours since she hit Jason and she was not accustomed to being exposed to ninety-degree temperatures for hours on end. Her body felt weak from the heat, especially since the last several months had been spent in the cool darkness of a bedroom. The beach bag she liberated from the unsuspecting swimmers had been a godsend. She was wearing the tan cover-up and sun visor, but left the inflatable pool float inside the bag. The bologna sandwich and peanut butter crackers had given her energy. She was nursing one of the bottles of water as she made her way south on the west side sidewalk of A1A. She turned the bag inside out, exposing the dull lining, folded the pool float, and pushed it back in with the beach towel. Cars of all types traveled in both directions. Many with lowered convertible tops and loud, chattering teenagers. She received catcalls and wolf whistles from two guys seated in lawn chairs in the back of a four-wheel drive pickup, but she wasn't in the mood to acknowledge them. Tina walked south against her better judgment. She was headed back in the direction of Cash's beach house, but it couldn't be helped. She had to rest and she remembered seeing something interesting on a previous ride in Jason's sports car.

And there it was, just a little further on the right. Adjacent to the sidewalk was a small, rectangular church, but it wasn't an actual church. Just a gray structure resembling a church, complete with a high pitched roof and steeple. It was no larger than the eight-by-ten storage building her father once built in their back yard. Lines of white posts sat in staggered rows the length of a football field behind the miniature church building and beyond them, another much larger building. An A-frame structure appeared to have been set atop a long, one-story building with a large porch. The first story was covered with rock facing, and the porch supported a balcony above. Jutting up from the stone structure was the high wooden A-frame with a doorway leading to the balcony. Above the doorway, a large cross hung at a strange forty-five degree angle.

Tina walked past the miniature church and saw what she had seen on the drive with Jason. A white sign mounted near the peak of the roof that read "Drive-In Christian Church." Inset into the wall siding was one of those three-line restaurant signs that can be changed by sliding individual letters into tracks. It read:

WELCOME RACE FANS
SUNDAY WORSHIP
8:30-10:00 AM

Tina had never seen, or even heard of, a drive-in church before. She would have been amused if she wasn't so tired. She walked behind the building and found what she hoped was there. A door. Tina looked both directions on A1A and slipped behind the building where no headlights could illuminate her movement. She grabbed the knob and it turned without resistance. She quickly pulled at the door when approaching headlights grew larger and brighter. But the movement stopped after about an inch. She ducked as the car passed. In the brief illumination she saw the padlock and hasp holding the door closed. She placed her right foot against the frame and pulled the knob as hard as she could. The door didn't yield. Two more sets of headlights, this time from the south. She flattened herself to the ground as a police cruiser slipped by. She laid flat in the rough grass for another minute. Thinking.

She stood when she could no longer hear approaching traffic. With her foot against the doorframe, she jerked at it in short, methodic movements. Four, five, six, seven, eight times. At the count of ten she felt the door give a little, then a little more. There was the sound of cracking wood, softened by years of moisture and salt-filled humidity. The tired frame was giving up the fight. On jerk eighteen the hasp came free from the frame, throwing two short screws against Tina's cover-up.

She stepped inside to darkness and shut the door behind her. A stale smell of gasoline and mold surrounded her. With no windows, she stood in total darkness. She cracked the door just enough to allow ambient light inside. A large riding lawnmower sat to her right. Two weed-eaters and a hedge trimmer hung on the opposite wall, along with an assortment of gardening tools. Underneath sat two red gas containers on the plywood floor. Several boxes of square plastic letters were lined up on a shelf against the far wall, apparently used to change the message outside. She briefly wondered if they ever changed it to read, "WELCOME RUNAWAY KIDNAP VICTIMS."

It was uncluttered and oddly clean for a storage shed. Plenty of open space was available for the pool float. She left the door slightly ajar and sat down to inflate the float. It took longer than she thought. The process made her light headed. She pulled the door closed and laid down. If someone found her tonight, so be it. She was too tired to care. She closed her eyes and drifted off to the sound of passing cars on A1A, just ten feet from her head.

☙

Colson walked around the charcoal-colored Honda Accord and gave the rent-a-car employee a thumbs up. The young man handed him the keys and told him it was a 2009 model with tinted windows, just as he had requested. The tinted windows for a Florida rental was a given. The color was chancy.

"We just had one charcoal Honda on the lot. You were lucky," the young man said.

"This is fine. Can you pick it up tomorrow?" Colson asked.

"Sure, just call the office when you're done. Don't forget to fill it up."

"I won't."

The young man stood, smiling at Colson. He figured he wasn't waiting for a handshake, so he pulled out a ten and handed it to him. The boy nodded appreciation and slipped into the passenger side of another rental, driven by a second young employee. He checked the interior of the car. There it was. A blend of sweat, perfume, food, puke, and alcohol from dozens of previous renters. All rentals smelled the same. Clean enough, but there was no getting rid of the familiar funk.

A strong ocean breeze rushed through the breezeway from the ocean side parking area. Colson turned toward the opening, breathed deep and exhaled. A red SUV drove slowly past him and through the breezeway. The front axle bobbed up and down over the first speed bump, followed by the rear axle, and then again over the second. It turned right, disappeared behind the building, and came back into view after turning left and pulling into an angled parking space. All four doors opened simultaneously. A man stepped from the driver's side, a woman from passenger side, and a boy and girl from the back seat. Both children immediately ran to the beach access gate and looked right and left. They bounced on the balls of their feet and beckoned the adults to join them. The woman walked to the excited children and followed their pointing fingers to various sites on the beach. The man was busy lifting the tailgate and setting luggage on the ground. It made Colson smile with the memories of the last twenty-five years here with Ann and Nichole. For a moment he thought about being a no-show and telling Beavers to shove it. Maybe that would make him mad enough to leave him alone. He shook his head. It would be the first time in over six months he had to be anywhere. Time to get it over with.

Colson rode the oil-scented elevator to the fifth floor and walked to his door. His go-bag was sitting on the kitchen table where he'd left it a week earlier. He slipped on his black BDU pants and navy shirt. He slid his go-bag across the counter and clipped his phone in the side pocket where he used to store an 800-megahertz radio. The camera and phone charger were zipped into pockets on the inside. He pulled his flashlight away from the wall charger, slid it into the slender outside pocket, and checked the opposite pocket for his ASP expandable baton. He lifted his Glock from the bag and held it up in one hand, pulling the slide back a fraction to ensure a round was in the chamber. He remembered one retired deputy who had made the mistake of pushing the slide back with his left hand in front of the muzzle and blew off a substantial portion of his palm and both his ring and pinkie fingers.

He pulled the photo of the target from the envelope and gave it another look. The man in the black golf shirt sported a high and tight military haircut. Career military types usually kept the hairstyle after decades of being used to it. Why bother to cut the other person from the photo? Obviously someone who didn't want to be associated with the man or this operation. He wondered for a moment if Beavers had been the second person in the photo. But why would he not tell him if that were the case? Maybe that was why he wouldn't take the photos himself. He slid the photo back inside and dropped the envelope into the bag. He checked his watch. 1910 hours. He stopped at the closet and plucked his Atlanta Braves ball cap from the shelf, pulled it down on his head, and then casually walked out the door.

The Rayford Inn was a modest, three-story hotel at the corner of A1A and Glenview Boulevard. Only twelve of its rooms faced the beachfront. Rooms numbering one through twenty-seven faced south and twenty-eight through fifty-four faced north. Visitors not fortunate enough to rent one of the coveted twelve oceanfront rooms were not totally out of luck. One could get a fairly decent view of the ocean from the balconies of the north- and south-facing rooms, but it was seldom anyone was seen loitering on the Rayford's balconies. Most who frequented the establishment had little interest in sightseeing and certainly had no desire to be seen.

Marcus Wituka stepped out of the convenience store on A1A and lit a cigarette. He glanced over his shoulder through the glass door and looked at the digital clock hanging over the cashier's head. 7:30 p.m. He took a long drag and walked to the corner, looking diagonally across the street at the Rayford Inn. Across from the Rayford on the ocean side of the street stood a ten-story motel at least twenty years newer than the Rayford. Wituka scowled at the thought of Pickett's choice of a meeting place. "That cheap cracker," he said aloud to no one. He should have asked for more than a hundred for the meet, especially since he went cheap on the room. At least he was going to get pleasure out of loading Langston up with a load of bull about Cash. He hated Langston like he hated all cops, including Pickett, but since Pickett was having him set Langston up with bad information on Cash, he didn't mind playing along. It didn't matter what Pickett's motivation was. When Langston left he would have money in his pocket and a room for the night. He had a quarter bag of pot in his shoe and a couple of his homeboys were bringing some high quality meth later.

He dropped his three-hundred-fifty-pound frame off the curb. With the exception of the square made by the two intersecting streets, the gray asphalt was unremarkable with its white and yellow lines and wide turning arrows. The intersection was paved with inlaid tan bricks to simulate the beach. Two-tone blue bricks made a pattern to simulate the surf in the center. The odd brick had been knocked out of place here and there by years of traffic, and the colors appeared faded from what would have been their original brilliance. Wituka paid no attention to the thoughtfully contrived street design or the traffic signal as he hobbled through the crosswalk, just as he paid no attention to the traffic coming from either direction.

The brakes of the dark gray Honda squealed and stopped two feet from Wituka's legs. He stopped and snapped his head to glare at the driver. The windows were dark, but he saw the man well enough through the windshield. He wore sunglasses and a ball cap. He just sat there. No horn blowing, no hand gestures, no lip movements. He just stared at him through his sunglasses. Wituka plucked the cigarette from his lips and flicked it toward the car, watching it bounce off the hood with a spark and slide off onto the street. He raised both hands in a taunt, silently challenging the driver to do something about it. The man sat and continued to stare. Unable to get a rise out of the cracker, Wituka offered a dismissive wave of disgust and continued plodding across the street.

∼

"Do you actually expect to get any reliable intelligence from that filthy, lying psycho?" Langston asked Reese when they climbed into the Tahoe.

Reese pulled the passenger door closed and clicked her seatbelt. "Anything we can get at this point is better than what we have now, which is not much."

"If your surveillance and investigative techniques haven't gotten you anything, then that should tell you something…you either haven't done enough or you're not looking in the right place. Anything come back on the name of that boat?"

"No. Nothing on the registry. It's going to be from Mexico, most likely."

"Do you have Cantrell en route to the hotel?"

"Yes, sir. He should already be there and set up. You think we need the backup? What if Wituka gets suspicious and leaves?"

Langston looked at Reese in disbelief. "Listen lieutenant, you always need backup. I don't care if it's a deal or just a meet. Nothing is worth getting dead over because you thought you could do it alone or were afraid the deal might not go if the target gets hinked up." He paused and shook his head. "I better never catch you doing something stupid like that."

"I understand, Sheriff."

Langston turned right on International Speedway Boulevard and crossed over the inner costal bridge. The police radio came to life with a lookout for a demented teenager who had been missing since early the same morning. "Reference a signal 56 on a fifteen-year-old white male missing since approximately 0600 hours this date from Port Orange. Subject last seen wearing blue jean shorts and red t-shirt. Subject reportedly signal 24 and left treatment facility on foot, no direction of travel. Any contact, hold and notify radio. Out of Volusia at 1900 hours."

Langston and Reese remained silent until the radio traffic ceased. Langston gestured to the radio.

"These kids get fried, and then they become dangerous. And it's because of people like Cash."

"Can I ask you something?" Reese said. "I understand why we're investigating Cash and we'll do everything in our power to have him prosecuted—"

"But?" Langston interrupted.

"But…is there something else? Something about Cash I don't know about? Something personal?"

Langston drove in silence for a long moment. The radio crackled and the dispatcher began rattling off the description of a vehicle driving erratically. He reached to the console and toggled the volume down.

"It's our job to take what crooks do personally," he said. "This is where we live. It's where most of our families live. You either turn a blind eye or you take care of business. All of our business is personal. I'm surprised you haven't figured that out yet, Reese."

Reese looked at her hands folded in her lap. "I understand what you're saying, Sheriff."

"Raise Cantrell and find out if Wituka showed up."

Reese reached for center console and raised the radio volume. She touched a separate toggle and skipped through the menu until "OCU Invest" appeared on the screen, and raised the microphone.

"801 to 803. Are you in position?"

"803, 10-4, across the street with eyes on the one-four side of the building. The target went in the office and is now in room two-seven."

"Received. We're about ten away."

"10-4."

"What did Pickett promise Wituka?" Langston asked.

"I don't know, why?"

"Because he's actually on time. That's unheard of with these people. They usually run on doper's time."

"What's that?"

"They're always late for meets, sometimes deliberately, to see if they're being set up, but most times because they're so screwed up they can't keep time. Doper time."

Reese nodded and adjusted herself in her seat. She reached behind her and adjusted the paddle holster on her belt.

"Why didn't you pull Pickett's part-time permit? Why let him work security at his stores to begin with?"

"I didn't. If you recall, I inherited all the old administration's garbage. The security job had been approved long before I took office. There hasn't been an issue until recently, so I let it go."

"So he's done some good then?" Reese asked.

"He's done squat!" Langston corrected. "He wouldn't know his ass from the business end of my Glock forty-five. He wants to wear the uniform, write tickets, and embellish war stories. He doesn't have the ability or intuition for the job."

"Then why leave him there?"

"Well, to use your words, we wouldn't want to make Cash suspicious now, would we?"

➤ Chapter Thirteen ➤

Colson gritted his teeth and pulled away from the fat-body Neanderthal who had just finished his territorial challenge and stepped onto the sidewalk. The Rayford Inn was on his right now, but he continued down the street fifty yards and turned left into the parking lot of what appeared to be a souvenir shop converted to a business office. The digital clock on the radio displayed 7:35. He swung around in the parking lot on the far side, nosed the Honda to the front corner, and pushed the gear into park, just in view of the Rayford across the street.

There was fat boy walking into the office. *Nice place for a romantic rendezvous,* he mumbled. He checked the time again. 7:45 and there was fat boy again, coming out of the office and around to the opposite side of the building and out of sight. He pulled the digital camera from his go-bag and hit the power button. The large camera screen filled the back side of the camera. He had used it many times during his last few years with the agency. Nichole had to have the latest high-resolution camera every other year, so he kept the hand-me-downs for work. He played with the zoom and pulled the entrance of the Rayford in to fill the entire screen, and then back out. He almost didn't catch the Tahoe pulling into the far entrance and disappearing out of sight.

He dropped the camera on the seat between his legs and pulled out of the lot, making a hard right and passing the entrance where the Tahoe turned in. The Tahoe's brake lights illuminated as it slowed. Colson sped the Honda up, shot through the intersection, and slowed to turn left into the high-rise parking lot next door. The entrance was blocked with short pylons driven into the asphalt. "Damn," he cursed himself for not being on his game. He sped to the next entrance and swung left. The Tahoe was out of sight now. Maybe there was still time. He drove around the front of the high rise and to the side parking area facing the Rayford. He slowed and backed into a space directly across from the parked Tahoe. No one exited the vehicle. Too late.

Colson settled into his seat. The idea was to get pictures of the couple going into the room. His arm would have been around her or hers around him. Maybe he would have been able to grab a photo of him carrying her over the threshold. Even better, maybe a hug and kiss at the door before going inside to carry out their fantasy. That would have been it. That would have been enough. But no. Now because of his laziness and poor planning, the best he could hope for was a picture of them coming out of the room. Spent. Maybe a parting hug and kiss—if he was lucky. He would have jumped all over his investigators for such piss-poor planning and execution of surveillance. Then there was the lighting issue. If this lasted an hour or two, the digital camera wouldn't record squat, even with the low-light capability. A thirty-minute project just turned into a possible all-nighter, and he was livid at himself. He pulled the camera charger cord out of the go-bag, stuck one end into the cigarette lighter, and the other end into the camera. He wasn't going to screw up the next opportunity. Now for the exhaustion of scanning the entire side of the building. Would the man park his vehicle right in front of the room? Surely not. That would make it entirely too easy for jealous wives to pinpoint. Would they even park on the same side of the building? He felt a little more at ease because they weren't out of sight long enough to have walked that far without him seeing them. No, they were on this side and probably on the ground floor. He had to watch all the ground floor rooms and be ready when they came out. He turned the radio to his favorite '80s station but kept the volume low. Loud music was distracting, but the background noise was needed to stay alert. "Work fast, my friend," he said.

Paranoia swept over Wituka as he peered around the heavy hotel curtain. Langston and his cute female lieutenant stood in silence by the television stand following their brief official greeting. There was something not right about the meeting, and now the cool cracker who almost ran him down had hauled ass around the building and backed into a space directly across the lot. He felt he was being set up and it infuriated him. They must want him to violate his parole, but why? His mind raced, thinking about what they might know. He had violated his parole countless times since his release. His problem was not knowing which crime they knew about. The drugs, the auto theft, the molestation? He darted his eyes to the bed without moving his head. His stash. If they found it, he'd be violated for sure.

"Marcus," Langston said, breaking the silence, "so what is this vital information you have?"

Wituka snapped around and pointed at Langston. "You're just harassing me, Langston. I ain't giving you shit since you had Pickett set me up."

"Look, Mason. I drug both of us out here to listen to your crap. You think I'm here to bust you when I've got bigger fish to fry? Don't flatter yourself. If I wanted you in jail, I'd send my youngest deputy to do my light work."

Wituka swung his index finger back to the window. "Then explain that cracker across the street in the Honda. He tried to run my ass down thirty minutes ago."

Reese looked at Langston. "We don't have anyone in a Honda, Marcus. Look, you're just..."

"No, you look," Wituka shouted. "If he ain't with you, then he's one of Cash's men. That means you ain't trying to set me up, you're trying to get me killed."

Langston shook his head, looked at Reese and stepped to the door. "Let's go Reese. I told you he's a psycho."

"Wait," Wituka yelled. "That's what you want. His men to kill me so you'll be rid of me, so you get Pickett to set me up like I'm giving you information I don't have. I ain't no snitch, even if it is a white boy."

Langston narrowed his gaze. "You mean to tell me you know nothing about Cash's operation or what he's doing?"

"Naw, man."

"And you don't have a way to get into his operation or get information from his people?"

"Naw, man. Nothing like that. Pickett said to feed you bogus information about him being a meth dealer and he'd pay me a hundred."

Langston took a long step to meet Wituka nose-to-nose. "So help me Marcus, if you're lying to me I will fulfill your paranoid fantasy and throw your ass in jail tonight."

"Sheriff, look at this," Reese said from the window.

Langston looked over her shoulder at the gray Honda across the lot. "He's still sitting there, looking in this direction and scanning the building."

"Raise Cantrell."

Reese lifted her portable, keeping her eyes on the Honda. "803."

"803, go ahead."

"Directly across from our position there's a dark gray Honda, you see it?"

"Got it."

"He's backed in. You'll need to go on foot. Go by and get the tag and get a look at the driver if you can."

"10-4, on my way."

Wituka sat his three-hundred-fifty pounds on the edge of the bed. "So you don't have anyone out there," he said mockingly.

"We don't have anyone in a Honda," Reese replied in the same tone.

"Pickett paid for the room," Langston said. "Then use it. We'll figure out what's going on and you stay as far away from this as you can. And keep your mouth shut, got it?"

Wituka looked down at his massive thighs and shook his head in silence.

ᔕᔑ

Colson caught the man's movement in his peripheral vision. He didn't see where he came from before he stepped on the sidewalk near the front of the building. It was almost sunset and here was another guy in a suit jacket walking around in eighty-degree heat. He kept his eyes on the building, but tracked the man as he approached behind him. He patted his knee to the steady footfalls of the man and found a rhythm. Gotcha! The man broke rhythm and slowed slightly as he passed behind the Honda. He caught his quick glance at the car tag in the rearview mirror. The man returned to his steady pace and walked in a side door. Not hotel security. Too slouchy and tired. Not one of Cash's thugs. Too subtle. Cash would make sure his man went out of his way to let him know he was being followed. It had to be a cop, but why? He hadn't been sitting in the lot for more than fifteen minutes. Uniforms would be dispatched to a suspicious vehicle, not a plain-clothes detective. It was something else. Something he had no desire to be a part of. He alternated looking at the Rayford Inn and down the sidewalk toward the street.

Two minutes was just about right. The plain-clothes guy was at the intersection and crossing the street. When he climbed into the sliver Taurus, he knew he was right. *We were watching the same guy.* Motion caught his attention across the lot. The couple walked out of the end room to the Tahoe. He raised the camera, played with the zoom, and took shots as quickly as the limited camera memory would allow. If this was a romantic interlude, it was too short. Ten minutes, tops. They walked fast and climbed into the Tahoe. No hug or kiss, not even an exchange of words he could see. The man had an angry walk, not the prance of the freshly laid. The back-up lights came on and the Tahoe screeched backwards, and then jerked forward and out onto South Atlantic. The Taurus immediately pulled out and fell in behind. He lowered the camera and stared at the wheel. He had either been used by Beavers, or both of them had been. For Beavers' sake, it better had been both. He started the Honda and laid the camera in his go-bag. He pushed the gear into drive and pulled out of his spot, and then stopped short. There was movement in the room and a streak of light from around the edge of the curtain.

He backed the Honda into the spot and waited. He pulled the camera back out, powered it up, pushed the zoom to the limit, and held it up to view the room. Lights off and movement of the curtain. Colson killed the ignition and settled into his seat. The job's not finished. It would be dark in an hour and time to find out what the hell Beavers had gotten him involved in.

∽

Cash jumped to his feet and glared at Jason. "What do you mean she's gone?"

"We went out to take the pictures like you said, and she hit me on the way back in," Jason said, rubbing his temple.

Cash rushed to the French doors, jerked one side open, and ran to the rail. He scanned both directions and turned to yell back into the house. "Why the hell didn't you say anything, you idiot!? How long has it been?"

Jason continued to rub his temple. Embarrassment and frustration made his head throb worse than before. "I don't know!" he snapped. "A few hours. I just woke up right before you came in. I can't help—"

"Shut up!" Cash shouted, and turned to Taylor. "She can't go far and she's not going to the police. You take Jason and go find her...now!"

Taylor nodded. "Mr. Cash, I can probably do better by myself."

"You take this dumbass out of my sight, Taylor. You find Tina and bring her back here. I've already accepted a deal and I'm not losing it."

"She might cause us a problem, depending on where we find her."

Cash realized Taylor was inferring a public kidnapping would draw attention. He walked to Taylor and pushed his finger close to his face.

"You bring her back here alive, Taylor. If it doesn't look like an easy snatch, then you stay on her until it is. You understand?"

Taylor nodded and turned to Jason. "Get your shoes on hotshot, and let's get going."

Jason snatched his shoes off the floor and sat down to pull them on. He wiped his long hair away from his face and glared at Cash, wanting to crack him in the temple with the same flashlight.

༺∾

Colson checked his watch. 8:40 p.m. He lifted the camera and zoomed in on the window of room twenty-seven. No more movement. Nothing since just after the couple left. He lowered the camera and eased back in his seat. He heard his cell vibrate and slid it from its case to look at the screen. Beavers. He would want to know if he got the pictures. He swiped the screen with his finger, sending the call directly to voice mail. "Well, there are a few things I'd like to know myself, Beavers. You can just wait," he said to his phone, and then slid it back into the pouch. Like why was this little rendezvous not even close to what was advertised, why the police surveillance, and who really is the target? Now a plain-clothes cop had copied his tag, dragging him into whatever mess or investigation they were doing. He had to find out what was going on before being named in an indictment or called as a witness to something he knew nothing about.

Movement again. Colson raised his camera and zoomed in on the room. The door had been pulled open about three inches, and then slammed shut. The light in the room was out and he couldn't see who was peeking from the inside. He tucked the Glock into the glove box. Without a level three holster, it could be just as dangerous to carry it. He had no intent to shoot anyone, yet, but getting into a scuffle could end with him being shot with his own gun. If he couldn't get the information he needed without a gun, he was really off his game. He pulled the ASP from the side pocket of the go-bag and slipped it into his right front BDU pocket. He stepped out of the Honda with the camera in his left hand and walked to the side entrance where the plain-clothes guy tried to disappear earlier.

Tourist hotels all had pretty much the same layout. In front would be a lobby with a long guest check-in desk off to one side. A bank of two elevators would be side-by-side across the lobby, or there would be two sets in side hallways. A total of four or eight, depending on total occupancy. In either case, there would be a rear exit to a pool or parking area. Colson jogged down the hall past a bank of two elevators and hooked left at the first intersecting hallway. Straight ahead was the back door with a red, glowing exit sign above. He pushed through the glass door to the rear parking area, cut left again, and then stopped at the back corner. The door was open again, but half-way this time. He lifted the camera and adjusted the zoom. Fat boy was on his cell phone, looking in the direction of the Honda. Fat boy? If there had been any romantic intent between the man and woman, it would have instantly evaporated at the sight of that slug. It was time for a talk.

Colson stepped from the corner. Wituka flipped the bar lock and stepped outside, resting the door against it. Colson froze. Fat boy wasn't leaving. He stepped back to the corner and waited. Wituka lumbered down the sidewalk and into the side office entrance. He must be alone, otherwise there was no need to prop the door. But he wouldn't be long. Colson jogged across the parking lot, pushed open the door and eased it closed against the bar lock. He announced, "Motel Security," while walking to the back of the room. He checked the bathroom. Clean towels and rags hung from a bar above the toilet. The soap and drinking glass were still in their wrappers.

Colson walked back to the door and pulled the heavy curtain back far enough to see as much of the sidewalk as possible. The room was as cheap as he expected. Two rough, fabric chairs sat opposite each other on either side of a plastic table in the front corner. A ruffled, flowery-print bedspread covered a full-size mattress, obviously disturbed by the load of fat boy's huge bulk. The air was still and hot. An aroma of musty humidity enveloped Colson. He reached down to the air conditioning unit below the window and turned the fan to high and the temperature to cold. He gave the room a quick survey. No papers, briefcases, or photos anywhere. No boxes or guns or drugs in view. Other than the disturbed bedspread, the room hadn't been used for long. Fat boy must have rented it shortly after he almost totaled out Colson's rental car.

He checked the sidewalk again. Fat boy came into view holding a can of soda in one hand and a bag of chips in the other. He pulled the retractable baton from his pants and stood behind the door. Waiting. The baton felt substantial and solid in his hand. When collapsed, the twenty-one-inch steel baton was only seven inches long, but still effective for close quarters combat or for applying pressure to certain points on the body.

Wituka pushed the door open with his back, letting it close and bounce off the bar lock. He put the soda and potato chips on the table and exhaled as though he had just run a marathon. Colson took a single step and reached around Wituka's neck with his left arm and pushed the rounded end of the baton under his jawbone, directly under his ear.

"What was your little meeting about?"

"What the hell?" Wituka screeched without turning to face the intruder. "What'chu want man?"

"Just what I said. What was your meeting about?"

"I ain't said shit to nobody, man."

Colson walked Wituka to the wall next to the bed and pressed the baton deep. "I don't care about you or your friends but the police had your meeting under surveillance and I want to know why."

A voice came from directly behind, at the door.

"What the hell?" the man said in a Hispanic dialect.

Langston cursed and lifted the radio microphone. "Cantrell. Did you get an ID from that tag?"

The radio emitted a moment of static and then Cantrell's voice. "Tag comes back to a local rental company. I'll have to go by tomorrow for the driver's information."

"Do it first thing," Langston said, and snapped the microphone back on the dash.

"Now do you see what I was talking about, lieutenant? It doesn't make sense. If Wituka hadn't been spooked, he would have given us bad information that could have ruined our case or sent us in the wrong direction."

Reese stared out of the passenger window in silence.

"What the hell is Pickett thinking?" Langston continued. "The only explanation is that he's working for Cash and it's not just part-time security." They rode in silence for a mile. "I should bring him in and find out."

"Sheriff," Reese said, "like you mentioned earlier. Cash will know something's up."

"I know what I said, lieutenant," Langston snapped, and shook his head. "I have no doubt Pickett's already told him about the investigation by now. That explains Cash's counter-surveillance at the hotel. If that's what we find out, Pickett will be indicted right along with Cash for felony obstruction of an investigation. You put a couple of investigators on him. I don't want him to take a shit without me knowing it, clear?"

Reese shook her head. "Yes, sir."

Langston turned right and shot into the left lane of the inner coastal waterway bridge. Sergeant Cantrell's voice came over the radio, advising he was out of service at headquarters. The radio crackled at the end of his transmission and the Tahoe was silent once again. Langston glanced to Reese as she continued to stare out the window.

"Look, Reese," he began, "I know you're trying hard to get this right. You can't allow personal relationships to direct an investigation."

Reese broke her stare and turned to Langston. "You think Pickett and I have a relationship?" She chuckled. "We dated twice. That's it. My job comes before any man and..." a moment of understanding crossed her face. "That's it, isn't it? You think we're an item and that's why you're so pissed at me."

"What?" Langston said.

"That's just the way I see it, Sheriff."

"Well, you see it wrong."

Reese smiled and nodded. "Okay. I apologize for getting it wrong."

"Do I think you're too good for him? Yes, but that's not my focus and that's not what makes my blood boil about Pickett. I've spent my entire adult life in this job and I can't stand these part-time wannabes who want the best of both worlds. They have their lucrative businesses because the county pay isn't good enough for them. But they also want to brag to their girlfriends about being super cop on the weekends. It's dangerous to give them arrest powers and a gun. After the next election all of them will be history. Especially since the trouble Pickett has caused. Case in point."

"I really don't know what to think. Wituka is a liar, you said so yourself," Reese said. "He could just as easily have been lying about Pickett."

"Think it through," Langston said. "Pickett set up the meeting. It was clear to me Wituka was scared to death thinking Cash's people were watching him. Only he and Pickett knew about the meeting. Now we just have to find out what the purpose of the meeting was to begin with before I pull Pickett's badge."

⇒ Chapter Fourteen ⇐

Confronting fat boy was a calculated decision. Colson knew he could have broken off and gone home. He had done the job, no matter if the photos didn't reveal the couple in an embrace or not. He could have gone home, told Beavers "Mission accomplished," turned over the photos, and then told him to pound sand. But he knew there was something ugly going on and he'd been dragged into it. The detective would have him identified by the rental agency first thing in the morning. Maybe even tonight, depending on how hard he pushed it. The choice now was to either wait for a knock on his door by the detective, or find out what was going on tonight and knock on the detective's door instead.

Colson recognized the risk of working alone and he would've never permitted his people to do it. He knew it was a necessity in exigent circumstances, but it was risky and dangerous. If an officer acted alone, at least he could fall back on his authority and the good faith protection afforded to peace officers acting under the color of law. But he no longer had that protection. What he had done could have been the ultimate display of stupidity if things spun out of control. He knew very well it could lead to criminal and civil liability, not to mention getting killed in the process. He had seen it too often in Internal Affairs. Officers getting involved in all manners of family and neighborhood disputes, injecting themselves in an official capacity when they should have divorced themselves from the situation. He had seen good employees lose their jobs, or worse—their freedom.

He spun Wituka around with the ASP digging deeper under his jaw. The two Hispanic men looked to be in their late twenties or early thirties. One in a tank-top wife-beater shirt and the other in a white t-shirt with cutoff sleeves. Both sporting a variety of tattoos on each arm. Some complete, but most outlines of uncompleted drawings and letters. The one nearest to Colson had a snake tattoo running from underneath his neckline, winding over the top of his shoulder, with its hissing head resting just forward and under his left ear. Both men had muscular upper torsos and the glassy gaze of seasoned methamphetamine addicts. Colson had seen the same gaze a thousand times.

"Cracker has a gun," Wituka said.

The first man grinned, glanced at his partner, and then back to Wituka. "Homie don't have no gun," he said with a nervous chuckle.

"What?" Wituka replied, cutting his eyes down, but unable to see what was in Colson's hand.

"Old man got the drop on you with that," Snake Tattoo laughed.

"What is that in your hand, Holmes? A jumbo-size Viagra bottle?" he scoffed.

Snake Tattoo drew a slender switchblade from his pocket and held it up for Colson to see. The blade shot forward with a quiet click as he slowly waved it in front of his face. "You won't need pills when I cut your pecker off and feed it to you, old man."

Colson sighed and rolled his eyes. The two Hispanics stood their ground. He waited for the obvious, but the two men weren't paying attention. Colson made an exaggerated glance to the propped open door. The second Hispanic caught his eye, flipped the bar lock, and then clicked the door closed. No possible witnesses now.

Colson snapped his wrist toward the floor, extending the ASP to its full twenty-one inch length with the clack of metal on metal, locking it in place. Without pausing for effect, he swung it forward, striking Wituka's calves at full speed. The impact of the Honda striking his legs would have felt similar, had Colson not stopped at the intersection. Wituka's legs flew forward. Colson watched him fall flat on his back. His initial look of shock was immediately replaced by terror and disbelief when he tried to take a breath without air in his lungs. He gulped and gasped for air. The combination of gravity and his huge gut fought against him.

Colson bladed his body and raised the ASP in a fighting stance. Snake Tattoo swiped the blade, cutting the air two feet in front of Colson. Snake Tattoo finished his air-slicing maneuver, and then lunged forward one step. Colson stepped back, out of the stubby blade's range, but still close enough to keep Snake Tattoo within his range. He swung the ASP down at an angle, catching Snake Tattoo's right forearm with the last six inches of the metal baton, snapping it in half with a dull crack. The knife bounced silently on the carpet as Snake Tattoo released a scream and dropped to the floor, clutching his arm just below the elbow. Colson felt a rush of hot air and saw the door slowly closing. The second Hispanic had wisely stepped out. He stepped on the blade and bent over to grab the handle, breaking it in half as he stood. Snake Tattoo was on his knees, clutching his arm and squeezing hard, quivering. Wituka struggled to his knees and was using the bed as leverage to stand.

Colson grabbed Wituka's left shoulder and spun him around. "Let's try again, fat ass. Who were you meeting and what was it about?"

Wituka spit, but his spew fell short, now dribbling from his chin. Colson readjusted his grip on the ASP and drove the rounded tip of the steel rod deep into Wituka's stomach, causing what little air he had in his lungs to rush back out. Wituka flopped back onto the bed and resumed his gasping exercise. Colson walked over to Snake Tattoo, patted his pockets, and pulled an eighth of an ounce of meth wadded and tied in the corner of a clear sandwich bag.

"You a Narc?" Snake Tattoo asked. "You broke my arm, man. I'm gonna sue your ass for excessive force."

Colson walked to the bathroom, tossed the bag in the toilet, and then flushed it. He turned back to Snake Tattoo and smiled. He rested the ASP on his shoulder and knelt nose-to-nose with him. "You screw with me again and I'm going to take this and turn you into a Mexican Fudgesicle. Comprende?"

"Don't screw with him, man," Wituka sputtered from his back. "He's one of Cash's men."

Colson snapped his head and stood. One of his questions was answered. No reason to make him think otherwise.

"Who was the couple you met?"

Wituka squinted confusion. "You don't see good? I didn't tell them anything, I swear to God, man. I didn't know anything to tell them."

"Tell who?" Colson raised the ASP above his head.

Wituka held his arms in front of his face. "Sheriff Langston, man. Damn!"

"What was the meeting about?" Colson demanded.

"Ask Pickett, man. He set it up."

❧

Tina was startled awake by the roaring plap-plap sound screaming through the walls of the utility shed. Thin slits of sunlight squeezed through cracks between the planks of the outside wall. Tina pushed up hard with her hands and slid her back against the wall, disoriented. The sound faded and regained intensity again and again. She looked around and saw the gas cans and riding mower. Her head throbbed and the roar from outside wouldn't stop. She pressed her temples with the palms of her hands and prayed. *Dear God, make it stop!* After what seemed to be an eternity of torment, the roar faded for the last time. Only as the noise receded did she recognize the source. Motorcycles. There must have been forty of fifty riding by the utility shed just a sidewalk's distance from the street. The swooshing of passenger vehicles afterward sounded like a spring rain in contrast to the motorcycle convoy.

She covered her eyes. What day is it? What was yesterday? Would the caretaker catch her when he came to mow the lot for Sunday service? Would they call the police on her for just sleeping in the shed? Maybe not, but for breaking the door? Tina rolled up the towel she used for a pillow and shoved it in her bag. She moved to the door and eased it open an inch, then two. No cars at the main building. She was thirsty and hungry. The main building looked like it was a mile away. How could she make it without being seen? Where else could she go? Just go.

Tina walked a straight path toward the front of the main building. Running on the beach didn't draw attention, but running to a deserted drive-in church might. A two-foot high chain suspended by short, white, metal pipes partitioned off the section of the property with the storage building. It wouldn't keep anyone out, but it did give each section a somewhat sacred feel of its own. She walked past a short, round fountain made of concrete, with large rocks piled in the middle. Seven large palm trees sat in random locations in the front section with mulch placed neatly around their bases. The wide-bladed tropical grass was manicured and apparently well maintained by whomever used the riding mower from the shed.

Tina stepped over the low chain and walked through rows of old speakers hanging from white-painted metal posts. The rows were arranged in a semicircle pattern stretching the length of a football field. Thirty total, if she had any interest in counting. A low one-story building stood near the middle of the old drive-in. She used it as cover and hugged the wall as she passed. She slowed her pace when she reached the front balcony to the large, wooden, double doors. The door moved a quarter of an inch when she pulled, but its movement was abruptly halted by a deadbolt. She walked to her right and around the side of the building. The rock wall facing looked old. The structure built above was covered with wide, vertical siding painted a dull gray, weathered from years of salty humidity and rain. She walked beneath a carport awning on the right side, but there was no door to check. She found two single doors in back. One near each corner. Both locked tight.

Hunger pains continued poking at her. She set her bag against the back wall of the building and slid down beside it. She dug through the bag's contents, praying she had missed seeing loose change or a dollar bill in a hidden corner. She had eaten the crackers last night. She looked up the wall of the building and wondered where the projection room would have been when it was a real drive-in. She thought about buttered popcorn and hot dogs and soft drinks. If only this was still a drive-in with a concession stand.

She suddenly jerked her head to the left, jumped up, and grabbed her bag. The building in the middle of the property. That would have been the concession stand. But surely not now. She ran to the south corner of the building and peered around the corner.

Tina trotted to the front corner and stopped. There was a sign above the door of the middle building, but she couldn't read it. The traffic was light on A1A. No one would be paying attention to the vacant church lot. She began walking toward the middle building, hoping each step toward the rear of the building provided more cover from nosey drivers. She kept her head down and moved quickly. The printing above the door came into focus as she got closer. No, not a concession stand anymore, but she smiled as if the sign had read "steakhouse." She read the wording out loud. "Rainbow Clothing and Food Bank." She placed her hand on the knob and closed her eyes. Turning slowly, the knob moved freely. The knob didn't stop. She pulled. *No!* she thought. It didn't budge. It was as if the door was playing a cruel game with her and having a silent laugh at her expense. She considered breaking the door, but she had nothing to use to do it. The shed door was almost rotten and the hasp had been cheap. There was no way to get inside.

She walked away from the door and held close to the rear wall. She almost didn't see the small, two-pane window. It was tiny and just above her head. She turned around and looked up at the window. She could only see the ceiling of the interior. It was faded to yellowish-beige. She reached for the glass and pushed with the palm of her hand. Nothing. She reached high, pressed both palms on the glass, and then pushed again. It moved up a fraction of an inch. Again. The lower pane shot up an inch. Again. She pushed the window until it was fully open, but getting inside would be a problem.

She grasped the windowsill and strained to pull herself up. She put her right arm in over the sill, then her left. The metal cut into her underarms like two parallel knives. She shoved her head inside and pulled herself halfway in. She groaned as the sill scraped her stomach. Someone walking nearby and staring at her legs dangling outside would call the police. She couldn't waste time. She found herself above a deep stainless steel sink. She held the sides of the sink and pulled herself all the way through, slamming her shin against the front of the sink and dropping to the floor. She grabbed her shin in agony and screamed through gritted teeth. She sat and rubbed her shin hard until the pain was tolerable.

She stood up and looked around the room. The stainless steel sink was attached to a stainless steel counter with boxes of plastic spoons and forks and rolls of paper towels. On the counter was a bag of paper plates, closed at the top with a twist tie. A stainless griddle sat against the back wall with an exhaust hood hanging above. It was the obvious source of the old grease aroma surrounding her. Two deep fryers were shoved in the corner next to a large stainless steel refrigerator. She ran to the refrigerator and pulled the door open. A large jar of pickles sat next to a half gallon of milk. She pulled out the jug and twisted the top off. She held it to her lips and instantly jerked it away. The sour funk wafting to her nose made her gag. She slid the jug back on the rack and slammed the door.

The adjacent room was lined with wire shelves. There were sporadically placed cans of food in what appeared to be random stacks. As she moved around the shelves, she saw the small labels taped to the bottom of the racks. The food was stacked in sections labeled alphabetically. Green beans above "g" and so forth. She walked further down the row and stopped in front of "s." She grabbed two cans of chicken noodle soup and ran back to the kitchen. Searching for an opener, she shoved loose items around in each drawer. It was right under her nose. The commercial can opener with a long handle was attached to the stainless steel counter. Although designed to open large cans, it should work. She stuck the can in the teeth of the opener and spun the handle. She set the first can on the counter and repeated the procedure with the second can. She grabbed a plastic spoon from the box under the counter and devoured both in less than a minute. She turned the faucet above the deep sink and held her head down for a long drink of water.

The room-temperature soup tasted wonderful. She pulled more drawers open until she found a small can opener and placed it on the counter. Running back to the soup rack, she pulled off the remaining four cans of soup and set them on the counter next to the opener.

Tina looked around and sighed. Her bag was lying on the ground under the window. She recalled the wording above the door: "Clothing Bank." She opened the door on the opposite wall. A plaque on the door read "The Rainbow Fellowship Hall." Folding tables were arranged end-to-end in three neat rows the length of the room. Large cardboard boxes sat on top of tables against the wall, under a row of windows. Each box was marked with sizes and mounded over with clothing.

∽

Officer Tim Sanders turned south off the beach access road onto A1A on his third patrol round of the beach. The temperature had already reached a mid-morning eighty-two degrees. Sanders rolled up the driver's window, turned the air conditioner to low, and lifted his cell phone. "I'm stopping for coffee, talk to you later…don't start, I drink coffee no matter how hot it is. See you, bye." He ended the call and tossed his cell in the cup holder when the radio came to life.

"Any units in the area of 3140 South Atlantic Avenue. The security company advises a motion detector was activated in building number two. The alarm company contact is not sure if it is the main or secondary building, but the facility should not be occupied at this time. No previous false alarms to date."

Sanders lifted his microphone. "504 radio, I'm close. I'll be code 8 to the location."

"Received. 1035 hours."

∽

Tina turned one box over, spilling the clothing across the tabletop. She held up t-shirts and blue jeans, checking the sizes whenever she could find a tag that hadn't been completely faded or torn off. She put aside two shirts and two pairs of jeans just as the beach patrol unit turned down the main road to the property. She froze, watching the slow moving police pickup move down the main road. She grabbed the shirts and pants and ran back to the kitchen. She quickly tied the bottom of one of the shirts in a knot and shoved the soup cans and opener down the neck, and then rolled all the clothing into a tight bundle. She ran back to the window in the kitchen. The patrol unit was parked at the main church building and an officer was checking the front door she had checked a half hour ago. She scanned around to her right and saw a door leading to the street side of the building, out of the officer's view. She ran to the door and stopped short. It would be locked just like the others. She reached for the alarm bar and hesitated. The cop would see her climbing out the same window, probably breaking her neck in the process. This was the only way out, alarm or not. She shoved the alarm bar and the door popped open. No alarm. She couldn't see what the officer was doing now. She just ran. She got to the side of the building and peeked around the corner. The officer wasn't in front, but his truck hadn't moved. He'd take the same route she had around the building, and then he'd see her. She ran straight for A1A with the bundle under one arm.

Tina saw the ocean between the condominiums across the street. She ran faster. Pain and shock shot through her when she propelled through the air and fell face down in the grass. Her right breast screamed with agony when the bundle of cans broke her fall. She rolled on the grass, cringing. She had been concentrating on the road and didn't notice the short chain barrier she'd stepped over earlier. Her left leg was bleeding just below the knee and both her legs stung. She got to her feet, snatched up her bundle, and continued. Stepping over the sidewalk chain, she was at the street. Once on the street side of the storage shed, she took another look back at the main building. The police truck still had not moved. Tina smiled in spite of the pain in her legs and breast. She had clothes and dinner. The hotel on her left across the street was an eight-story building. The condo to her right was twelve stories and built in two side-by-side sections, giving the illusion of two tall, narrow buildings from the front. In between and behind the buildings she could see dozens of palm trees in the foreground of the ocean. Just left of the larger building was a driveway leading to an underground garage. The driveway angled down from the entrance and disappeared to the right. Tina waited for traffic to clear and ran across the two-lane road.

～

Sanders checked the front, side, and rear doors of the main church building. All secure. He stepped close to a rear door and listened. Other than the dull hum of the air-conditioning unit, nothing. A false alarm, just like the other ninety-nine percent of burglary calls. This was not an extravagant church facility with expensive chandeliers and a safe full of Sunday morning cash offerings. They would be fortunate to receive enough funds to pay their power bill. This was a place for religious tourists to visit, those who felt the obligation to attend church even while on vacation.

Sanders made his way to the front of the main building and saw a girl crossing A1A with something under her arm. He took mental note. Could be something—probably nothing. He climbed into his unit. "504, radio. Code 4 at this time. I'll be checking the next building near the roadway and will advise further."

"10-4. 1050 hours," the dispatcher replied.

Sanders walked to the first door of the one-story building and found it locked tight. He stepped around to the side and saw the open window with the discarded beach bag beneath it. He stood under the window and listened. No sound. He moved around to the door facing the road and instinctively flipped down the top strap above his pistol.

"504, radio. I have an open door at the front building. East side. I'll be checking the interior."

"10-4, 1052 hours."

Sanders eased up to the door with his hand on the butt of his pistol. He moved to the far side of the door, against the wall. He pushed the door open and took a quick glance inside. He stepped into the doorway and surveyed the fellowship hall. The two overturned boxes of clothing caught his attention.

"504, radio."

"Go ahead."

"The building appears code 4. Start another unit to assist in clearing the entire facility and make contact with the security company for the property owner to respond. Looks like someone ransacked the place."

"Any suspects believed to be on scene, 504?"

"Unknown until we clear the entire building. A young female, approximately eighteen to twenty, brown hair—medium length, and wearing a blue bikini was crossing South Atlantic as I approached the building. She was carrying something, could have been clothing. Advise beach units she's a possible suspect."

"10-4, 1058 hours."

➺ Chapter Fifteen ❦

Cash uploaded the last photo of Tina and closed his laptop. "So, Pickett, how did your ridiculous plan work out with the good sheriff?"

Pickett adjusted his gun belt and slid his handcuff case from the small of his back so it wouldn't dig into the soft leather couch. "Beavers had the photos taken last night. I should have them soon."

Cash leaned forward and cocked his head. "And just what do you think you'll accomplish with them, huh? The man's already getting a divorce. You think you can blackmail him by threatening to give his ex-wife just one more reason to hate him?"

"That's not what I was thinking, I…"

"Then what were you thinking, Pickett?"

"Mr. Cash, Langston has a decent reputation so far, his pending divorce notwithstanding. But if the local press were to be given photos of him going in and coming out of a hotel room with a subordinate, no less a lieutenant he'd just promoted who has far less experience than any other candidate, they'd have a field day. The commissioners will want him gone when half the department files suit. Not to mention how the liberal press already hates him for his stance on illegal immigration."

Cash sat back in his recliner and silently nodded. He looked at the ceiling in thought. "So what's the rest of the plan? And I know you want something else."

Pickett smiled. "Langston is smart and I don't think he'll want the photos going to the press. There are three things that could be accomplished here."

"Three things? What, other than dropping the investigation into my affairs and clearing Jason's charge?" A look of understanding formed on his face. "Of course. Number three is what you want, isn't it? Look, Pickett, you get nothing from me unless and until Langston is stupid enough to bite on the first two demands. Understand?"

"Yes," Pickett nodded. "First of all, I plan on sending him the photos anonymously. He would do everything in his power to make my life hell if he knew I was involved. I think he'll comply with the demands. I'll know if he doesn't. Let things cool off on your end until two months out from the election. Then I'll release the photos to the local press. He'll think it was over and done with, but the timing will be about perfect."

"Perfect for what?"

Pickett's radio chirped before he could answer. "All units reference possible signal 7 suspect. Burglary occurred approximately ten minutes ago at the Drive-In Christian Church on South Atlantic. Possible burglary suspect seen leaving the area is a white female, eighteen-to-twenty years old, approximately five-two, slender build, straight shoulder-length brown hair, and wearing a blue bikini. Last known direction of travel was eastbound on foot from the roadway. Any contact, hold and notify. Nothing further. Out of Volusia at 1115 hours." Annoyed by the interruption, he reached to adjust the volume switch.

"Wait," Cash snapped.

"What?"

"What was that? On your radio, what was it?" he demanded.

"Just a look-out for a possible burglary suspect, why?"

Cash glared at Pickett. "Before you start giving me your wish list, there is one other problem you need to help me fix."

"What now?"

"You need to find that girl before your buddies do."

"What? Who is she?"

Cash leaned back and nonchalantly raised the lid on his laptop. "Let's just say it's Jason's girlfriend who got cold feet," Cash looked up from the laptop and met Pickett's eyes. "I'll put it this way, Pickett. You get absolutely nothing if she is arrested."

Pickett made no attempt to hide his shocked facial expression. "So now you want me to commit a capital offense and kidnap this girl?"

Cash nodded and held up his hand. "No, no, Pickett, you just find her. I'll send Taylor to bring her home. It's that simple."

Pickett stood in silence. "Anything else?" he asked flatly.

"You forgot your demands. I'm surprised at you."

Pickett turned and walked to the door. He stopped and turned. "You finance my run for sheriff from the end of August through November. Television ads, billboards, yard signs, brochures, everything."

Cash grinned. "You pull this off and I'll be happy to own a sheriff."

Pickett pulled the door shut behind him with a click. Cash typed in a password on his keyboard and pressed enter. The chat room flashed on the screen. Cash checked the time at bottom right of the screen. 11:29 a.m. No activity in the private chat room, but there was one minute to go. He refreshed his screen and there he was. A little box appeared above the time, indicating one member in chat. Cash typed in the box: "Good afternoon, Avid Collector," and then he pressed "Enter." His comment flashed on the screen. He waited.

"Good afternoon. Is the delivery of my vehicle confirmed?"

"Fifty-five thousand. Tax, tag, and title."

"Fifty is what was agreed to."

Cash smiled as he typed. "That was prior to another bid being received."

"How do I know it will not go up yet again?"

"I will accept your final bid and close the sale if you will take delivery in three days."

Cash expected a delay, but not a long one. He would give Avid Collector exactly thirty seconds before he logged out. He watched the time at the lower right of his screen. There was no seconds counter, but the time had just changed to 11:31 a.m. He decided to be generous and wait until 11:32 appeared before logging out. He estimated his wait was no longer than fifteen seconds before...

"Fifty-five thousand. That is my final bid."

"Excellent. Delivery will take place in seventy-two hours as agreed."

"Very well."

Cash logged out and closed the laptop. He stared out the French doors at the sun's reflection off the waves on the horizon. "You better find her, Pickett," he said to the empty media room.

Colson set his coffee cup on the kitchen counter, spun the bar stool around, and sat in front of his laptop. He pulled the memory card from the camera and pushed it into the adapter, and then the adapter into the flash drive port on the side. The drive came up on the screen ten seconds later. He selected one of the photos and pressed print. The wireless printer came to life and shot out a piece of photo paper. He pulled the page off and placed it next to the laptop. He closed the flash drive, clicked on the Internet icon, and typed "Volusia County Sheriff's Office" in the search box. He clicked on the home page and was mildly impressed with the website. It appeared up-to-date and not too busy. Easy to navigate.

He found what he was looking for on the left side toolbar and clicked again. A photo of Stuart Langston popped up in the center of the screen. Under the photo was a lengthy, professional biography and accomplishments of the Sheriff of Volusia County. He held up the photo he had taken less than twelve hours ago. Same guy. It looked as though he had lost weight, but stress can do that. He looked over to the female in the photo. She didn't look like any deputy sheriff he had ever seen. The wife probably would be jealous, even if they were conducting legitimate police business.

Colson picked up his phone and saw five missed calls from Beavers. He had to know what was going on, and it disappointed Colson. Beavers had to have known who the target was. Not a high-ranking church member carrying on with a secretary. What made it worse was he was working with someone like Pickett. Colson knew these people. He had interviewed them for employment and rejected them. They were applicants from category number one. The ones who just wanted the badge and gun for personal gain and gratification. Even when one scammed him well enough to get the job, they exposed themselves soon enough and became his pet project until they were run off, fired, or prosecuted. He wouldn't even care if Beavers hadn't involved him. They could play all the games they wanted because those kinds of people were no longer his problem. He thought for a moment, pulled the memory card, and shoved it back into the camera. There were a couple more photos to take.

Colson finished printing two additional photos on glossy paper and slid them into a legal-size manila envelope. He placed a piece of clear packing tape on the flap and pressed it down firm. He picked up his cell and pressed Beavers' name on the contact screen. He answered after the first ring.

"Colson! Where you been? I've tried calling—"

"Calm down, Beavers. Let's get this over with," Colson said without hiding his disgust.

"You get the photos?"

He ignored the question. "Where are you?"

"At home. You want me to come to your place?"

"No. There's a souvenir shop at the corner of South Atlantic at the foot of the Port Orange Bridge. I'll be in the parking lot in fifteen minutes."

Beavers hesitated a beat. "I have to finish up here. I can be there in an hour."

"Fifteen minutes, Mike, or you can take your own pictures."

"Fine. What's with you?"

"Just be there."

Colson ended the call. Still uncertain of how dirty Beavers and Pickett were, he had no intention of giving them time to plan for the meeting. And he would only meet in public. What he intended to say to Beavers would certainly end whatever friendship had developed, so there was no reason to give him privacy. He didn't want to give himself or Beavers the opportunity to get physical. Since he had been dragged into this mess, he would have to play it out and remove himself from the situation. But something told him it wouldn't be that easy. He should have used better judgment from the beginning and not met with Beavers in the first place. It was too late now.

Colson grabbed the envelope and his keys. He took the stairs instead of the elevator and jogged to his car. He turned south out of the parking lot and floored the Corvette, easing back when the speedometer read seventy-five miles per hour. Just one night of driving the Honda made him temporarily lose his feel of the muscle car's accelerator. He checked his mirror, expecting to see blue strobes closing in, but there was nothing but receding traffic. It was another beautiful Daytona afternoon and the soft leather seats of his personal rocket felt like they had been molded to the form of his body. He lowered both windows, allowing the warm breeze to rush in, and turned up the radio. Believing this childish game to be ending soon made him grin with the exhilaration of the drive. His mood soured as he passed one of Cash's liquor stores on the right. This one looked nothing like his main store on Nova Road with its numerous neon signs hanging inside high, glass-panel walls, large parking area, and tall, swaying palms in manicured grass islands. This store was a squatty, older building with an attached lounge for low-life mid-morning drunks. It shared a parking lot with a grocery store of similar appearance.

Colson's timing was right. He cruised through the next three lights under green and turned right on Dunlawton Avenue, and then immediately left into the rear parking lot of the gift shop. He backed into a space and checked the digital clock. Eleven minutes total. He'd give Beavers another three minutes. He was reminded of visiting every gift shop on A1A with Ann and Nichole at some point over the years. They all were the same. The only difference was the placement of the items inside. But he enjoyed every minute of walking from one to the next and seeing Nichole's excitement about this or that item, buying beach towels, t-shirts, flip-flops, and sunglasses. He didn't really want to go in any of the shops now. No reason without his girls.

The red SUV darted right into the parking lot and nosed in next to Colson. Beavers walked into Colson's view from around the truck and stood with his hands held out in a questioning manner. Colson grabbed the envelope from the passenger seat and stepped out.

"What the hell, Colson?" Beavers said. "What's all the drama about?"

Colson walked three steps and put his foot on the front bumper of the SUV. He fanned himself with the manila envelope and looked back at the gift shop. "You know, Mike," he began, "I learned a lot working in Internal Affairs. I had to pretty much memorize the policy. At first I thought it was a pain, but the more I read it and applied it to the cases, I began to understand how vital it was to maintain integrity in an agency. Maintaining discipline. You know why, Mike?"

Beavers gave him a blank stare. "What's this all about and what in the world does it have to do with anything now?"

Colson shook his head and pointed at Beavers. "You're making my point, Mike. What does it have to do with anything now? I don't know how you guys behaved, but honesty and integrity aren't supposed to be left in the locker when you go off duty. That's not necessarily expected if you work in a factory or on a farm. Law enforcement officers are and should be held to a higher standard, on and off duty. We had to police ourselves because we were the only ones who could do it. The public doesn't trust us to begin with and if we fail to correct our own problems, we're worse than the criminals and politicians."

"Look, Grey," Beavers said, "I don't know what you're driving at or what bug got up your ass this morning, but just in case no one has told you, we're retired." Beavers drew out the last phrase as if Colson was mentally challenged.

Colson continued as if Beavers hadn't spoken. "But we figured out something about a year into my assignment in IA. We figured out the stupid things employees were doing were not specifically covered by policy. Then we realized you can't have a policy for everything, so you know what we did, Mike?"

Beavers resigned himself to being lectured. "No, Grey. What did you do?"

"We adopted a Code of Conduct. We used it more than all the other hundreds of pages of policy combined. Almost everything we do is driven by our conduct. What got our people into the most trouble was when their conduct reflected poorly on the officer, agency, or on the law enforcement community. It makes the public lose faith and trust in all law enforcement."

Beavers crossed his arms. "Tell me what this has to do with—"

"You know exactly what I'm talking about," Colson snapped, jerking his foot off the bumper. "You feed me this bullshit about some distraught wife and the entire time you're helping some other demented officer set up Sheriff Langston for God knows what." He poked Beavers on the right breast with his index finger. "It's time for you to start explaining."

Beavers held his hand up in surrender and took a step back. "Look, man. There's no reason to get bent out of shape. I didn't know everything about it. He could be screwing his lieutenant for all I know. We're just the paparazzi."

"We, hell," Colson said. "If you knew that much, you also had to know Pickett was up to something dirty. Yes, I'm retired, but I didn't spend almost thirty years of my life trying to do the right thing, only to turn into what I despised and I will not be a part of it. You copy that traffic, sergeant?"

"Fine," Beavers said. "I don't know what Pickett's motives are, I just needed the business." He gestured to the envelope. "Those the photos, I hope?"

Colson slapped the envelope on Beavers' chest. "You can stick one up your ass and the other up Pickett's. Don't call me again." He turned and walked to his car.

"You forgot your money," Beavers said.

Colson opened the door, crawled in and pulled it shut. He picked his sunglasses up off the console and slid them over his nose. "I'm sure there'll be room left for you to stick that too." He hit the power window switch and the window shot up. His tires barked as he pulled from the space and squealed out of the parking lot.

❧

"What do you mean you can't find her?" Cash said, scowling. Taylor and Jason sat on the couch, slouched over as if they had lost a fortune gambling on the Super Bowl.

"She's gone," Taylor said.

"I've been here while you two have been running around in circles for two days and even I know more about what's going on that you do." Cash stood and walked to the French doors. "She broke into a church clothing bank this afternoon and is somewhere in the Port Orange area, most likely wearing jeans and a shirt that's two sizes too big for her."

"How do you know that?" Jason said.

"Pickett's looking for her now." Cash pointed at Taylor. "And when the police find her, you're going to get her and bring her back."

"How are we supposed to get her from the police?" Taylor asked. "I mean, unless it's Pickett."

Cash stood silent for a moment tapping his fingers on the bar. "It's just trespassing and minor theft. No one except Pickett will be looking very hard for her. If one of those beach bum police types bump into her, we'll post her bond and get her that way. If Pickett gets to her first, it will cut out a step. Believe me, Pickett's motivated."

Taylor said, "We won't be able to bond her out when they find out she's wanted out of state."

"Then I guess you better find her first," Cash said.

"She can't get far," Jason said.

Cash threw a look of disgust at Jason. "She got away from you easy enough. The next deal has been set up for less than..." he looked at his watch, "thirty-six hours from now."

Jason said, "But what if they don't find her by then?"

"With respect," Taylor offered. "It's a legitimate question, Mr. Cash. Will you be able to delay delivery?"

Cash looked from Taylor to Jason and gestured his head toward the bedroom. "Go in there and get Lacy cleaned up. You need to bring her out here and get her sobered up. Tell her we're sending her to be with Kara or something. We'll substitute her for Tina if it comes down to it."

"If..." Taylor corrected himself. "Since the deal was made for Tina, how should we handle the transaction if the buyer gives us a problem?"

"You'll just have to be persuasive, won't you, Taylor?" Cash answered with a grin. "Negotiate the deal down a little if you have to. You'll tell them we'll cut a good deal for Tina when she's ready. Tell them Tina is sick and I didn't want to deliver her in that condition, but as an act of good faith we delivered our next best at a discount. I don't care, Taylor. Make it up and make it sound good."

"Hey!" Cash shouted at Jason. "I said go wake Lacy up and throw her in the shower. Taylor, you tell Fuller to set up just like before. If you have any problems on delivery, you know what to do."

Taylor nodded understanding. "I'll take care of it."

"Good."

Jason walked out of the bedroom and sat back on the couch, looking at the floor.

"Well?" Cash said.

"It's Lacy." Jason looked up from the floor.

"What about her?"

Jason dropped his eyes. "I think she's dead."

⇒ Chapter Sixteen ⇐

Colson watched the tan Taurus circle the rear parking lot from his balcony. The spaces were numbered and reserved for renters and their guests. This driver was neither. If you have a reserved space, you don't have to drive around the lot three times to find it. The car finally nosed into a space at the sea wall and a man stepped out. Colson recognized him almost immediately. Today he wore a green polo shirt and tan slacks. There was enough time to finish making his sandwich. Colson laid a large slice of tomato on top of the bologna and salami. He squeezed a generous amount of mayo on top before pressing down the top layer of bread. He folded the sandwich in a napkin and pulled a bottle of water from the fridge. As he walked to the condo door, he stopped and turned. He grabbed a folding beach chair from the closet and went out the door.

Colson met the man as he stepped off the elevator. At first the man walked past Colson, and then stopped and turned. He didn't bother to step on the elevator and make the man find him. Colson wanted to talk to him.

"Less than twenty-four hours. Not bad," Colson said.

The man stared at Colson. "Excuse me?"

"Less than twenty-four hours to find me. You would have had to visit the rental agency first. You must have come straight over after you ran my information."

"Major Colson," the man said with a nod.

Colson grinned and held out his hand. "Please, just call me Grey."

The man took Colson's hand. "Sergeant Cantrell. Volusia County Sheriff's Office. You weren't exactly difficult to find."

"Innocent people typically aren't, sergeant."

Cantrell nodded. "I need to talk to you about an incident last night. Can we go back to your condo?"

"I'd rather you follow me if you don't mind. Beach scavengers, you understand," Colson said.

Cantrell gave him a look of confusion. Colson clarified. "They'll steal my stuff."

Cantrell's expression changed to understanding.

"Besides," Colson continued, "I brought you an extra chair. Would you like a sandwich?" he asked, holding up the napkin-wrapped lunch.

Cantrell shook his head. "No thanks. I'm good."

They stepped onto the elevator and rode to the ground level. Cantrell followed Colson through the hallway and out onto the hot asphalt of the rear parking area and then to the beach access gate. Colson punched in the code and they descended the stairs to the sand.

Cantrell followed Colson across the beach road to the canopy. Colson unfolded the chair and offered it to Cantrell. Colson sat and looked over to Mr. and Mrs. Hammond. Mr. Hammond waved and Colson returned the gesture.

"Nice little setup," Cantrell observed.

"Thanks. Mrs. Hammond over there keeps an eye on it when I make lunch."

Cantrell nodded and slipped on a pair of sunglasses. "An assault complaint has been made against you."

"Is that a fact?" Colson asked.

"The complainant wants you arrested for busting into his room and attacking him."

Colson nodded and took a bite of his sandwich. "Did you tell him that people in hell want ice water?"

Cantrell chuckled. "So you did go in there and tune him up a little?"

"Not what I said, sergeant."

"He's serious."

"So am I. I don't know your complainant Sarge, but he sounds like a low-life snitch to me. If so, you know when he's lying because his mouth is moving. But that's not what this is about, is it? I imagine you didn't come looking for me because some three-hundred-fifty-pound snitch got pushed around."

"Who said he was three-hundred-fifty pounds?"

"Good catch, Sarge."

Cantrell said, "Your record was easy enough to understand. Nearly thirty years at your department in excellent standing. Uniform until '87. Four years undercover in narcotics. The following years in fugitive until you made sergeant in the late '90s, as I remember. Lieutenant a few years later and finally retired as a major on the command staff, in charge of Internal Affairs."

Colson watched Cantrell recite a fairly accurate summary of his career. "I'm impressed. You dug deep real fast, sergeant."

"The summary was on a cached page of your retirement party announcement."

Colson nodded. "Sure. The Internet. You guys are light-years ahead of the old investigators. We would have killed to have the resources in the '80s you have now."

"Okay, Major...I mean, Mr. Colson. Are you willing to tell me what was going on last night and why you were there?"

Colson finished the last bite of his sandwich and took a swig from the water bottle. Cantrell had already pulled a note pad from his back pocket and flipped it open. He gave Cantrell the rundown about his hesitant relationship with Mike Beavers and their meeting at Inlet Harbor.

"So," Cantrell said while reviewing his notes, "Beavers led you to believe you were taking photos for a distraught wife who believed her husband was fooling around on her."

Colson nodded. "That's it."

"Then why not take the photos and leave? Why would you..." Cantrell paused to rephrase his question. "For argument's sake, why would you then confront the room's occupant?"

"It was obvious that's not what this was about. Not with the police conducting counter-surveillance and that tub of shit in the room with them. I don't like to be played, sergeant, especially by someone who is supposed to be a professional friend and retired officer. I needed to know I was right before I told him to shove his photos and pound sand. So now, why don't you tell me what's going on with the Sheriff?"

Cantrell flipped his pad closed. "I'm sure you of all people understand I can't go into a case with you."

"Sure I understand," Colson said. "How about I go into it and you correct the parts I get wrong."

"What do you mean?" Cantrell asked.

"There is something rotten in your agency, or should I say *someone* by the name of Pickett. He's probably tied to Martin Cash, who I'm guessing is one of your targets. Why he wanted those photos is still an unknown unless it's for the purpose of blackmail. Either way, you have a mess to clean up."

Cantrell stared at Colson with his mouth partially open.

"Am I right or am I right?"

Cantrell pulled a business card from his wallet. "I appreciate your cooperation, Major." He handed over the card. "I strongly suggest you stay away from the investigation. I know your involvement was inadvertent and you wouldn't want to be involved any further."

"Thank you sergeant," Colson said while examining the business card. "I severed my short relationship with Beavers early this afternoon."

Cantrell stood and knocked sand off his shoes. "You mean you went along with the deal and gave him the photos?"

Colson shook his head and smiled. "I gave him a couple of photos, but maybe not the ones he was hoping for."

"I don't want to know," Cantrell said, holding further comments at bay with a raised hand.

Colson stood and shook Cantrell's hand. "That assault complaint. You say there was just one?"

Cantrell squinted. "Yes, why?"

"Just curious. You stay safe, sergeant. You know where to find me if you need anything."

Cantrell nodded and walked out from under the canopy. Colson watched him climb the stairs to the parking lot. Mr. Hammond waddled to the edge of the canopy as Colson leaned back in his chair.

"You know, Grey," he said with a grin, "the city's going to come after you if you don't watch it."

"Why's that?" Colson asked.

"Because I don't see a license hanging in here and you conduct more business on the beach than the umbrella rental guy."

Colson chuckled. "Thanks for watching the tent."

Hammond laughed and turned to walk back to his umbrella, shaking his head. "Think nothing of it."

Tina jerked awake again, but this time she immediately recognized the sound of laughing children in the parking garage. She peered around the room, rubbing her eyes, and running her hands through her hair. The women's locker room was adjacent to the underground parking garage and had been deserted and quiet all night. It seemed like such a waste of space. Who works out on vacation? She started to stand, but dropped to her butt as the pain in her shin screamed. Sleeping on the floor for two nights, combined with her bruised shins and breast felt like she had been in a car accident. Tina rolled to her knees and steadied herself with her hands. She stood slowly. She walked in place and rolled her neck to loosen up. She shivered. The locker room was clean, but the air conditioner made it feel like a walk-in cooler. At least stowing away here hadn't been the adventure she endured at the drive-in church. The garage gate had opened, she waved at the people in the car as they drove out, and she walked right in. She decided she could talk her way around anyone who challenged her about being there. At least stall them long enough to run away at the first opportunity. She was too tired to worry about it. It was a nightmare. She still didn't know what time or day it was. Right now jail didn't sound like that bad an option. At least there were cots and food. She had been in captivity for months anyway; how much worse could it be?

The blue jeans and t-shirt were too large, but she was happy to be wearing them. She would have certainly frozen in the bikini. She shoved the bikini inside the knotted shirt with the remaining soup cans and pushed the locker room door open. The vehicle with its back-up lights on was on the far side of the underground garage. She concealed herself behind a concrete pillar as it backed out of the space and drove to the steel mesh door. The weight of the vehicle stopped on a pressure plate in the concrete slab, activating the door motor. It made a screeching sound as metal gears turned, complaining from lack of lubrication. The mesh door jerked and began its slow ascent. She tried to time her walking with the movement of the door, just as she had yesterday afternoon. As the door reached the top, the car moved forward with Tina walking ten feet behind. She slowed so as not to overtake the slow-moving car being driven by a squat, elderly woman with snow-white hair. The old lady seemed so focused and worried about scraping the sides of the garage opening, she barely moved at all. Tina had to stop or she would have walked into the back of her car. The car mercifully moved on and she stepped out to the ramp and into the sunlight. She continued up the ramp and over to the public beach access walkway.

Tina stood with her hands on her hips, looking north, but for what? She knew she had made no progress. Wandering aimlessly. Nowhere to go and no one to help her. Nothing but a few cans of soup. She had to make a decision, but turning herself back over to Cash was not an option. She would turn herself in to the police first.

The sand was soft and the sun was blistering. She walked north, thinking. She was determined not to spend another homeless night looking for a vacant shed or locker room to sleep in. She was tired and depressed. There had to be someone who would help. The only person who helped her during this entire ordeal was that man on the beach. Maybe he was just showing off. Maybe he was a pervert, thinking she would fall at his feet, thank him for saving her, and beg to repay his valor with sexual favors. That's how men were, especially the older ones.

But could it be any worse than what she faced by going to Cash and begging forgiveness? If the gray haired man was a cop, he'd probably turn her in. But he wouldn't know she was a fugitive. How could he know? But he would insist she go to the police about Cash, so she couldn't tell him. She stopped walking and tilted her head back. A squiggly line of huge seagulls flew overhead, along the top floor of the condo on her left. It's a stupid idea, but her only option. But how could she find him?

⁓

"I should have asked for twenty-five hundred." Beavers took a long sip of beer and set it on the wet napkin.

The bar was on a deck overlooking the Atlantic. The night breeze was warm and smelled of sea salt. A few beach stragglers were taking advantage of the cooler evening, walking hand-in-hand along the shore as it crept inland with each wave. Calypso music played from remote speakers dangling from the bar's inner rafters. Strings of large multi-colored Christmas lights were lazily draped around old, wooden posts, strung from one to the next. Beavers took another sip and glanced over his mug at Pickett, who sat across from him in a t-shirt and shorts.

"Two thousand was agreed to. That should be plenty for what, two pictures?" Pickett said.

Beavers became riveted by Pickett's explanation of his true motive for wanting the photos, although he conveniently omitted his relationship with Martin Cash. Beavers did not need to know about the criminal investigation, but Pickett figured a small dose of the truth would keep Beavers quiet and invested in his plan.

"There could be a problem," Beavers said. "It's a gamble with Langston. You don't know that he'll pull out of the election because of a couple of photos of him and Reese going into a hotel room."

Pickett took a long pull from his beer and looked out over the ocean. "That's true, but if the media gets the photos it should cause enough controversy to hurt his chances. You remember what happened with your sheriff when the media got on his case about mowing his yard during working hours? You and I both know he wasn't doing anything wrong, but that didn't matter to the public. They saw the pictures and he couldn't intelligently defend himself. Who cared if he spent eighty hours a week managing the agency? Not to mention nights, weekends, and holidays? All the public cared about was he was mowing his yard during business hours and they ran him out of office."

Beavers shook his head. "I know, but this is different. We know Langston's not doing anything wrong and this is deliberate blackmail. There's something you're not telling me."

"No," Pickett insisted. "The man is a horn dog. He's slept around with every female in the agency. So we got photos of him with the wrong woman, but that's only because we didn't have the opportunity to get photos of him with the right women. Stop over-thinking this and lighten up, Mike."

Pickett paused as a young waitress asked if they needed another beer. She put a small black folder on the table after Pickett told her no. Pickett set ten one-hundred-dollar bills inside before closing it and sliding it across the table.

He grinned. "Here's the rest. You better take that before the waitress thinks it's her tip."

Beavers tapped the top of the folder with his finger for a moment, and then slid the bills out and shoved them in his pocket before handing the envelope over to Pickett.

"I still think this is a bad idea," Beavers said, and downed the last of his beer. "You should have just put that money toward your election campaign and beat him straight up."

"Don't worry about the campaign. I'll remember your work, Mike. Or should I say, Colonel Beavers."

∽∾

Taylor spread a thick sheet of plastic on the floor and grimaced. He had no problem breaking men's jaws or noses. There was no hesitation or regret if his opponent was rendered unconscious or suffered a brain injury. They would do the same to him if given the opportunity, but most didn't have the skill or speed. But after all the blood and stinking sweat of the octagon, this was Taylor's first experience with a dead body. Lacy was not bloody or broken. She appeared to be sleeping deeply. No iron stench of blood, sweat, or feces. At least not yet. She didn't deserve to die.

He suddenly felt nauseated. Beads of sweat formed on his brow and upper lip. He rolled Lacy onto her back, slid his arms under hers, and then lifted. He nodded to Jason to lift her legs and they gently laid her on the plastic. The look on Jason's face was not one of regret or even apathy. His was the look of a spoiled child who had been ordered to take out the garbage. The disgust Taylor already felt for Jason was multiplied by a thousand. It was one thing to make a profit off of homeless girls. They were destined to prostitute themselves at some point with or without Cash's help, but this girl was dead and there was no remorse. He had joked about death, even threatened it, but this was real and he was part of it. He could have killed the doctor, but held back. He could have killed any number of opponents over the years, but that had never been the goal. Taylor won respect through strength and hard work, not cruelty or profit.

Jason exhaled as if he had been digging ditches all day and jerked one side of the plastic over Lacy's body. Taylor grabbed Jason's wrist and shot him a dead stare. He jerked away and rubbed his wrist.

"What the hell's wrong with you?" he snapped.

Taylor squatted down and folded the other side of the plastic over the body. "Just go get me the tape. I'll take care of it from here."

"Fine," Jason said and stormed out of the dark room.

Taylor pulled the plastic away from Lacy's face and examined her features with his one eye. She had been a pretty girl. He whispered, "I'm sorry," and folded the plastic back over her face. He felt something hit his back and saw the roll of tape bounce on the floor next to him. He jerked his head to the door but Jason was already out of sight. He pulled lengths of tape, wrapped the ends of the plastic together like a garbage bag, and lifted the body in a fireman's carry.

Cash appeared in the doorway. "I'll tell Fuller to get the boat ready."

"I think it's an unnecessary risk," Taylor replied.

Cash cocked his head. "You go out five, ten miles and it shouldn't be."

"People are nosey, Mr. Cash. I can have this taken care of in an hour and there will be no risk of fishermen or the Coast Guard just happening up on us during a ten mile cruise. It gives Langston too much time if he's still got surveillance on us."

"And you have a better idea?"

"Just quicker and cleaner."

"What?"

"An incinerator."

Cash looked at Taylor for a long moment and nodded. "You just remember," he pointed at Taylor, "anything goes wrong and it's your ass as much as mine."

Taylor nodded and walked around Cash with Lacy's wrapped corpse. The sedan was at the side of the beach house and the trunk was open. Taylor paused just before backing out and stuck his head out the door to look down the beach side of the house. No one was walking along the shore. A quick glance toward the high privacy wall on the street side and down the long line of foliage at the property line, but no one could watch from the street unless they could see through stone. Satisfied, Taylor lowered Lacy's small, wrapped frame in the trunk.

Cash stood, watching Taylor from the door. "Taylor. Fuller's going to help Jason look for Tina. They're running the ATV's up and down the beach. Apparently you've scared the piss out of Jason. You find Pickett and see what he's come up with. You have just a little over twenty-four hours or you'll be looking for another job."

Taylor finished closing the truck with a quick slam. Without a word he climbed behind the wheel and pulled away from the house. Cash watched the sedan wait for the gate to open and then turn right on A1A and drive out of sight. What neither he nor Taylor saw was the man standing amid the dark green foliage at the edge of the property or the Corvette parked a hundred yards behind him at the water department.

♈

The twenty-minute downpour blew inland and out of sight. The sun blazed down on the thick St. Augustine grass and caused steam to rise from the streets and sidewalks. The quiet of the bedroom was interrupted by the click of the thermostat on the wall and the hum of the air conditioning unit coming to life. Kim Reese slipped from under the sheet nude and took the Volusia County Sheriff's Office t-shirt off the dresser. She pulled it over her head and walked to the window. Pickett swung his legs over the side of the bed and pulled on his boxer shorts. She heard him moving but kept her attention on the drying grass outside.

"You're not telling me everything," she said.

Pickett laid his hands on her shoulders and kissed her neck. "There's nothing else to tell," he whispered.

"It was stupid," she snapped and pulled away. "That idiot informant blew your counter-surveillance and now Langston knows something is going on. There's nothing I can do about it. You're at the top of his shit list."

"Look," Pickett said, "you and I both know what a hothead he is. Bi-Polar Bear is what the guys call him. You can smooth this over and in a couple of months he'll be too occupied defending his ethics to worry about anything else."

She shook her head. "It just wasn't necessary. You didn't have to set up this elaborate scheme to catch him in a hotel. I could have led him on and he would have been there with me in a second."

Pickett spun her around and held her shoulders. "No. I won't have you sleep with him. Not when we can accomplish the same thing by other means."

"I'm not stupid," she said. "There's something more. Why are you helping Cash?"

"I'm not helping him. He's helping me. He's simply a successful businessman and that flies all over Langston. Its harassment, pure and simple." He walked back to the bed and sat on the edge. "And he's going to finance my campaign."

She sat next to him. "It just feels too risky to me."

"Nothing dirty about it," Pickett said, lifting the manila envelope from the nightstand. "He won't be able to explain these away and you'll just say 'no comment' when the press asks. He'll expect you to deny having sex with him on duty, but you won't confirm or deny. That will do him more harm than if you gave a full statement. You don't have to lie, just say nothing."

"Those the pictures?" she asked, holding out her hand.

He smiled and handed them over. "Yep."

She pulled the tape from the flap, wound the string loose, and opened the envelope. She pulled the eight-by-tens out and held them side-by-side. She looked at Pickett, then back to the photos.

"What?" he said.

Reese slid them back in the envelope and handed it to Pickett. "You should have gone with my plan."

❧ Chapter Seventeen ❧

Internal investigations and criminal investigations had their differences, but were similar in many ways. Instead of violations of the law, Internal Affairs investigators address violations of agency policy. Of course, an officer could be investigated for criminal activity, and then be hit with a double-whammy of an administrative investigation. The violation would be based on the policy that states no employee will commit a crime. In such cases, the officer could be charged criminally in addition to receiving administrative disciplinary action. That is, if they remained employed.

In his career, Colson had been both a criminal and internal affairs investigator. Recent events resurrected memories of both. He had never anticipated the unbelievable situations some cops got themselves into until he saw it with his own eyes. Even criminal behavior at times. The percentages were far lower in the law enforcement community, but they were still there. "Liquor and women," as he learned in Internal Affairs. The two things that get cops in trouble more than everything else combined. Almost thirty years on the job and Colson still shook his head at some of the crap officers would get into both on and off duty. "Bizarre behavior."

Colson sat with his feet propped on the balcony rail, looking at the horizon without seeing it. The sky had cleared completely. The only evidence of the sudden afternoon storm was the steaming pavement and the trickle of water in the drainpipe. Two young men were the only occupants of the beach following the rain. One carried an object Colson didn't recognize as a kite until they released it into the air. The kite grew in shape as it rose higher and closer to Colson. The strong inland wind pushed it nearer the condo as the young man released a steady length of string. It made small 'S' shaped movements, and sporadically jerk wildly in a broad 'S' shape pattern. Colson squinted at the kite and saw it was a replica of an old bi-plane. He lifted his binoculars and found the young man through the lens. The boy held two plastic handles, one in each hand, directing the kite's movements. He set the binoculars down and propped his feet back on the railing.

"It just doesn't fly," Colson said. As commander of Internal Affairs, he knew what was going on in the agency. Every minor complaint and every major investigation. He could make sense of things because he had information no one else knew. In an agency of over eight-hundred sworn officers, that was a lot of information to know and be trusted with. Now he was an outsider and knew almost nothing. That was fine if he hadn't been pulled into it, but he had. And he didn't like being in the dark.

He walked into the kitchen, flipped open his laptop, and sat at the counter drumming his fingers on the fake granite top. He could learn more about Cash in fifteen minutes from his office in Clay County than Sergeant Cantrell could learn in fifteen weeks. Colson had built hundreds of contacts over his twenty-eight year career and what he couldn't find out on his own, a contact with another state or federal agency would happily find for him. A quick phone call to DEA Agent Pettigrew and he would know if drugs were Cash's specialty with an instant inquiry through the Narcotics and Dangerous Drug Information System, or NADDIS. Even if Cash's name had been merely mentioned during the course of an investigation, he would know it. If drugs weren't his game, another call to Agent McCann with the FBI would do the trick. But he was a civilian now. As such, those resources were no longer available to him. He could still make the calls, but those unofficial inquiries were not legal and certainly not ethical.

He opened his laptop and typed *Florida Department of State* in the search engine and clicked. A list of options appeared. He selected the Division of Corporations, then Inquire by Owner Name. As expected, a long list of links appeared in the screen. Cash 4 Gold, Cash in Advance, Cash in a Pinch. Sprinkled among them were individuals with the last name of Cash. He scrolled down and there he was—two names from the bottom of the list. Martin Cash. The link embedded in his name opened the filing information page, listing the corporation's mailing address and owner's address. In this case, they were one in the same. Cash, Martin, 4301 South Atlantic Avenue, Ponce Inlet, Florida. He wrote the address on a sticky note and closed the laptop.

Colson slid the patio door open and walked to the rail. The sound of surf and smell of fresh sea air was invigorating. A staggered line of seagulls glided in the warm updraft near the top of the building. The strong breeze kept them aloft the entire length of the building without flapping their wings. He watched the line of birds lose altitude as they passed the structure, and waited for them to begin flapping. He hadn't been in his new hometown for a month and this Cash guy had already become a permanent pain in his ass. Colson had never been questioned in a criminal investigation. He had always been the one doing the questioning. He had never been unwittingly or willingly involved in unethical activity. He had always been the one stopping it. He looked north up the shoreline to the pier and thought, *Maybe I could assist the good sheriff. On the other hand, he might make things worse.* He shrugged. *Time to poke the tiger.*

～

Pickett looked back and forth at the two eight-by-ten glossy photographs with shock frozen on his face. Kim walked back into the room with two short glasses of whiskey and soda and set one of them on the end table. She sat on the bed next to him and craned her head to take another look at the photographs.

"Nice," she said, with intended sarcasm.

Pickett shook his head. "I don't believe this shit," he said, and slapped the photos on the bed next to him.

"Something tells me the press won't have much interest in publishing those," she said with a laugh.

Pickett stood and snatched his pants from the floor. "I'm gonna kill Beavers." His words seared through gritted teeth. "I paid him two grand for that shit," he said, gesturing at the discarded photos on the bed. He pulled the phone from his pocket and touched Beavers' number. Muffled loud thumping and screeching greeted Pickett after five rings. He jerked the cell away from his ear and grimaced.

"Yeah." Beavers yell was barely audible through the noise.

Picket held the phone in front of his face. "Beavers. Where the hell are you?"

"Oh, I'm at Biggins, why? I can hardly hear you."

"Biggins? You stay right there," Pickett shouted and pointed toward the wall as if Beavers was standing in front of him.

"Do what?" Beavers shouted back into the phone.

"I said you stay right there. I'm on my way to you," Pickett repeated, and then ended the call and slipped his t-shirt over his head. He crammed the photos back into the envelope and started toward the bedroom door.

"You should take my car," Kim said. "Someone tells Langston an S.O. unit is parked in front of a strip club and he'll take your bike away from you."

Pickett glared at her. "It's not his damned bike!"

"It is with all that equipment and Volusia County written all over it."

"Whatever," he said, snatching the keys off the dresser and stomping out.

Reese lay back on the bed and closed her eyes. She knew half the department hated her for making lieutenant, but she didn't care. She deserved it as much as anyone else. If it was partially due to her being an attractive young woman, so be it. She pondered Pickett's plan to discredit Langston and run for his office. It had potential. Sex scandals had ruined many a politician's career. She knew Langston wouldn't give up that easy, but another promotion excited her and she would play along for now. If it appeared that Pickett's plan was going to fail, she would vehemently deny Langston's alleged misconduct and stand by him. Either way she would win. Pickett's plan would have had more teeth had he gone along with her idea, but she would never tell him she would have enjoyed sleeping with Langston. The cell phone interrupted her daydream. She answered on the second ring.

"Lieutenant Reese," Langston said.

"Hello, Sheriff. Is everything all right?"

"I've had to make a couple of temporary reassignments. Both of the homicide investigators will be in training for two weeks. I've assigned Sgt. Cantrell and another one of the OCU investigators to their spot."

Reese sat up on the bed. "With all due respect, sir, I won't have enough people to do surveillance in the Cash case."

"You let me worry about that. Cash will still be around two weeks from now when you get your people back."

"The only reason I asked is because you seemed so—"

Langston interrupted. "I said don't worry about it, lieutenant. Just put the case on hold until I advise otherwise."

"Yes, sir."

Those driving south on A1A could only see the green metal roof of the Ponce Inlet Water Department over the solid mass of palms and undergrowth. The main drive off A1A split left and right thirty feet from the road, making a rounded-off square access road around the complex. The acre of land between the complex and the inner access road had been left to flourish like a tropical jungle. The same dense wall of plant life surrounded the facility on all four sides, leaving it camouflaged from view. Small one-by-two-foot signs hanging from two light posts at the entrance were the only clue to let visitors know where they needed to be to pay their bill or have their water turned on. There was nothing secretive about the water department, nor were the buildings in the complex in disrepair. The buildings were of appropriate tan stucco and the grounds were manicured and well maintained by inmates under the supervision of county workers. But the wealthy residents along this part of Daytona Beach Shores had no desire to see a lowly government complex from the windows of their six-thousand-square-foot beach homes.

That was Colson's assessment of the situation as he turned the Corvette onto the access road. He had made two passes by Cash's address on the sticky note and was satisfied he was in the right place. Not much to see. Just a glimpse of the roofline over the huge stone fence and a fraction of a second peek through the wrought iron gates in front. On his return pass he saw the side stone wall ended where the dense foliage on the water department's property began.

He backed into a parking space at the far side of the lot, grabbed the camera, and stepped out. A woman came out from the Water Department main entrance and walked to her car. Colson stretched and acted like he was punching numbers into his cell. He raised the phone to his ear as the woman backed out and disappeared down the access road. Colson dropped the cell phone in his pocket and walked north across the access road to the undergrowth where a "No Trespassing" sign stood in the wide-bladed grass. From the road he estimated the foliage stretched seventy-five to one-hundred yards to the property line. His high estimate was accurate. It took him over twenty minutes to negotiate his way through the think undergrowth before he caught a glimpse of a clearing ahead.

The beach house was at least four stories high. The back portion of the top floor had a railing with glass panel inserts. He could see the tops of umbrellas and a pergola on the roof deck and two large balconies jutting out on the beach side from the third and second floors above the sand. Colson let out a light whistle. Must be nice. He raised the camera and focused on the side of the house. A dark sedan was parked under a carport with the trunk open. He couldn't see the tag from the side, but zoomed in and took a couple of shots. He pulled back on the zoom and took shots of the entire house. He wanted shots from the rear, but didn't dare expose himself by stepping out into the open. It would take too long to cover the hundred or so yards through the thick mess to the rear of the property. He pulled one of the full-house shots up on the screen and zoomed in on the small black objects mounted on the front and rear corners of the house. Just as he suspected. Security cameras set on rotating mounts. They may not be constantly monitored, but they were most certainly recoding their images to a hard drive. Colson decided to watch and wait for a half hour, but five minutes was all it took.

Colson saw movement at the side door. Taylor's back was to him, his broad shoulders filling the doorframe. He was backing out the door looking from side-to-side. Colson raised the camera and took another shot. The zoom confirmed it was Taylor, holding something draped over his arms. Colson knew what the object was the moment Taylor turned to walk to the trunk of the sedan. "My God," he whispered, and momentarily lowered the camera in disbelief. He realized his error and jerked it back to his face, clicking as fast as the camera's memory would allow. Taylor lowered the body into the trunk and closed the lid. Taylor's attention was focused on the side door. Colson widened the zoom and took shots of Cash in the doorway talking to Taylor as if he had stopped by to pick up an area rug for delivery to the cleaners. Cash and Taylor exchanged a few more words before Taylor climbed into the car and drove out the front gates.

He had been hearing the buzz of what sounded like a dirt bike for over a minute, but it suddenly grew louder in the past five seconds. Colson took two steps back into the foliage. The man riding the ATV shot twenty feet past him before hitting the hand brake and sliding the knobby tires in the thick, damp grass. He had already turned and moved into the thick brush when Randy Fuller yelled, "Hey"!

He took long, high strides through the thick undergrowth. Every few feet he caught a glimpse of an unusually shaped branch or flattened foliage where he had stepped on his way in. He could hear the man entering the thicket now. "Hey!" the shout came again. Colson stopped and listened. The man was twenty feet behind him and following his path. He cut to his right, off of the makeshift path, sat on his heels and waited. The man must have heard him stop moving and slowed his progress in turn. He heard slow, deliberate steps coming closer. Then the man's head became visible, scanning the area around him. A few more steps and he became visible from the waist up, still scanning. But now Colson could see the stainless steel semiautomatic pistol he swept back and forth with the motion of his head.

There was no doubt in Colson's mind the man had seen him watching Cash and Taylor. There was also no doubt this man worked for Cash and wouldn't hesitate to kill a witness. So there was no doubt about what Colson had to do now. He pulled the collapsed ASP from his back pocket and held his position. Three or four more feet. The man took another step and then another, still scanning. He moved past Colson, but close enough. Colson stood when the man turned away from him. He snapped the ASP skyward, extending it to its full length with a clean click. Not immediately recognizing the metallic sound, Fuller was a moment too slow in turning. Colson came down with the ASP across Fuller's right hand, snapping the metacarpal bone of his index finger. Fuller screeched in surprised agony as the pistol dropped to the mossy carpet of the undergrowth with a muffled thud. Fuller snapped his head to see Colson and shot his left hand down for the pistol.

Colson recalled ASP training very clearly. A solid eight hours of everything from disassembling the simple weapon to striking a man-sized dummy hundreds of times, using a dozen striking techniques. They were trained to disable suspects without causing serious damage by striking areas called green zones, or to cause permanent damage by striking red zone areas of the body. The bones of the hand fell well within the green zone. Although deploying an ASP was considered less than lethal force, the ASP could be a twenty-one inch stick of solid metal death if not used properly. Colson knew the proper defensive strike resembled the shape of an "X." From a fighting stance the ASP is held tip up in the strong hand. With a jerk the hand is raised as if cocking it for a hammer fist strike. With a flick of the wrist, the ASP would fully extend. The officer would strike downward at the attacker across the chest in a diagonal motion and continue in a fluid motion, raising the ASP and striking a second time, making the shape of an imaginary "X" across the attacker's chest.

But Fuller's chest was not exposed. He was bent over, reaching for the pistol. Colson held the ASP low to his side. He turned his hand palm-up and swung as if lobbing a tennis ball. The ASP crushed the cartilage in Fuller's nose with Colson's follow-through swing. Fuller's head snapped back and his eyes rolled back into his head. His upright body appeared to pause for an instant, then stiffen, and finally go limp as he toppled backward in the spongy cushion of moss.

Colson knelt and listened. Fuller lay unconscious on his back, but his chest rose and fell with regularity. He would survive the broken nose and finger, but it would take a week for his headache to subside. He picked up the gun, dropped the magazine, and then racked and cleared the chamber. He tossed the magazine in one direction and the gun in the other. A few weeks in this salty jungle would disable the gun and make the ammunition worthless. He rolled the man onto his side and pulled one knee to his chest to maintain his position. Satisfied he wouldn't choke on his own blood, he slid the man's wallet from his back pocket and flipped it open. A flattened pack of rolling papers fell to the ground. He picked up the papers and slid them back in the wallet. He was still breathing steady and sleeping like a baby. Colson checked the remaining contents of the wallet. A condom, credit card, forty dollars cash, and a driver's license. He slid the license from its slot and read the name: Randal A. Fuller.

Colson pulled a pen from the pocket of his fatigues and wrote the name and license number on the palm of his hand. He closed the wallet and stuck it back in Fuller's pocket. He patted Fuller's other back pocket and almost missed it. He passed the left back pocket the first time, but something didn't feel right. He pulled the top of the pocket back to avoid being cut by a blade or poked by a needle and pulled out a folded piece of computer paper. "Tina Crowder" was written in the center of the page. Colson flipped the paper over and saw a color photo of a young girl forcing a smile. It was the girl who was assaulted on the beach by the slug son of Martin Cash. He added her name on his hand under Fuller's. He folded the paper and put it in the pocket of his fatigues. He felt around Fuller's belt line and found his cell phone. He snapped it off the belt and slid it out of the holder. He touched the screen, then the contacts shortcut. Most of the contacts didn't sound familiar. There were numbers to three liquor stores. All Cash's of course. He saw the number for Jay Taylor, Martin Cash, and a one-name contact—Pickett.

Colson pulled the paper from his pocket and documented all the names and numbers he recognized under Tina's name. Beads of sweat ran into his eyes and his palms were wet. The notes he had written on his hand were beginning to smudge. Fuller groaned. He was conscious but in pain. Colson was sliding the cell phone back into the belt clip when it rang—

Cash checked his watch and looked to the line of dense foliage at the edge of his property. What was Fuller doing in there so long? It was too hot to be waiting on Fuller while he was doing God knows what. He stepped inside, pushed the door closed with a slam, and walked to the bar counter. What had Fuller seen? He pushed up the lid of his laptop and clicked on the camera icon. Four equal-size blocks filled the screen. Each, a slowly sweeping view from the four roof mounted cameras. He hovered the cursor on the southwest camera and clicked the pad. The scene filled the entire screen above a DVD-type toolbar at the bottom. He clicked the reverse button once and the scene started to reverse in slow motion. He looked and waited. This was taking too long. He cursed and clicked reverse twice. The swift camera movement irritated Cash. He had to concentrate to catch the area of the property line he was interested in. In a flash the four-wheeler was there and then gone. He clicked pause and then one-half forward speed. He didn't notice the figure among the foliage for a moment because he was looking for Fuller and the four-wheeler, but then he saw something out of place. A shape foreign to the line of palms and thick hedges. He moved the cursor to pause, and then zoom. He squinted at the screen and moved his face closer. "Damn," he said, pulling his cell phone out and punching Fuller's contact icon.

⇒ Chapter Eighteen ⇐

There were two cars in the Biggins Gentlemen's Club parking lot at two-thirty in the afternoon. The majority of its patrons didn't arrive until much later in the evening. A few businessmen frequented the dimly lit establishment in the early afternoon to escape the blazing Daytona heat, have a drink, and flirt with the topless waitresses.

The one-story building was well maintained and not very remarkable in the daylight. The creamy yellow exterior was accented with half-round, sand-colored, faux-roman pillars attached to its façade in front and one-third the length of its sides. Few tourists paid attention to the building as they drove north and south on A1A. Their focus would be drawn to the bright yellow and red neon sign erected thirty feet above the hot pavement that read BIGGINS in huge lettering. It could be seen for a quarter-mile during the day and nearly a half-mile after dark when the neon came to life. Passersby would either laugh hysterically or convulse with shock while trying to formulate an explanation for their children who inquired about the name from the back seat. Parking in front could prove hazardous to those timid about backing into traffic, especially if they had been drinking. The four front spaces were a short car length from the sidewalk, and two of those were reserved for the handicapped. Patrons who knew the value of discretion parked their vehicles in the main parking area on the north side of the building.

Mike Beavers loosened his tie and slid on his sunglasses as he walked across the parking lot. It was his first time in the bar and he was somewhat surprised how clean it was. But it was early in the day. The meeting with the owner had gone fairly well and the job should be easy enough. Find his twenty-five-year-old former bartender, dig into his finances, and find proof he was the person who had stolen the eighteen thousand dollars from the office safe. Beavers did a quick calculation in his head. Locating the former employee could take three or four days—let's say a week. Running his credit history, identifying his accounts, and possibly finding a safe deposit box would take another week. The money could be in a girlfriend's account or in a shoebox under his bed. That would add even more man-hours of work, but from what he had been told, the bartender was not that bright. The owner could very well get a bill exceeding the amount stolen from him and Beavers told him as much.

"It's for my satisfaction," the owner replied with a smirk.

Beavers didn't bother to ask the man why he just didn't leave it up to the police. He already knew the answer. They had taken the report and sent an investigator to interview the current employees. The suspected bartender was long gone by then and there was no physical evidence for an arrest based on probable cause. Now the case would be sitting in a file cabinet, never to be opened unless the bartender walked in and offered a confession.

Beavers smiled as he walked to his SUV. "That's where I come in," he mumbled. He hadn't had lunch, and the three free beers he drank during his hour-long meeting with the owner had made their way through his bloodstream and into his brain.

The front tires of the Jeep screeched and bit into the pavement. Pickett swung into the side parking lot and spotted Beavers' SUV parked near the back. Beavers climbed into the driver's side, not paying attention to the Jeep speeding into the lot and stopping behind him. Beavers sent an annoyed look at the Jeep through his side mirror. It was just sitting there. He jumped in his seat when Pickett jerked open the passenger door and climbed in next to him. Pickett slammed the door and waved the manila envelope in Beavers' face.

"Where do you think you're going, you piece of shit?" Pickett demanded and threw the envelope. Beavers jerked his hands up to keep it from hitting him in the face and it fell in his lap.

"What's wrong with you?" Beavers questioned. Pickett's ridiculous outburst scared him at first, but was now pissing him off.

"I told you to wait. You thought you'd just rip me off and I wouldn't find you?"

"Look. I couldn't understand a word you were saying on the phone. Now what's the problem?"

"Open it!" Pickett demanded, pointing at the envelope.

Beavers picked the envelope up and slid the photos out. He looked at the first photo and then back to Pickett. He slid off the top photo and looked at the second. "Where did these come from?"

Pickett slapped the dash with his hand. "Where the hell do you think?" He pointed at Beavers' face and shouted, "You!"

"I…" Beavers stuttered, "I…I didn't take them."

"What do you mean you didn't take them? I paid you to take them."

Beavers shrugged. "It doesn't matter. I paid my guy to take them. I had a lot going on and couldn't be in two places at once. It was an easy job."

Pickett snatched the envelope from Beavers and shook it violently.

"Then how do you explain these?"

Beavers shook his head and muttered to himself, "Colson was pissed."

Pickett straightened in his seat with a look of disbelief. "Colson? Don't tell me you involved him in this!"

Beavers looked confused. "He acted like he knew *you* for some reason? He wouldn't accept the money anyway."

"But you didn't have any problem taking the money!" Pickett screamed.

"I didn't look at the pictures. I trusted him," Beavers pleaded and slurred, revealing his mildly intoxicated state. "I'll give you back the money. I still have most of it left."

Pickett's screaming increased a decibel. "I don't need the damned money. I need the pictures!"

"I said I'd get them. He has them and I'll get them for you," Beavers insisted. "You just need to calm down Pickett, you're acting crazy."

Pickett squinted at Beavers. His breathing became erratic. What would Cash do if he couldn't get Langston off his back? How in hell did Colson get involved and what does he know about his relationship with Cash? Probably everything. The wheels of his plan were falling off fast. His head was spinning. Beavers kept talking but his words sounded muffled, as if he was hearing everything from under water. He felt numb. What was Beavers saying?

"Pickett," Beavers repeated. "Have you lost your mind?"

Pickett appeared to find his focus and met Beavers' eyes. Beavers recognized Pickett's moment of clarity and regained his half-drunk composure.

"I'll go right now and get the photos from Colson. I'm sure it was just a bad joke. Meanwhile, you might want to see the department shrink. I worry about you sometimes, Pickett. I'm not so sure you're cut out to be the top law officer in my county. I should probably save you from yourself and have a talk with Langston." He nodded toward his side mirror and reached for his seat belt. "Now, if you don't mind moving that Jeep," he said, pulling the shoulder harness across his body, "I have work to do."

Pickett felt numb. Overwhelming rage instantly possessed him. He snatched the envelope from Beavers' lap and threw it in the floorboard. The photos slid halfway out of the open flap. Pickett clinched Beavers' wrist with his right hand and held it down on the driver's seat. He leaned toward Beavers, using his upper body weight to press his wrist into the seat. "I don't think so," Pickett growled.

"What do you think—?" Beavers began to protest, but Pickett shot his left hand out and grabbed Beavers' loosened tie and jerked hard, cinching the knot tight as it slid to the side of Beavers' neck. Picket pulled the tie toward him, causing Beavers to lean to his right. He gasped and clawed at his neck with his free hand but couldn't find the knot. Pickett rose to give himself more leverage and jerked the tie back between the seats. Beavers continued to claw at his neck and gasp, but now it slid further from reach. Pickett groaned and strained until Beavers' arm stopped flailing and fell limp in his lap. He realized he'd been holding his breath and exhaled hard. He dropped back into his seat and looked at Beavers. The face of death. He had seen at least a few dead bodies on duty, but not like this. For some reason this one looked different.

Pickett looked out the tinted driver's window at the parking lot. No new cars. No witnesses. He snapped his head toward the dash clock. 3:41p.m. Not much activity at the bar between the noon and night crowds. He sat back in the passenger seat, still breathing hard. He forced himself to think. Had he touched anything? Nothing but the envelope and door handle. He used his shirttail to open the inside door latch and stepped onto the asphalt. He exhaled sharply out of his nose and gave Beavers one last look. "I'll take care of it myself," he said to the dead private investigator. He wiped the outer door handle with his shirt. He reached for the partially exposed photos and envelope in the floorboard and gently pushed the SUV door closed with his knee until it made a soft click.

He walked to the back of the SUV and took one last look at the parking lot and the passing traffic on A1A. He pulled himself into the driver's seat, almost losing his balance. He realized his hands were trembling. He could hear his own heavy breathing as if someone was holding their hands over his ears. He became lightheaded and he saw darkness in his peripheral vision. He was about to pass out. He put his hands on the steering wheel and rested his forehead on them. He had to get away from the scene, but not in this condition. He couldn't risk having an accident in this area. It would document him being near the scene of the crime at the approximate time of death.

He allowed himself a minute to regain his composure and motor skills. He looked down at the photos. They were no good to him, but Colson may want them back since Beavers said it was probably just a bad joke. He knew it wasn't a joke. The two eight-by-ten glossy close-ups of a man's hand giving him the finger was not even a little funny.

∽

Sweat ran down Colson's neck and back. His shirt and waistband were soaked. He wiped his eyes with his sleeve and looked at the cell phone. He hesitated for a moment and considered not answering. *Time to poke the tiger,* he thought once again. Colson pressed "answer" and held the phone to his ear without speaking. Silence for a count of two, then: "Fuller?" Cash sounded a little impatient.

"Sorry, Martin," Colson said pleasantly. "Your boy can't come to the phone right now."

Another pause, but this one made it to the count of three. Cash seemed to be controlling his voice. "What are you doing, Colson?"

"I came to complain about my water bill."

"Where's Fuller?" Cash said, ignoring Colson's answer.

Colson looked down at Fuller, who was regaining consciousness. He was emitting a muffled groan with his hands over his nose and mouth.

"He's right here with me."

173

"Put him on the phone," Cash demanded.

"Well, he can't talk right now. He came after me with a gun so I had to drop him like a bad habit."

"You're trespassing, Colson."

Colson shrugged.

"Maybe on Water Department property and that would make it none of your business. He shouldn't be waiving a gun around. I would bet he's a felon, making it illegal for him to even have it."

"And that," Cash emphasized, "would be none of your business. Look," he said, attempting to even his voice, "we should talk. Seriously. Just bring Fuller back up to the house."

"And what should we talk about, Cash? Maybe criminal activity more serious than trespassing? Concealing a death? Murder possibly?"

"You have no idea what you're talking about."

"I know what I saw."

"You can't leave anything alone, can you? Fine, just help Fuller to the treeline and get the hell out of here."

"Your concern touches my heart."

Colson wasn't a fool and had no intention of exposing himself, but decided to check on Fuller before going back to the car. He squatted and pulled Fuller up to a seated position, then scooted him over to a tree and leaned him against it. He heard the thump of the round burying itself in the moss a split second before the unmistakable sound of the rifle caught up to it. He ducked instinctively, but knew he couldn't be seen this far into the foliage. He moved quickly through the thicket, trying to make as little noise as possible. A second and third shot rang out without the warning sound of a round striking the ground or tearing through the trees. Whoever had the rifle was taking pot shots, hoping to hit something. Fuller was just as likely to catch a stray bullet as he was.

He picked up his pace, counting on the ocean breeze and the rustling palms to mask the sound of his movement. The deeper into the foliage the better. He emerged from the foliage within five feet from where he entered and scanned the parking lot. No new cars or activity. He tossed the phone back into the trees, wiped his brow with his sleeve, and walked to his car. The rifleman had given up. Cash's property was large. It's doubtful anyone could have recognized the bark of the rifle since there were virtually no acoustics at the coastline. He and Ann would frequently have to raise their voices against the roaring ocean breeze to have a conversation. If you were not in the direction of the sound, you most likely wouldn't hear or recognize it.

The passive key remote in Colson's pocket unlocked the driver's door before he reached to open it. He started the engine and cranked the air conditioner to its highest setting. The blast of air took five seconds to cool off and it felt like a cold shower. The control panel read ninety-three degrees, but it would have been over a hundred if he hadn't parked in the shade.

He put the 'Vette in drive and jerked from the parking space, allowing the wide rear tires a quick bark. He swung around the access road and north out onto A1A. He pulled a business card from the middle console and punched numbers into his phone.

"Sheriff's Office Organized Crime Unit," answered a female voice.

"Sergeant Cantrell," Colson said.

"He's not in right now. May I take a message, or can someone else help you?"

Colson craned his head back, having expecting the answer. "Please ask him to call Grey Colson."

He ended the call and dropped the phone in the passenger seat. He thought about Nichole. He hadn't heard from her in over a week.

♋

Nichole picked her cell phone out of her purse and touched the screen, but it stayed blank. She sighed and dug around in the center console for the charger. A horn blew behind her. She glanced up to see the traffic moving again. She eased up fifty feet to satisfy the impatient driver behind her. She moved quickly to plug the charger into the dash outlet and the USB connection into her phone. She had planned on calling Dad to let him know she was coming for a visit, but wasn't sure she would be finished with her finals on time. She hadn't given that little detail enough thought before booking the flight.

Traffic crept forward again and she followed suit. Finals or not, she may not make the flight with the absolutely ridiculous traffic on Interstate 285. It was eight lanes wide in some places and there still wasn't sufficient room to accommodate Metro Atlanta traffic. She remembered going with her parents to Daytona every year. How Mom and Dad insisted on leaving at five in the morning to get to the other side of the city before rush hour. It didn't matter the day of the week; the traffic was horrid. She picked up the cell phone. This time the screen came to life with the little battery icon flashing. She slid the screen to contacts and touched Bobby's picture icon.

"Hey, Babe," Bobby said. "How was the final?"

She sighed. "Fine. I guess I did okay. Didn't take as long as I thought."

"You okay?"

"Yeah. I hate I-285 traffic. I'm just tired."

"I'm gonna miss you this weekend."

"Me too. Thanks for understanding."

Bobby paused. "Did you call your dad?"

"I meant to, but I wasn't sure I could make it with my finals today."

"You didn't call?" he said with concern. "What if he's not there? I mean, what if he has company or something?"

"What? Who would he have as company? And he's not gone. He lives on the beach, for heaven's sake."

"Well. He might have a lady friend or something."

"That's crazy. Just take care of Marty and Bella and I'll be home late Sunday."

"Okay," he said. "Do you want me to call him?"

She thought for a moment. "No, I'll call him when I land."

"After you call me?"

"Of course."

"Okay, you be safe and have a good flight."

"I will. Love you."

"Love you back."

Nichole slid her phone back into her purse. The pace of the traffic picked back up once she had passed the Interstate 75 interchange. Checking the time on her dash, she calculated she could make it, but the wait time through security was an unknown. Good thing it was a late flight.

⇢ Chapter Nineteen ⇠

Cash scanned the treeline through the riflescope and saw nothing but a solid green mass of leaves and undergrowth. He thought he saw Colson move through the thicket and had no idea if the shots made contact. If so, Colson would never be found. He pulled the rifle away from the railing and sat back in the lounge chair. He saw movement at the edge of the tree line near the ATV. Cash stood, raised the rifle to his shoulder and put the scope to his eye. It was Fuller holding one hand under his armpit and his nose with the other. The front of his t-shirt looked like it had been painted red. "Damn," Cash uttered under his breath, "what a dumb ass." Fuller paid no attention to the ATV and walked around it, straight for the beach house.

Cash lowered the rifle, walked to the roof elevator and rode it to the main level. Fuller was leaning over the sink, splashing handfuls of water in his face when Cash walked in the kitchen.

"Don't be bleeding all over my kitchen, Fuller."

Fuller didn't reply.

Cash raised his voice. "You hear me?"

Fuller casually turned his head. "You could have killed me, man. I heard the first shot hit three feet from me."

"Ah," Cash mocked, "I knew what I was shooting at. Did Colson get away?"

"He broke my hand and nose!" Fuller shouted. "I'm gonna kill that son of a bitch!"

Jason walked into the room from the deck. "What's going on?"

Fuller turned to expose his blood soaked t-shirt. Jason's eyes grew wide with surprise. "What the hell?"

Cash turned to Jason. "It was your friend again. Colson. He came here snooping around and did this to Randy." Cash gestured to Fuller, who had returned to hanging his head over the sink.

"Why?" Jason asked.

"Because he doesn't have a life. Because he thinks he's still some kind of detective. Hell if I know. But there's one thing I do know. I've been in this county all my life and employ a lot of people. That Georgia cracker just moved down here. I don't care what he saw or what he thinks he saw, it's his word against mine."

Jason looked at Fuller, then back to Cash. "So what do we do now?"

"Nothing right now. We have just twenty-four hours to get Tina back, and then we'll deal with Colson."

"But what if he goes to the police?"

"Go to the police with what? Is he going to tell them he was trespassing and assaulted one of my security men?"

"There's a problem," Fuller mumbled.

Cash turned to Fuller, who now was leaning back against the counter. "What problem?"

"I got a pretty good look at Colson before he ran back into the brush."

"And?" Cash said impatiently.

"He had a camera."

∾

Tina was tired and ready to give up. She had eaten the last can of soup earlier and the hunger pains were back. It was stupid to think a stranger would help her. People don't help other people; it's too dangerous. What made her think she was any different because she was a young woman? She remembered the women in the county jail dormitory. The worst experience of her life, with the exception of being held captive by Martin Cash. The female inmates were mean, dirty, and violent. She overheard one of the deputies say that the women fought more than the male inmates and she believed it. She witnessed dozens of fights in her relatively short time and was amazed most of them were over other women. Tina's entire focus was to stay to herself and keep a low profile. She avoided the fights, but it cost her half her dinner tray and every dessert. Not that it was worth eating, but even the thought of bland jail food made her hungry now.

She tried to recall landmarks near the section of beach where she and Jason had been. She wondered why Jason even bothered taking her to this section of the beach since their house was right on the beach, but it didn't take long once they got there. It was only legal to drive on this section of Daytona Beach after paying a five-dollar fee at the access road. After driving back and forth for Jason to show off his eighty-thousand-dollar NSX, they parked and talked until the little scumbag tried to feel her up. She closed her eyes, trying to visualize something familiar. A person could walk ten miles on the beach and most everything would look identical. People, pool chairs, kids building sand castles, and something else. What was it? Tina's eyes shot open. Parasailing. She had seen people parasailing in only one place during their drive on the beach and she had wanted to watch. She looked south and saw it maybe two or three hundred yards away. The distance was difficult to estimate, but she didn't care. She had passed right by without realizing it. She walked back the way she came with renewed hope—but it would probably be for nothing.

Pickett's finger hovered over Cash's contact number on the screen, but he decided against it and dropped his cell phone into the cup holder. He couldn't tell Cash he screwed up again, and being talked to like a child was getting old. He gripped the steering wheel tight and shook it. "Damn it!" he snapped.

Langston already wanted his badge. His only hope would be to get those photos and threaten to give them to the press. He should have squeezed Beavers for Colson's address before he had made him do what he did. He shook his head violently. He couldn't believe how he had reacted, but Beavers had pissed him off. Called him crazy. "I'm. Not. Crazy!" he shouted inside the Jeep. "Think," he commanded himself. Cash had the address, but he wasn't going to call him to announce his blunder. No, he was a cop and could get it himself. Then he would get the photos and finish it. He was in it as far as he could go. Further than he thought it would go, but there was no time to worry about it now.

Pickett turned left on International Speedway Boulevard and snatched the gears, making the six-cylinder engine strain to keep up. He checked his rearview mirror every other second and reminded himself to take it easy and not get stopped. His buddies would cut him slack and wouldn't write him up for speeding, but it would be his luck after

Beavers was found for them to remember something odd about the encounter. And even some of his best buddies would say something to make themselves look good. He eased off the accelerator and turned left on Nova Road, throwing a disgusted glance at Cash's main store. He passed the sheriff's substation at the corner of Orange Avenue, turned into the lot, and then parked the Jeep behind the building.

It was cool inside the small, one-story substation. Deputy Munoz sat near the public information window, quietly typing at the computer. This would be his day to work the desk and no one else appeared to be there. He glanced over the screen at Pickett.

"Hey, Pickett, you working today?" he asked, looking at a wall calendar.

"Uh," Pickett hesitated. He hadn't considered anyone would question him. "No, I just need to use the computer for a minute."

"On your off day?" Munoz questioned as he gave him a confused look.

"Well, I have to pick up a marked unit. Sheriff's got me doing a public relations thing tomorrow. Free fingerprinting for kids at Volusia Mall. You know, for kids' IDs. And I've got this subpoena and need to see what the case is about before court. I figured I'd kill two birds while I was here."

"Fine with me." Munoz turned back to his screen and started typing. "Hell if I'd be here on my day off."

Pickett sat at a desk across the room and logged in. He clicked on the Master Name Index icon, typed Colson's name in the query box, then clicked ENTER. He sat back to wait, but the information box flashed on the screen before he could relax. He peeled a sticky note from a stack on the desk and jotted down the address. Pickett looked at the box labeled "Incident Type" where "Speed Warning" had been entered, and replayed the incident in his mind. The guy was a smartass and he should have put paper on him. Retired cop or not. The radar had read fifty-two miles per hour, but most people won't argue it. Colson didn't argue either, but he was smug and condescending, cruising around like a playboy in his little Corvette.

He looked at the address. 1303 South Atlantic Avenue, unit 510. He closed his eyes to visualize the long stretch of A1A running north and south in that area of the county. With the exception of a few demolished condominiums, there were still dozens, and most looked identical. He queried the address in the computer for the complex name. Sundowner Condominiums appeared on the screen. Pickett shook his head in recognition and stood.

"I'm going to grab some keys," Pickett said.

Munoz gave a dismissive wave and continued typing, never taking his eyes off the screen. Pickett walked to a pegboard with two rows of keys hanging on hooks, each below a label indicating the unit number. He lifted the clipboard hanging next to the keys and looked at the entries where the deputies signed them out for the past week's duty. He looked over to Munoz, who was still focused on whatever he was typing. He hung the clipboard back without signing it, grabbed a set of keys, and then walked out.

The sand was hot and the tops of Tina's feet were sunburned. She walked down to the shallow surf and made her way south. The aroma of hamburgers and steaks grilling poolside made her stomach growl. She walked on and struggled with what to say if she found the man from the beach. Her mind was made up. If she couldn't find him or he refused to help, she would have no choice but to turn herself in and then just take her chances with the female inmates.

Four red buoys floated in the shallow surf, marking a path for a motorized raft to take excited customers out to meet a larger boat. The customers were strapped into a harness and given safety instructions on their way out to deeper waters. She watched a pair being pulled like a giant kite about a half-mile off shore. She didn't know how high they flew, but it looked like they were higher than any condo she had seen on the beach. She stepped under the canopy where two folding tables were set up with brochures and a price list. A young girl in a bikini handed her a brochure. Tina thanked her and walked away. She dropped the brochure in a garbage can and looked up at the condominium complex. It had to be the right one. The lots on either side of the building were vacant. She saw the remains of short, wrought-iron fences where there had been pools for vacationers to swim and play during better economic times. But the buildings had been torn down and the lots wiped clean as if nothing had ever stood there. Between the vacant lots sat a renovated five-story complex.

She knew the beach access gate would be locked, so she waited. It was difficult, if not impossible, to see anyone walking in the parking area from this low angle. The stairs rose at least six feet above the sand against the sea wall, with a small landing for the gate. She wouldn't be able to get to the gate in time if someone stepped out. She walked slowly and hoped her timing would be right. She knew security had to be decent at the beach complexes or non-residents would use the parking spots constantly.

The thick, powdery sand near the sea wall was searing hot. She heard giggling children at the pool and an occasional screeching girl, probably being tossed off her dad's shoulders. Everyone was having a good time but her. She reached the foot of the stairs and turned to look at the ocean. Waiting. The sun was bright and hot, but the breeze made the wait tolerable. She heard a faint whistle and saw the lifeguard stand from his perch, frantically waving a yellow flag back and forth and blowing his whistle in short, sharp bursts.

She held up her hand to block the sun and focused to see what made the lifeguard so excited. She couldn't see anything unusual at first, but then she made out the two dark dots bobbing several hundred feet off shore. Now the lifeguard was looking through binoculars and waving his flag with one hand and blowing the whistle with more urgency. She became so focused on the careless swimmers she almost missed her chance. The electronic gate latch clicked and the children were on the landing before she knew it. She ran to the top of the stairs just in time to keep the teenage boy from letting the gate click closed.

"Hey!" Tina said. "Hang on a second."

The teenage boy grinned and held the gate while Tina climbed the metal stairs to the top. She gave him a smile and thanks when she stepped in the parking area. She looked down at the two-foot-wide band of light-gray concrete bordering the hot, black asphalt and cringed. It would be scorching hot. She walked to the low showerhead and turned it on, alternating her feet under the lukewarm spray, rinsing the sand from between her toes. She followed the narrow band of light concrete along a wrought-iron fence beside the pool. She looked up as she approached the ocean side of the condos. Balconies stacked one upon another. Some occupied by people in shorts or bathing suits. A shirtless man on the third floor leaned over the rail, nursing a can of beer and watching the poolside activity.

She reached a brick walkway and turned left along the length of the building, looking around the parking lot for the man's face. She made it to the breezeway where the wind almost blew her off balance. A man stepped out of a car in the narrow front lot leading to the street. It wasn't him. She grew discouraged, thinking it would be impossible to find the man. She backed away from the sidewalk to take another look up the five stories of balconies and didn't notice the woman on the bottom floor, ten feet from her.

"Are you looking for someone, honey?" Faye Cox said. It made Tina jerk. She looked down at the woman in the white bathrobe but didn't know what to say. She had been telling lies for months about who she was, where she was from, her parents, he life, everything. She was mentally and physically exhausted. And hungry.

The encounter with the beach policeman flashed through her mind. The false name she had given him at the time made her so scared she couldn't even move. Tina knew they would not only arrest her for jumping bail, but charge her with giving a false name. Maybe they didn't check because she was a victim. She didn't know, but the cop allowed her to leave. Telling the truth to the police and in court had done her no good, but she was tired of lying to everyone. She looked at the woman and sighed, ready to see how much good the truth would do her now.

Faye set her drink down and stood. "Are you okay? Aren't you the girl from the beach? The one the boy slapped.? My name is Faye."

Tina nodded.

"What's wrong?" Faye asked.

Tina saw a genuine look of concern on the woman's face. She took a couple of steps, introduced herself by her real name, and then told her the story. About the night out with friends, being arrested, and running away before her trial. She told Faye about Jason, Cash, the last two homeless nights, everything. She didn't even remember sitting down at the small table, but when she finished it felt like a terrible weight had been lifted from her shoulders.

Faye sat through the entire story with her mouth partially open. She occasionally would reach over and touch Tina's hand when she brought up a particularly sensitive part, like being held captive, the other girls, and sleeping in the tool shed.

"My Lord," was all Faye could utter. She had gotten far more than she had bargained for with her simple query. She took a long sip of her drink and set it back on the table.

"What are you going to do, go home?"

"Maybe," Tina said. "I didn't know where else to go but to the police, but I lied to that cop about my name that day."

She pointed to where Jason slapped her around. "I wondered if that man who helped me would be willing to—"

"Mr. Colson?" Faye cut her short. "He's a very nice man. Retired from somewhere in Georgia where he was a policeman."

Tina nodded her head. "I thought he might be. I need police advice, but not from a cop who's still working. You know, he wouldn't really have to report me that way."

"Well, I don't know how that works, but I think he would be willing to talk to you. Very nice man."

Tina brightened. "Do you know which condo is his?"

"I think it's on the top floor, but I don't know the number. I see him on the balcony on the far left. It has to be the last door."

Tina smiled and stood. "Thank you."

"Wait," Faye said. "He's not here right now. I saw him drive out earlier and he hasn't been back."

"You sure?"

"Honey, believe me. I know everything that's going on here."

"Okay. I'll sit by the pool and wait."

"Oh, no you won't," Faye said in a motherly tone "I'm going to make you something to eat."

⌘

Officer Matt Sanders was the first unit on the scene. It was 7:30 p.m. when the signal 48, or person dead, call came over his radio. He was in the middle of dinner. Most calls can hold or be diverted to another unit, but he was close and this wasn't a routine loud music or barking dog dispatch. He threw a ten-dollar bill on the counter and jogged to his truck. By the radio log, it took him fifty-eight seconds to arrive in the parking lot of Biggins.

The SUV was parked nose-first in a space against the building. It wasn't dark yet, but the sun was not as intense in its low position in the sky. The front of the SUV was in the shade of the building, making the interior more visible to passersby. An ambulance had been dispatched and arrived one minute after Officer Sanders. He was at the driver's side door when the paramedics jumped from the ambulance and trotted to the passenger side. The doors were unlocked.

Beavers' body lay across the center console with his head in the passenger seat. His face was a gray-purple color and his mouth and eyes were partially open. Sanders observed signs of lividity on the man's face where it rested on the seat. He was clearly dead and had been for a while. The paramedics quickly concurred. He saw a necktie draped across the man's back, but couldn't see the knot due to the position of the body. He knew the procedure. Do not move the body. Protect the crime scene and take statements until a detective arrives. He confirmed the report to the radio operator and requested a second unit and a homicide detective. He pulled a roll of crime scene tape from the truck and waited for the second patrol unit. A sheriff's deputy arrived and assisted in cordoning off the SUV. The deputy stood by the crime scene with his note pad to record the names of anyone entering or exiting the restricted area.

The night manager told Sanders a customer noticed the man slumped over his seat after parking next to the SUV. Thinking he was drunk, the customer didn't report it to the manager until two hours later when he returned to his car and saw the man in the same position. "You should probably check on the guy out here," the customer told the manager before driving off. He wasn't a regular, so he didn't have a name to give Sanders. The young manager was visibly shaken.

"I blew it off for a while because we were getting busy," the manager explained. "I just figured he was sleeping it off," he said, gazing past the yellow tape at the SUV and shaking his head. "We've never had this kind of trouble here."

Officer Sanders jotted notes on his pad. He wrote down the manager's name and personal information.

"You couldn't have done anything," he said. "I'm just getting general information for my report. The detective will be more detailed."

"I'll just be inside," he said, turning away from the crime scene and walking away.

Sanders squeezed his collar microphone. "504, radio. I need the time I went out on this call," and waited for a reply. The radio operator would have recording the time he arrived in the 911 computer system.

The female voice responded, "1931 hours."

He wrote the time on his pad as a dark gray sedan and a white SUV pulled into the lot. The SUV had a gold star outlined in green lettering: "Volusia County Sheriff's Office" and "Crime Scene Unit."

Sanders knew most people thought it was like TV and the crime scene technicians were the investigators who collected evidence and arrested the bad guy or girl. It was a television fallacy. The majority of crime scene technicians were not law enforcement officers at all. At least not in Volusia County. They were trained to collect and log evidence, lift fingerprints, spray Luminol to reveal bloodstains, and take photographs of the crime scene.

The man driving the sedan got out and walked to Sanders. He wasn't wearing a suit jacket, just a white dress shirt and a dark blue tie, hanging lose around his unbuttoned collar. A paddle holster held a Glock on his side and a Sheriff's star was stuck on his belt. He was wearing dark wraparound sunglasses and looked to be in his mid-thirties. He offered a small grin as he approached.

"Sergeant Cantrell, Organized Crime," he said, offering his hand. Sanders shook it and looked mildly puzzled.

"Officer Sanders. You said organized crime, right?"

"Yes," Cantrell said. "I worked homicide before my transfer. Our two Crimes Against Person's detectives are in training, so I guess I'm it for now. What do you have so far?"

Sanders pointed to the SUV. "Not a lot. I've only been here twenty minutes, but I spoke with the manager who was alerted to the body by a customer who thought the dead guy was just a drunk sleeping it off."

Cantrell nodded. "Any identification on the victim?"

Sanders shook his head. "We haven't moved the body. The tag comes back to a Michael Beavers, Ormond Beach address. We still don't know—"

Cantrell held up his hand for Sanders to stop. "Hang on. What did you say his name was?"

Sanders looked down at his notes. "Michael Beavers."

"Shit!" Cantrell turned, pulled his cell phone and held up his index finger. "Stand by for a minute." He walked to his car, poking his finger at the screen.

∾

"The sheriff is not in his office," the young deputy said at the metal detector. Colson looked at his watch. 7:40 p.m. He closed his eyes and shook his head. He had already forgotten agency higher-ups don't work nights. He was so accustomed to working all hours, especially night shift, it hadn't occurred to him during his thirty-minute drive to Deland. He had never known the sheriff of Clay County to work nights unless there was a major incident the media wanted to speak with him about or a political fundraiser he would benefit from attending. He almost made it to the day shift club, but Major wasn't quite high enough for it to be unthinkable to work past five o'clock.

Colson thanked the well-pressed twenty-something-year-old deputy, stepped back through the metal detector, and collected his pocket items from the plastic tray. He wondered if Langston permitted his home address and number to be listed in the public directory as his sheriff had. It was worth a try. He climbed into his car and pushed the Internet explorer icon on the screen of his cell phone. He typed Langston, Stuart when the little text box popped up. He had to backspace three times for inadvertently pushing microscopic letters with his fat fingers.

He found the only Stuart Langston with an address on North Summit Avenue in an area called Lake Helen. He navigated to maps and typed in the address. From his current position, it appeared to be about seven or eight miles along his route back to Daytona. He started the 'Vette and drove back in the direction from where he came.

He checked the address again once he turned onto North Summit Avenue and pulled into the driveway of a modest ranch house. The black Tahoe he had watched at the Rayford Inn sat in front of the closed garage door. The house sat on a flat, narrow lot flanked by two scruffy trees. The exterior was painted a light tan and trimmed in off-white. A front door with an outdated oval window stood behind a screen door. A worn concrete stoop lay on the ground at the front entrance. Colson had seen identical houses in older neighborhoods in Clay County. Probably built in the early '70s with less than twelve-hundred square feet of living space. A little small and low-rent for the chief law enforcement officer of the county. A sheriff's salary was usually based on the size of the population he was entrusted to protect, and Volusia was not that small of a county. He checked the address again and looked at the dash clock. 8:05 p.m. It was almost dark and a light was on in the front room.

Colson walked to the door and knocked. The door opened almost immediately. Langston must have heard him drive up.

"Major Colson," Langston said, pushing the screen door open "Please come in."

"Thank you, Sheriff," Colson said, and stepped into a small, but tidy, living room. "We haven't met, have we?"

"I've seen your picture," Langston said. He was holding a small glass half-full of amber liquid. Colson could smell a slight aroma of bourbon as Langston swirled it around two ice cubes, which made a tinkling sound against the glass. Langston was not stammering, slurring his speech, or unsteady on his feet. He had either just started drinking or was a professional drunk. Colson understood. He had almost attained a doctorate in drinking after losing Ann. Langston motioned for him to follow and they walked on a linoleum floor through the kitchen and out onto a screened-in porch.

"It's nice out tonight. The no-see-ums can't get to us in here." Langston sat on a plastic chair made to resemble wicker, and then motioned for Colson to have a seat.

"You said you had seen my picture," Colson said. "From the research Sergeant Cantrell did?"

Langston shook his head. "No, I mean Cantrell probably has a license photo or something. I looked at the Clay County website. It still has a picture of you, except you were a lieutenant at the time."

Colson grinned and nodded. "Yep, sounds about right. They update the website every ten or twelve years, whether it needs it or not."

Langston lifted his glass. "Something to drink?"

Colson shook his head. "No, but thanks. You haven't asked why I'm here."

"Don't need to. You didn't take Sergeant Cantrell's advice and are still messing with this investigation."

"You know why?" Colson asked.

"Probably. I think we're a lot alike in that respect, Major. We both have made mistakes in our career. We made what we thought was the best decision and it turned out to be the wrong decision. Although we thought we were doing the right thing, it still pissed us off. What did we do? We fixed it. Am I close?"

Colson looked through the screen into an empty back yard. Patches of sand scattered in random spots where grass refused to grow. The yard backed up to a scruffy treeline behind a tattered doghouse.

"Something like that," Colson said. "Where's the dog?" he said, pointing to the back yard.

Langston took a sip from his glass. "With wife number two down in Fort Myers."

"Sorry."

"Ah, I'm good with it. I didn't deserve her."

Colson looked down at his hands. "I know what you mean." He looked back to Langston swirling his drink. "I went out on water department property today and took some photos of Cash's beach house."

Langston stared straight ahead and nodded. Colson leaned forward in his chair.

"I don't think you understand, Sheriff. I saw them carry a dead body out of the house, put it in the trunk of a car, and drive away. Then one of his men, Fuller, came after me with a gun."

Langston looked over to Colson. "Looks like you came through all right."

"Better than he did."

"Colson, you'll have to trust me. I know what I'm doing."

"With all due respect, Sheriff, I inform you I've seen a dead body being carried from your target's house and what do you do? Sit on your porch sipping bourbon."

"I can understand why you think that, but I assure you I know what I'm doing. Like I said, we are more alike than you think."

"You'll have to do more to convince me of that. Don't forget I'm a registered voter in Volusia County now."

The sat in silence for what seemed like five minutes. Colson broke the silence. "What's your email address?"

"My email address?"

"Yes."

Langston recited a list of letters and numbers as Colson typed them in his cell phone screen. He continued to push selections on the screen when Langston finished.

"What are you doing?"

"I'm going to send you the photos and names and numbers I found in Fuller's phone later." Colson handed Langston the folded piece of paper with the girl's photo, stood up, and then walked to the kitchen door. "They're no good to me. Do with them what you wish," he said, and disappeared into the house.

Langston took another sip of bourbon and stared at the doghouse. Two wives, two dogs, and no children ago he had been relatively happy. He hadn't been old enough to remember his father, but loved his mother dearly. What she had put up with during her second marriage made him seethe with hatred for his stepfather. His mother married him when Stuart was six years old and he couldn't recall a single moment when she had been happy. Of course she supported and encouraged Stuart through public school and college, and provided his every need.

That was the only reason she married the bastard. For him, so she could give him what a single mother couldn't. But she was privately miserable, being treated like a slave in her own house by both her husband and his son. He didn't dare tell her he was almost as miserable as she was living in that man's house, with him and his equally disgusting stepbrother. He hated them and they hated him in return. The man never adopted him nor gave him his last name. For that, Langston was grateful, but it was the only thing he had been grateful for. He was glad his stepfather was dead. He had driven his mother to an early grave. It was only fitting that he died alone in hospice. Langston didn't attend the funeral and wasn't invited to the reading of the will. Why should he be? The man was leaving him nothing and he had wanted nothing from him. In the months following his stepfather's death, he overheard a couple talking at a restaurant about his stepfather's estate and estimating how much it was worth. He walked up to the couple waiting in line for a table and politely interrupted them,

"I know how much he left," he said.

The man's eyes widened. "You knew the family?"

"A little," Langston replied.

The woman spoke up. "How much did he leave?" she asked in a mysterious tone.

Langston smiled at her. "All of it," he said, and walked away without bothering to see their reaction.

Langston hoped the years and marriages had made him a wiser, more mature man. He had never treated his ex-wives like his stepfather and stepbrother treated his mother. If anything, he felt himself the victim. He thought Reese might have been a good prospect for wife number three, but now he knew better. Any woman who slept with the likes of Pickett wasn't worthy of being with a real cop. He had to focus on his task and not concern himself with women. He had to finish what he set out to do from the first day he was sworn in as sheriff. And that was to see justice done for his community, for himself, and especially for his mother. Lock up the last person alive from her tormented marriage and watch him rot in prison. Better still, that he resist arrest and commit suicide by cop.

Langston gulped his last sip of bourbon and crunched one of the ice cubes. The amber liquid felt warm sliding down his throat. His focus adjusted from the patchy back yard to the screen window as he summoned a picture of his stepbrother from a distant memory. His mind's eye superimposed the image over the screen and there he was. Just as he remembered him the last time he saw him up close before leaving for college. A much younger, but just as evil, Martin Cash.

❦ Chapter Twenty ❦

Pickett couldn't believe his eyes or his luck. He had pulled into the Sundowner parking lot, driven through the breezeway, and nosed into a space at the sea wall. All the close spaces were filled. He would have taken advantage of the privilege of parking the cruiser at the curb to avoid the walk, but there wasn't a curb per se, just spaces along the perimeter of the wall and one row in the middle. The spaces were angled such that you drove under the right breezeway and made a right, driving around the center isle of cars and either selecting a perimeter or middle space.

He glanced in his rearview mirror after shifting the cruiser into park and there she was. He wiped sweat from his eyes and looked again. It was the girl from the photo, no doubt about it. Tina and an older woman in a bathrobe, walking into a condo on the ground floor directly behind him. Maybe he really would be killing two birds with one stone, as he told Deputy Munoz. But how would he do it alone? Colson and the girl. The logistics weren't right. If he went to deal with Colson on the fifth floor, the girl could be gone when he returned. If he grabbed the girl, he couldn't just leave her in the cruiser while confronting Colson about the photos. His hands were trembling again. Pickett punched Cash's contact on his phone. It rang once. An exasperated Martin Cash answered.

"What is it, Pickett?"

"I've got the girl," Pickett said in a nervous, but prideful, tone.

"Well, good job Pickett. You surprise me. Bring her to the house."

"I mean, I know where she is. I'm parked thirty feet from the condo she's in."

"Well, go get her, Pickett. Don't call me until you really have her and are on your way," Cash said, with emphasis on the word "really."

Pickett considered telling Cash to send someone else for the girl so he could confront Colson, but he knew he'd be told to forget about Colson for now and bring the girl. He could hear it in his head as clear as if Cash had already said it. He and Cash had differing objectives, but there had to be a way to satisfy both. In the relatively short amount of time he had known Cash, he knew he only wanted to deal with one thing at a time. He was so hell-bent on finding this girl, nothing else mattered. Colson was more his problem right now than Cash's. He would send Taylor to deal with Colson for his benefit, not Pickett's. Cash made it clear from the start he thought his blackmail idea was ridiculous. No, he had to convince Cash this was about getting the girl quietly, not the photos. If he played it right, he could do both.

"She'll bolt out the back if I go to the front door. From where I am now I can watch the back and almost see if she goes out the front through the breezeway."

"What are you saying?" Cash said.

"I'm saying I don't want to lose her. I need to move the marked car or she'll see it through the glass doors. I need another body down here to cover the back when I go to the front."

"Where the hell are you?" Cash said.

Pickett hesitated. "The Sundowner on A1A."

"The Sundowner? That's where Colson lives. What are you doing, Pickett?"

"I thought you'd be pleased I found her," Pickett said sternly and lost his composure, shouting into the phone. "Now are you going to send help or not, goddamn it?"

Cash held the phone away from his face and looked at it in disbelief. "Where the hell is Taylor?" he shouted to no one in particular. Fuller sat on the couch, scratching the area around the splint on his finger. Cash thought he looked ridiculous with the bandage over his nose.

Fuller mumbled as if he was speaking through a terrible head cold. "I don't know. He hasn't called."

Jason walked into the common room holding his cell. "I've called ten times and it goes straight to voice mail."

Cash looked at Jason and then to Fuller. "Pickett's found Tina. Get your asses over to Colson's condo."

"She's with Colson?" Fuller asked.

"No, but she's in the complex. You'll have to take the SUV. Taylor has the car. Get going."

Fuller pushed himself up from the couch and walked to the counter. He snatched up his keys and went to the side door. "Where is this place?"

Cash said, "Do I need to hold your hand and lead you there? Call Pickett and he'll tell you. It's on the same damn road we're on. Figure it out. You have another gun?"

Fuller nodded and stepped out, mumbling to himself, "A lot of good it will do if I can't shoot left-handed."

Cash walked to the window and watched Fuller and Jason climb into the SUV and drive to the gate. "Where do I find these people?" he said, shaking his head. He set the laptop on the bar and lifted the screen. Once it came to life he typed in an address and waited for the chat room to load. Cash suspected his customer would be anxious for a confirmation and checking the chat room frequently. He grinned and typed "Avid Collector. Confirm pick up of vehicle at time and place agreed to, tomorrow night" and then pressed ENTER.

⚬⚬⚬

Taylor drove the sedan up to the vacuum attendant, put the gear in park, and stepped out. The Hispanic attendant handed him a slip of paper and proceeded to pull the car mats from the floorboard and feed them into a short, boxy machine. It resembled his grandmother's old washing machine's clothes ringer. A second, young Hispanic pulled the mats from the opposite side and began running the vacuum hose over the floorboards at a furious pace. He looked to his left at the cars waiting in line and walked to the rear entrance. The man seated behind dark, tinted windows in the blue pickup two cars back watched Taylor disappear behind the door.

It wasn't unusual for people to take a long look at Taylor because of his massive build, dark sunglasses, business suit, and confident walk. The combination suggested he would be best left alone and given a wide berth. They would look until his dark sunglasses turned in their direction, then—they'd look away. The workers quickly finished the sedan. One jumped in and held the door partially closed as he drove it expertly between the guide rails. Once the roller caught the front wheel, he sprinted back to the next car waiting to be vacuumed. The two young workers repeated their routine with the next car without delay. The man behind the wheel of the pickup truck stuck a toothpick into his mouth and moved up behind the car ahead of him.

Taylor walked down the narrow hall of the car wash. To his right was a half-wall covered with plain, white sheetrock. The wall from his waist up was a solid sheet of glass, allowing customers and amused children to observe vehicles moving through the suds and spinning brushes. A young boy, maybe six or seven, stood on his tiptoes with his nose pressed to the glass ten feet in front of Taylor. He was so mesmerized that he didn't notice the menacing figure walking toward him. He stepped around the boy and into an open waiting and retail area. License plate frames, cup holders, and rearview mirror air fresheners of a dozen varieties hung from metal pegs on the walls and display racks.

He walked to the counter near the front door and handed the clerk his ticket and a ten dollar bill. Through the front glass door he saw three wet cars being attacked by more Hispanics armed with drying towels in each hand. He didn't wait in the air conditioning. He pushed through the door, sat on a wooden bench seat, and watched the attendants run around the cars. The attendants wasted no time drying with both hands, spraying glass cleaner, and applying tire shine.

Taylor had washed and dried more cars than he could remember during his eighteen months in the state prison. State Trooper units, state prison transport vehicles, local sheriff's office patrol cars, unmarked administrator's vehicles, and four-wheel-drive ATVs used for maintenance on the prison campus. He didn't mind the work. The days passed more quickly and he wasn't stuck in his cell. He looked forward to the work details as long as it kept him out of that tiny cell and away from his cellmate. He was a punk, armed robber who constantly bragged about frightening old women with his gun while taking their money and jewelry. Taylor despised the site of him. Had he not maintained self-control, he would still be prison for beating his eyeballs out like the optometrist.

He discovered a way to kill an additional two hours per day after dinner by using the prison law library computer. The Internet access was extremely limited, to keep the convicts from surfing porn sites. Most everything not related to issues of law or educational material was blocked. He made good use of his time. He could no longer fight for a living, but he could learn something new. Something he could be proud of again. So he read everything he could access about computers, software, and websites. After a few months of research, he was confident he could build a website to rival any other. It was a talent he never knew he possessed. He understood code and could write it in his sleep. He could diagnose some software problems, install programs, and speed-up hard drives. But with no technical school diploma, no one would even entertain an interview for a job. The few who did were immediately intimidated by his size and disability. Who wanted a one-eyed ogre as their computer tech guy when there were a thousand to pick from in the struggling economy?

He snapped from his thoughts when he heard the attendant's whistle. He hadn't noticed the sedan being driven out of the wash, and it was ready to go. The attendant stood by the driver's door waving his drying towel as a signal. He stood and shoved his hand into his pocket for a tip. He pulled three objects out. A ten dollar bill, his sales receipt, and a flash drive. He folded the bill and receipt around the flash drive and walked to the attendant, who held out his hand. He slapped the items in his hand a little more forcefully than the attendant expected to ensure he felt the extra bulk. The attendant looked down and squeezed the ten dollar bill, feeling the object inside. He looked back to Taylor and smiled.

"Gracias," he said, and stepped aside.

"Sure," Taylor replied flatly, and dropped into the driver's seat. He pulled into traffic and grabbed his cell phone. It took thirty seconds for the phone to cycle through its routine and load programs. When it finally found a signal, the top information bar flashed an icon. Five missed calls. All from Jason Cash.

A red, compact car rolled slowly from the mouth of the washing tunnel and came to an easy stop against the speed bump at the end of the line. An attendant jumped into the driver's seat and moved it to the center of the lot where two other attendants swarmed it with fresh drying towels. The young, female driver stepped outside with her claim ticket in hand. It took another minute for the next vehicle to emerge from the tunnel. The attendants scurried to keep up the pace.

The man in the ball cap wore a white undershirt, blue jeans, and tennis shoes. He browsed through a car magazine he had no interest in as the attendants worked on the red compact and released it to the young woman. He tossed the magazine on top of the others and walked outside. The blue truck emerged from the tunnel and was now being attacked by the drying attendants. He walked to the truck where one of the attendants was spraying glass cleaner on the inside windshield.

"That's good enough," he said. The attendant looked puzzled.

"Es Bueno," the man replied. The attendant climbed out and trotted around the front of the truck with his hand out. But the man held up his hand for him to stop and waved for the attendant who was drying the rear bumper. The second attendant watched the man peer at him over his sunglasses, remove his ball cap, and hold it out as if asking for a tip of his own. The attendant reached in his pocket, dropped the flash drive in the man's hat and pulled out a folded twenty-dollar bill. The man tossed the ball cap onto the passenger seat and climbed in. He grinned as he shut the door. The two attendants argued under their breath in Spanish about splitting the twenty as the man drove from the lot.

Colson watched the waitress refill his coffee cup and thanked her with a smile. He poured in a little cream, no sugar, and looked through the large window as he swirled the mixture with a spoon. He always tried to park where he could keep an eye on his car. It was nearly twenty years old and not worth ten grand in the blue book, but he still didn't want some hoodlum messing with it. Ann had promised he could buy another Corvette when they were financially able. He had driven one when they dated, but traded it for practical reasons. She was excited for him when they were able to afford a used one after eighteen years of marriage, so the car was special to him. Special because Ann had ridden in it.

"Are you ready to order?" the waitress asked politely.

"No, thanks. Just the coffee."

She walked away and Colson looked back to the parking lot and beyond it to International Speedway Blvd. Traffic was light-to-moderate, moving east and west. He could see the glow of the large "Welcome to Daytona Beach" sign on the over walk, spanning all four lanes and welcoming visitors to the most famous beach in the world. He briefly wondered about the claim, but that's how it was advertised. He took a sip of coffee and sighed. It had all been a waste of time and energy. It was like trying to put together a child's puzzle with two or three pieces missing. It couldn't be that complicated, but no clear picture was emerging from the few pieces of the puzzle he'd found.

The encounter with Cash and his punk son, Jason. Being duped into taking surveillance photos and sucked into an investigation of Cash by Langston's organized crime unit. Then to learn Reserve Sergeant Pickett had set up the meeting for some insane reason. He was obviously delusional. But the real disappointment was Sheriff Langston. Until tonight he assumed Langston was honest and on the ball. Why had he reacted so nonchalantly with the information and photos? You don't sit on your porch drinking bourbon when you receive that kind information, especially when you are already working on it as a top priority. Even Sergeant Cantrell didn't question him extensively that afternoon on the beach. Just a strong suggestion that he stay away from the investigation. Were they incompetent, dirty, or just lazy? There had to be another possibility.

He stood and dropped a ten dollar bill next to the half-empty coffee cup and gave the waitress a wave on his way out. Whatever the reason, it was a missing piece of the puzzle he was never going to find because he was going to stop looking. The thick night air smelled good. Heat radiated around his legs from the asphalt cooling from another hot day. He hadn't been to the beach in days, but that would change tomorrow.

✌❀

Tina closed her eyes and let the water run on her face and through her hair. She washed her hair for the third time, just to spend a little more time in the shower. She stepped out, dried her hair with a towel, and wrapped herself in it. The small bathroom was steamy, but she didn't care. She flipped on the exhaust fan and combed out her hair. The sweat and salty humidity washed away, she walked into the guest bedroom where Mrs. Cox laid out a clean pair of shorts and t-shirt. A pair of tennis shoes and socks lay on the floor at the foot of the bed. The woman had been very nice. They had talked while Tina devoured two sandwiches, a half bag of potato chips, and a large glass of cold milk. Mrs. Cox had done all the talking. About her husband the preacher and their daughter who still lived up north and never visited.

She was a gracious but lonely woman who just needed someone to talk to, or talk at was more accurate. She told her the clothes belonged to her daughter. She moved them here in hopes she would need them when and if she ever came. They fit perfectly. The tennis shoes were about a half-size too large, but they would do. She sat on the edge of the bed and slipped them on. The bed felt comfortable under her. She wanted to lie down and sleep for a week in the dark coolness of the room, but she had to see if Colson would help her. She walked out of the bedroom. Mrs. Cox still wore her bathrobe, sitting on the couch with her legs pulled up under her. She looked over the magazine she was reading.

"Those fit fine, dear. And the shoes?"

Tina smiled. "They're fine too. Thank you for everything."

"You're very welcome. You look like you feel so much better. A good shower always does that." She patted the couch with her hand "Come have a seat. We can finish what we were talking about."

Tina hesitated. "I really want to, and again I appreciate everything, but I really need to talk to Colson."

"But he's not home, dear. Remember"?

"Maybe he came in while we were eating or while I was in the shower. We wouldn't have been able to see him pull in the garage."

"I guess so," Faye said. "I could call but I don't have his number. He never seems to have time to talk for very long. No one does."

Tina saw the disappointment in Faye's eyes and could hear the loneliness in her voice. She had only known this woman for ninety minutes and it felt like she was her grandmother. She glanced around the room. On a small table by the couch was an eight-by-ten photograph in a brass frame. A much younger Faye Cox with a stocky, serious-looking man. The man was standing behind a seated Faye, his arm around her right shoulder. To the left of Faye stood a young girl with long, straight hair in ponytails. The man looked like what she pictured a preacher would. Standing straight and official in his three-piece suit. Faye and their daughter were modestly dressed up to the neck. Faye's hair was a poufy brown like pictures of women she had seen from the 1970s. Faye followed Tina's glance.

"Look at that old picture," Faye said, lifting it from the table and pointing. "The Reverend Cox and our daughter, Carol."

Tina smiled and nodded. "It's a nice photo of you."

"I was much younger then. This was taken for our church directory. That was when everyone had a church directory of all the families. Do they still do that?"

"I don't know," Tina said. "I really don't remember going to church."

Faye's eyes widened a little. "Really? Well, I haven't been since Mr. Cox passed. Sometimes I think it's overrated."

Faye held the frame at arm's length and examined it. Tina heard a slight sniffle and suspected she had probably gone months without even noticing it. Now the memories were coming back and it was her fault. She knew what it was like being nineteen and being alone. She couldn't bear the thought of being alone at Faye's age.

"Faye. Can I ask one more favor?"

Faye seemed to snap from a daydream and looked at her. "Of course, dear."

"I just need to talk to Colson for a little while. I don't even know if he can help, but maybe he can give me some advice. I still need a place to stay tonight. Could I possibly use your guest room? We could talk some more tonight if you like."

Faye beamed a smile. "Absolutely! I think I have cake mix in the kitchen. You go on up and see if he's home and I'll get started."

Faye walked to the kitchen area and began opening cabinet doors. Tina followed her through the small kitchen and reached for the handle.

"Oh, no dear," Faye said. "Just go out the front door, turn right, and walk to the elevator. It's shorter."

"Okay."

Tina turned and went out the front and down the hall. She rounded the corner to her left and saw the elevator door closing, but the young woman inside noticed her at the last moment and held it for her. Tina smiled and thanked the woman with the rolling suitcase at her feet. She looked at the bank of buttons to the right of the door. Number five was lit. The young woman held her hand out as if to press another floor.

"Which floor?"

"Same. Fifth. Thanks," Tina replied.

∽

The breezeway was located on the far right side of the complex if viewed from the street. Yellow PVC pipes hung horizontally from short chains above both the entrance and exit lanes with "8 FT" in black lettering to warn drivers of the maximum clearance. Pickett stood by an island planted with a ten-foot palm tree and neatly manicured flowers. He looked at his watch for the fourth time in as many minutes. He couldn't watch both the front and back doors of the condo from anywhere he positioned himself. His best guess was the girl would leave the same way she entered. Through the back sliding doors. The only thing he could do until Fuller arrived was to act like an impatient husband waiting for his wife to meet him at the car. He didn't have to pretend to appear impatient and even somewhat frustrated. He nervously hoped to God the girl hadn't left while he moved the sheriff's cruiser to the opposite side of the complex. It took no longer than a minute, so the odds were on his side.

He paid little attention to the dark compact car coming through the breezeway. It slowed at the bright yellow speed bumps and parked in an open parking space in the middle row. He looked over the car at the burnt orange sky above the ocean and kept the sliding doors in his peripheral vision. The young, slender woman distracted his thoughts for a moment when she stepped out of the car and pulled a rolling bag from the back seat. She wore brown slacks and a modest blouse. Her hair was dark brown and a little longer than shoulder length. And she was beautiful. She extended the handle on the suitcase and pulled it behind her. She glanced up at the building as she walked in his direction. They exchanged a polite grin and nod before she walked through the breezeway and disappeared down the inner hallway.

Nichole was tired. More from her finals than the drive to Hartsfield-Jackson airport. The added aggravation of security and the long wait at the terminal didn't help. At least the rental car process went well and she had arrived just before dark. She called Bobby from the rental lot, but decided not to call Dad. He would be so surprised. She expected to see him sitting on the balcony as usual, but he wasn't there. She smiled as the familiar aroma of the ocean wafted around her. This was her second home, even if it had only been for one week a year. Her friends didn't understand why she enjoyed vacationing at the same place every year. Most of them visited extravagant resorts and booked a variety of cruises, returning with fascinating stories, photographs, and souvenirs. But she was glad it was different for her. She had lifelong memories of a familiar home away from home. A place she would bring her children and make new memories as she had with her parents. She walked to the elevator with a smile.

∽∾

Cash grinned when his account balance appeared on the computer screen ten thousand dollars fatter than the previous day. Avid Collector didn't waste time locking in his purchase and transferring the deposit. His last customer must have been satisfied with Kara, and he was slowly building a reputation. He wished he had gotten into the business years ago. The money would have been endless and tax-free. They say recessions bring out the best in the entrepreneurial spirit. He closed the laptop and walked to the window. Jason and Fuller better not screw this up. The house perimeter lights illuminated a fifty-foot halo around the beach house against the darkness of the lawn and driveway beyond. Two gatepost lamps brightened a small area where the long driveway met A1A. He watched the headlights and tail lights of vehicles blink past the iron gates. Then a set of lights turned toward the gate and stopped. Cash squinted for a better look as the gates began to swing inward and the vehicle moved down the long driveway. "Taylor," Cash mumbled. He met him at the side door.

"Where the hell have you been?" he demanded. Taylor walked around him into the media room, draped his suit jacket over a chair, and sat.

"I was taking care of business, and then ran the car through the wash."

"Where the hell did you go, Tampa? And why didn't you answer the dozen times we called?"

"Look Mr. Cash," Taylor said. "Sorry about the phone, but the battery went dead and I didn't realize it. I took care of the problem the right way. No one will ever be the wiser. I thought you would be pleased."

Cash sat in his recliner. "What about the friend who helped you? Dragging a witness in was a bad idea."

Taylor shook his head. "I was alone. I have access to his place."

"What place?"

"Let's just say he's in the funeral home industry."

Cash snapped his head up at the smart tone in Taylor's reply. When he asked a question, he expected a straightforward, respectful answer. Not some ambiguous, flippant answer from an employee who suddenly has an attitude and apparently thinks he's some sort of partner. He stood, but didn't walk over to the former ultimate fighter. His anger hadn't yet turned into blatant stupidity.

"Let's just say HELL, smartass. Let's say that we do things my way from now on. This isn't the Terrible Taylor show. It's the Martin Cash show. I let you do this your way, but that was before you decided to start playing games with me. When I call, I expect you to answer. And when I ask you a specific question, you damned well better give me a specific answer. Is that clear enough for you?"

Taylor nodded.

"Jason and Fuller have gone to pick up Tina."

Taylor's eyes widened. "They found her?"

"Pickett says he did. Over at the complex Colson lives in. It's too much of a coincidence. You're going to have to deal with Colson sooner rather than later. I hope you left that incinerator on when you left."

Taylor stood and grabbed his jacket. "You need me to meet them there?"

"No. First things first. You have enough to do getting ready for tomorrow night at the pier. I don't want you doing anything else tonight to draw attention. After tomorrow, you take care of Colson."

Taylor walked to the side door. "I'll set everything up at the rental house."

"You do that."

❧ Chapter Twenty-One ❦

Sheriff Langston was still sitting on the porch when his cell phone rang. He turned up the small glass and let the last of the bourbon slip into his mouth while fumbling with the phone.

"Go ahead," he said.

"It's Sergeant Cantrell, Sheriff. I know we've been pulled off the Cash case, but there's been a development."

"What kind of development?"

"Mike Beavers has been found dead in Biggins parking lot. It's clearly a homicide."

"Beavers? Isn't he the former cop who hired Colson to take photos at the Rayford Inn?"

"The very same."

Langston was silent in thought for a moment, *Why would anyone kill Beavers? Surely it wasn't over a couple of worthless photographs. Sergeant Cantrell said Colson didn't give the photos to Beavers. What nut case would...*

"Sheriff," Cantrell said, "are you there?"

"Pickett," Langston said. "Did anyone see a motorcycle near the scene?"

"I haven't been able to identify any witnesses. The place was practically deserted when we believe the murder occurred. Do you really think Pickett..."

"Right now he's the main suspect," Langston said. "He knows he's going to get canned for misconduct and interfering with the investigation and he's the only connection with Beavers crazy enough to lose control."

"Since I've been reassigned, you want me to notify Lieutenant Reese?"

"No. You communicate directly with me," Langston ordered. "Lieutenant Reese is in bed with him, literally, and he'll find out we suspect him if she knows. Send an unmarked car out to look for him. Two detectives. Remember, the crazy bastard is armed."

"And when we locate him?"

"You call me. We don't know what kind of forensic evidence we have on scene. We'll need all we can get. If he killed Beavers he'll be acting erratic."

"I'll get a unit on the way to his house," Cantrell said.

Langston said, "Send another unit to Colson's condo. If he was pissed enough to kill Beavers over a couple of photos he didn't deliver, Colson may be the next logical stop."

Cantrell stepped to the sidewalk and looked north on A1A. Colson's complex was too far north to see, but only a fifteen minute drive at most. His conversation with Colson had been short, but it didn't take long for Cantrell to like the man. He seemed like someone he would have enjoyed working for. He hoped the sheriff was wrong about Pickett. He didn't like or even respect him, but any time a law enforcement officer is involved in a crime, it makes them all look bad. People like Pickett were the reason law enforcement officers had to constantly struggle for the respect and cooperation of citizens who were tired of being talked down to like children. Their perception was that all cops were just alike.

"We're about finished here. The medical examiner's on-call investigator has taken the body and I've got a uniform supervisor making the death notification. I'll check on Colson myself."

He pocketed his phone and jogged to his car.

ℳ

Nichole paid little attention to the girl riding the elevator with her. She might have recognized a few faces of those who vacationed during week twenty-three, but she had no idea what week this was on the vacation calendar. She remembered Dad saying they were there to relax, not socialize. He and Mom had never been social animals.

The door slid open on the fifth floor. Nicole pulled her suitcase behind her and started down the exterior hallway. She didn't sense anything out of the ordinary until she passed the unit just before 510. She could hear the scratch of tennis shoes on the concrete as she neared the condo door, knowing the girl was either going to the stairwell or to her

206

dad's place. There was no reason to go to the stairwell when she could have easily taken the elevator to any floor. She stopped short of the door and turned. The girl stopped abruptly behind her.

Nichole said, "Are you looking for someone in particular?"

"Ah," Tina hesitated. "I was looking for Mr. Colson."

"He's my father. And you are?"

"My name is Tina. He may not remember me and I don't think he knows my name."

Nichole felt a lump in her throat for a moment. What would this girl want with Dad and why would he know her and not her name? Maybe she should have listened to Bobby, but surely Dad wouldn't be in some sort of perverted relationship with this teenager. She was afraid to ask, but did anyway.

"How do you know my...Mr. Colson?"

Tina looked down at her feet. "A few weeks ago he helped me when he saw a boy slap me on the beach. I got away from him for good a few days ago and now he's after me. I didn't know at the time that Mr. Colson had been a policeman and I came to ask him for advice."

"Why not go to the police here in Daytona? That would be the best thing for you to do."

Tina looked up at Nichole. "I can't."

"Why not?"

"Because they will arrest me."

"For what?"

"Something that was not my fault in Alabama last year."

Tina crossed her arms as if hugging herself and tears welled in her eyes. She looked down again, hoping Nichole wouldn't notice.

"I thought this was a bad idea. I shouldn't have bothered you. I'm sorry."

Tina spun on her heels and started back down the hallway. Nichole watched her for a moment, wondering if this girl was telling the truth. She knew what her dad would have done if he had ever seen a boy slap her. As mild mannered as he was, any act of violence against her or Ann would have been met by an immediate and equally as violent reaction from her father. Nothing like that had ever occurred, but she had no doubt.

Nichole said, "Wait."

Tina stopped and turned.

"Let me knock. There's no reason you can't speak to him at the door."

Nichole knocked, waited, and then knocked again. Tina stood behind her against the railing, looking out at the red, blue, and green neon lights of souvenir shops and restaurants on A1A. Cars and motorcycles moved north and south at a lazy pace. She pictured Taylor or Jason or Randy driving one of the cars, looking side-to-side at pedestrians walking along the sidewalk, hoping to find her. She thought about Kara and wondered what they had done with her. Whatever it was, she didn't want the same fate, no matter what. Cash wasn't running a home for wayward girls with the intent of helping them. Nothing but bad things would have happened if she stayed or if they found her now. She heard Nichole knock for the third time.

Tina said, "Faye said he probably wouldn't be home."

Nichole turned. "Faye? Who's...never mind. I have a key. We can sit on the balcony and wait for him."

Tina grinned. "You don't mind?"

Nichole shook her head. "It's okay. I don't have a clue what Dad's up to, but he's always getting into some project." Nichole fumbled for a key in her purse, unlocked the door, and stepped in. She dropped the key in her purse and pulled out her cell phone. "I'll call him."

Tina followed and pushed the door closed with a click.

Colson got to his car and dropped into the driver's seat. He usually wouldn't drink coffee this late, but the caffeine gave him a little burst of energy. He started the engine and slipped in one of his favorite CDs. The '80s rock band was perfect for the ride home, but something was missing. He looked up through the smoked-glass roof panel and smiled. He hadn't driven around this late for a long time. Most of his evenings were spent enjoying the sights and sounds of the ocean from five floors above the sand. It was a little muggy, but the breeze would break that up on the drive home.

He opened the center console, removed the small ratchet stored inside, and loosened the two bolts holding down the roof panel on the driver's side. He climbed out and moved to the passenger side to repeat the process, and then he lifted the rear hatch. He laid the roof panel in the brackets behind the seats, closed the hatch, and got back in.

The Corvette was practically a convertible now. He lowered both windows and cranked up the music. The factory speakers were top-notch for 1994 and sounded crisp and full. The last time he had gone to the trouble to remove the roof panel, he and Ann were driving home from a craft show. He couldn't remember the subject of their conversation, but they laughed like teenagers all the way home. It began when he rolled up parallel to some kid in a tricked out, low-riding Honda with a muffler designed to make it sound faster than it ever hoped to be.

The kid looked over at Colson and revved his engine. In a flashback from his teenage years, Colson felt possessed and instinctively floored the gas, jerking him and Ann back in their seats. He could hear the Honda scream with agony as the young kid tried to gain ground and overtake him, but it was to no avail. His better judgment slowed him down about a quarter of a mile later when he lost sight of the Honda. He could sense Ann glaring at him and expected her to complain about him acting juvenile and say he should know better. Instead, they both just laughed.

He grinned at the thought when he pulled to the exit of the parking lot. He paused and looked both ways. If he turned east on International Speedway, he would be home in fifteen minutes. Simply not enough time to enjoy the ride. He turned west and gunned the engine toward I-95. He hung his arm out the door and relaxed into his seat. The weather and music were perfect. The humid breeze buffeted around him and the car sounded like a purring monster. He never heard his cell phone ringing in the console.

ᔐᔐ

Pickett saw the SUV turn into the lot off of A1A and park next to a dumpster near the entrance of the breezeway. The driver's side door opened and Jason slid out of the seat. He waved them over when Fuller came into view from the other side. The bandages on Fuller's nose and hand stood out in the reflection of the florescent lights of the breezeway.

Pickett said, "You look like hell, Fuller. What happened?"

"Colson happened. I'll tell you about it later, but I look better than he will when I find his ass. Let's get this done so we can get the hell out of here. Where is she?"

"This ground floor condo," Pickett said and nodded toward the sliding glass doors twenty feet away. "She should still be in there. I couldn't cover the front, but I can see enough of the front from here if she went out that way."

Fuller looked at the sliding doors. Vertical blinds hung across the entire length of the glass. Thin slits of interior light escaped between the individual blinds being disturbed by either an air vent or people inside moving around them.

Fuller said, "She hasn't seen you before. You should go to the front. We'll watch the back."

Fuller looked Pickett up and down and said, "Where's your uniform?"

"I've been busy," Pickett snarled, and walked through the breezeway to the front.

ᘒᘒ

Faye Cox hummed one of her favorite southern gospel songs and set the oven temperature to three hundred fifty degrees. She poured globs of yellowish batter into the pans, slid them in the oven, and set the timer. She smiled when she heard a knock. She adjusted her robe and fast-walked to the front door.

"I told you he wasn't home," Faye said as she pulled the door open. Her smile vanished at the sight of the man holding a wallet open in front of him. A gold, seven-pointed star reflected from the hall light just inside the door. She instinctively began to shut the door, but the man stopped it with his free hand.

Pickett said, "Sheriff's office ma'am. I need to speak with you."

Faye grasped the top collar of her robe and held it closed tight under her chin. "About what?"

Pickett glanced past Faye into the condo. The short hall opened up to a living area with cream colored floor tile and light yellow walls. The back glass doors were visible. There was no other way out.

"Let's step inside," Pickett said and pushed the door open.

Faye took a step back as the door swung closed. Pickett gave it a quick shove to ensure it was locked.

Faye said, "I asked you what this was about."

"And I told you we had to talk."

Pickett reached back, lifted his gun from the small of his back, and pointed the muzzle in Faye's face. She went pale and propped herself against the wall with her free hand. She had never owned a gun, held a gun, or even seen one close up. The muzzle of the nine-millimeter pistol looked like a cannon. She wanted to scream, but she was too shocked to even speak. Pickett waved the gun toward the living room.

"Sit down over there and be quiet," he ordered.

Pickett watched Faye stumble backwards and catch her balance on the coffee table. She sat on the couch and pulled her legs up under her. She was visibly shaking and her lips quivered. Pickett took a quick glance into the bedroom to his left and went straight for the sliding glass door. He slid it open and motioned Fuller and Jason inside.

Faye felt like she was having an out-of-body experience she had read about in books. What was happening could not be real. Her heart pounded as adrenaline raced through her body. The edges of her vision began to darken and she was light headed. She was looking but not seeing. Sounds and voices were muffled. The air was too thick to breathe and she was both cold and hot simultaneously. Her eyes were locked on an intersection of grout, dividing four pieces of tile against the far wall. She was too terrified to look away. Then the feeling of being strapped into a roller coaster on rough wooden rails and someone seated next to her screaming in terror. But what were they saying?

"Where is she? Where is she?"

Faye looked up from the tile against the wall at the dirty hand squeezing her right bicep, and then to the face of Randy Fuller. Two blackened, bloodshot eyes filled with hate, divided by white gauze. She cut her eyes left where he pressed down on her shoulder with a rough hand in a plaster cast. Not the first man, but another hideous madman.

This time Faye didn't try to scream. The sound rose from her diaphragm on its own, without her being aware.

The shrill scream made the hairs on Jason's neck stand up. The woman had been quietly sitting in a fetal position until Fuller starting shaking her. Tina was gone again. They had searched the small, two-bedroom condo quickly. In each closet, both bathrooms, under the sink, and under the beds. She simply was not there. Jason stepped next to Fuller and slapped the woman hard.

"Shut up, bitch!"

She wasn't fazed at all and didn't stop. It was as if she didn't need to take a breath. Jason grabbed a throw pillow off the couch and covered her face. Fuller pushed her over on the couch, onto her back, but the muffled screams continued. Jason leaned his weight hard on the pillow, muffling the sound further. Fuller sat his weight on her stomach.

"Shut up, damn it!"

The screaming turned to moaning, then to gasping, then to nothing. Jason took his weight off the pillow and Fuller stood. Pickett stood watching from the hall after completing a second search of the condo.

"Let's go," he said.

Fuller said, "You said she was here."

"She was here," Pickett shouted "but she's not here now, is she? Let's get out of here."

"Where are we going?"

"We are not going anywhere. You two go out to the SUV and wait."

Jason said, "Where are you going, Pickett?"

Pickett turned and walked to the front door. He eased it open a crack and listened, then pulled it open all the way and looked down the exterior hallway. Fuller and Jason moved up behind him.

Pickett said, "I'm going upstairs."

≫ Chapter Twenty-Two ≪

Tina followed Nichole inside. The condo had clean, tan walls and the same tile as Faye's place, but the layout was different. Instead of the kitchen area being in the rear, leading out the sliding doors, it was on the right as they entered. Nichole pulled her suitcase into the first door on the left and stepped back into the living room. Tina walked to the sliding doors and looked out over the ocean. The comfortable coolness of the condo kept her from opening the door and stepping onto the balcony.

"By the way, my name is Nichole."

Tina turned and smiled. Nichole slipped off her shoes and sat back in a recliner. She looked around the modest room with the one recliner, a couch, and a coffee table fashioned to look like old ship planks. A modern flat-screen television hung on the opposite wall above an entertainment center that didn't match the coffee table theme.

Tina said, "These condos are nice."

Nichole looked around the room. "I've been coming here all my life for vacation. They renovated about five years ago. Everything is new, including the walls and floors, with the exception of some of the salvaged furniture."

"How long was your dad a cop…ah, policeman?"

Nichole closed her eyes as if trying to remember. "For as long as I remember."

Tina nodded. She looked at the two photos on the entertainment cabinet. She recognized Colson and Nichole. The attractive woman with them had to be her mother.

"Does your mother live here or are they divorced?"

Nichole's eyes dropped. "She died late last year. It was just before Christmas."

"I'm really sorry."

Tina walked to the couch and sat down. The cushions felt hard, as if the couch was there for decoration only. She felt awkward after the last question and hoped Nichole would break the silence or turn on the television. They sat in silence. Before she could think of something else to say, they both impulsively jerked at the loud knock at the door.

Nichole snapped her head to Tina. "Is there someone with you?"

Tina shook her head. "No."

Nichole squinted. "Are you sure?"

"I'm not lying. There's no one with me."

Nichole stood and walked to the door on the balls of her feet. She swung the bar lock over the door peg and put her ear close to the metal door. She was startled by another knock and stepped back. The thick, steel door deadened the sound of traffic on A1A, but it amplified the sound of someone knocking to the point it could wake the dead. She moved back to the door and held her ear close.

"Who is it?"

"Sheriff's office for Mr. Colson."

Nichole looked behind her. Tina now stood in the middle of the living room, watching her.

"He isn't home. Who are you exactly?"

"Detective Pickett, ma'am. It's very important that I speak with him."

Nichole turned the deadbolt and opened the door until the locking bar caught it. The tall man was wearing a dark polo shirt, khaki pants, and tennis shoes. His brown hair was cut short and neat, but he hadn't shaved in a couple of days. His brown eyes looked sincere but tired. The gold star he held looked familiar. Nichole had seen many. They were commonplace around the house, but she had never examined one closely. He held his wallet closer to the three-inch opening. Nichole thought the badge looked genuine and substantial like her father's, not a cheap imitation. She glanced at the identification card to the left and caught the name Pickett and Sergeant.

Nichole said, "I thought you were a detective."

"Detective sergeant," Pickett said flatly.

Nichole nodded. Her dad had been a detective sergeant once. Years ago when she was eight or nine years old. She looked up at Pickett as he slid his wallet back into his pocket.

"I saw you downstairs," Tina said

"Yes ma'am. I had to wait for my partner."

"What's going on with my dad? Is he all right?"

Pickett glanced at his watch and said, "That's what I'm here to find out. There's not much time and I need to see him. It's vital I talk to him now. May I ask who you are?"

"I'm his daughter, Nichole."

"Then you're in danger as much as he is. Please ma'am, can we speak inside?"

Nichole's eyes widened "Danger? Danger of what? This is crazy."

Pickett glanced back at the front parking lot and back to Nichole.

"Do me a favor. If that's the bedroom window, go look out to the front parking lot. You'll see where I parked my patrol car."

Nichole nodded and closed the door. She was back ten seconds later, flipped the bar lock, and then opened the door. Pickett nodded and stepped inside. He saw a nervous Tina sitting on the edge of the couch cushion with her hands folded on her lap. His heart rate climbed. He had to think on the fly. How to do this quietly?

Nichole paced in front of the sliding doors until Pickett stopped in the middle of the room. He took the opportunity to look around the living room and kitchen. The door to the bedroom he passed was open. The bed was made and a suitcase sat just inside the door. The bedroom door directly to his left was also open with another made up bed. Colson didn't seem the type to hide. Criminals hide, not retired cops. They get in your face and want to know what the hell is going on. The daughter was telling the truth. Colson wasn't here. But where could the photos be? The only pictures he saw were propped on the entertainment center under the television. One eight-by-ten of Colson, a woman who was probably his wife, and a younger Nichole. The other was a three-by-five of an older Nichole in a graduation gown, smiling from ear to ear.

Nichole said, "Tell me what's going on."

Pickett took a breath and looked from Nichole to Tina and back to Nichole, taking time to formulate his answer.

"We've been working on a criminal case and have a wiretap on a man named Martin Cash." Pickett saw Tina sit up straighter at the mention of the name. He could see this story might actually work. He felt a sudden exhilaration as if he really was a detective sergeant working a case. His fatigue turned into a relaxed confidence. He continued as though he was giving court testimony.

"Your dad was a witness in an assault case involving his son."

Nichole said, "Why would we be in danger for that?"

Pickett held his hand up. "That's not all. Let me finish, please. We're investigating Cash for more serious crimes, and Mr. Colson became involved after Cash and one of his men tried to intimidate him and keep him from pursuing the assault complaint."

Tina broke her silence. "That sounds like them."

Tina sat with her hands folded in her lap, but she now rested her back against the couch.

Nichole said, "That's who you were talking about? The one who hit you at the beach and is looking for you?"

Tina nodded.

"And today," Pickett continued, "Mr. Colson assaulted one of Cash's men."

Nichole put her hands on her hips and glared at Pickett. "That's crazy. My father wouldn't..."

Pickett raised his hand again. "I'm not saying it wasn't justified, just that it happened. The reason I'm here is to place him in protective custody. The information we received from the wiretap tonight was that Cash is sending his men here." He made a show of looking at his watch again. "We have to get you two out of here now."

Nichole said, "And go where?"

"Just to the substation for now."

"But what about my dad?"

"There's an unmarked detective unit with me. I'll wait here for your father and escort him to meet you as soon as he arrives."

Nichole dropped her arms to her side and sighed. "I can't believe this. How did Dad get involved in this? He hasn't been down here two months."

"Please," Pickett insisted. "Take whatever valuables you need and let's go to the station. My partner can answer any other questions you have on the way."

Nichole reluctantly walked to the bedroom and unzipped a side pocket on the suitcase. She pulled out a clutch wallet, went back into the living room, and noticed Tina still sitting on the couch.

Nichole said, "You can't stay here anyway, and running away is not the answer. Let's go."

Tina stood and followed Nichole to the door. Pickett walked close to the entertainment center, palmed the small photo of Nichole, and held it to his side. He followed Nichole and Tina out the door. He pulled the door almost closed, allowing the latch to click as it contacted the stop plate, but not catch.

The three made their way down the exterior hallway to the elevators. He glanced over the rail and saw the dark SUV parked along the sidewalk. He couldn't see through the dark-tinted windows, but could feel Jason and Fuller watching the walkway expectantly. They stepped into the elevator and Pickett checked his watch for the third time. The first two times were for show and he hadn't even noticed the time. Now it was 9:23 p.m. He stepped out with Nichole and Tina in tow and they followed him to the SUV.

Pickett hesitated before opening the rear door for Nichole "We'll have you back here as soon as the threat has been eliminated. I'll call the station when I make contact with your dad."

Nichole nodded and he opened the door. The interior was dark as she climbed in. She was so caught up in the bizarre story, she didn't notice the dome light hadn't come on inside. The vehicle interior was large, making it easy for her to step over the middle console and make room for Tina. Nichole felt a light breeze of cool air blow against her legs from low-mounted vents. Other than random car headlights moving along A1A, they sat in darkness and silence.

The door shut with a dull thump. A silhouette of the driver's arm moved the SUV gear down to the "D" and they moved slowly to the exit. Nichole looked over to Tina. She could see the outline of her face against the glowing vertical sign of the Sundowner. Black lettering at the bottom of the sign hadn't changed since she and her parents first stayed there. It simply read: "Welcome Home."

The SUV turned south on A1A and picked up speed. Nichole could make out the shape of the front passenger turning in his seat and reaching up to the headliner above the middle console. There was the sound of a soft click and sudden light from the ceiling. The man with the bandaged nose had moved into an awkward position in his seat and held a gun in his left hand, pointed at her stomach. Tina gasped, grabbed the door handle, and jerked violently. Nichole's heart began to race at the macabre scene of the bandaged man.

Randy Fuller looked back and forth between Tina and Nichole, moving the gun from side to side.

"Stop it, bitch. You can't get out and you know I'll shoot you before you get away again. The doors are locked, so keep your mouths shut and be still."

Nichole was paralyzed. She focused on the gun, then back to the passenger. His eyes told her he was seriously pissed and meant what he said. The only sound now was the whirr of the tires on the road and Tina's muffled crying. She looked to see Tina bent over in her seat with her face in her hands. Then she felt eyes on her from the rearview mirror. She looked up and met the driver's eyes.

Jason said, "What's your name, sweet thing?"

Pickett cursed and slammed the condo door. If the photos were inside, he couldn't find them. He looked in every drawer, cabinet, cubbyhole, under both beds, and between the sheets. Colson didn't have a reason to suspect anyone would ransack his apartment, so where could they be unless he destroyed them? But he had something just as good. Nichole. If the photos still existed, Colson would tell him where they are. The last resort was the laptop he found on the kitchen counter. Pickett carried it to the cruiser, sat in the driver's seat, and opened the laptop. As expected, a little box demanding a password appeared when it powered up. He closed the top and dropped the computer onto the passenger seat.

⇝ Chapter Twenty-Three ⇜

Sergeant Cantrell saw the patrol car pull out of the Sundowner from an eighth of a mile south on A1A. He sped up his unmarked sedan. The patrol car shot past him. Cantrell could not read the small unit numbers through his rear view mirror. He lifted the radio microphone.

"OCU unit to the county unit southbound on A1A from the Sundowner condos."

No response. Cantrell repeated his request. "OCU unit to the sheriff's unit that just left the Sundowner condos, respond."

He waited, but again no response.

A female radio operator transmitted. "Radio to OCU unit, no calls have been received from that location and no units are on the log as being in or out of service at that location."

Cantrell said, "10-4," and replaced the microphone in its clip on the dash. For a moment he had thought something already happened to Colson, but it must have been just a routine patrol by a young deputy who had his head up his ass and not listening to the radio. He turned into the lot and parked.

Pickett heard Cantrell's call loud and clear but ignored it. He couldn't have seen the unit number going the opposite direction, especially at night, or he would have called it specifically. Why in hell would the OCU unit care about him pulling out of the Sundowner? Pickett pondered the possibilities. Unless they had put it all together. Pickett, Cash, Colson, and Beavers.

"No," Pickett said aloud. "They're not that good and not that quick."

He dismissed the idea and continued south, hopeful that the photos were on the laptop. He was confident Cash would be impressed by his cunning capture of Tina. And the bonus of Nichole would take Colson off his back. It was a win-win scenario unless Jason and Fuller got there and tried to take all the credit. Pickett pushed the cruiser to catch up to the SUV. No one was going to take the credit but him.

"Damn it!" Pickett barked when he saw the green Corvette shoot past him on the opposite side of A1A. The speed of the low vehicle caught his eye as it swung left off of Dunlawton Avenue a fraction of a second before the light went from yellow to red. There was no mistaking Colson in the glow of the streetlights with the roof panel off. Colson was spinning the steering wheel with one hand and the resting the other on the side mirror, like a teenager on spring break. "That prick!" Pickett said, and hit the switch to activate the blue LED light bar. He braked and spun the wheel to whip the cruiser through a U-turn.

"Well, hell," Colson said to the rearview mirror when the cruiser crossed the center turn lane. He didn't bust the light, but did take the intersection a little fast. He sighed, turned on his blinker, and pulled into the Treasure Island Hotel parking lot before the cruiser even got close. Why wait when it was obvious who he was after? He turned the radio and engine off and waited as the cruiser pulled in behind him. He pulled his license and insurance card from his wallet and dropped his retirement identification in the console. He wished he had taken the time to get his Florida license.

Colson didn't want special treatment and would rather take the ticket and be on his way. He placed both hands on the steering wheel to put the officer at ease as he approached. But something suddenly made Colson uneasy. The blue LED lights went off. It didn't make sense. They were in a parking lot, so traffic safety wasn't an issue, but that wasn't the only reason officers leave their lights on for the duration of a traffic stop. It's about officer safety. If help is needed, the emergency lights are a constant beacon for back-up units to find you fast, especially at night.

The figure of a man exited the cruiser and quickly approached his window. No slowing to check the hatch, no flashlight in hand, and he was wearing civilian clothes. Colson dropped his hands from the wheel as the man stopped, turned, and leaned his back against the car behind the driver's door. Pickett nonchalantly looked over his shoulder at Colson.

Colson said, "You know, Pickett. I just can't seem to enjoy myself down here for you stopping me every other week. I would complain to the sheriff, but I'm convinced he's as incompetent as you are."

Pickett spun. He placed one hand on the corner of the windshield and the other on the roof post behind Colson's head. He leaned forward and glared at Colson.

"You listen to me, smart ass. This isn't about you and your little green go-cart this time. You owe me two photos that you were paid to take."

Colson said, "It's going to hurt my feelings if you tell me you weren't happy with the ones I sent? I thought they were quite fitting and I wanted you to have them for free. But since you just stopped to chat, Reserve Sergeant Pickett, why are you not in uniform? Surely that's against policy. But then again, I'd be surprised if Langston even had a policy—"

"Shut up!" Pickett shouted. "Get out of the car!"

He put his hands back on the wheel. "Let me explain so even you can understand it, Pickett. This is the way it works. You can bitch me out or write me a citation, but not both. If you're not putting paper on me, then the bitch session is over and I'm leaving. So either get to writing or get to driving."

Pickett pulled the Glock from behind his back and leveled it at Colson's head. "You're not going anywhere smartass. Now get out of the car."

"Am I under arrest?"

"No, I'm just going to shoot if you don't do it now. Keep your left hand on the wheel and open your door from the outside with your right."

"So you did learn something in the academy. I'm proud of you Pickett."

Pickett shouted, "Do it NOW!"

Colson did as instructed, crossed his arms, and leaned back against the driver's door. Pickett glanced from side-to-side and lowered his gun to drawn less attention, but kept it leveled on target. Colson cocked his head slightly.

"You must not realize that you just shit and fell back in it."

Pickett ignored the comment. "All I need from you is the password for your laptop."

"What are you talking about?"

"That's where they are, right, on the laptop?"

Colson said, "At this point, Pickett, I couldn't care less about those pictures. No one around here seems to give a tinker's damn about

221

doing the right thing, but you're not getting any passwords. Follow me to the condo and I'll even load them on a decorative calendar if you like, you psycho bastard."

Colson could see Pickett grinding his teeth and his eyes appeared to fixate. He decided not to push him further. The man before him was about to snap and that's not healthy when the wrong person has the gun. He wondered if he had already pushed Pickett too far. And although it could be assumed most people have laptop computers, why did Pickett sound so certain he did? He had to be careful with his words.

Colson said, "Fine. But as I said, you'll have to follow me. There's nothing we can do in the middle of this parking lot."

Pickett swallowed. "Just give me the password. I already have the computer."

The words threw Colson. He had to control his anger and sarcasm. "And how did you do that, Pickett?"

"Nichole. Your daughter let me inside. It was on the kitchen counter."

Colson felt his heart skip a beat. He knew that was impossible, but the mere thought made his legs weak. He felt himself take a quick breath as if the air had been knocked out of him. Maybe he did break into the apartment, but how could he know about Nichole?

"I don't think so, Pickett."

Pickett pulled something out of his back pocket and held it up for Colson to see. It was the photo of Nichole he had taken from off the entertainment center.

"There's a rolling suitcase in the guest room. She must be visiting. You give me the password and I'll check it out. If it's good, they'll let her go."

Colson's face flushed. "My God, Pickett. Who will let her go? I swear to God, I'll kill you, Pickett. You better be bullshitting me."

What was initially a practice in hostage negotiation just became a matter of life and death if Pickett was telling the truth. Colson felt panic rising; he had to maintain control because now it was Nichole's life in jeopardy. There was no more time to deal and debate with this madman. The sooner he could hear Nichole's voice, the better. He had trained every year for this type of scenario, but as the years passed and he was assigned administrative duties, defensive tactics played a smaller role in his career. But the repetitious training served its purpose and flooded his memory. He had to compel Pickett to extend the gun and almost literally hand it to him. He would have to count on Pickett to be as slow to react as the average human. It would take a fraction of a second for him to react to Colson's move, then another fraction of a second to adjust his aim, and yet another to pull the trigger.

Colson took a quick step forward. Pickett instinctively raised the gun. Colson took his next step forty-five degrees to his left and swept his right arm up to block Pickett's attempt to adjust and move the gun in his direction. He simultaneously grabbed Pickett's wrist and jerked his arm toward the ground, but he didn't drop the gun. They spun around twice as Pickett attempted to pull away from Colson's grasp. Colson grabbed Pickett's wrist with his left hand and held it with both as he swept his leg to drop Pickett from behind. It only caused both to stumble backwards against the hood of the cruiser. Pickett pushed hard against Colson's face with his free hand.

Colson yelled, "Drop the gun!"

Pickett stubbornly continued to clinch the butt of the gun, his hand turning pale as Colson squeezed and twisted his wrist. Colson moved his right hand over Pickett's fingers and pulled hard, trying to leverage the gun from his hand by twisting it to the outside and out of his natural grip. Pickett tried to pull away and the two spun again. He rammed Pickett with his shoulder, slamming him back against the rear door. Colson felt the strength in his arms diminish. A struggle that had lasted only twenty seconds felt like hours. He knew he was not the younger man in this fight and it had to end now.

Prying the gun from Pickett's grasp was not working. If the gun was what he wanted, then he would get it. Colson pulled Pickett's arm away from his body once again, knowing he would resist. Pickett pulled back inside. Colson helped him by pushing the same direction until the muzzle was flat against the middle of his stomach. Colson stuck his finger in the trigger guard over Pickett's finger and squeezed.

Firearms instructors called it a "press contact" shot, appropriate during close-quarters struggles. Colson had practiced it hundreds of times on the shooting range with paper targets. One reason for the practice was to demonstrate the difference in surface trauma between a slug striking a body from several feet away and the effect of muzzle explosion in direct contact the skin. Without looking, Colson knew the entry wound in Pickett's stomach wasn't a small, neat hole. Most likely it would be large enough for him to stick his fist through. The expanding gas from the explosion behind the slug buried itself under the top layer of skin, but finding no room to dissipate, was forced outward from the body, disintegrating flesh in its wake. The muffled blast had the effect of a referee blowing his whistle at the end of a boxing round. The struggle immediately ceased. Pickett's eyes froze and locked onto Colson's. They stood face-to-face, pressed against the police cruiser. Pickett squinted slightly but said nothing. Colson felt Pickett's hand relax and drop the gun.

Colson said, "Listen, Pickett. Who has Nichole? Where is she?"

Pickett coughed and his legs went limp. Colson slid him to his right and opened the rear door. He held Pickett's shoulders and sat him sideways one the edge of the seat with his feet on the asphalt. He knelt down so his face was even with Pickett's.

"Tell me where my daughter is."

Pickett's eyelids fluttered as if he was about to drift off to sleep. Colson shook him until his eyes widened momentarily, and then they closed. Colson laid Pickett across the back seat, grabbed his ankles, and pushed his body in until he was able to close the door. The familiar smell of iron filled the air around Colson. He looked at the smear of blood down the side of the door and the dark, wet droplets on the black asphalt.

If what Pickett said was true, Nichole had to be at the beach house. He ran to his car and took his cell phone from the console. He picked up Pickett's Glock on his way back to the police cruiser and dropped it behind the wheel. He looked at his phone and saw two missed calls. He touched the icon and Nichole's number appeared. He pressed the number and held the phone to his ear. Nichole's voice came on after five rings stating she was away from her phone. Pickett was obviously insane, but he had to be certain that his claim of having Nichole was not just the lie of a delusional psychotic. He pushed a second contact number on the screen and waited. A voice came on the line before the first ring finished.

"Grey," said Bobby with an urgent tone.

Colson knew there was no reason to panic a man over three hundred miles away. "Hey Bobby."

"I've been trying to call Nichole for two hours. Did she make it all right?"

Colson said, "You mean make it to Daytona? I've been out half the day, driving up and down the coast. You mean she's coming for a visit?"

The tone in Bobby's voice didn't change. "Yes, yes, she left hours ago. She called when she rented the car, but she was supposed to call once she got to your place. So you're not there? You haven't seen her?"

"I'm sure she's fine. She has a key, and I'll be there in less than an hour."

Bobby was silent for a moment. "I'm sure you're right. I just don't like her traveling alone. Please ask her to call when you see her."

"Absolutely."

"Thanks Grey."

Colson laid his phone in the cup holder in the dash and headed south on A1A. His breathing became heavy and he found himself staring far beyond the cars ahead of him toward the dark horizon. He weaved the cruiser from lane-to-lane around slower traffic. Training in emergency vehicle operation and pursuit driving rose from their slumber in Colson's subconscious and moved his hands on the wheel by muscle memory. Advice in self-defense he tried to give Nichole countless times played in his mind. Explaining he wouldn't always be around to protect her. Warning her to always be aware of her surroundings, to use her car windows as rearview mirrors before getting in, to run and scream if anyone tried to attack her, and then to go straight for their eyes or groin if they grabbed her. How did this happen?

The traffic light was red at Dunlawton and A1A ahead. He forced himself to slow and activate the lights and siren at the intersection. He passed the stopped cars in the turn lane and cleared the intersection, turned off the emergency equipment, and pushed the accelerator to the floor. He knew the proper thing to do in normal circumstances would be to call 911, make a report, and let the police do their job. But what would he say? *I just killed a reserve sergeant and could sure use a little help with my missing daughter?* The Clay County Sheriff's Office policy he memorized prohibited him from acting in an official capacity in personal matters, but this was a time-critical situation and he had no official capacity. Not anymore.

❧ Chapter Twenty-Four ❦

"It was just daddy calling," Jason said, looking down at the glowing cell phone screen. He looked back at Nichole through the rearview mirror. She was a dark silhouette in the back of the SUV except when passing streetlights briefly illuminated her features. When her face flashed into view, all Jason saw was a look of disgust and hate. She sat silent. Not whimpering like Tina. This one would be harder to intimidate. Jason stared at her through the mirror, waiting for her to look away, but she didn't. He pushed the sunroof button and the top slid back with a hum, followed by a slight buffeting, hot breeze. Jason held his eyes on Nichole as he flipped the cell phone up and out of the sunroof. She still didn't look away. No reaction.

Fuller snapped, "Shit!"

Jason looked down and jerked the SUV back into the lane.

"Watch the road!"

Jason turned to Fuller. "She's going to be a problem."

"Just watch the road."

Jason looked out the side mirror. "Is Pickett back there?"

"He went back upstairs to look for something."

Jason nodded and smiled. "Two for the price of one." His smirk began to fade as Nichole's stare felt like it was beginning to burn a hole through the back of his skull. He glanced back to the rearview mirror and met Nichole's glare. "But I guess that's not always a good thing."

Sergeant Cantrell wrote the words "Call me ASAP" on the back of his business card and pushed the corner into the thin rubber gasket surrounding the sheet metal door of unit 510. He knocked and waited for at least three minutes. Colson would have answered if he had been there. He needed Colson's cell number, but it was stuck in his file and no one would be in the office at this hour. The last thing Cantrell thought he'd be doing tonight was trying to find Grey Colson. Would he have opened the door for Pickett before he got there? Maybe. If Pickett had gone off the deep end, he could be inside holding a gun on Colson right now, or he might already be dead.

He rode the elevator to ground level and walked to the office. It was dark, but he pulled on the door to satisfy himself it was locked. A sign on the door declared the office closed at ten o'clock, but also listed an after-hours number for security. He dialed the number and received a "Sundowner Security" greeting in a tired sounding male voice. When he informed the guard who he was and needed assistance, the voice brightened. "I'll be right there."

Cantrell hoped the guard wasn't expecting to be his partner on a TV reality show. The guy must have been walking the perimeter because the thin, sixtyish, and mostly bald security guard rounded the corner of the building fifteen seconds later. Cantrell flashed his credentials and shook hands with the older man.

Cantrell said, "I need to do a welfare check in unit 510."

The thin guard rubbed his chin. "That's Mr. Colson, isn't it?"

"Yes."

"Is he okay?"

Cantrell tried to hide his sarcasm. "That's why we need to check."

"Did you knock or call?"

"Yes."

The guard turned and Cantrell followed him to the elevator. They rode to the top floor in silence. The old man fumbled with a ring of keys as he walked down the exterior hallway and stopped at the door. Cantrell sighed impatiently as the guard pulled a pair of skinny glasses from his shirt pocket, slid them on his nose, and plucked the card from the door. He flipped it over to read it and handed the card back to Cantrell. He gave Cantrell a nod and knocked. "Mr. Colson?"

Cantrell spoke behind the guard. "I've already done that."

The guard looked over his shoulder and nodded. He fumbled with the keys again and slid one into the lock. Cantrell pushed past the guard with his gun out as soon as he heard the lock click open.

"Hey," the guard said, "I thought this was a welfare check."

Cantrell barked over his shoulder, "Close the door and stay outside."

He called out, "Colson!" as he moved down the short hall. He quickly cleared the bedroom to his left and stepped back into the hallway. He glanced right into the kitchen nook and swung his gun left across the living room. He cleared the master bedroom and bath. Nothing. Cantrell holstered his gun and stood in the middle of living room. Drawers in the kitchen and bedrooms were left partially open. Papers on the counter top were disheveled. Someone had clearly been looking for something. The suitcase in the guest room suggested he had a visitor. He walked out the front door to a disappointed security guard.

Cantrell said, "Mr. Colson may be in serious danger but that's all I can tell you right now. Did you see him leave or see anyone out of place here earlier?"

The guard shook his head. "There are renters and permanent residents here. Different people always coming and going every week, but maybe…"

"Maybe what?"

The guard grinned. "Follow me."

They rode back down the elevator and walked through the breezeway. Few parking spaces were vacant for a Friday night. Cantrell suspected people on vacation must be dining in more these days. They stepped through the breezeway and into the rear parking lot. The guard stopped walking.

Cantrell said, "Where are we going?"

"Right here." The guard gestured to the sliding doors on his left. "Mrs. Cox sits here pretty much all afternoon and evening with a cocktail. I'm surprised she's not out here now. She sees all the comings and goings." The guard leaned close to Cantrell and grinned. "She even hit on me a time or two."

Cantrell nodded. "Very nice, but she's not out here."

"She probably just stepped inside. See? The lights are on and the door is cracked open. She won't mind us asking. I hope you're not in too big of a hurry 'cause she can talk the bark off a tree."

The guard stepped up to the small open space in the door and called out "Mrs. Cox." He paused a beat and called again, easing the door open further with his finger. "It's security Mrs. Cox...hello."

The sliding door was now open enough for the guard to stick his head through. The shrill sound breaking the silence came from directly overhead. He instinctively jerked, banging the back of his head against the metal doorframe. A small, bright red light accompanied the non-stop screeching.

The guard clutched the back of his head and stumbled backward. He would have tripped off the curb if Cantrell hadn't steadied him. Cantrell eased the guard into a patio chair and slid the glass door full open. Smoke curled from around the oven door and rose to the ceiling. Just enough had accumulated to flow into the smoke detector and set it off the moment the guard stuck his head in.

Cantrell took two quick steps into the small kitchen and pulled the stove door open. A mushroom cloud of smoke wafted in his face. He stepped back and waved his arms to disperse the smoke. He coughed and turned the temperature knob off. Two flat, smoldering black discs sat on the baking rack. A partially nude figure on the couch caught his eye. He ran to Faye Cox and knelt by the couch, checking both her neck and wrist for a pulse. The robe she wore had slid open, exposing the right side of her body. Cantrell pulled the robe closed and checked her pupils. They were fixed and dilated. He listened for breathing, but there was nothing.

The guard spoke from behind. "Dear God. Smoke inhalation?"

Cantrell turned. The guard stood in the middle of the kitchen, rubbing the back of his head.

"Do me a favor. Step outside and make sure no nosey neighbors come in."

"You want me to call 911?"

Cantrell shook his head. "I'll take care of it."

He pulled his phone out and pressed Sheriff Langston's icon. He picked up in two rings.

Langston said, "What's the story Sarge?"

"We have another one."

"Colson's dead?"

"No, I don't believe Colson is dead, but the Reaper is following him around like the tail on a dog."

Langston was quiet for a moment. "There's only one other logical place for him to be. Call radio and have them dispatch any available units."

"Isn't anyone watching Cash's house now?"

"No," Langston said, "nothing was supposed to happen tonight."

∽∾

Nichole felt along the wall of the pitch-black room until she came to a heavy fabric on the wall and pushed it aside. Moonlight washed over Tina's curled up body on the floor against the far wall. She was not whimpering any longer, just balled into a fetal position. She covered her eyes as if a floodlight had suddenly been shined in her face. Nichole walked to her, gently raised her by the shoulders, and leaned her against the wall.

Nichole said, "You can't give up. We need each other right now. Tell me what's going on."

Tina looked into Nichole's eyes and shook her head. "I can never get away from them. They'll kill us. Kara's gone and Lacy isn't here. They didn't let them go no more than they'd let me go."

Nichole squeezed Tina's arms. "You still haven't told me what's going on. Why are they doing this, Tina?"

Tears began to stream from Tina's eyes. She jerked her arms away and covered her face with her hands.

"I don't know…I don't know." Her voice rose. "I don't know…I don't know!"

The muffled shout came from outside of the room. Someone pounded on the opposite wall three times. "Shut up in there, damn it."

Jason lowered his fist from the wall and dropped onto the couch. "Stupid bitches."

Cash stood looking at his own reflection in the French doors. He turned around. Jason and Fuller sat on opposite ends of the couch. Fuller's head was leaned back and his eyes were closed.

Cash said, "Don't get too comfortable. When Pickett gets here I want you to move Tina to the rental house at the pier. The meet is less than twenty-four hours from now and you'll already be in place. Everything is being set up now."

Jason said, "But the electricity isn't even on there. Are we supposed to sit in the dark all night? And what about the other girl?"

"You'll do what I tell you!" Cash snapped. "Colson will come back out here for his daughter, but that's fine. He won't be such a badass as long as we have her. I'll have Taylor take care of them both."

The side kitchen door opened and Taylor walked in. He dropped the keys on the counter, jerked the necktie away from his collar, and then sat down at the bar. He took a handkerchief from his pocket and wiped his brow and the back of his neck.

Cash said, "Is everything set up at the rental for tomorrow?"

Taylor shoved the handkerchief back into his pocket. "It's all set, but it's hot as hell in that place."

Jason slapped his hands on his knees and looked at Cash. "See what I'm talking about?"

"Shut up!" Cash snapped again. "Taylor's been busy. You've never done a hard day's work in your life. You think manual labor is the name of the Mexican who does our yard work, for God's sake."

∽

Colson slowed the cruiser, looking for the gate lights. He had driven this road more times than he could count and admired the beachfront homes, but never had to search for a specific residence this late at night. When he was here earlier it was broad daylight and street numbers were easy to read, but he couldn't see at night like he could when he was twenty-two years old. And earlier he was relaxed and searching out of curiosity, not extreme urgency. He felt a rush he had never experienced during his law enforcement career. The adrenalin that kept him alert during a major drug bust, or searching a dark house for an aggravated felon, could not compare to the jet fuel coursing through his bloodstream at this moment.

He had never been directly involved in a kidnapping case. That was always left up to the feds. But he knew enough to know every second was precious; and for every moment wasted in senseless

231

negotiation and investigation, the probability of recovering the victim alive reduced exponentially. He knew where Nichole was and he had to act immediately without regard for his own safety or worrying about probable cause tying his hands. He wasn't a cop anymore, and now was the time to start acting like it.

He saw the two bright lantern lights perched on stone pillars at the gate entrance to his left. He slowed and nosed the cruiser to the gate. The intercom box was positioned evenly with the driver's side window. He pressed the red button and waited. He dropped the magazine from Pickett's Glock and saw eleven rounds still loaded. He shoved the magazine back in and pulled the slide back slightly. One round was in the chamber. As he had hoped, the low, electric whine of a motor came to life and the twin gates began a smooth swing inward.

He eased the cruiser forward at ten miles per hour along the lazy curve of the driveway, flanked by squat driveway lights staggered on both sides. Their dim wash of light illuminated the concrete just enough to keep him off the grass. The four-story beach house ahead was front-lit by spotlights hidden behind decorative shrubbery along both sides of a double-wooden front door with wrought iron hinges. Banks of dual spotlights were mounted on the front corners of the house. He had to assume the same would be true for the back. A glow rose from the roof where someone had taken potshots at him earlier in the day. The only other light shone through the ground floor windows. That was where Cash and his thugs would be.

He pulled up to the side carport, stopped a car's length from the door, and grabbed the small flashlight and his ASP. He had to move fast and quiet. He shoved the Glock into the waistband of his pants at the small of his back and stepped into the darkness at the front corner of the house. Colson's counterparts at the police department would often argue about what was the most dangerous scenario for a cop: a traffic stop or searching a house. Of course both scenarios are dangerous, but Colson argued that entering a suspect's residence was far more dangerous than a traffic stop. The state could regulate tinted car windows, but there was no such regulation or law to prevent a homeowner from hanging curtains or shades. He was entering a large, unknown territory. He had to even the odds. They still wouldn't be in Colson's favor, but they would improve. Buried electrical lines would require him to take a tour around the house to find what he was looking for.

He stooped and ran along the outside of the shrubbery, across the front of the house. It was very unlikely that the supply box would be mounted on the front. He cut right at the corner and ran along the left side toward the rear. He felt the ground slope downward as he ran. There would be a partial-underground level with daylight exposure in the back. He reached the back corner and stopped. He aimed the flashlight down the length of the house and clicked it on to get a flash glimpse and quickly clicked it off. The breaker box was almost arm's length away. The small door was hinged at the top. A metal tab extended through the door at the bottom through a narrow slot, secured by a metal zip tie. Colson pulled his ASP and snapped his arm to extend it. The small end of the ASP slid easily through the loop in the metal zip tie—and with a twist, it popped off and dropped to the ground.

Colson took a deep breath to calm down. He was getting ahead of himself and needed to slow his pace. He walked back to the rear corner and looked down the length of the house. The moon provided sufficient light and his eyes were adjusting. There was a deck above him with a stone patio beneath. A floodlight illuminated the small back lawn before yielding to the sand and surf. He felt confident he couldn't be seen by the roof-mounted camera up against the side of the house. One single French door led to the patio, but there were no windows at this level. Colson slid his back along the rear wall to the door and craned his head to look inside. It was totally dark. He turned the doorknob slowly and pushed. He wasn't surprised when the deadbolt held it firm. He rested his head back against the stucco and thought.

He moved quickly, standing the ASP against the wall at the breaker box, and retracing his path back to the cruiser. He pulled the driver's door open to the smell of coagulating blood from the back seat. He stuck the keys in the ignition and started the engine. He pressed the parking brake halfway to the floor with his hand, turned on the headlights and blue LED lights, slid the gear into reverse, and pressed the door locks. He closed the door as the cruiser began backing slowly, the partially engaged parking brake preventing it from gaining too much speed.

He ran back to the front corner of the house and watched. The cruiser rolled back, missing the black NSX by two inches. It dropped off the driveway and over a small row of low, flowering shrubs. The blue LED light bar on the roof lit the large front lawn and stucco of the house in random flashes of electric blue. The alternating strobe headlights bobbed up and down on the uneven lawn, casting white light on the front of the house in a jerky pattern.

➤ Chapter Twenty-Five ◄

Cash looked at his watch and stood from his recliner. Randy Fuller was snoring with his head laid back on the couch and Jason sat on the other end with his eyes closed and arms crossed. Taylor sat at the bar, staring at his own reflection in the French doors. Jason and Fuller were startled awake when Cash broke the silence.

"What the hell is Pickett doing? I let him in fifteen minutes ago."

Jason stood. "I'll go see what he's doing," he said, and walked through the kitchen. The blue flashes of light reflecting off the walls of the hallway caught his eye. He had seen plenty of cop-car blue lights from the house, but only quick flashes as they sped past the front gates. These blue flashes seemed to be coming from the front yard.

Jason muttered, "What the hell?"

Cash followed Jason through the kitchen to the side door and stepped outside. Fuller staggered behind, scratching his wrist above the cast. They stood bewildered at the slowly backing cruiser making a lazy arc across the lawn. Taylor stepped to the door and watched from inside. Cash jogged to the front corner of the house as if he could span the thirty yards to the cruiser, but stopped short.

Cash shouted, "What is he doing? Is he drunk? Turn off those lights, you idiot!"

They watched helplessly as the cruiser's rear bumper struck the inner wall at a forty-five degree angle and briefly bounced forward. The fiberglass rear bumper collapsed, allowing the steel inner bumper to crack the stucco façade, knocking dinner plate size flakes to the ground. The lights continued flashing and the tires continued a slow reverse spin, digging small trenches in the grass.

Cash called to Jason, "Go see what's wrong and turn those damned lights off."

Jason sprinted across the lawn. He was halfway to the out-of-control cruiser when its struggle with the wall caused it to slip sideways and begin traveling parallel to it, screeching metal against concrete as it made its way to the side wall.

❦

Colson stayed out of view at the opposite corner of the house when he heard Cash shouting at the cruiser. He knew such a macabre scene would get the attention of anyone in the house. He watched Jason sprint across the lawn and decided it was time. He ran back to the breaker box, flipped up the small door and hesitated. The breaker should kill the exterior floodlights. He had to be quick. He snapped the main breaker to the left. The floodlights went dark, leaving only moonlight. He dropped the small door over the metal tab, laid the shaft of the ASP across the top, and pressed his weight downward. The tab bent, delaying anyone from switching the power back on.

He ran back to the rear door, punched the tip of the ASP through the section of glass nearest to the lock, and raked shards of glass from the frame. He reached in, turned the deadbolt, and stepped into the darkness, darting quickly to his right. He knew one of the most dangerous aspects of entering a room under potentially hostile circumstances was for an officer to be silhouetted in a doorway, or fatal funnel. He went to one knee, collapsed the ASP against the stone tile floor, and then slid it into his front pocket.

He raised the flashlight in his left hand and rested his right forearm on his left wrist, holding the Glock. He could turn the flashlight on and off just long enough to check his surroundings and potential threats, and then move immediately to cover. Anyone shooting at his light would likely miss. He clicked on the flashlight and moved twice, catching brief glimpses of the large, lower level of the house. It was as though he was taking a photograph and he could only see when the camera flashed. There was a poker table in front of him. A bar stood beyond the poker table in the center of the room. Its polished wood gleamed as bright as the large mirror hanging behind it. Black leather stools with chrome legs were evenly spaced along the front of the bar. There was no movement and no sound. Colson pointed his light at the floor and clicked it on.

He walked around the bar. His light caught narrow, double doors at the back of the room. On closer inspection they were elevator doors decorated with judges paneling. No one would be using them without an electrical backup source and there was no sound of a generator. Not even emergency lights. With cameras mounted at every corner of the house, Cash had neglected to include an important component to his security system. He moved along the wall to the far end of the room where he could see faint ambient light from another doorway.

It was the entrance to a short hallway, leading to a stairway that rose to a landing. A window at the top of the landing allowed faint moonlight to seep down the stairs. He stood at the bottom of the stairway and listened again. Someone was shouting, but not from inside the house. It was the muffled voice of Martin Cash.

✌∾

"What happened to the perimeter lights?" Fuller said, looking back at Taylor standing in the doorway. Taylor looked back through the kitchen, pulled his gun, and guided himself along the wall to the living area. He found the door to the locked bedroom and twisted the knob. Still locked. He spun his gun around when he heard the shouting.

"Bust the window!" Cash yelled. He watched Jason jerk violently on the doors of the cruiser to no avail. The blue LED lights seemed brighter for some reason, and it was just a matter of time until some other cop saw the insane flashing against the house and stopped to investigate. Cash turned to Fuller, but he was already halfway across the lawn with his gun. Fuller stopped at the passenger door and struck the side window twice with the butt of the gun. It took a total of five strikes to shatter the glass. Fuller reached through the window and turned off the ignition. The wheels ceased their slow spin, but the lights continued to flash. He looked between the seats at two radio consoles, both with a dozen illuminated buttons labeled with abbreviated siren selections. The last thing he needed was to turn on a siren he couldn't figure out how to turn off. He noticed two red toggle switches and quickly flipped both. The lights mercifully ceased.

Fuller hadn't noticed the smell of blood until then. He was surprised he could smell at all through his swollen sinuses, but the odor was pungent. He drew his head out of the window and peered in the back. The figure of a man lay crumpled and face down against the back cage of the patrol car. He pulled up the door lock and opened the passenger door. The dome light lit up the interior. A dark smear of blood covered a large portion of the tan vinyl bench seat and a long pool collected where the bench seat met the backrest.

Fuller looked at Jason. "It's Pickett."

∽◠

Colson knew they wouldn't stay outside forever. He ran up the stairs with his gun at a high-ready position and stopped when he reached the top. Through the window he saw two figures at the patrol car. A quick flash of his light revealed a long hallway to the rear of the house. He moved along the wall, gauging the distance in his mind and pausing before entering the room. He swung his gun left and clicked his light on and off. Nichole had to be somewhere, if she was here at all. There was nothing to lose at this point. It was not likely they would hear him from the front lawn. He walked to the center of the room and called out, "Nichole...Nichole!"

The voice came from the far door on the left. "Dad?" The voice came louder and someone was pounding on the door from the inside. "Dad!"

Colson ran to the door, turned the knob, and shoved with his shoulder. The deadbolt didn't yield. He stepped back and kicked hard above the lock. The hollow-core door cracked as the bolt tore through the casing and swung open. Nichole appeared through the door and threw her arms around him. Relief and urgency mingled as he hugged Nichole and kissed her forehead. She cupped her hand over her mouth and began to cry. Tina stood outside the door, looking at Colson through puffy, red eyes.

Colson said, "We have to get out of here now."

It must be the same tunnel vision I experienced, Taylor thought as he heard Colson talking to the girl. Colson was so focused on busting in the door he never saw him standing on the far side of the room. He was within an arm's reach of Colson when the lights came on. He lifted his gun to Colson's head.

"Don't move, Colson," Taylor said, holding his hand out for Colson's gun. Colson stood with his arms around Nichole. He could see their small reflection in Taylor's glasses. Tina backed against the wall, slid to the floor, and covered her face with her hands. Cash and Jason walked through the kitchen and stopped in the middle of the room. Cash put his hands on his hips and smiled at Colson.

"I knew you'd come here, Colson. Thanks for taking care of Pickett for me. He was a pain in the ass."

Colson looked at Cash and back to Taylor, who held the gun steady. He looked back to Cash and said, "The only reason I'm here is to take my daughter home. You can tell your watchdog to stop pointing that gun in her direction."

Cash's eyes narrowed. The elevator doors opened. Randy Fuller stepped out and said, "Someone broke in downstairs." He turned, saw Colson, and took two long strides toward him.

"Stop," Cash said, not taking his eyes off Colson. "He hasn't handed over his gun yet. Give Taylor the gun, Colson."

Colson hesitated. If he had been alone, there was no way he would give up the gun. People who were not proficient with firearms were bad shots, especially when it came to hitting a moving target with a handgun. Had he been alone, he could run in at least two directions he could see at the moment. Back toward the hall he came from, or into the dark room three feet from him. The dark room being the best option. Anyone coming in would step into their own fatal funnel and be shot. But he didn't have the luxury or time to warn Nichole or the other girl, let alone brief them about a plan. One of them might be shot and he wouldn't be able to live with that. He had to buy time. He held the butt of the gun with his thumb and index finger and handed it to Taylor.

Cash walked to his recliner and sat. "You put on some show, Colson. Then you break into my house."

Colson lowered his arm to cover the bulge of the ASP in his pocket. "I admit I'm a little unpredictable when my daughter is kidnapped."

"How long have you been here, Colson? I mean living in Daytona?"

"Long enough to become acquainted with a dirty, wannabe cop, the cheesiest dressed crook in town, and a steroid freak."

Cash responded as if Colson hadn't spoken at all, "Well, I have lived here all of my life. My father built his business here and I have worked my ass off trying to do even better. But the entire time someone or something has been trying to screw me over. Either this ridiculous recession, the IRS, or your buddy, Sheriff Langston. But that wasn't enough. You had to come along and start nosing around and become yet another pain in my ass. You so-called public servants just can't stand for someone like me to have a little more money or a nicer house than you."

"It seems to me the good sheriff isn't interested in you anymore. I figured you paid him off. But it's not about what you have, but how you get it that separates the low-lifes from honest, tax-paying citizens. "

"You don't know anything about me, smartass."

"In your case, Cash, it's simply a lack of self-discipline. I have no reason to doubt your family made big money legitimately, but when times got tough, you were too lazy to stay honest and turned into a slug. Jason losing control on the beach that day is the perfect example. Like father, like son—and you only have yourself to blame. The reality is that a person can either exercise self-discipline or it will be imposed on them. There's no way of getting around it. Like the laws of nature, you can't break them, you can only demonstrate them."

Cash flipped a dismissive wave and stood. "It doesn't matter. I'm done with you." He turned to Fuller. "Have you got everything in the truck?"

Fuller shrugged.

"Then go check and drive it to the carport!" Cash screamed. Fuller turned and jogged out the door.

Colson said, "So what was all the drama about the pictures of Langston?"

Cash blew air out of his mouth in disgust. "I had nothing to do with that. It was Pickett's crazy scheme to embarrass Langston out of the race so he could be the next sheriff. God only knows why anyone would want the job. The question now is what to do with you two."

"Mr. Cash," Taylor said, his gun still trained on Colson. "Think about it. Colson is a cop killer. He kills Pickett and steals his car. Then he breaks into your house. The evidence will be overwhelming. You have the right to be protected in your own home. Hell, they'll probably give you a medal for it."

Cash's eyes widened with the implication and a smile crossed his face. "But what about the girl?"

"What about her?" Taylor said. "She could be as crazy as he is. How were we supposed to know?"

"I knew you were valuable, Taylor. That's why I hired you."

Taylor gestured toward the hall with his gun. "Let's go."

"Where are you taking them?"

"Downstairs where they broke in. Makes more sense." Taylor stared through his dark glasses at Colson. "I said GO!"

Colson's mind was racing. He felt the weight of the ASP in his right front pocket, but there was no clear opportunity—yet. He couldn't live if something happened to Nichole. She depended on him to keep her safe. He couldn't believe she was here and this was happening. There was no question that if any harm came to Nichole he would already be dead, because he would fight to the death before allowing it. He tried to recall the layout of the lower level. The bar, the poker table, the large mirror. They were walking in front of Taylor down the stairs. They passed the landing and turned left down the final flight.

Colson held his arm tight around Nichole's shoulder as they walked off the final step. He could feel her quivering in his grasp and heard her sniffle. She laid her head on Colson's shoulder. "Daddy," she said low, terrified. Colson kissed her temple. She sounded like she was six years old. His heart skipped a beat thinking about those years. He held her tighter. "It's all right, baby. You're with me and I won't let anything happen," he whispered.

"Over by the door and stop," Taylor ordered. They walked around the center bar. Colson glanced back to Taylor.

"Listen, Taylor. This won't look right and you're smart enough to know it. People don't break into houses with their daughter. She's too terrified to do anything. Let Nichole leave."

"Keep walking," Taylor said.

Colson eased his hand near the ASP in his pocket. He would have to strike quickly and simultaneously shove Nichole to the side if they were to have a chance. Taylor would have to move closer, but he didn't dare look back. He clutched Nichole's shoulder and slowed his pace. They were ten feet from the door. He tried to reason with Taylor again.

"You're a fighter. An honorable man and honorable men don't hurt women. I don't care if you kick my ass from here to Miami Beach, but you're not scum like Cash."

"No, I'm a steroid freak—remember?" Taylor mocked.

"Even steroid freaks don't murder innocent people. You wanted a piece of me at the beach. Put the gun away and it can be me and you right here...unless that fear in your heart is still in the way."

"Turn around, Colson," Taylor said.

⇉ Chapter Twenty-Six ⇇

The young, male paramedic carried the automated external defibrillator, or the AED, in one hand, and a bright orange box in the other. He was followed by a female paramedic rolling an empty stretcher. He opened the rear doors of the ambulance and slid the box full of first aid equipment to the side. The female pulled a lever to collapse the legs of the stretcher and rolled it inside. They had done everything they could to revive Faye Cox. Their initial observations were accurate, but the final determination was made by the emergency room physician over the phone. They climbed into the ambulance and circled the parking area to the breezeway.

Kim Reese met the ambulance as she pulled into the street-side entrance of the breezeway. A uniformed deputy stood guard at the front door of the condo on her immediate left. He nodded as Reese drove by. She pulled into the rear lot and stopped behind the dull-white medical examiner's van. She jerked the gear into park and climbed out, slamming the door behind her. Another uniformed deputy stood outside the sliding doors with a pad and pen in his hand. A weary looking security guard stood off to the side. One strip of yellow crime scene tape spanned the glass door at head height. Reese marched up to the deputy who eyed the gold badge dangling from a chain around her neck.

She said, "Lieutenant Reese," and ducked under the tape. The deputy annotated her name and the time on his pad. A stretcher sat in the middle of the living room. One crime scene tech stood with her back to Reese, taking photographs of a pillow lying by the couch. A female investigator from the medical examiner's office and Cantrell hefted a body bag onto the stretcher and lifted the side rails. Cantrell moved to the foot of the stretcher and helped the investigator raise it. He noticed Reese watching from the kitchen. He pressed a number on his cell and turned away. Reese rested her hands on her hips and stared at the back of Cantrell's head for the thirty-second phone call. He turned around and met her gaze.

"Sergeant Cantrell," Reese said from the kitchen. "Step outside."

Cantrell ended the call and thanked the on-call investigator. She shook his hand. "Is it safe for me to go home after this, or should I get coffee and wait for another call? This is two tonight, you know."

Cantrell chuckled. "I can't guarantee anything, but we'll try not to bother you again."

The investigator nodded and rolled the stretcher past the deputy, who made another note in his pad. Cantrell stepped out and met Reese at the rear of her car. The look on her face and tightly crossed arms warned Cantrell of her mood.

"Sergeant Cantrell," Reese said, "have you forgotten the concept of the chain of command?"

"No, ma'am."

She narrowed her eyes. "Well, it seems to me you have. I know you're assisting Homicide for a few weeks, but you still answer to me. I had to hear about this over the radio. My first thought was maybe you hadn't had time to brief me yet, then I find out this is the second homicide of the day and you didn't even notify me about the first one. Sheriff Langston will have both of our asses when he finds out."

"The sheriff already knows."

Reese fumed, "What do you mean? You went over my head?"

"Maybe you should talk to the sheriff about it."

"Damn straight I will, but right now I'm talking to you, sergeant" She drew out s-e-r-g-e-a-n-t to remind Cantrell he was a lowly subordinate. He would enjoy the turn this conversation was going to take.

"Yes, we are talking, so let's talk about it. Where is Pickett right now?"

"What are you talking about?"

"When and where did you see him last?"

Reese looked shocked. She stood speechless for a long moment as though someone had just told her a loved one had suddenly died. She couldn't find the words to respond at first. She was a lieutenant, and a defiant sergeant was talking to her like a suspect.

"You dare question me?"

Cantrell pulled a note pad from his jacket pocket and a pen from his shirt. He held the pen up, clicked it and flipped the pad open. He scribbled on the top of the page and looked back to Reese.

"Yes, Lieutenant. This is a criminal investigation and your boyfriend is the main suspect. Should I read you your rights before we begin again?"

Reese's face flushed. She leaned against the side of her car and looked at the deputy standing at the glass doors, and then back to Cantrell. The weary guard was gone. It was silent, other than a few muffled voices from the balconies above where curious onlookers leaned over the rails, enthralled by the police activity below. The voices seemed to diminish as the medical examiner's van disappeared under the breezeway, but another set of headlights bounced up and down. A dark sedan rolled over the speed bumps and into the rear lot. Two figures stepped from the sedan. A man and a woman. At twelve-thirty a.m., the parking lot was too dark for her to recognize who they were, but there was no doubt about the vehicle with government tags. It was another unmarked county unit.

The dark-skinned man, wearing a white shirt and dark slacks, walked ahead of the woman, who was thin and short. She also wore dark slacks and a white top. Both with a star clipped to their belts, situated in front of small-framed, compact Glocks in paddle holsters. When they reached Cantrell and Reese, the man extended his hand. He was holding a cell phone.

The man said, "Sheriff Langston on the phone for you, lieutenant."

Reese looked at the man and woman. They looked vaguely familiar. She took the phone, turned away, and then held it to her ear.

"Lieutenant Reese."

"Lieutenant," Langston said sternly, "you may recognize Sergeant Martin and Detective Hunter with Internal Affairs."

Reese looked back at the two I.A. detectives. "I think so."

"They are going to drive you back to their office for an interview. I expect you to be extremely forthcoming and cooperative."

"Can I ask what this is about?"

"I'm not going to play games with you, Reese. You know what this is about. You just do as instructed and we'll go from there. Understand?"

"My car is here. Can I just—"

"No," Langston interrupted. "Leave your keys with Sergeant Cantrell. A two-man unit will be dispatched to drive it back."

"Yes, sir."

"Put Sergeant Martin back on the phone."

Reese handed the phone back and walked to her car. She pulled a soft leather brief case from the passenger seat and the keys from the ignition and returned to Cantrell. He resisted a smile. Reese held the keys in front of her face, dangled them for a long second, and then dropped them into Cantrell's hand without a word. The I.A. detectives turned and Reese followed them to the car. Detective Hunter opened the back door and let Reese slide inside. Sergeant Martin paused before opening the driver's door and spoke into his phone.

"I understand, Sheriff. We'll take care of it. Do you want me to place her on administrative leave after the interview?"

"No," Langston said. "I want you to convince her to do the right thing."

"Yes, sir. I'll do my best."

"Do better than that, sergeant. Make it happen. One more thing. Before you drive her home, be sure to take her firearm and credentials."

"Yes, sir."

❧

Fuller walked in the side door and saw Cash in his recliner, typing on his laptop. Tina sat on the floor with her knees pulled to her chest and head down, just as she was when he walked out. Jason sat on the couch with a gun in his lap. He walked over to Jason and looked around the room.

"Where's Taylor and Colson"? He asked.

The answer came from behind him. He turned to Cash, who didn't look up from the laptop. "Taylor took them downstairs. When he's finished, you two take Tina to the rental and I'll call 911 about our intruders. It'll be a couple of hours of answering questions about Colson's erratic behavior, but—"

"Damn it!" Fuller said, "I wanted to do Colson." He pulled his gun and ran to the stairs, taking two at a time.

Jason spoke up from the couch. "You think it's a good idea? I mean, calling the police out here?"

Cash looked up from the laptop. "You heard Taylor. Colson killed Pickett. One of their own. Don't think for one minute those dirt-road deputies are as smart as those on the TV shows you watch. They screw up a thousand cases for every one they get right. We'll be handing them a cop-killer on a silver platter."

Jason inadvertently jerked when a shot rang out from the lower level below his feet. The sound was accompanied by a short scream. A female voice. Two seconds later, another pop, but no scream. Cash grinned and closed the laptop.

"Go ahead and put Tina in the car."

Tina tightened her arms around her legs. Her whimpers turned to sobbing. Jason stood, walked around the couch, and stopped, towering over her compressed form on the floor.

"Let's go," he ordered.

"No!" She shook her head violently, still buried in her knees.

Jason grabbed her bicep and jerked her to her feet. Tina swung her free arm and slapped him across the face before he could block it. The strike stung his cheek. He was momentarily dazed and surprised and tasted a trace of blood in his mouth. He shoved her hard against the wall. Tina spun and deadened the impact with her hands. She turned only to be propelled back against the wall, Jason's fist sinking deep into her stomach. In one instant, her breath was pushed from her lungs and she crumpled to the floor. She knelt on all fours and gasped violently.

"Bitch!" Jason yelled. "That's for slapping me, and this is for hitting me with the flashlight."

Jason swung the gun in a wide arc, aiming for the side of her head, but his forward motion was stopped. He snapped his head around to see Cash firmly holding his wrist in check.

"Stop it!" Cash demanded. "You've made your point, but she's merchandise that's supposed to be in good condition upon delivery. The customer isn't going to pay us for a black-and-blue girl who needs stitches because you couldn't control your temper. Take her to the car and wait for Fuller. I swear to God, if they don't take delivery because she's damaged I'll beat your ass to death myself. Do you understand me?"

Jason glared at Cash and jerked his hand free.

"Do you understand?" Cash narrowed his gaze at his son. Jason nodded and looked down at the floor. He grabbed Tina and lifted her to her feet. Her breathing was slowly returning to normal as he led her to the side door.

Cash shook his head and walked to the top of the landing. "Fuller," he yelled down the dark stairwell, "Let's go!"

⇒ Chapter Twenty-Seven ⇐

Colson had seen many gunshot victims in his career. Unless it was a suicide, it was rare the victim had only one hole. One of his deputies had been shot in the stomach at nearly point blank range. The bullet had entered just below his Kevlar vest and had destroyed a portion of his liver. He had lived to tell about it and was still on the job. Colson wasn't an expert marksman. Not all law enforcement officers were, but that is why they were required to train and qualify at least twice per year. He learned from the beginning it's not always one shot, one kill, unless you were a sniper. With handguns, they practiced two shots to the chest, one to the head. There were cases in which suspects who were high on meth or other stimulants required an entire magazine emptied in them to bring them down. He was counting on Taylor's aim not being accurate. The man's shoulders were broad and his movement would be limited and slow. Give him a moving target and his chances of a kill shot were greatly reduced. That should buy enough time for Nichole to escape. But he would have to move fast and push Nichole out the door. He prayed she would run to the brushline and disappear. Even wounded, he could join her if he could take Taylor out.

Colson turned to face Taylor. He kept Nichole on his right, where he could grab the handle of the ASP undetected. He held it firm, waiting for the best moment to shove her away and deploy the metal shaft.

He looked past Taylor at the sound of feet pounding down the steps on the opposite side of the bar. "Hey," Fuller called out, and rounded the bar in a trot, gun in his uninjured hand. "Colson is mine."

He pulled his ASP and jerked it to extend the shaft when the gunshot rang out. He saw Fuller stop suddenly, his blackened eyes wide in shock. He dropped to one knee and laid his gun on the tile to prop himself with his uninjured hand. He seemed to realize what had happened, and placed his hand back on the gun. The second shot exploded before he could raise the gun from the floor. Taylor stood over Fuller until he collapsed on his back. He turned back to Colson.

"You're right, Colson. I'm not like that scum and I couldn't let them kill you."

Colson hugged Nichole and nodded, looking into Taylor's dark sunglasses. He moved Nichole to the door and opened it. "What's going on, Taylor?"

"You need to tell them what happened here. Fuller was going to kill you both."

"You know I will, Taylor, but what's going on?"

"The feds can tell you. I'm working with an agent. But they'll probably be pissed that you screwed up their plans."

Colson grinned, "They'll get over it. You say 'their case,' so you're an informant?"

Taylor slid the glasses off his nose and faced Colson and Nichole. His left eye squinted in the light, but the right socket held a hazy, lifeless orb. "They don't hire many convicted, one-eyed steroid freaks as agents, do they?"

Colson collapsed his ASP on the tile and slid it back in his pocket. "Thanks, Taylor," he said, and ushered Nichole out the door.

Taylor pulled out his cell and held it to his ear when they disappeared from sight. He kept his eye on the stairs until there was an answer and said four words: "My cover is burnt."

⌘

Taylor hated the term "snitch" and appreciated Colson not using it. A snitch was a seven-year-old boy who tells on his eleven-year-old brother after seeing him kiss the neighbor's daughter. A snitch was only interested in obtaining favor or gain for himself instead of helping someone or seeing justice served. Otherwise every cop in the nation could be considered a snitch. That was how Sheriff Langston explained it to him after his release from prison.

He was freed with no job, no money, and nowhere to live. He had received a copy of his eviction notice from the apartment complex the year prior. It was forwarded through the State Department of Corrections. His few belongings and cheap furniture had been dropped on the curb for human vultures to pilfer. There was no hope to return to ultimate fighting, and his criminal record made his chances of being hired as a trainer or computer tech extremely remote. He took the public transit bus with his fifty-dollar release fund and was deposited on Peninsula Avenue just west of the inner coastal bridge in Daytona. He had been offered a job on the day of his arrest. It was his only option short of finding a homeless shelter.

Taylor had only worked for Cash two weeks when Langston confronted him at the car wash. The unmarked Crown Victoria moved slowly behind Cash's black SUV on the conveyor through the suds and rinse. Langston sat on the bench next to him. He wore a black golf shirt and tan slacks. Not the typical sheriff's attire.

"Mr. Taylor, I'm Sheriff—"

"I know who you are," Taylor said, cutting him off. "Are you following me?"

"We follow all of Cash's people at one time or another."

He turned to Langston and considered him through his dark glasses. Langston wore an almost identical pair.

Taylor said, "Is there a problem?"

"You don't know?" Langston said evenly.

"I've only worked for the man for two weeks. Making bank deposits, throwing stock in the liquor store, and washing his cars."

"I believe you. That's why I wanted to talk to you."

"That's good to know."

"Listen, Taylor. I don't think you're like Cash and his other men. I remember your case and the circumstances around your arrest. I read the file."

Taylor chuckled. "So you think I'm a good guy?"

Langston shook his head. "That's not what I'm talking about. You're case made the local news. Sure you beat the eyeballs out of that doctor. Given the same circumstances I might have done the same. What I mean is, you were an athlete with no criminal record. No history of violence, except when it was permitted in the octagon."

"So."

"So, I need to know what Cash is into."

"And you expect me to snitch for you, is that it?"

Langston watched an attendant jump into the seat of the SUV and drive it across the lot. Two others attacked it with towels and spray bottles. He sighed and looked back to Taylor.

"What I'm saying is I believe you to be a man of integrity. You didn't give my deputies a minute of trouble when they came for you. You didn't even want to take the case to trial. You accepted your punishment like a man and then they released you for good behavior. That tells me a lot."

Taylor stood as one of the attendants held up his drying towel, signaling he was finished. Taylor pulled a couple of bills from his pocket, but didn't move. Langston stayed in his seat.

"That doesn't mean that I'll betray my employer. I didn't see you at the bus stop, offering me a job or place to live."

"That's true," Langston said. "You're just running errands for him now. But I have a feeling your better judgment will prevail when he takes you into his confidence and you see what's going on. My guess is you won't want to be involved in whatever it is. It's not being a snitch, it's simply doing the right thing."

Langston stood and pulled a piece of white paper from his pocket, the size of a Post-it note. "This is my cell number. Don't lose it."

Taylor stood still. The man with the towel was still waving. The Crown Victoria ended its journey through the wash and an attendant sat behind the wheel, waiting for the SUV to be moved out of the way. He glanced back at Langston, took the note, and then slid it into his pocket.

〜

Officer Matt Sanders stepped out of the Quick Mart carrying a grape slushy. He sat the cup on the hood of his unit and stretched. The gun belt, vest, and the equipment strapped around him added twenty-five pounds. After ten hours in the heat, it felt like fifty. He spent the last two hours writing incident reports on the MDC computer—or Mobile Data Collector—in his unit. One report of a stolen purse, two arrest reports for drunks fighting on the beach, and one involving a sunstroke victim. The report running him into overtime was the supplemental for the detective to include in his homicide file for the Biggins incident. He took a long sip from the slushy and started the truck. The vents blew cool air in his face and around his neck. He leaned forward and pulled his shirt and vest away from his chest to allow the trapped heat to escape.

His eyes were tired. His chest burned and itched under the vest, but he couldn't reach it to scratch. His undershirt stuck to his torso like a second layer of clammy skin. He would pull everything off and jump into the shower as soon as he gassed up and drove home. The female voice on the radio made him groan.

"Radio to any available units in the area of 4301 South Atlantic Avenue, sheriff's office requests assistance reference possible disturbance at that location. 10-0, use caution as suspects may be armed. Set perimeter but do not approach the residence at this time. Sheriff's units will be enroute for back up. If contact is made with a Grey Colson subject, white male, approximately forty-eight to fifty years of age, hold and notify sheriff's radio. Out of Volusia at 0050 hours."

Sanders rubbed his eyes. He couldn't recall why the name was familiar. He reached for the microphone and hesitated. He looked out the window to his left and shook his head. It was no more than two miles at the most. The number of units on morning watch was far fewer than evening watch, and it was just his luck to be this close. He reluctantly spoke into the microphone.

"504, radio. I'll be code 8 from South Atlantic and Dunlawton."

Sander's put the truck in gear and screeched southbound out of the lot.

⌁

Colson led Nichole around the side of the house to the front corner and stopped. He checked left, across the front side. No activity. The white cruiser gleamed, reflecting the glare from the security spotlights. The reflective green SHERIFF lettering stood out in contrast to the polished paint of the cruiser. He held Nichole around the waist and they bolted across the yard.

The cruiser had wedged against the side and front perimeter walls. The trunk lid was slightly ajar and bent from the initial impact with the wall and the driver's side door was locked tight against the front wall. Nichole ran along silently. Colson wanted to console her, but there was no time.

"We'll have to get in through the passenger side," Colson said.

He pulled the passenger side door open and slid in, fighting the computer stand away and throwing his legs over the radio console. She climbed in after him and shut the door. A high-pitched scream made the hairs on his neck stand. Nichole clamped her hand over her mouth to cut the involuntary scream short and slammed her eyes closed. Colson had hoped she wouldn't see the body, but the smell of blood was overwhelming. He put his hand on her shoulder and squeezed gently.

"It's all right, babe. Hang in there with me," he said.

"The other girl is still in there," Nichole said.

"I have to get you out of here first."

∽

Cash stepped down to the landing and yelled again. "Damn it, Fuller. I said let's go." He caught movement in his peripheral vision through the window. Seeing Colson and his daughter running across the front yard made no sense. He had heard the gunshots himself. He ran up the stairs two at a time, out the side door, and pulled Fuller's rifle out of the SUV. He heard what sounded like fingernails scraping a chalkboard as he rounded the front of the SUV. Jason watched his father from the driver's seat with bewilderment. He had been too busy scolding Tina to notice the two escapees crossing the yard. Now the cruiser was moving along the wall and Cash was raising the rifle to his shoulder.

Colson started the engine and pulled the gear down to "Drive." The rear tires spun in the damp grass. He eased off the gas, dropped the gear into "Low" and tried again. Sheet metal and stucco fought against each other as the side of the cruiser scraped in protest until Colson maneuvered it away from the wall. He would have to arc away from the wall for a better angle on the gates. He put his arm around Nichole and pulled her shoulder to him.

He saw Cash sprint from the house to the back of the SUV and emerge with a rifle. "Put your head down," he said, controlling the urgency in his voice. The loud "THUNK" sound of a rifle round striking the hood of the cruiser and the ricochet spark were simultaneous. The report of the rifle occurred a millisecond later. Colson spun the wheel to the right and gunned the cruiser when the tires gained traction. A second rifle crack rang out, but there was no impact or spark this time. Cash was not proficient with a rifle, even when he could see the target. The cruiser rolled onto the driveway. Colson aimed for the gates and floored the gas pedal. The enhanced, fuel injected, V-8 engine in the police interceptor jerked him back as another shot cracked from behind. He held Nichole's shoulder firmly when the cruiser impacted the gate at fifty miles per hour. Mainly designed for aesthetics, the double gate instantly yielded to the aircraft-grade aluminum push bumper mounted to the nose of the thirty-five-hundred-pound cruiser. Being forced in the wrong direction, the left gate broke off its hinges, cartwheeled one revolution, and slid flat across both lanes of A1A. The left side remained upright and slammed against the intercom column, shattering it and launching chunks of stone and concrete block down the length of the outside wall.

Colson spun the wheel hard right when the cruiser's nose dipped onto the road. The warped trunk lid dislodged and bounced up and down. He stood on the brake when a set of flashing headlights swerved directly into his lane. The anti-lock brakes grabbed and slowed the cruiser to a stop, nose-to-nose with Officer Sanders' truck.

Sanders stepped out of the truck and squinted to see the driver of the sheriff's unit. Colson stepped out and held his hands to his side, causing Sanders to move his hand to his holster.

Colson held his hands higher. "You're the officer from the beach, right?"

Sanders didn't lower his guard, but stepped closer to get a better look. His expression turned to one of recognition.

"And you're Colson." Sanders touched his shoulder microphone. "504, Radio. I have contact with the Colson subject in the roadway."

"My daughter's in the car with me. There are at least two armed suspects in there and an informant." He walked around the back of the car and noticed a Remington pump shotgun lying in the trunk. "They have a female kidnap victim."

Sanders looked confused. Colson suspected the young officer had never encountered such a volatile situation. It was a lot of information to process in a short period of time, but that's what police work is. Huge chunks of boredom, occasionally interrupted by instantaneous spurts of violent chaos. Daytona Beach was not Clay County, and although their procedure for responding to active shooter incidents may vary slightly, the basics would be the same. Colson knew the playbook and what to expect. The beach patrol officer's role would be to isolate, contain, evaluate and report until backup arrived. In this case, SWAT or a tactical unit. But there was no way to keep Cash and his insane son contained when there was a hundred acres of tropical scrub and brush available to hide in. And then there was the young girl.

He knew it would be the better part of an hour before a perimeter was set up and a SWAT team arrived. This couldn't wait.

Sanders raised his voice as Colson came closer. "Keep your hands where I can see them."

"Officer Sanders," Colson said, after glancing at his nameplate, "I have to help the other girl and you need to protect my daughter out here."

"We're not going anywhere. I'm calling this in and waiting for backup. If you are retired cop, you know better. My instructions are to hold you and report in. SWAT will handle it from here."

Colson nodded and turned. Sanders pulled his Glock and leveled it at Colson's back. "Stop, Colson."

Colson opened the passenger door and helped Nichole out. He put his arm around her and walked her to the truck. Nichole was visibly shaking. Her blouse was disheveled and torn. Sanders holstered his gun. He turned to Colson, but he was walking back to the rear of the sheriff's cruiser.

"Colson," he yelled.

Colson rounded the rear of the cruiser and lifted the shotgun from the trunk, holding it low and out of Sander's sight as he walked to the driver's side. "You take care of my daughter, Sanders. I have no doubt your policy allows that."

"Damn it, Colson. We were told to maintain our position."

"You were. I wasn't," he said, sliding the shotgun across the seat and dropping behind the wheel. He flipped the toggle for the roof light bar, slid the gear into reverse, and smoked the rear tires.

⇝ Chapter Twenty-Eight ⇜

Cantrell ran to his car when officer 504 announced Colson was at Cash's beach house. The officer's voice sounded stressed and his radio traffic was sporadic, but he said something about shots being fired and a hostage at the residence. He jerked the radio microphone to his mouth.

"803, radio, I'm enroute to 504's location." Cantrell hung the microphone back on the dash, but jerked it out again and spoke. "803 to 504, do you still have contact with the Colson subject?"

There was an extended pause. The radio traffic was heavy with sheriff and police units announcing they were responding to the scene, their sirens wailing in the background. The radio operator placed the frequency on emergency status, keeping unnecessary radio traffic to a minimum. Cantrell called again, articulating each word for the lone officer at the scene.

"*803 to 504, do-you-still-have-contact-with-the-Colson-subject?*"

"Negative," came Officer Sander's reply. "I have his daughter. He drove back inside the perimeter of the property. I tried—"

Cantrell cut him short. "Understood. Hold your position."

"10-4," Sanders replied.

Cantrell cursed under his breath and punched the accelerator when he pulled out of the Sundowner parking lot. "Damn it, Colson." He lifted the microphone again.

"803 to all responding units: be advised the Colson subject is a friendly, I repeat, a friendly."

He dropped the microphone onto the passenger seat and shook his head, scolding Colson as if he was sitting next to him. "You're just determined to get yourself killed, aren't you?"

༺∿༻

Cash ran to the SUV and jerked the passenger door open. What had been the faint scream of a distant siren began to multiply and grow in intensity. He saw flashing blue lights just beyond the gates right after Colson crashed through, but no siren. He thought that Colson had probably been knocked cold from the impact with the gate, or one of the rifle shots had found him.

"Get us the hell out of here," Cash snapped and slammed the door, holding the rifle between his legs. "Every cop in the county will be here in sixty seconds."

"Look," Jason said, pointing through the windshield.

The rear tires of the sheriff's cruiser barked and spun in reverse. Cash looked out the gate just in time to see the car disappear to the left of the wall, then reappear, running full speed toward the house. He threw the door open and dropped out of the SUV with the rifle. He ran to the front of the SUV and raised the rifle, firing twice. The cruiser kept coming. Cash knelt for a better aim. His eyes were level with the flashing headlights. He fired blindly into the barrage of white and blue flashes as it grew closer.

The flashing headlights were having the desired effect. Colson had the driver's door partially open. He leaned out the door, keeping his head low and the barrel of the shotgun resting on the window frame. He could probably hit Cash with the scatter gun from this distance, but he would waste time chambering another round if he missed. Cash didn't have a handicap with the semi-automatic assault rifle. He could keep shooting until the magazine ran dry. He decided to get within twenty feet, hit the brakes, and then take his shot.

Cash squinted and fired into the middle of the flashing lights again. The cruiser didn't slow down. He had to move. He stood and ran to his right and raised the rifle for another shot. He squeezed the trigger. The rifle recoiled at the same moment a powerful hand grabbed his wrist, forcing the rifle skyward. Taylor's face looked surreal in the blue and white flashes.

"Enough!" Taylor shouted, clamping down on Cash's arm. Cash jerked the butt of the gun upward, striking Taylor's jaw, but his grip didn't weaken. Cash struggled to swing the rifle in the direction of the cruiser for one last shot and squeezed the trigger.

The last shot penetrated the cruiser's windshield where Colson's head would have been under normal circumstances. Colson temporarily lost his bearings when the round exploded the windshield. He jerked the wheel left and right, dropping the shotgun in the grass. He felt the rear tire of the cruiser roll over it. He looked over the steering wheel at Taylor struggling with Cash. They both froze for an instant as Colson drew closer. Colson jerked the wheel to the right to avoid Taylor. As if reading Colson's mind, Taylor shoved Cash backwards. Colson couldn't avoid what happened next. Cash's awkward stumble looked like a drunken dance as he attempted to regain his balance, flailing an empty hand with the other clutching the assault rifle.

Cash pulled the trigger once after he fell in front of the SUV, striking Taylor in the stomach. The last thing he saw was a black tube bracketed between two flashing headlights. The aluminum push bumper caught Cash just above the bridge of his nose and drove his head into the grill of the SUV. The impact exploded the airbag in Colson's face and knocked him back in his seat, dazed.

Tina screamed from behind as Jason watched in horror from the driver's seat. The SUV was knocked back five feet from the impact. The hood of the cruiser buckled and steam spewed from the sides. He turned the ignition key. Nothing but the glare of a red Check Engine light. He pulled his gun from the center console, pushed the door open, and then dragged Tina from the back.

Taylor groaned. He had fallen to his knees and was lying in the fetal position. Colson was moving again, but slowly. Jason pushed Tina to the black NSX and opened the door.

"Get in!" he yelled, fighting off Tina's flailing arms. He ran to the other side and fell behind the wheel. Tina clawed in the dark for the door handle and found it an instant after Jason locked it from his side. He slammed the door and started the three-liter, V-6 engine. At idle, the NSX engine ran quiet compared to Colson's Corvette, but screamed like a true European sports coupe when revved.

"It's over!" Tina screamed, and blindly slapped at Jason's face with both hands as if swatting away a swarm of hornets. "Let me out!"

With less room than a phone booth to maneuver, fighting was almost impossible. Jason raised his right elbow and snapped it forward into Tina's nose. The slapping mercifully ceased as she gasped and covered her face. "Bitch, I'll kill you if you don't stop that shit!" He shoved the gear into first, dropped the clutch, and shot down the long driveway.

∽

Colson heard the whine of Jason's car and saw the tail lights speeding down the driveway. He put the cruiser in reverse and backed into the grass. The tires spun and dug ruts in the manicured lawn, fishtailing until the tires bit concrete. He floored the accelerator. The engine hesitated, coughed, and came back to life. Jason turned right on A1A and was out of sight. Colson swung the cruiser to the right on A1A, then immediately hit the brakes and lowered the window. Officer Sanders stood behind his truck door, clutching his right arm. A black dent was punched deep into the driver's door. Nichole stood outside, steadying Sanders by the elbow.

"He was just standing by the door when the car came out. It hit the door and caught his arm. I think it's broken."

Colson nodded. "Get him in the car and lock the door. I hear more units coming. I'll be right back."

"Dad!" Nichole scolded, but Colson had already pulled away. The rear of the cruiser dropped slightly as it caught low gear and sped north on A1A. Nichole could smell radiator fluid in the fog of the cruiser's wake.

The tail lights of the NSX were a small horizontal line in the distance. Colson estimated Jason was a half-mile ahead of him. He pushed the cruiser over eighty miles per hour, but he was losing ground on the sports car. It was fast. He had driven one that had been seized from a drug deal and knew its capabilities. The NSX was light with a top speed of at least 170 miles per hour. The bulky cruiser would never catch up. Radiator fluid coated the windshield and the headlights were broken. The wipers only smeared the greasy fluid reducing his visibility. He saw the neon Treasure Island hotel sign ahead and swung the cruiser into the lot. He ran to the Corvette, leaving the cruiser hissing and steaming in the parking lot.

He pulled onto A1A. There was no traffic to be seen in either direction at two a.m. Colson shifted into third gear and reached 105 miles per hour. The tail lights of the NSX came into view, turning left on Dunlawton Ave. With no other traffic in sight, Colson shifted again, topping 120 miles per hour. Two marked sheriff's units met him traveling south, both running their lights and sirens, but neither paid attention to him. He should have used the radio in the cruiser. He punched 911 into his cell, ignoring the five missed calls from his son-in-law, Bobby. He put it on speaker and set it in the cup holder.

◠◡

Sweat beaded on Jason's face. He looked in the rearview mirror. No one was behind him. Not Colson or the police. He slowed the NSX to forty-five miles per hour and stopped at the first red light on the inland side of the Port Orange Bridge. There was no sense in running traffic lights and drawing more attention from the cops. Tina sat stone-faced in the passenger seat. He couldn't believe Cash was dead. Jason caught himself smiling. The man had never been a father to him. He always disrespected him and treated him like shit. But one thing about the old man, he did know what to do when everything went to hell.

He had to get Tina to the rental house. He could still finish the deal and walk away with enough cash to disappear for a long time. The headlights appeared as the light turned green. He didn't notice the light had changed, keeping his eyes in the rearview mirror. The polo green Corvette rolled up to the NSX in the right lane. Colson grinned and waved as though he were an old friend.

Colson said with a smile, "We're at the light at Dunlawton and Ridgewood Avenue." Jason jerked the gear and pulled away fast, turning the NSX right and almost clipping the nose of the Corvette.

"Now heading north on Ridgewood," Colson said to the phone, and turned to follow. 120 miles per hour was as fast as Colson had ever driven the Corvette, but he knew from his research the LT1 engine was capable of reaching a top speed of 168 miles per hour. He didn't intend to provoke Jason and get the girl hurt, but he would keep up with the NSX and report their location to 911. As he learned over the years, it's not the car that matters, but the experience of the driver. The Corvette and NSX were a good match, but the drivers weren't in the same league.

He kept his distance from the NSX and updated their location to the 911 operator. "Passing Beville Road, exceeding eighty-five miles per hour." Colson pictured sheriff's units speeding across the Port Orange Bridge. He hoped they sent a few units on a parallel course north on A1A, just in case.

Just as he thought, the NSX made another right. "Now turning east on Orange Ave, back over the bridge." If it hadn't been for all the drama, Colson would have enjoyed riding around all night. The breeze was cooler than earlier, Nichole was safe, and Colson was in his element. He almost felt homesick, but put the thought out of his head. He dreaded explaining this adventure to his new son-in-law. He would never stand for Nichole to visit him again.

Colson picked up the phone. "Where are the units?"

"They're on their way to you," was the curt reply from the operator.

"From where? Omaha? Ah, the hell with this," Colson said, and dropped the phone back in the cup holder.

Colson pushed the Corvette faster, closing in on the NSX. Close enough to see Jason's surprised eyes in his rearview mirror. They topped the Orange Avenue Bridge at 115 miles per hour. The two sports cars speeding across the concrete seams in the road reminded Colson of someone firing an assault rifle, two rounds at a time. Pla-plap—Pla-plap—Pla-plap. The NSX darted into the left lane. Colson had to react quickly, not seeing the slow moving car ahead of Jason. The NSX darted back into the right lane. Colson stayed left to keep his eye ahead of the suicidal teenager. He downshifted as they ran the light at South Peninsula Drive. He thought about Jason's driving habits during their little road race. He had a tendency for right turns. It was time to convince him to make another one.

Colson stayed in the left lane, allowing the NSX to move ahead, and waited for the inexperienced punk to do just exactly what he wanted him to do. Make the right turn too fast. Jason cut the wheel hard right, back south on A1A. The low center of gravity kept the car on its wheels, but the turn was too tight, causing it to slide sideways. Colson downshifted, swung the Corvette in a wide arc, and made the turn smoothly. The NSX was now behind him. An experienced criminal would have used the opportunity to hit the brakes and flee in the opposite direction. But Jason was a spoiled punk, full of piss and vinegar. He wanted to show Colson who had the fastest car. He couldn't resist.

Colson slammed through the gears and pulled away from the NSX, making the temptation irresistible. Jason cursed and worked the gears. Colson heard the gears of the NSX grind as the frustrated teen botched his hand-foot coordination with the clutch. He watched the headlights swerve in his right mirror and grinned. Almost time.

Jason finally wound the NSX out to fifth gear and pushed his foot to the floor. The rear of the Corvette grew on the road ahead. He dropped the gear back to fourth and darted to the left, but Colson matched his move, leaving no room to pass. Jason jerked right, but again,

Colson stayed in his way. Then everything seemed to stand still. Colson cut the steering wheel left and pulled the hand brake, spinning the car. Billows of black smoke rose as the pavement burned an eighth of an inch of rubber off the wide rear tires.

Jason instinctively hit the brakes and cut right to avoid Colson. By the time he straightened, it was too late to avoid the curb. The impact sheared the front right wheel off the axle of the NSX, freeing it to bounce across the Quik Mart parking lot at fifty miles per hour. Tina had been silent until now with both hands bracing her against the seat. She screamed as the nose of the NSX shot upward and slammed back down on the bare metal hub of the axle. Sparks flew from the undercarriage as it slid at an angle toward the gas pumps. Plate glass exploded when the tire bounced up and through the front of the store, obliterating a display of ball caps, souvenir magnets, and ceramic mugs.

Raja had not seen a customer in three hours, but he didn't care. The old portable television made the time pass until the delivery guy arrived at five a.m. He sat behind the counter watching a reality show rerun, keeping one eye on the door in case someone walked up. If they looked like a tourist, he would push a button under the counter to let them in. If they looked like a thug, he would duck under the counter and hide until they gave up and went away.

He grabbed a candy bar from the display and unwrapped it. He was reaching to turn the TV channel when he heard the squealing of tires outside. He expected to hear the crash of metal on metal a second later, but didn't. He stood from behind the counter to look. The explosion of the plate glass window made him jump and bang his head on a display of cigarettes behind him. He fell to his knees and covered his head as shards of glass flew overhead and dropped behind the counter.

The grinding of the axle slowed the NSX. Its momentum carried it another fifteen feet where it stopped short of a gas pump sitting atop a small concrete island. Colson watched the door open and Jason slide out holding a gun. He drove the Corvette into the lot and got out fast. Jason ran to the entrance of the convenience store and pulled on the door, but it was locked. Colson ran up behind Jason and body-blocked him against the door, knocking the gun free from his hand. It made a clacking sound on the sidewalk. Jason fell to the sidewalk, knocked out cold.

Colson pulled Pickett's handcuffs from his pocket and rolled Jason onto his stomach. He grabbed one arm and held one cuff above his wrist. He hesitated when he noticed the thick aluminum handles on the glass door. Colson grinned and lifted Jason to his butt with his back against the door. He opened one cuff and ran the end through the quarter size, black ring in the middle of Jason's deformed earlobe. The other he ratcheted to the door handle. He slid the gun into his waistband and helped Tina climb out the driver's side of the NSX. She seemed to be gazing at something a mile away. She was in shock. He walked her to his car and sat her down.

Raja appeared from the store when the sheriff's units arrived. Sergeant Cantrell pulled up in his sedan and met Colson in the middle of the parking lot. Cantrell gave Jason a look and turned to Colson.

"Sort of an unconventional method to detain a suspect, wouldn't you say?"

Colson saw Jason wincing. He was coming back to life. "I suppose, but this way you don't have to babysit him."

"The sheriff wants you to give a statement tonight."

Colson nodded. "I figured as much. Nothing will drag a sheriff off his back porch like a kidnapping and a few dead bodies."

Cantrell squinted. "What are you talking about?"

"Never mind. Will you do me a favor, Sarge?"

"It's real ballsy of you to ask for a favor after all the hell you raised tonight, but what is it?"

"Will you assign a female officer to take Nichole home and sit with her until I get back? I know she'll have to make a statement too, but surely it can wait until tomorrow."

"Consider it done. You ready to get this over with? A couple of deputies will be assigned to clean up your mess here."

Raja stepped around Jason and held up his palms. "What's going on?"

Colson turned. "Well, if it isn't Roger. Did I make you proud?"

"It's Raja," he said, dropping his hands to his waist and rolling his eyes.

"Whatever," Colson said with a dismissive wave. He felt the presence of someone behind him and turned around to Tina. She appeared more settled than when he helped her from the car. She dropped her eyes.

"I just wanted to say that no matter what happens to me now...thank you."

Colson hugged her and patted the back of her head. "It's all right, dear. I would expect someone to do the same for Nichole."

Jason tried to stand. The cuffs jerked his ear down, tearing the skin at the base of his deformed earlobe. "Ahhhh, SHIT!" he screamed. "Screw you, Colson!"

Colson walked to Jason, stooped over, and looked into his eyes. "You know, you need to save your sweet talk for the boyfriends you'll meet in prison."

⇛ Chapter Twenty-Nine ⇚

The interview room was ten by twelve feet. It had brown carpet and beige walls. There was no one-way mirror, but a closed-circuit camera was mounted high on the wall in the far corner. Colson recognized the ceiling-mounted microphone disguised as a smoke detector. He had a similar set-up in his interview room. There would be someone monitoring and recording the statement in another room not far away. Probably the next room.

Agent Frank McCann leaned back in his chair and laughed. Colson grinned from across the cheap laminate table, resting his chin in his hand and grinning. Sheriff Langston sat at the end of the table with a confused look. He looked back and forth between McCann and Colson.

"You two act like you know each other."

McCann turned to Langston, trying to control his outburst. "I guess you could say that. Colson and I used to share information over the phone when he was with the county and I worked out of the Atlanta Field Office. We only met each other in person once, at a metro agency conference."

McCann turned his attention back to Colson. "It's a good thing, Grey. Anyone else would have a hard time believing you. But then again, we knew what was going on."

Colson raised his hand. "That's what I've been trying to figure out. Since we're finished with my statement, how about clueing me in on the whole thing. Six hours ago I was convinced that the sheriff here was either dirty or an incompetent boob."

Langston spoke up. "I couldn't say anything at the time, Colson. You're a civilian now."

"It's over now and I'm all ears," Colson said.

Langston seemed to be in thought for a moment, formulating a summary of events. "It began with a NCIC audit. You know, where they reconcile the logbooks with case numbers to make sure histories and inquiries are being run legitimately."

Colson nodded. "Yeah, I'm familiar with that."

"There were several that reflected bogus case numbers."

"So that's where Pickett comes in, right? He was running inquiries against NCIC rules."

"No," Langston shook his head. "Not at the time. He was having a civilian technician run them, but we didn't know that yet. It took a while for Internal Affairs to narrow it down. Anyway," Langston continued, "all the names he ran were young females, and all were wanted for a variety of felonies or were on felony probation."

"So why didn't Internal Affairs confront Pickett then?"

"They were in the process of confirming he was involved around the same time we started the investigation into Martin Cash's activities and the thugs he was hiring. I smelled a rat when I found out Pickett was running an off-duty security operation at Cash's liquor stores. I knew there was a connection, but wasn't certain what it was."

"Speaking of thugs," Colson said, "what's the story with Taylor?"

"I was on scene the day he was arrested for aggravated battery. He literally beat the eyeball out of an optometrist he claimed negligently caused his blindness. He had no prior criminal history. Not even a speeding ticket. Cash obviously hired him as a heavy, but Taylor had no idea what he was getting into."

"So you turned him on Cash?"

Langston nodded. "We knew Cash was losing his ass with the significant drop in tourism. I first suspected he was dabbling in drugs and or prostitution, but no, he was trying to go big-time in human trafficking."

"Why didn't you search his house for other girls or evidence?"

"We didn't have probable cause for a search warrant then. Our surveillance didn't observe any females coming or going from the beach house. Even if we had, they were all of adult age and could stay there if they wanted to. It's not a crime."

"Well," Colson said, "when did you develop the probable cause?"

McCann spoke up. "When the good sheriff called me."

"Come on, Frank," Langston said. "You didn't even know what Cash was doing at the time." He turned back to Colson. "I called Frank and told him he may be interested in looking at Cash. He had a couple of agents mirror our surveillance and saw one of the exchanges with a Mexican national. The girl's name was Kara. Taylor got information about the time and place, but had no idea if the deal would go or not. I passed it to Frank and he ran parallel surveillance on the swap. Taylor's information was good, and the FBI had the Coast Guard pick up the boat as soon as it left the inland waterway. Three suspects in custody. The girl was in the hospital for two weeks for heroin detox, but was otherwise no worse for wear."

"What about the body I saw Taylor drop in the trunk and drive away with?"

"There was nothing he could do to stop it. Cash had her so doped up her heart stopped. Taylor called me as soon as he left the beach house and met us at the morgue with the body,"

"Hell," Colson said. "That and Taylor's statement should have been enough probable cause to go in and get Tina right then without a warrant. Exigent circumstances."

Langston held his hand up again. "We would have without hesitation, but Tina wasn't there. Taylor said she had escaped two days prior and no one knew where she was hiding until Pickett saw her going into Faye Cox's condo."

"Faye Cox?" Colson said. "What did she have to do with Tina?"

"She was looking for you but you weren't home. Tina told us Faye invited her in to eat, shower, and rest until you came home. She was trying to find you. She called you 'the man from the beach.' Damn shame."

"What do you mean?"

"Faye Cox is dead."

Colson put his head in his hands. His involvement had cost an innocent life and almost took his daughter away from him. Colson felt regret for anyone being harmed because of his involvement. He told himself it was not directly his fault, but it didn't help. It was five-thirty a.m. and Colson was exhausted. He spoke to Langston without raising his head.

"At your house you acted like you weren't even interested in the evidence I gave you. Why didn't you bring Cash and his crew in for questioning? The poor woman might still be alive."

"Look, Colson. There was no way of knowing what would happen. She was at the wrong place at the wrong time. It wasn't our fault and it wasn't yours. When Frank became involved, I pulled my people off the investigation."

"Whatever happened to agency cooperation?" Colson asked. "We used to do it all the time with the feds. That's exactly why Frank and I know each other."

"I had to. It was personal," Langston said. "Martin Cash was my stepbrother."

Colson lifted his head and looked at Langston "Your stepbrother? Then you should have never been involved in the first place. You should have turned it over to Frank or the Florida Department of Law Enforcement from the beginning."

"You're right. I violated my own policy."

Colson placed his hands flat on the table. "I'm in no position to judge you, sheriff. I violated every paragraph in my code of conduct tonight. I always thought I would be embarrassed to admit it, but I'd do it all again if I had to for my daughter. Speaking of Nichole, you guys got everything you need from me? I need to get back to her."

Agent McCann and Sheriff Langston stood and shook Colson's hand. "I hate it about Taylor," Colson said.

"He's in ICU, but they said he will live. He'll probably have to piss in a bag for a while, though."

"What's going to happen to Tina?"

McCann said, "We'll do what we can. Her case sounds shaky to me, but she jumped bail and that never looks good. But under the circumstances, we may be able to talk the district attorney to agree to a year of probation. I think we can keep her from doing jail time. If she successfully completes the first-offender program, the charge will be wiped from her record."

Colson opened the interview room door. He stopped and turned. "Just one more question."

McCann chuckled. "What is it, Columbo?"

"What were you guys waiting for? Me to kill everyone so you wouldn't have to prosecute them?"

"No, smartass," McCann said. "We were right on schedule until you decided to come out of retirement."

"On schedule for what?"

"Cash was going to make a trade for Tina tomorrow night." He looked at his watch. "I mean tonight."

"With who?"

"Me."

"You?"

"How rude of me not to introduce you to my Internet persona," McCann said, holding out his hand. "Avid Collector, at your service."

⇒ Chapter Thirty ⇐

Deputy Duncan squatted in front of a stack of cardboard boxes in the back of the property room, searching for a medium size Stetson hat. He found two at the bottom of the stack and pulled one out. An excited new recruit peered around the corner from behind the counter in front. Deputy Duncan carried the box to the counter and dropped it in front of the twenty-something-year-old recruit.

"Sign here," Deputy Duncan said, spinning a property inventory card around. The young deputy eagerly signed, scooped up the box, and pushed on the door, knocking Sergeant Martin back a step.

"Slow it down, son," Sergeant Martin scolded.

The recruit's eyes widened and he stopped in his tracks. "Yes, sir...sorry sir." Sergeant Martin gave him a quick nod and the recruit scurried down the hall. His tennis shoes squeaked on the shiny linoleum floor until he disappeared around the corner.

Sergeant Martin set the box he had carried in onto the counter. Deputy Duncan dropped the inventory card into a file cabinet and turned to face him.

"What'cha got for me, Sarge?"

"Well, Duncan. Another one bites the dust. You know the drill. Check all the property against what was signed out and let me know if anything is missing."

"Right away, Sarge. What happened with this one?"

Sergeant Martin cocked his head to the side. "Same answer as last time. We don't discuss Internal Affairs cases," he said, and walked out without another word.

Deputy Duncan opened the lid and pulled out a hat and five uniform shirts and pants. A duty belt and two pair of high-top boots were next. A Kevlar vest lay on top of the remaining items. A small, black box containing a Glock, three full magazines of .45 caliber rounds, a flashlight, two pairs of handcuffs, paddle holster, Taser, and an identification wallet.

He reached for the wallet and flipped it open. His eyebrows instantly rose. He couldn't suppress the slight grin creeping across his face as he read the name aloud.

"Lieutenant Kimberly Reese. Ain't that some shit."

~~~

Colson dropped his keys on the dresser and loosened his tie. The funeral for Faye was a quiet farewell in a small white church in Port Orange. In spite of being the wife of a preacher for over thirty-five years very few, if any, former church members made the trip to say goodbye. That could explain the overabundance of flowers arranged near the casket in their absence. If it had not been for the brief national news coverage of her murder, tied to Cash's ridiculous illusion of being a world-renowned human trafficker, they probably would never have known what happened to her.

He recognized a few residents of the Sundowner who accounted for a majority of the congregation, including Mr. and Mrs. Hammond. Colson offered his condolences to Faye's daughter after the service. She introduced herself as Carol Swafford, a fairly attractive woman in her forties. She smiled through drying streaks of tears and was graceful, considering she was talking to complete strangers about their relationship with her mother. Colson wondered if Faye had left instructions for her ashes to be sprinkled on the beach, but decided not to ask.

He finished changing and walked out on the balcony. A hot July breeze blew his hair back. It was two o'clock in the afternoon and the balcony was shaded. He sat and looked out over the beach. Cars, trucks, bicycles, motorcycles, and people moved up and down the beach as they had the first time he and Ann vacationed in Daytona. It seemed as though nothing ever changed here, no matter what happened, short of a thermonuclear war.

Colson said, "I'm glad you could stay, Honey."

Nichole smiled from her chair and brushed the hair from her eyes. The hot breeze blew it back across the front of her face. "If I leave you alone, you'll get in trouble."

"I love you."

"I love you, Dad. You worry me, though."

"Don't worry about me. I'll keep myself busy"

"That's exactly what I'm worried about, Dad"

"I'm glad you stayed, but I hope it's not a problem for you to miss class. How is that going anyway?"

"It's kicking my ass."

"Art is? You're kidding. I thought you just showed up and painted or something."

Nichole shook her head and laughed. "There's a little more to it than that."

Colson nodded. "Well there should be, for thirty grand in tuition per year. Is Bobby still mad at me? He could have stayed a few days longer."

"He just wanted to make sure I...we, were okay. He was in the middle of a case and had to get back. He's afraid of his boss."

"He should be more afraid of you."

"Oh, give me time," Nichole chuckled. "He will be."

Colson grinned and touched her hand. "You're just like your mother."

The End

❯❯ About the Author ❮❮

Christopher Griffith was born in Maryville, Tennessee, but spent his young adult years living in the northeastern United States. With a love of music, Chris traveled and sang on a part-time basis with Southern Gospel Quartets until 2010, when he began to pursue his strong desire to write a crime novel. Chris was twenty-two years old when he accepted the privilege of joining the Cobb County Sheriff's Office in Marietta, Georgia. In the past twenty-eight years, Chris has been assigned to the Sheriff's Office Undercover Narcotics Unit, DEA Task Force Atlanta Field Division, Fugitive and Fraud Units, and Internal Affairs. He currently holds the rank of Deputy Sheriff Major in the Operations and Investigations Division.

Christopher Griffith currently lives in Dallas, Georgia with his lovely wife Beverly, his equally lovely daughter Brittany, and their dogs Marty and Bella. Chris and his family vacation in Daytona Beach each summer and can be found in the shade of their canopy, reading their favorite novels.